THE CHRONICLES OF THE KARIONIN

At the end of the Second Age of Tamar, the Five Gods, the Lorincen, played with the dice of history. Tarat, self-styled ruler of the Gods, and Kyra, once the Chronicler, now the Destroyer, urged their worshippers, the larin, to war upon mankind. Miune, the father of mankind, could do little to ward off the malice of his stronger kin, but he knew his children's hidden strength. He taught his worshippers to hate. Maera of the Mists and Jehan, known as Player, sought a different path . . .

THE RED BOOK OF CHRONICLER RADAM
1111TH YEAR OF THE AGE OF EMPIRE

Thallassean

Onchan

Bria ILWHEIRLANE

Outer

Adun · Lutra

Islands

Ninkarrak

Sea of

Strait
of Zamarga

Belarrai

ISIN Jaen

ESTERIAS

Canth

Astara

· Larsa

KAILANE **Sea** YPANE
Mara

*Marshes
of
Sikkar* Krydani *Dalossian
Archepelago* **JALMAR**

Svdik Ruffin· Ai Bay
Gwatar · Kavarna **SUSSEY** of Khor

Nadrum **RAVAAR**

Ravach

DARENJE

LAMASH Kappar **AMRIOTH**

Dariel Jaora

Lara

SARDOM Caruiz **ANAT**

Belkova **MAHRAN**
Ranaodh Aodh

THE CHRONICLES OF THE KARIONIN

LYSKARION
The Song of the Wind

J. A. Cullum

First Edition

Canadian Cataloguing in Publication Data

Cullum, Janice A., 1944-
  Lyskarion

ISBN: 1-894063-02-3

1. Title

PS3553.U34L97 1998   C813'.54 C98-910462-1

CREDITS

AUTHOR / MAP	J. A. Cullum
ILLUSTRATION / BORDER:	Michael Dashow
TEXT / COVER DESIGN	Gail Pocock
LAYOUT:	Daniel Blais
PUBLISHER:	Edge Science Fiction and Fantasy Publishing

FONTS

R Stempel Garamond, Imprint MT Shadow, Arial

LYSKARION: The Song of the Wind is a work of fiction

Edge Science Fiction and Fantasy Publishing
P.O. Box 1714, Calgary, Alberta, Canada T2P 2L7

(20020122)

To all the authors who have inspired me, and
particularly to Poul Anderson and Randall Garrett
who helped to teach me that writing
is also a craft.

GENEALOGY OF THE ROYAL HOUSE OF SUSSEY – THE HOUSE OF ANIFI

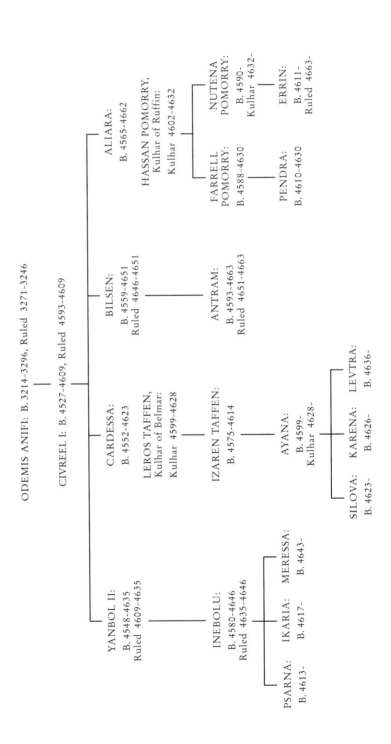

ODEMIS ANIFI: B. 3214-3296, Ruled 3271-3246

CIVREEL I: B. 4527-4609, Ruled 4593-4609

YANBOL II:
B. 4548-4635
Ruled 4609-4635

CARDESSA:
B. 4552-4623

LEROS TAFFEN,
Kulhar of Belmar:
Kulhar 4599-4628

BILSEN:
B. 4559-4651
Ruled 4646-4651

ALIARA:
B. 4565-4662

HASSAN POMORRY,
Kulhar of Ruffin:
Kulhar 4602-4632

INEBOLU:
B. 4580-4646
Ruled 4635-4646

IZAREN TAFFEN:
B. 4575-4614

AYANA:
B. 4599-
Kulhar 4628-

ANTRAM:
B. 4593-4663
Ruled 4651-4663

FARRELL
POMORRY:
B. 4588-4630

PENDRA:
B. 4610-4630

NUTENA
POMORRY:
B. 4590-
Kulhar 4632-

ERRIN:
B. 4611-
Ruled 4663-

PSARNA:
B. 4613-

IKARIA:
B. 4617-

MERESSA:
B. 4643-

SILOVA:
B. 4623-

KARENA:
B. 4626-

LEVTRA:
B. 4636-

Cast of Characters

Adun

Adun, Elise – *Heir to Adun*

Adun, Jorum – *Son of Elise Adun*

Adun, Moira – *Elise's grandmother, the Adun of Adun*

Anifi, Errin Yar Pomorry – *See Anifi family tree*

Farswimmer, Ankor & Pela – *Children of Tarle and Renala Farswimmer*

Farswimmer, Manata & Renala – *Wives of Tarle Farswimmer*

Farswimmer, Tarle – *Chief huntsman then arrage of the wiga which often summered on Adun*

Reeve, Brennan – *Anitra Adun's husband*

Sharkbiter, Incal & Imra – *Arrage & arragel of the wiga when Elise was a child*

Skane, Timmon – *Moira Adun's agent and Jorum Adun's father*

Sussey

See Anifi family tree

Carredos, Delanan – *Wizard and member of the Varfarin*

Elgan, Das 'Elgan' – *Descendent and student of the Wizard Cormor*

Menabe, Jao – *Wizard, member of the Varfarin*

Taranta, Galen – *Wine merchant in Ruffin*

Ilwheirlane

Ashe, Paule 'Ashe' – *Wizard and member of the Varfarin*

Braydon, Palus – *Commander-in-Chief of the Armies of Ilwheirlane*

Cinnac, Vanda III – *Estahar of Ilwheirlane*

Derwen, Enos 'Derwen' – *Esalfar, High Wanderer, of the Varfarin*

Durgren, Otto – *Jerevan Rayne's valet*

Kindric, Eten 'Kindric' – *Wizard who began Jerevan Rayne's training*

Lesho, Entanu & Oumaroo – *Childhood friends of Del Maran and Elise Adun*

Maran, Charna & Ethan – *Del Maran's cousins*

Maran, Del 'Arrun' – *He studied wizardry with Elise Adun*

Maran, Orris – *Lanrai of Luro, Commander of the Shore Guard, and Del Maran's father*

Rayne, Danor & Nadira – *Jerevan Rayne's parents*
Rayne, Jerevan – *Hetri of Leyburn*
Vordal, Emin – *Admiral of the Navy of Ilwheirlane*

SOUTH COAST AND THALLASSEAN SEA

Aeloin, Hathi – *Chairman of the City Council of Darenje*
Elpine, Bryant – *Retired member of the Council of Darenje*
Jabiren, Escan – *High priest of temple of Jehan in Darenje*
Kamrasi, Aketi & Saranith – *Wizards and arrain in the Senangan navy*
Kanakar, Lucian – *Commander of the military unit from Turkel Qualog*
Kelpdancer, Zetan – *Arrage and commander of the military unit from his wiga*
Korsen, Amale – *Chairman of the City Council of Darenje*
Larkin, Kennar – *Kovarai of Lara, Chairman of the Council of Kovarin of Samrah*
Latrem, Fellis – *Chairman of the City Council of Darenje*
Marcos, Semley 'Myrriden' – *A wizard trained by the Wizard Agnith*
Massif, Bokal – *Ring Master of the Carnival of Wonders*
Morec, Jula – *First Class Healer trained by the Kindred of Maera*
Olaven, Gaya – *High priest at Sanctuary of Maera in Darenje*
Ortigel, Lyle – *Admiral of the Fleet of Ilwheirlane*
Quanat, Petrel – *Member of the Kindred of Maera and First Class Healer*
Roka, Mekan – *Member of the Kindred of Maera, First Class Healer*
Rudbar, Saman 'Rand' – *Wizard, member of the Varfarin*
Scurek, Balen – *Journeyman wizard who trained with Jerevan Rayne*
Tidewater, Annais – *Fat lady of the Carnival of Wonders*
Yolande, Zenobia – *Member of the Kindred of Maera, sibyl*
Yosevi, Alden – *Member of the Kindred of Maera, First Class Healer*

LYSKARION

The Song of the Wind

PROLOGUE

MONTH OF CERDANA

> *Members of the Varfarin pledge not to interfere with the right of*
> *sentient beings to govern themselves as they see fit. Still, that*
> *pledge does not abrogate the duty of each member to strive to*
> *insure that all the sentient beings so governed have an equal say*
> *in such government . . .*

— EXCERPT FROM <u>ILVARFARIN: THE OPEN ROADS</u>, BY THE WIZARD CORMOR

"WHEN I DIE, YOU'LL BE THE NEXT HEAD OF THE VARFARIN," the Wizard Cormor said quietly.

A log collapsed with a crack and a hiss in the marble hearth, sending sparks flying. The Wizard Derwen, seated in one of the two padded chairs in front of the fireplace, ignored both the sound and the ember that barely missed his foot. "Why me?" he asked, his attention fixed on the man in the opposite chair.

Only Cormor's head moved, but the ember returned to the fire, leaving the edge of the carpet unsinged. "You don't feel qualified?"

Derwen shook his head. "Even today, with so few of us left, you'd have no trouble finding half a dozen wizards stronger than I am. So why choose me?"

Cormor's austere face looked thoughtful. He fingered the large, egg-shaped crystal set into the hilt of the sword lying across his lap. "You have a right to know, but my reasons aren't easy to explain." He paused, and Derwen watched the blue light in the heart of the crystal pulse to the beat of Cormor's heart. Cyrkarion, the Blue Crystal, was one of eight living crystals created during the Age of Wizards. Called the Sword of Cormor due to its setting, it was both the source and the symbol of Cormor's power. That power often frightened Derwen, but never more than now, when he had just been told that the title of Esalfar, the mantle of leadership of the Varfarin, would be his on Cormor's death.

And Cormor was dying. Derwen's jaw clenched. Since Belis' death a little over a year earlier, Cormor was the last surviving Great Wizard, those who had qualified for the Council of Wizards. His death had been inevitable from the moment that Belis had died; they had been mind-linked, joined through Cyrkarion in a way that no one who had not experienced such a linkage could imagine. Without Belis, Cormor lacked a part of himself. He had no wish to live beyond the time needed to settle his affairs, and that time was almost over.

"It isn't true that I foretell the future," Cormor said, startling Derwen out of his musings. "Not even the gods do that." He raised a slender hand, and the brandy snifter on the table by his chair floated up so that his long fingers could close about the stem. He took a sip and returned the glass to the table. "But I have been blessed by Jehan and I shared his vision. The Varfarin, after all, was created to serve his will. What the gods see are possibilities."

"The multiple threads of fate," Derwen said.

Cormor inclined his head. "Precisely."

"So what possibilities does my becoming Esalfar bring into being?" Derwen asked, running a blunt-fingered hand through his hair. The room beyond the circle of firelight was dark. He felt himself isolated with Cormor in a moment of calm.

"If I name one of the stronger wizards to succeed me, say Balek or Sura," Cormor said, "either one would do a decent job for a time, but neither of them is my equal. Nor would they devote enough time to seeking someone else, someone who could become my equal."

"No one's been your equal in two thousand years."

Cormor raised a hand in protest. "There may have been many who could have been. We've tested perhaps ten percent of the children in Ilwheirlane, and our record is much poorer in the rest of Tamar."

"You want the testing of children made a priority?" Derwen leaned forward. "Balek would do that, if you told him to; any of them would."

"For a time, but the press of events would shift their priorities. After a few hundred years their search would falter." Cormor snorted. "After less than a hundred, more likely. Balek, Sura, all their paths lead to the same end."

"A few hundred years is a long time." Derwen closed his eyes. Beyond this room, this moment, lay a terrible abyss of duty and responsibility.

"We live a long time."

"Are you saying it will take hundreds of years to find someone to replace you?" He heard a quiver in his voice.

Cormor shook his head. "I don't know. My vision showed no dates. But I need you to do more than simply pursue a search for potential wizards. I need you to make sure, when you find someone who could be my equal, that person does become my equal."

Derwen swallowed. "What do you mean?"

The esalfar's face twisted in an expression of regret, and Derwen felt shaken anew by the lines of age and pain thus exposed, lines that had not been there a month before. He forced his attention back to his master's words.

"It can't have escaped your notice that the study of wizardry isn't popular today?"

"For good reason," Derwen said, grimacing, but at least the subject was a familiar one. "The uneducated fear us. They always have, of course, but since the awful destruction caused by the Bane, and the exposure of the atrocities committed by Rav and his allies, their fear has grown. One can't blame them."

"No. The Bane terrified me. The waste of it. Hundreds of kilometers of fertile land, reduced to a poisonous desert, and most of the wizards on Tamar dead." Cormor sighed, his eyes full of regrets. "And since then there have been so few of us. We haven't been able to mingle with the people as we once did. The unknown is always more frightening than the familiar." He rubbed his forehead. Then, straightening in his chair, he swept his hand away as if pushing his thoughts aside as well. He focused on Derwen. "What if you find someone with talent, and that person doesn't want to be trained? What would you do?"

Derwen stared back. "You can't force someone to learn wizardry."

Cormor smiled. "Are you sure? I can think of ways it might be done."

"What do you want of me?"

Cormor shook his head. "It's not what I want. It's what the future of Tamar demands. You must be single-minded and ruthless on the Varfarin's behalf. You must find someone with the potential to be my equal, no matter how long the search may take, and you must make sure that, when you have found such a person, he or she receives training, no matter what that person's personal views on the subject may be."

BOOK I

THE YOUNG WIZARDS

Acadam mend lar bat na,
Acadam ikval jeram iflat al idom amid.

Every old man was once a child,
Every ancient crone dreamt of first love.

— ESLARIN PROVERB

I

4621, 463RD CYCLE OF THE YEAR OF THE DRAGON
MONTH OF CERDANA

Of were-folk there are races six;
Be careful now, don't get them mixed.

. . . An ingvalar is lord of the sea,
When he takes the form of a dolphin free.
He loves to play with anything,
But best of all, he loves to sing.

— EXCERPTS FROM "THE WERE-FOLK", PUBLISHED IN A CHILD'S GUIDE TO THE LARIN AND OTHER BEASTLY TAILS, BY ENOGEN VARASH OF ELEVTHERAI, 4557

ELISE ADUN CLAMBERED UP THE STEEP INLAND SLOPE to the crest of the hill and gazed down at the shore. The tide was out. Great, kelpy boulders studded the cove, their mollusk-encrusted sides drying in the morning sun.

She was tall for a seven-year-old, and skinny, the slight awkwardness of early youth apparent in her movements despite her agility in climbing the rocks. The breeze tugged at the wisps of red hair that had escaped her pony tail. She turned her face to windward and inhaled the salt breath of the sea. Then she laughed with the ecstasy of the moment and took another deep breath of the northwest wind. Its taste was sweet, but it felt cold in her lungs, with none of the warmth of spring. The sun, however, was hot.

It was the first day of the month of Cerdana. Elise had seen ardethin and crocuses blooming amid the roots of the sparse, wind-twisted trees on the inland slopes of the hills, and the sea folk had come. The day before, the cove had been empty of all but rocks and shingle. Today a village of neat, round sharkskin cauraks covered the shore.

Elise had known the sea folk would be there, having sensed their arrival as she had each year since the age of four. She had slipped out of the house early to escape her grandmother's eye, but she had taken the time to fill a basket with a pot of butter, two jugs of milk and a handful of candies made from the honey of the old woman's bees.

She hesitated at the top of the hill, looking down at the camp. Her grandmother, Moira Adun, had forbidden her to visit the sea folk this year. Mother Adun, as she was known to everyone in the Outer Islands of Ilwheirlane, had said she had grown too big to play with primitives and romp in the waves as though she were a naked savage herself, but Elise did not care if Pela was a primitive. Pela was her best friend.

She sighed, her pleasure in the morning dimming. The sea folk only stayed on Adun for three months in the spring and early summer. Being lonely the rest of the year was hard enough. She would visit Pela and the others while they camped in the cove, and accept whatever her grandmother meted out as punishment, even a spanking with the silver-backed hairbrush. After all, the old woman had never objected to her friendship with the children of the sea folk in the past. What made this year different?

Bunching up her skirt and petticoats, she scrambled down the slope to the edge of the village, then picked her way across the strip of shingle lining the shore to where the waves lapped at her bare feet. She rarely remembered to wear the leather shoes her grandmother had bought for her on the mainland, and her feet were thickly callused, accustomed to the feel of the stones, but the water felt cold.

Elise knew from other years that despite the early hour, most of the young men and women of the wiga would already have gone hunting. Only a few of the remaining sea folk were about: a fat old man repairing the lines between a float and a lobster pot; a heavyset woman watching two chubby children playing in the waves at the water's edge; and another, younger woman laying out strips of raw, salted fish on a board to dry in the sun. Their lack of clothing startled Elise on her first visit of the year, as she inevitably forgot in the months between that the sea folk went naked except on ceremonial occasions. Clothes, after all, were a handicap for shape-changers.

She studied the line of skin cauraks, then went to the largest and most beautifully decorated. Outside it, she called out a greeting in Eskh. A tall, heavy woman emerged, naked except for a leather apron. She frowned at the sight of Elise, but greeted her politely, "Good day, youngling. How may I help you?"

"Good day, Imra Sharkbiter. I came to play with Pela, the daughter of Tarle and Renala Farswimmer, if they're still with the wiga." Elise lifted her basket. "I brought gifts."

Imra's face relaxed and she nodded. "I remember you now. You've grown, young Adun, or I would have recognized you right away. If you come back before you leave, I have a gift you can take to your grandmother for me."

Elise swallowed. She couldn't explain; the sea folk would never allow her to play with their children if they knew her grandmother had forbidden it. She couldn't refuse to take the gift, either. Maybe she could get Joady, the handyman, to give it to her grandmother. She forced a smile. "I'd be happy to."

Imra's head tilted and Elise felt herself being examined, but Imra only said, "You want the third caurak from this one, the one painted like a debarra. Have you brought us milk again? Incal's so fond of it."

Elise pulled out one of the jugs of milk and handed it over, relieved at the change of subject. "I remembered." She grinned. "He told me he was going to have to learn to milk a whale when the wiga left here. Did he try?"

Imra laughed. "Get on with you."

Elise skipped down the line of cauraks to the one painted in the brown and orange markings of the debarra, the entrance looking like the rounded mouth of the great, deep-sea fish. Larger than the others, the home of the wiga's chief hunter was second only to Incal Sharkbiter's. Again, Elise called out a greeting in Eskh.

Renala Farswimmer recognized her immediately. "Good day, little Adun. Come in. You're in time to share our breakfast. Pela isn't even out of bed yet." A tall, buxom woman, she wore her long, black hair in a braid that reached past her hips.

Elise grinned and slipped through the entrance, sniffing the aromas of hot fat and baking bread. "Mmm. I am hungry. I remember your cooking."

Renala smiled. "We have smoked debarra and shad roe this morning, with a loaf fresh from the baking oven. It's good to be living on land again. The sea has its own delights, but I miss the foods of the land." She bent down to tend an iron skillet on a grid over the fire in the center of the skin house, beneath an opening where smoke could escape. "Which reminds me," she added, "Pela has talked of nothing but meldarcanin for weeks. Did you bring her any?"

"No honey cakes, but I brought candies for Pela and milk and butter for you."

"Wicked child, you remember all our weaknesses," Renala said, laughing as she accepted the gifts. "Pela, wake up! Elise Adun has come to visit. Get your sleepy head up out of bed."

Elise saw a pile of skins stir on the sleeping platform. Pela's black-haired head poked up from the middle. "Did you bring meldarcanin?" she asked, rubbing her eyes.

"No, but I brought honey candies. Will they do?"

Pela grimaced and sat up. "Today I will control my sorrow, if you bring meldarcanin tomorrow," she intoned in one of the rhyming chants the sea folk loved.

Elise shook her head. Pela had always been quick at rhyming, while Elise could never think of any. "How can you do that when you're not even awake?"

"I don't know. I think that way sometimes," Pela said, standing up and coming over to Elise to look in the basket. She had grown as much as Elise over the past year and they were almost the same height, but, like most of the sea folk, Pela was plump. She took one of the candies, unwrapped it, and stuck it in her mouth. Her face smoothed into in an expression of ecstasy. "Ummm. Every year I think I know how good candies are, but when I taste them, they're always better than I expected."

Elise laughed. The islanders never seemed to enjoy anything, but the sea folk savored every moment, every sensation.

When they finished breakfast, Pela said, "I'm supposed to meet Errin to dig egastin this morning, but if you help we'll have time to ride a few waves."

"Ugh! Who wants to eat sand worms?"

"My father," Pela said, grimacing.

Renala laughed. "Tarle likes them poached in milk. He must have expected you to come today."

"Errin Yar is still with the wiga?" Elise asked. "He told me last year he was going back to Sussey to live on the land like his mother."

"He went back," Renala said, her tone disapproving. "He spent five months there, but then he came back to the wiga as he does every year. He doesn't get on any better with his mother's relations on land than with his father's second wife here, so they divide up his year - five months with the wiga and five ashore going to school like the land-born."

"Come on," Pela said, starting for the door. "I told Errin I'd meet him at Huler's Beach. We'd better go now, or we won't have time for surfing."

Elise saw no sign of Errin when they arrived at the beach, but Pela pointed at the water. *Wretched beast. He's started to surf without us,* Pela thought in the mind-speech she and Errin had taught Elise when Elise had been four. They were careful not to use it with Elise in front of adults, but among themselves it had become natural.

Elise looked out over the water and saw a small dolphin leap beyond the point where the waves started to curl. *Errin,* she thought.

He sensed her call. She felt the tingle of his awareness link with hers and the strange twisting feeling in his mind as he shape-changed back from dolphin to boy. Then, as though he had just become aware that they were linked, his mind closed to her. She swallowed, feeling rejected. Mind-speech was just a superficial exchange of information. A mind-link went deeper. After Errin had taught her to link the previous summer, and up until just before he left, they had spent most of their time together in linkage. She missed that intimacy.

He rode the next wave in, gaining his feet at just the right moment to avoid getting scraped by the sand. He looked taller than Elise remembered him, and thinner, too thin for an ingvalar. She could make out the outline of each of the ribs in his lean, angular torso, and his shoulders were bony. She wondered how he managed not to freeze in the icy water.

Pela said I could join you, Elise thought, raising her chin when he stared at her as they walked up to him. He was three years older than she was and she had thought that she must have done something to displease him near the end of the previous summer but she couldn't think what it could have been to have kept him angry with her until now.

"Then I guess you can." He used words instead of mind-speech, his voice gruff, but he smiled. His eyes were a mixture of green, blue and gold, reminding her of the sea when the sun first catches it after a storm.

THREE HOURS LATER, ELISE TIPTOED THROUGH THE KITCHEN of her home into the hall. She had to get upstairs before her grandmother saw her clothes. She hated to think what her punishment would be if the old woman caught her with her dress wrinkled and sandy and her petticoats wet from being used as towels after body surfing. It would be something worse than the hairbrush, she felt sure.

"She went down to the shore today, even after I forbade her."

Elise froze at the sound of her grandmother's voice coming from the parlor. Why would the old woman be downstairs at this time of day? And how did she know where Elise had been?

"Aye. I saw her go."

Her father, as well! Elise swallowed and flattened herself against the wall. She would never make it past the parlor entrance with the two of them there. They knew where she had gone, anyway. Maybe she should just go in and confess and take her punishment. With her father present, how bad could it be?

"Did you talk to her?"

Elise hesitated. Mother Adun was using her bossy voice, the voice she used to make Elise's father and others do things they didn't want to do. Not a good time for a confession. Maybe, if she could get up to her room without them seeing her, she could make them think they'd been wrong about where she had been.

"I tried, but . . ."

"But you haven't."

Elise pictured her grandmother's position from the sound of her voice. The old woman was in the wing chair near the fireplace, sitting with her back as straight as a ship's mast, her gnarled fingers resting on the antimacassars on the arms. She always sat there when she gave people orders, Elise thought resentfully. And when she sat there, she could see the entryway and the bottom of the staircase without even turning her head.

"She'll take na harm from tha sea folk," Elise's father said. "You know that. She's safer wi' them than she would be alone, swimming about tha rocks." Brennan had the soft drawl of the islanders that Elise loved, gruff, but musical, but she got punished when her voice slipped into the same accent. Her father's voice broke off and she heard his boots on the wooden floor as he walked over to the window.

"As her mother took no harm." Moira's voice was sharp, and Elise wondered what she meant. Anitra Adun, Elise's mother, had died when Elise was very young, but her death had nothing to do with the sea folk. She had slipped on the rocks at the top of a cliff during an autumn storm.

The silence in the parlor lasted for several moments before Brennan protested, "Elise just turned seven. Tha sea folk dinna seduce children." Elise could almost see him, slow and steady, bracing himself against the lash of her grandmother's tongue. She sometimes wondered why Moira had allowed her mother to marry Brennan, when the old woman seemed to hold him in such contempt.

"If she plays with them now, she'll play with them later. The ingvalarin count a woman grown when she has her first flow."

"Even that's years away," he said.

"Not so many, Brennan Reeve. Three or four years, five at the most. She's like her mother; she'll ripen young."

With her father by the window, Elise pictured her grandmother turned to face him. She flattened her body to the floor and peeked through the entryway. She had given up all thought of letting them know of her presence, but she wanted to see them. They were discussing her, after all.

"It's not just her playing with tha sea folk that's worrying you," Brennan said, turning back to face the old woman. "There's been something ta do wi' Elise eating at you ever since that wizard came ta visit. What did he tell you, Moira? Don't you think I have tha right ta know?"

"He only confirmed what I've suspected for years, that Elise has wizard talent. She's tried to conceal it, but she's learned mind-speech from the sea folk. He wants me to send her to the mainland for training."

Elise gasped and pulled her head back from the entryway, putting her hands over her mouth. Had they heard her? Brennan's boots clumped across the wooden floor. She held her breath, but the sound of his footsteps changed as he crossed onto the rug near where her grandmother sat.

"You told him na, didn't you?" His voice sounded harsh, angry. Elise couldn't remember his ever using that tone with her grandmother.

"I said I'd think about it." Moira's voice was cold. Hearing it, Elise shivered.

"You'd sell your own granddaughter ta wizards? You must be mad, old woman. You may be the authority on these islands, but I've called her my daughter for too many years ta let you send her away ta such a fate as that."

"Don't be a fool," Moira said. "I have no intention of selling her, as you put it. She's my heir."

"Then why didn't you tell tha wizard that? Wizards are chancy folk ta keep dangling, even for you."

"What do you think they do with children, anyway? Eat them?"

Elise cowered in the hall. She had never heard either her father or her grandmother so angry.

"I don't know that I'd put even that past them," Brennan said. "I've heard of worse things done in Ravaar before they wiped most of themselves out with tha Bane."

Elise's grandmother sighed. "There are no followers of Rav in Ilwheirlane. The wizards of the Varfarin are honorable people, dedicated to Jehan, the second branch of his priesthood. I took training from one myself in my youth. How do you think I learned my healing skills?"

"I thought you trained wi' tha kindred of Maera." Brennan sounded shaken, and Elise dared to peek through the entrance again. Stand up to her for once, Da, she thought. Don't let her send me away. But deep down she knew it was hopeless. No one defied Mother Adun, least of all her father, who had been one of her grandmother's tenant farmers before her mother married him.

"It's true I trained at the Sanctuary of Maera in Clutha," Moira said, "but the Varfarin used to have a wizard teaching there. They've always worked closely with both the kindred of Maera and the ajaren of Jehan."

"Why can't you teach Elise what she needs ta know?" He had his back to the fireplace and rocked back and forth from his heels to his toes.

"Because I'm old and my talent's weak." She turned in her chair to face him. "I summoned the wizard who came here. I wanted her tested. She needs to learn a healer's skill, if she learns nothing else."

"So why can't they send a wizard ta train her here?"

"Times are hard these days. The were-folk's raiding increases every year. Even when I trained at Clutha, there were others learning with me. The Varfarin can't spare a wizard for each child that needs training, unless the child has the talent to be a great wizard and is going to continue the training the whole way. Even if Elise has that level of talent, the last thing I want to do is ask the Varfarin to put that kind of an investment into her. Then I'd never get her back."

"So you do recognize tha danger," Brennan said. "Once they have Elise away from here, who's ta say what they'll do wi' her? Wizards have made monsters out of children in the past."

Moira sighed. "I can't deny that there have been evil wizards and mad ones. There may even be some left today. But I've never heard of any crime proven against a wizard of the Varfarin. They are sworn to Jehan."

"That may be. But where there's power such as wizards wield, who's ta say where the end of it is? Power can twist tha mind."

"Power twists the minds of those who seek it, if those who seek it aren't twisted to begin with. Most of us find it only a burden." She sighed again, and Elise heard an unusual note of tiredness in her voice. "But I wouldn't, in any case, send Elise to a wizard to raise. They know nothing of the sea, or these islands, and she's my heir."

"Then why . . ."

"No! Not to a wizard," Moira Adun continued, ignoring Brennan's interruption, "but I'd send her to Enole Lehar in Bria. He's my cousin, my uncle's grandson. I wrote to him when I heard there was a wizard living in the town. He's agreed to take her, if I decide to send her. There's a day school, too. The Wizard Derwen himself is staying there while he trains another child. The wizard who came here said Derwen would be glad to train Elise as well. She could visit us each fall, when the ingvalarin have gone south."

"It all comes back ta your fear of tha sea folk." Brennan glared at Moira. "Tell me you'd be sending her away, if it weren't for that!"

"Don't I have reason to fear them?"

"Because she runs off ta play wi' them when they camp on tha shore?" he asked impatiently. "Of course she plays wi' them. The sea folk children are tha only children she sees. She's lonely."

"You think I don't know that?" Elise flinched at the anger in her grandmother's voice. "All the more reason to send her to the mainland where there are other, human, children for her to play with."

"If you send her away, you'll lose her. We'll both lose her. Once tha wizards take her, you'll never get her back."

"That's a chance I must take." The old woman frowned. "I can't arrange a marriage for her until she turns eighteen, but I'll do it quickly enough then. She may come back. She's a good child, and she loves the sea."

"Na." Brennan turned away and began to pace the room. "I'll not have her turned inta a monster because of your fears." Elise ducked back behind the wall.

"She'll not be a monster. I admit wizardry's not what I want for her, but you're showing your ignorance, Brennan, when you speak of it the way you do. Humankind needs wizards, and there are few enough of them as it is. If she has as strong a talent as the wizard who tested her says, that ought to be reason enough to send her." The old woman paused. "But you're right, I'd have been too selfish to consider that, if it weren't for the rest of it. There's too much of the sea in Elise's blood. I see it pulling her."

"Even if that be true, she's only seven. She's safe for years yet. Wait until she's older."

"That won't work. The older she gets, the harder the training is to start. The Varfarin rarely takes children over five. Derwen's never taken a child over ten. She'll be nearly eight when she reaches Bria now, if I wait until the end of summer."

"So you'll give her up. What good is that going ta do you?"

"I may lose her. But she'll have babes, and they won't be of the sea. One of them can inherit. A baby born far from the shore, a baby who won't have played with the sea folk, won't feel the pull of the waves. The chain will be broken."

"You hate them so much?"

"Hate them?" Moira laughed, a high, cackling laugh that cut through Elise's shock and forced her to peek into the sitting room again. "Yes, I hate them. Hate them and love them; how can I help it? I'm Adun of Adun. Their blood runs in me, too." She paused. Then she continued, her voice steady and cold, laying bare the iron will that Elise had watched people bow to all her life, not just on Adun but on all the surrounding islands. "I watched the sea folk destroy my daughter. I won't stand by and let the same happen to Elise."

Elise pulled her head back carefully, wanting to cover her ears and pretend she hadn't heard what her grandmother had said, but the words, like the sound of her grandmother's laughter, echoed inside her head. She crawled across the hall to the kitchen and slipped out of the house. Then, heedless of the chill wind on her damp dress, she fled.

The sea folk had killed her mother, and her grandmother was going to send her away. Her grandmother would never let her see her friends again. Yet, how could sea folk be her friends if they had killed her mother? She ran, half-blinded by tears, for the hills.

ERRIN FOUND HER LATE THAT AFTERNOON as the sun was sinking through a haze of multi-colored clouds. The curlews cried mournfully, flying home to their nests on the cliff beneath her feet.

Errin's father, Lothar Yar, had urged him to look for her. "You're better than the rest of us at climbing these hills. You get more practice," Lothar had said, and though the words had stung, Errin had absolved him of malice. After all, his differences from the others of the wiga hurt his father as much as himself. "Someone needs to go after the child," Lothar had continued. "You're older, and you relate better to the way the landborn think than the rest of us."

Errin had flinched again, but Incal Sharkbiter, the chief, had agreed. Their arguments had not included the best argument of all, that he could mind-link with her, because that was still a secret known only to himself and Pela. So Errin had set out to look for Elise. She had not been hard to find, perched on the top of the highest hill on the island, but it had taken a stiff climb to reach her.

"Your grandmother's worried about you," he said, being careful to use ordinary speech. He had been seven when he helped Pela teach Elise mind-speech, wanting to show off. Last summer, when he had shown her how to mind-link, he had been nine and should have known better, but he had still felt the desire to show off in front of her. He had forgotten the danger until he felt how the link could deepen, how he could lose control over it. He had shied away then. When he admitted to his teacher in Sussey what he had done, the Wizard Delanan had warned him again of the harm a linkage could cause. So now he was cautious.

"She sent for you to come home and we had to tell the messenger you'd left hours ago." He sat down near Elise on the rough ground a meter back from the precipice. Accustomed to the support of water around him, heights made him nervous, and had done since his first time on land at the age of three when he had tripped and fallen with only air to catch him.

Elise eyed him. The wariness of her expression chilled Errin. This morning she had looked at him with admiration, despite her disappointment at what she interpreted as a rebuff.

"Why are you dressed?" she demanded.

He grinned, relieved, and looked down at his worn gray corduroy pants and brown sandals. "My skin isn't hardened to these rocks the way yours is. I need to protect myself to climb them." His eyes went back to her face and he saw traces of tears. "Why did you come here?"

She sniffed and swallowed. "This is where my mother died."

Errin grimaced. "You come here often?"

She shook her head. "I never thought about it until today. It's pretty here, and you can see so far. I don't remember her much."

"Why did you think about it today?"

"My grandmother said the sea folk killed her." Elise picked up a stone and tossed it out into the air beyond her feet.

Errin watched it fall out of sight. He couldn't hear it land over the sound of the surf on the rocks at the foot of the cliff. After a time she turned back to him, but he didn't know what to say. What she had said was impossible, unreal. Finally, he managed, "Your grandmother really said that? She actually told you an ingvalar killed your mother?"

Elise looked away. "She didn't say it to me. She said it to Da, but I overheard."

"I don't believe it."

Elise stiffened. "She's Adun of Adun. She never lies."

"Then you misunderstood what she said."

Elise shook her head. "I didn't." She scrunched up her face, remembering. "She said, 'I watched the sea folk destroy my daughter.' And my mother died here, on these rocks." She stared at him defiantly.

Errin sighed. He was ten. He knew the songs and the stories of the ingvalarin, and, because of his mixed background, he knew them from the point of view of both the sea and the land. But Elise was only seven and had grown up in near isolation. How could he explain? "You don't understand," he said finally. "You're too young. There's a difference between destroying someone and killing them."

"My mother died."

He glanced toward the cliff. "You're not afraid that I'd push you, are you?"

She looked startled. "Of course not!"

He nodded. "Ingvalarin don't fight wars, and we don't kill larin, or even malarin. You know that. But sometimes we do hurt humans, not physically and not because we mean to, but because that's the way we are. Do you see?"

She shook her head. Her eyes fixed on him, glowing in the reflected light of the sunset like two pieces of amber caught in firelight. He wanted to link with her to show her what he meant, yet he knew this would be the worst time of all to do so, with both of them under the stress of strong emotions. He swallowed and forced himself to use words. "Sometimes when people get hurt, and they think they can't deal with the hurt, they decide they don't want to live."

"You're saying my Ma killed herself? That she jumped off the cliff?"

He looked away. "I don't know. I don't know what happened to your mother, but that's another thing your grandmother's words might have meant. There are probably other meanings, too. I don't know what's true, but nor do you."

She sniffed and her eyes narrowed as though she were calculating something in her head. Finally she said, "It was autumn when she fell. I remember. A cruel, cold day, with the fog so close I could scarcely see my hand at the end of my arm. I overheard when the fishermen came to tell Mother Adun and I ran outside to find her, but I never got farther than the barn." She swallowed.

"So they had to hunt for you that day, too." Errin felt sad. "You've got long ears for a child."

Her chin rose. "They didn't hunt for me. Da was in the barn. He took care of me. He told me that at least I'd always have him."

Errin shrugged. "Then your mother's death could have been an accident, with the weather that bad. Even your grandmother can't know for sure."

Elise looked up at him and nodded grudgingly. "Your people never come here that time of year." Then she started to cry again. "But she's going to send me away. She never changes her mind once it's made up. And then I won't even have Da. She doesn't want me to play with you anymore, so she's sending me to the mainland to go to school and be taught by wizards."

He studied her. "You have talent or you couldn't have learned mind-speech. Have you been tested?"

Her eyes widened and she turned to him, wiping her face. "Wizards don't scare you?"

He shook his head. "Of course not. Why should they?"

She bit her lip. "Da says wizards do horrible things to children, and turn them into monsters."

He grinned. "Can you see your grandmother standing by while anyone turned you into a monster?"

Her lips formed an 'O' of surprise and then turned up into a smile. "Oh no! She'd have their hides . . ."

"Tacked to the yardarm," he finished. Their eyes met and they burst out laughing.

He walked her home under the fading salmon and pink glory of the sunset sky.

II

MONTH OF REDRI

> *To rule well one must first have command of oneself . . .*
> *Yet self-control should never be taken to the point of rigidity. A*
> *ruler must be open to the flow of new ideas no matter what their*
> *source. A beggar off the street may sometimes give insight to a*
> *problem where the wisest counselors and philosophers have*
> *failed . . .*

— EXCERPTS FROM THE ART OF GOVERNMENT, BY VYDARGA V OF ILWHEIRLANE

THE AUDIENCE CHAMBER OF THE ESTAHAR OF ILWHEIRLANE in Ninkarrak formed a vast semicircle. Long windows cut the curved wall, floor to ceiling sheets of a clear substance as strong as the stone of the walls and as transparent as glass. Only a great wizard could duplicate the material of those windows, which were invisible from an exterior view. To one outside, the Black Tower appeared to be constructed of solid blocks of black stone.

Rich tapestries from Mahran draped silver-gray panels of sylvith wood on the straight wall. The vast woolen carpet covering the floor came from Amrioth and had taken fifteen years to make, each knot tied by hand.

The room was filled with the cream of the aristocracy of Ilwheirlane and all the high officers of state, everyone dressed in their finest: silk and satin, velvet and lace, damask and jewels.

"This piracy must be stopped, Your Majesty," Orris Maran, Lanrai of Luro, demanded of Vanda III, Estahar of Ilwheirlane. "The eastern shores have been decimated, and now Senangans raid the Thallassean coast as well."

Palus Braydon, the Commander-in-Chief of the Armies of Ilwheirlane, eyed the speaker cynically, taking in his height, the bold features and the unruly thatch of dark brown hair. A good-looking man, but Braydon distrusted the brilliance of Orris' blue eyes, the intensity of his expression. Orris looked like a fanatic, and a highly placed, noble fanatic could be a nuisance. Still, the man had presence.

"You think we haven't tried to stop the piracy?" Vanda asked, examining the petitioner as carefully as Braydon had done. She wore a gown of crimson and gold that accentuated her pallor. The jeweled crown looked heavy on her head.

"Not hard enough, Your Majesty," Orris said. "Half of the people of Halek are dead: men, women and babies lying ripped apart in the streets, some of them half eaten. The tiger folk must be stopped."

Braydon grunted, hearing the gasps and murmurs of shock from around the room. From across the room, the Wizard Derwen waved at Orris, trying to get his attention. The young lord had no tact, but he was enlivening a dull afternoon. Braydon hated the waste of time involved in attending public audiences. Pomp and ceremony irritated him, but such functions were command performances. At least this session promised to be entertaining.

Vanda had stiffened at Orris' words and a glint of anger flashed in her gray eyes. She answered obliquely, "You've spent time at sea, Lord Luro?"

Orris looked disconcerted. "Yes, Your Majesty. I served in the Navy until my mother died and I retired to take responsibility for my lands."

"They say that Ilwheirlane rules the sea. Do you agree?"

"Of course, Your Majesty."

"Then you're a fool," she said. "No one rules the sea. Ilwheirlane may have the largest navy on Tamar, our trade routes may circumnavigate the globe, but our coastline is vast, and we can't even successfully guard the Strait of Belarrai."

"I don't understand, Your Majesty. Our navy is the greatest in the world. We should make it a priority to block the gateway to the Inland Sea, to keep out linlarin ships, and to hunt down those in the Thallassean."

"Admiral Vordal." Vanda gestured to the tall, weathered man twisting his bony hands in agitation nearby.

Vordal stepped forward and glared at Orris. He looked impressive despite his age, dressed in the blue dress uniform of the Royal Navy. "The Strait of Belarrai is more than sixty kilometers across at its narrowest point, Lord Luro, and the reefs and currents are fierce. We lose ships on the rocks there every year, as you should know."

Vordal paused, his expression grim, and turned to the Estahar. "We haven't enough ships or wizards to blockade the Strait without stripping protection from our ports and trade routes. Even if we had the ships necessary, we still couldn't stop all sea traffic without starting a war with our allies."

"Thank you, Admiral Vordal," Vanda smiled at the grizzled man, "but I'm not the one you have to convince. Lord Luro has accused us of inaction. Tell him how simple it is to hunt down all the pirate ships in the Inland Sea."

Vordal snorted. "Can't be done."

"Why not?"

"Think, man," Vordal said impatiently. "We aren't the only nation with shipping in the Thallassean. A linlarin ship only has to fly the flag of Sussey or Isin or even one of the human nations. After all, most of the pirate fleets stole their ship designs from Sussey. Unless we have a wizard aboard, we can't tell from a distance what breed the sailors are. And there aren't many wizards around in these days. How long could we keep peace with our allies if we stopped every ship we met?"

He pounded his right fist into the palm of his left hand. "We patrol our coastal waters. We attack any ship that flies the flag of Senanga, Mankoya or

Gatukai, and, if we have a wizard aboard who can tell the difference, any ship manned by linlarin. But that's all we can do. That, and return their raids in kind on the coasts of Cibata."

"You see, Lord Luro, we do what is possible," Vanda said. "We realize that sometimes that isn't enough. We're sorry for the losses the coastal regions suffer, but we're doing all that we can do."

"But it isn't all you can do," Orris insisted. "If you can't fight the linlarin at sea, then defend people on land. Set up forts and lookouts along the coast."

"We have forts along the coast." Vanda frowned. "There's a fort at Onchan and at Lutra, but the troops couldn't reach Halek in time."

"There are only three forts along the whole length of the west coast. It took the military more than a day to get to Halek from Lutra. You need a fort in every village."

"Not enough soldiers," Braydon said, startled into speaking out.

Orris turned to him. "You wouldn't need professional soldiers if you'd create a Shore Guard, a volunteer force made up of local citizens." He turned back to the Estahar. "Your Majesty, the villagers wouldn't even need to be paid. Just put one instructor in each village and have him train the volunteers. The villagers themselves would build the forts and man them, if you'd teach them how. They'd supply you with lookouts up and down the coast, and all they'd need is help with material and supplies."

Braydon stared at the man and took in the silence around the room. Clever idea. Might even work. He wasn't surprised when Vanda turned to him.

"Well, General Braydon, is what Lord Luro suggests possible?"

"Might be, Your Majesty. Lots of things are possible." Braydon scowled. "Question is whether it's economically feasible. All very well to say we wouldn't have to pay the villagers, but material and supplies are expensive. So are men capable of the sort of training he's talking about."

"The idea's ridiculous," Vordal said with a snort. "The expense would be prohibitive, and what purpose would it serve? To protect a few fishing villages? The Navy patrols the coast. That's always been adequate in the past."

"Lord Luro has a point, Admiral. The raids have increased in recent years," Wizard Derwen said, speaking for the first time.

"If we fortify the coast they'll increase even more. The isklarin will take it as a sign of hostility. We're at peace with the lizard folk at the moment. I wouldn't want to precipitate a war right in the Thallassean," Vordal protested.

"The taking of Ardagh was an act of peace?" Derwen asked.

Vordal stiffened. "That took place forty-five years ago and Ardagh was a nest of pirates. The isklarin only wanted a port to open up trade. But they'll see the increase in our fortifications as an act of hostility."

"I wasn't aware that the opinion of Gandahar determined Ilwheirlane's internal policies," Vanda said, turning back to Braydon. "You think the idea has possibilities?"

Braydon grunted, wondering, not for the first time, why Vanda had chosen him to command her military forces. He was the son of a teamster, and had enlisted in the army at seventeen to get away from his father's heavy hand. Oh, he had come up with a few good ideas, but most of his success could be credited to careful preparation and sheer tenacity, not the kind of performance that normally drew the attention of royalty.

He shrugged and brought his eyes back to Orris, unaware of the fierceness of his expression. He always looked angry when deep in thought, and Orris had given him a lot to think about. "System like that can't spring up overnight," he said. "Take years. Largest towns first, if they're strategically placed. Have to take some smaller, even the distances. Troop of men per town for training. Exposed areas first. Fort every fifty miles to start. Ten, fifteen years, just the first stage."

Braydon paused and looked around, surprised to find everyone, including Vanda, staring at him. The attention, however, did not lessen his aggressive posture or lower his voice. "Interesting idea, Your Majesty. Expensive, of course. Put my staff to work on it, with your permission." He bowed, reluctantly remembering the formalities but anxious to get them over with as soon as possible. He would need to get hold of Wizard Derwen. Jehan, he didn't even know the length of the coastline. Narrow inlets wouldn't count, though, would they? Have to get a cartographer.

Vanda nodded, her expression indicative of amusement. "Of course, General Braydon, you may be dismissed. But first," her voice checked him as he started to leave, "how long will it take your staff to give you the initial estimates on timing and expenses?"

Braydon shrugged. She would ask that. "Week. Break the lot of them if they can't come up with something by then." He looked round for Derwen and signaled to him. Then he turned to Orris who looked a little stunned. Good. No tact, but maybe a trace of common sense. "You come with me. Your idea. You implement it. Need someone with ideas instead of excuses." The man might be a fanatic but his idea was sound. Use the tools available.

Vanda inclined her head. "You are also excused, Lord Luro. I think you've found the right forum for your ideas."

EIGHT DAYS AFTER ORRIS' INITIAL AUDIENCE WITH VANDA, Braydon eyed the Lanrai across his desk in his own office, a small, bare room with walls haphazardly papered with maps. Orris was useful. He had a keen mind when he kept his emotions under control. Braydon didn't want to lose him.

"I have to return to my estates, General," Orris said.

"Not under my orders," Braydon said. "I can't keep you, but if you want that Shore Guard of yours, you'll take care of your business, then come back."

Orris was startled. "Your feasibility study came up with positive results. I thought there was no question of it not being carried through."

Braydon gave a short barking laugh at Orris' political naivete. "Oh, there'll be a Shore Guard, or some form of it, someday. Whether it'll resemble what we've mapped out this last week remains to be seen. Needs you to ride guard on it."

"Won't you see to it yourself?"

Braydon shook his head. "Commander-in-Chief. Given this project more time than I should already. Have to hand it over. Rather hand it to you than one of those fool aides of mine or some outsider. You've got the motivation to keep it moving."

"I'm not even in the Army,"

"Just as well. Make you Commander of a new service. Able to draw on Army and Navy for assistance. Better that way. High ranking lord, no question about eligibility. Officer in the Navy, checked you out. Smooth feathers over having Army begin the project," Braydon said, rubbing his hands together and thinking about Vordal's anger over the whole proposal. Orris had his head so far up in the clouds he wouldn't notice Vordal's objections. Only way to treat the old reactionary; run right over him.

"I'm retired. I've been retired for four years. I have estates to manage."

"Got a wife; she's been running your estates for years when you've had to travel," Braydon said. "Won't need to live in Ninkarrak. Better if you live at home on the coast, closer to your command."

"Does anyone ever say no to you, General?"

Braydon snorted but for a moment a twinkle flashed in his eye. "Not often, if I can help it."

Orris shook his head doubtfully. "What you describe would require a royal appointment. Won't Her Majesty have a man of her own to put forward?"

"Already agreed to you. Talked to her last night, when I showed her the preliminary figures. You're her choice, too." Braydon chuckled. "Clever woman. May lack wizard talent but never underestimate her."

"I can't give you an answer now." Orris paced the width of the small office. "I have to go home to Cliff House and talk to my wife. My son is still a small child."

Good, Braydon thought. He hasn't said no. He'll come round. He's the type, but it wouldn't hurt to add some pressure. "Give you three months. Have to know one way or the other by then." He paged through the papers on his desk as though anxious to get on to something else. "Dunrough can get the wheel turning. He's the buck-toothed seral you met outside. Good at staff work. Can't make a decision." He looked up and glared at Orris, gauging the effect of his words. "Have to appoint someone else, if I don't hear from you in three months."

"You'll hear from me."

III

MONTH OF AGNITH

At ragewe ma.

Fate cannot be ruled.

— ESLARIN PROVERB

"MARRY," FARRELL POMORRY NEARLY CHOKED ON THE ORANGE JUICE he was drinking. "You think I need to marry again? Are you out of your mind, Ayana?" He put his glass down on the table next to his chair. "My marriage to Iddina was a disaster. The happiest years of my life have been the ones since she died. I have no intention of repeating my mistake."

"But you have to," Ayana Taffen said.

Farrell reclined on a lounge chair on the patio of his home near Ruffin on the Isle of Sussey, overlooking the Bay of Aelos. Ayana had refused one of the other lounges, and had pulled an upright chair away from the table so that she could perch on it and glare at him.

Farrell sighed. He had been enjoying the warmth of the sun blazing down from the cerulean sky. It would have been too hot, but for the cooling southwest wind that whipped the waves across the bay to frothy whitecaps. The sound of the surf breaking on the rocks below often lulled him to sleep. He wished Ayana would go away and let it do so now. Ayana ranked as his least favorite cousin. Furthermore, he had drunk too much wine the night before and had a headache, which she was making worse.

"Why? What concern is it of yours?" he demanded.

"Well," Ayana said, pursing her lips, "Pendra's too young, so you don't have much choice, unless you want to risk having your estates go to that animal?"

"What animal? What are you talking about?" Farrell took another gulp of juice. He was never at his best before noon, but he didn't think the fault all his this morning. Ayana was talking gibberish.

"The danger of your inheritance going to Errin Yar, the child of that creature Nutena ran off with. He was born in a wiga. He's part fish."

Farrell shook his head, and latched onto the easiest point. "Dolphins aren't fish, Ayana. I always thought Cardessa should have insisted you spend the traditional month or two of your childhood with one of the wigan. I had to, and I made sure Pendra did."

"Fish or dolphin, what difference does it make?" Ayana wailed. "Kyra forbids the larin to breed back to the beasts. All the wigan folk are damned, and as it stands at the moment, only you, your daughter, and Nutena stand between Errin Yar and the Kulharion of Ruffin."

Farrell blinked at her, realizing that, while he had known Ayana since her birth, he really did not know her at all. She looked the same as she always had: a short, stocky woman with dark hair and dark eyes, earnest and intense. She was wearing something fussy in a shade of pink that did not become her and was clutching a large purse. He had never detected a sense of humor in her side of the family. She had to be serious.

Farrell thought about that for a moment, then said, "If it comes to that, Ayana, since your father died, unless you or one of Inebolu's daughters produce a son, only my daughter's potential male offspring and myself stand between Errin Yar and Lyskarion and the throne of Sussey. Yambol and Bilsen are too old to marry again, Inebolu has no intention of doing so, and Antram's said he won't."

Ayana grimaced. "It's not fair that Lyskarion requires a male bearer. Why couldn't it have been like Vyrkarion, or one of the other stones that need a woman?" Her jaw clenched, and she added, "But you needn't worry about the throne of Sussey. I'll produce a son, if I have to consult a wizard to do so."

Farrell blinked. "I'm not worrying. I don't care who inherits Ruffin after Pendra, much less Lyskarion, but the odds are pretty good she'll produce a child at some point. Right now, she's still a child herself."

"Don't you care that Nutena's brought that animal into your home?" Ayana demanded.

Farrell sighed and took another drink of his juice. Right now, hangover or not, he wished it were wine. "Why should I? He's a quiet boy, not much trouble, and he's only here half the year. The other five months he spends with his father's wiga."

"You permit that?"

"It's none of my business, Ayana. I'm the boy's uncle, not his keeper. If you want to complain about the way he's being raised, complain to my mother."

"I'm amazed Aunt Aliara lets him live here. She's a member of the House of Anifi. She shouldn't have to put up with scum."

"But my dear Ayana," Aliara's voice said silkily from the doorway, "I put up with so many things. The presence of a mere boy of questionable breeding hardly counts. And actually, compared to most of my family, his manners are rather good."

Farrell looked up with relief at the arrival of his mother. Despite her nearly sixty years and the silver that lightened her once black hair, Aliara Anifi was still a strikingly handsome woman with the regal bearing befitting the sister of the current Ahar of Sussey. She could handle Ayana. Maybe he would get a nap this morning after all.

"Aunt Aliara, I didn't realize you were here," Ayana said, coloring.

"No, I realize that," Aliara said, walking forward and seating herself on another of the chairs by the table. "If you'd known I might overhear, you would have wrapped the dirty linen a little more neatly." She smiled quite amiably, but Farrell noticed that Ayana's hands had started fidgeting with her purse. His mother often had that effect on people.

"I was merely expressing my concern about an impossible situation."

"Impossible? I hadn't realized any laws of nature were broken," Aliara said, cocking her head as though curious. Her eyes were a limpid golden brown.

Ayana inhaled sharply. "You know what I mean."

"Yes, unfortunately," Aliara said, her eyes narrowing, "I know exactly what you mean. You're the same sort of paltry bigot as your mother. I never could get along with Cardessa. And for your information, we are not worshipers of Kyra the Destroyer in this house. Now, I think you've upset my son quite enough for one day. You may go."

Ayana rose and glared at Aliara for a moment, but when Aliara's gaze didn't falter, she sniffed and said, "Well then, good bye." She stalked off the patio into the house.

Farrell watched her depart then looked at his mother. "Did Nutena hear any of that?"

"No, thank Jehan. She went into Ruffin this morning," Aliara said.

"Well, that's a blessing. I could hardly believe Ayana was serious at first."

"Oh, she was serious. She's the image of her mother. Unfortunately for my brothers, Cardessa had a hand in choosing both their wives, and they all had that same mean-mindedness." Aliara shook her head. "Inebolu's daughters, Psarna and Ikaria, aren't any better. If you weren't much too lazy to rule, I might wish that they all bear nothing but daughters."

ERRIN SWAM ALONG THE COAST OF THE BAY OF LURO, his senses automatically sorting the multitudinous and diverse sensory input from his dolphin sonar and his ingvalar were-sight. The whole melange of sensation and sounds combined to create what the ingvalarin called the song of the sea, the most beautiful music in the world. Errin never ceased to marvel at its melodic richness, or to rejoice in his ability to hear it. He listened to the slow, background rumble of the tidal currents, the quick, darting notes of schools of fish, the irregular booming of sonar echoes from the sloping bottom, and the rhythmic dance of leaves in the copses of kelp forest. Every sound and movement became a part of a great, eternal symphony.

All those who heard the song of the sea were drawn back to it, yet he wondered sometimes if his own fascination was not intensified by the fact that he might so easily never have known it. If the conditions of his birth had been different, if his mother hadn't been living with the sea folk when he had been born, then he might have been fated to live on land all his life.

He shuddered at that thought and his tail swept down with extra force, swerving him momentarily from his course. He made an adjustment and reassured himself. He had been born among the sea-folk, and he had inherited the ability to shape-change. Therefore, despite his other deficiencies, the sublime rhapsody was his to enjoy. He rose to breathe, jumping all the way out of the sea with a flip of his tail, then dove again, sending out a trilling whistle of his own to join the music and echo back to him.

The sea floor began to slope more steeply. The water in the bay felt warmer than the water in the open sea. He could taste a lack of salinity and a trace of silt, signs that he approached the shore near the mouth of a stream. Errin rose to the surface, blew and dove again.

He wasn't sure what had brought him this way. It would take him days to catch up to the rest of the wiga as they started their migration south, but he had wanted to visit the mainland for a long time. Adun had not been the same the past three years without Elise. Even Pela had been a little subdued in the human child's absence.

He had decided to visit Bria and see for himself how well Elise was taking to the study of wizardry. He knew she had potential; she had learned mind-speech quickly, and had always had an instinctive feel for the sea. Such feelings were a sign of ability. But believing that she would do well did not satisfy the itch he felt in her absence. He could not forget the time they had spent mind-linked, or the last summer, when the knowledge that she would be studying wizardry had drawn him to her even more.

He had managed to keep from linking with her after Delanan's warning, but it had been hard. After all, the two of them shared a bond. If she succeeded in her studies and learned to see with her inner eye, she would see the world the same way he did, which was not true of the other members of his wiga. He had been born with the half-blind outer eyes of humankind, just as Elise had.

His body twisted as he changed direction to avoid a grove of giant kelp. While he enjoyed swimming through the majestic growths with the dancing leaves his sonar echoed as cascades of tinkling notes. It was dangerous when wearing a pack harness. The straps could tangle in the thick growth and, if they did and the victim panicked, he could drown. He had found one of the children of the wiga drowned like that once, unable to untangle himself even after switching to human form, and he had been wary of kelp forests ever since. He rose to the surface, blew, and dove again. The bottom sloped up steeply to a beach ahead. If the directions Incal had given him were correct, it ought to be the beach belonging to the village of Bria.

He shifted just beyond the point where the waves began to curl and rode a breaking wave in his human form. The pack on his back disturbed his balance, and he nearly stumbled before getting his legs under him. When he had recovered and made it out of the water, he looked around for witnesses to his awkwardness, but there were only two old men repairing fishing nets more than halfway down the beach. He wondered at the disappointment he felt. Surely he hadn't expected Elise to be waiting for him? It was nearly noon. She was probably sitting down to lunch.

He carried his pack up the sand to a point above the tide line and unsealed it. Then, remembering that Bria was a human village and not one regularly visited by ingvalarin, he opened the pack and got out a pair of pants and a cotton shirt as well as his sandals.

Dressed, he walked down the beach to where the men sat on a pair of barrels, their nets spread out in the sand around them. They were ancient and as alike as identical twins, their skin weathered by the elements where it wasn't covered with faded blue sailcloth overalls, cotton shirts and straw hats.

"Good day, gentlemen," he said in the human tongue.

"G'day," one of the men said, not bothering to look up.

The other old man raised his hand and tipped his round, wide-brimmed hat back on his head, surveying Errin from head to toe. "Don't get many of you folk in Bria. You come to see someone special?"

Errin swallowed, reluctant to admit to this stranger that he had come so far just to talk to a child. He said, "I hear there is a wizard living here."

The fisherman, satisfied, said "Oh, aye," and returned his attention to his needle.

"Could you tell me where to find him?"

The old man looked up again, glanced toward the village, and then back to Errin. "Don't reckon he's home. Couldn't rightly tell you where to look this time o' day." He went back to his sewing.

"Could you tell me where he lives?"

The other old man said abruptly, still without looking up, "Anyone in tha village tell you that. Big gray house wi' blue shutters. Can't miss it. But you won't find nobody there."

"Thank you. Thank you very much," Errin said, and headed toward the village.

Despite his native caution regarding the fishermen's directions, and the fact that all the houses were gray, having been built with marinwood shingles that weathered to a silvery hue, Errin did find the wizard's house unmistakable. The house with blue shutters was the largest structure in the village. No one answered his knock, however, and the house appeared as empty as the old men had warned him it would be.

He looked up and down the main street. No adults were in sight, only two boys playing in a yard surrounded by a white picket fence in front of the house next door.

"Good day. Can you help me?" he asked them, walking up to the fence. "I'm looking for the Wizard Derwen."

The boys broke off their game, and the taller, older one, who looked to be about Elise's age, stared at Errin. Errin noted by the construction of their eyes that both boys had were-sight.

When he had completed his examination, the older boy walked up to the fence. Stocky, with dark brown hair and solemn brown eyes, he had on a pair of corduroy pants and a faded cotton shirt, half unbuttoned. "Good day to you, master," he said, stumbling over the formal courtesy. "The wizard's giving lessons up the hill. You came out of the sea, didn't you?"

Errin nodded, seeing the look of longing in the boy's eyes. The half-blooded who had sight but not the ability to shape-shift often heard the call of the sea, but had no way to answer it. He wondered if the boy's parents were similarly crippled and felt a surge of pity, and relief that his own fate had been different. He, at least, had been born with the ability to shift, even if he hadn't been born with were-sight and had to learn to see in his human form. He shielded his emotions before the boy could pick them up and asked, "What's your name?"

"Entanu. Entanu Lesho."

"What's up the hill, Entanu?"

"The big house. The wizard usually doesn't get back til late when he goes up the hill." The boy hesitated, his eyes round and bright. "What's it like in the sea?"

Errin sighed. He understood the boy's curiosity, but satisfying it would not satisfy the boy's longing; might, in fact, intensify it. Still, the child had asked. Errin would do his best to answer. He called up a fragment of song in his mind and projected it as hard as he could. Most of those with were-sight could pick up mental images, if the images were sent clearly. Such impressions were different from the formalized images of mind-speech, which the child would not have been trained to understand. Mere impressions were subject to different interpretations, but music was easiest of all to understand.

Entanu's eyes widened and his face smoothed in an expression of bliss. Then the second boy, who looked several years younger, came up to the fence and said, "Me, too!"

Errin nodded and projected the images again to the younger child, who shared the same brown hair and eyes as well as the same vision as the older one.

Entanu broke out of the trance the images induced and frowned at his now raptly smiling companion. "You shouldn't have shown Oumaroo. Now he'll long for it, too."

Errin shook his head. "He would anyway, just as you do. But with a wizard here, you both should be studying with him. You might have the ability to learn."

Entanu shook his head. "He's the court wizard. We couldn't pay him."

Errin was shocked. "The wizards of my experience seek pupils. They don't drive them away."

"The Wizard Derwen came here to teach the son of the Lanrai," Entanu said. "He isn't interested in us."

"But he already has another pupil, doesn't he?"

"The heir of Adun." The boy nodded. "How did you know?"

"I know her. My wiga camps on Adun in the spring and early summer. In fact, it's Elise I really came to see." He found that easier to admit to other children. "But if the wizard already has two students, why wouldn't he take more?" He thought of the classes he attended every fall and winter in Sussey where as many as twelve children gathered around the Wizard Delanan and he recruited anyone willing to learn.

"She's the heir of Adun and we're half-breeds," Entanu said. His teeth gnawed at his lower lip. "People here would be afraid of us, if we tried to learn wizardry."

Errin had heard of such bigotry and even Elise had expressed a fear of wizards, but, living in Sussey or with the wiga, such prejudices had never seemed real to him. Nor could he imagine a wizard sharing such provincialism. He shook his head. "In Sussey there'd be no lack of teachers anxious to teach you."

Entanu's eyes widened. "You've been to Sussey, too?"

"I live there half of each year."

The boy nodded. "You weren't born with were-sight. You had to learn."

Errin inhaled. Not many of the were-folk could tell that merely by looking at him. He had long ago changed the formation of his eyes to fool the casual observer. Knowing that the boy had seen through his defense left him feeling exposed, reminding him of the years before he gained his vision when he had no control over even the form of his own body. "Your sight is sharp. That's a good sign if you ever do want to study."

Entanu shook his head. "I'm sorry. I didn't mean to offend."

"No apology necessary." Errin forced himself to smile and to proffer the message of reassurance with his mind as well as with the muscles of his face. "We all have sensitivities, but mine are no fault of yours. Tell me, if the wizard is going to be up the hill until late, will Elise be there too? Surely that's a long time for a lesson."

Entanu grinned, glad of the change of subject. "No. She should be down any time now. The wizard only gives lessons in the morning."

"What house does she live in?"

"That one there." Entanu pointed at another silver gray house, this one with dark green shutters and trim.

Errin examined it. "Thank you."

Less than an hour later he watched as Elise came down the hill, kicking an irregular gray and white stone. She was tall and thin, her red hair bound into two ragged braids around her narrow, finely boned face.

Kick. The stone skidded sideways across the path. Errin could see her annoyance. She took eight steps to the left and kicked again. This time the stone flew downhill but also all the way across the road to the other side and into the brush at the edge. Elise had almost reached the bottom of the hill before she looked up and saw him watching her. She broke into a run.

"Errin! Errin Yar!" She stopped in front of him. "What are you doing here?"

He grinned. "I'm glad to see your studies haven't damped your spirits."

She eyed him curiously. "Why are you here?"

"What reason could I have but to see you?"

"I don't know." She shook her head, but her face broke into a smile.

"I didn't think I'd ever see you again. I'm glad you're here. How long can you stay?"

He frowned. "Not long. I only came to see how you're doing, so I could take news of you back to Pela and the others. I'll have to swim hard now, if I'm to catch the wiga before they reach southern waters."

"Oh." She bit her lip.

"Don't pout, Elise. Do you have lessons this afternoon, or can we ride a few waves before I leave?"

Her face brightened. "We can ride waves. Come on, I'll stop by my cousins' to tell them where I'll be." She grabbed his hand and pulled him toward the house with green shutters. "I'd skip my afternoon lessons for a chance to go surfing with you, but I don't have any today, anyway."

"Don't sound so disappointed," Errin said, letting her tug him along. "Are the lessons hard?"

Elise shrugged. "It's not that they're hard. They make my head hurt sometimes, and I'm not very skilled." She reached the gate in front of her house and opened it. "Wait here. I won't be a minute."

When she came back a few minutes later she wore a strange looking garment fitted at the top, but with a short, voluminous skirt. "What's that you're wearing?" he asked.

She giggled. "A bathing costume. Here on the mainland we have to wear clothes no matter what we're doing."

He shuddered. "Is it as uncomfortable as it looks?"

She nodded, giggling again at his expression. "It's worse than it looks. Mainlanders are weird."

Errin was glad to see her smiling again, but her earlier disparagement of her talent bothered him, and he couldn't stop himself from returning to the subject. "You know, you shouldn't expect too much of the early part of your training. Three years isn't much time." He frowned when he saw her expression take on a discontented pout. "You can't expect to become a wizard overnight."

Elise turned away from him and started to walk toward the beach. "But Del can do things I can't, and he's only nine."

Errin caught up with her. "Then he's been studying longer than you, hasn't he?"

Elise tossed her head. "I'm still a year older. I should be stronger."

He shook his head. "It doesn't work that way. Hasn't your master explained that to you? It isn't age, but the amount of time you've spent in concentration. How old was the boy you're studying with when he started his training?"

"I don't know exactly. Somewhere around two or three, I guess. He got tested early, because he's a descendent of one of the great wizards."

"So he's been studying for six years, to your three. That means he should be twice as good as you, despite your relative ages, if your talents are perfectly matched. I'd have thought Derwen would have explained that when you started your studies." They reached the top of the sandy, sloping beach and he grabbed her hand, pulling her around to face him. "Didn't he explain that to you?"

"I don't know. I don't remember." She looked up at him and wrinkled her nose. "I don't want to talk about lessons anymore. Can't we just go surfing?"

He nodded and let her drag him down the beach. She was just a child, after all. He couldn't imagine why he'd been so concerned, and what it was about her that had drawn him here.

THE WIZARD DERWEN STOOD ON THE HEADLAND and watched as Elise played in the surf with an ingvalar. The sight disturbed him. What was a child from one of the wigan doing on the mainland? Why had he sought out Elise Adun? She was a steady child, a good student. What could she have in common with one of the sea folk, idle nomads who never did a day's work, but devoted their lives to the pursuit of pleasure?

At least it was only a single visit - he had scanned the boy's mind and made sure of that - but there had been other things in the boy's mind that disturbed him, and he hadn't been able to read more than surface thoughts before the boy had sensed him and raised his shields. And that in itself was a puzzle; an ingvalar of the wigan folk shouldn't have been so sensitive or had such an impenetrable shield. He shrugged. Well, it wouldn't be his problem much longer. Just one more thing he would have to mention to Ashe.

IV

MONTH OF ILFARNAR

> *Remember, there is an art to ruling well. That art demands that one see all sides of any question, examine every point of view . . . The resolution of a difficult situation is never simple or obvious. If it were, there would be no problem. Further, the true resolution of any situation should benefit, or at least satisfy, all the parties concerned.*
>
> — EXCERPTS FROM THE ART OF GOVERNMENT, BY VYDARGA V OF ILWHEIRLANE

A DELIBERATELY NONDESCRIPT MAN, the Wizard Ashe had sand-colored hair and a face devoid of a single distinctive feature. Slightly above average height, he did not appear tall. Even his pale blue eyes, surrounded by almost colorless lashes, had a quality of opacity that deprived them of expression.

Sitting in the Wizard Derwen's private chambers in Ninkarrak, the Black Tower, Ashe wondered why he had been summoned. Ninkarrak, after which the capitol city had been named, was the heart of the human lands. He was accustomed to the borderlands, but Derwen was head of the Varfarin. So Ashe, being summoned, had come.

He felt he had the right to an explanation, but Derwen had not offered one. In fact, the stocky little man had ignored Ashe for the last hour, busy writing at his desk. "Sit down, I'll be with you presently," had been all he had said.

So Ashe waited. Born Paule Ashe in Duragan, he had grown up in the far northern court of Akyrion after his affinity for the telepathic karothin drew the attention of the Wizard Kaaremin. Kaaremin and his mate, Andamin, had taken Ashe as an apprentice. When Ashe qualified as a wizard, he had wandered for years before joining the Varfarin. He had never before been in Ilwheirlane.

The Black Tower itself awed him with the sheer perfection of its engineering, but his present surroundings were less impressive. Derwen's study was paneled with dark wood, and the Esalfar's furniture appeared old and cumbersome. Ashe found himself thinking that the room suited Derwen and shielded his thoughts. He might be unimpressed by his superior, but it would be unwise to let the Esalfar know that.

"Well," Derwen said, finally turning to Ashe, "that's taken care of. Glad you could get here so promptly."

Ashe inclined his head. "Perhaps you could explain the urgency?"

Derwen rose and crossed the room to a table where a serving tray had been set out, pouring them each a glass of wine. "There's a meeting I want you to attend with me." He gave one glass to Ashe and swirled the wine in his own. Despite being overweight, with his clothes untidy and his cravat askew, he had a certain ponderous dignity. "It's always a good idea to have a witness when one makes a royal request," Derwen said, "especially as I expect the petition to be denied."

"What petition?"

"Balek wants military aid for Cassinga. Sent a fast courier ship with the request. He really wants Ilwheirlane to come and fight his battles for him, which isn't going to happen. But I have to pass on his petition, and then I'll have to go to Cibata myself. At least that's what he wants me to do and, while I may be head of the Varfarin, Balek's a stronger wizard. So I try and heed his appeals as best I can."

"Why would Balek want you in Cibata?"

Derwen snorted. "He says my presence will be a sign of the Varfarin's continued support of human rule there. I'm not sure that's his real reason, but, as I said, I can't afford to offend him. If Vanda doesn't authorize military aid for Cassinga, I'll have to sail within the week. Which brings me to the other reason I summoned you."

He hesitated and took a swallow of his wine. "I need to take you away from your present assignment. When you applied to join the Varfarin, I contacted Kaaremin. He indicated that you have a particular gift for dealing with the young and that your vision is extensive." His eyes met Ashe's with sudden intensity. "He said that you could be a great wizard, if your dedication to that goal matched your talent."

Ashe shrugged. "Kaaremin is given to exaggeration."

Derwen's eyes narrowed. "Perhaps, but it's your skill as a teacher that interests me most. Did Kaaremin exaggerate in that regard as well?"

Ashe raised one eyebrow. "You have someone in particular you want me to teach?"

"That depends." Derwen drew in a deep breath. "Your application to join the Varfarin said nothing of your experience as a teacher."

Ashe took a careful sip of his wine. Acidic, but drinkable. He looked back at Derwen. "I wasn't, at that point in time, interested in teaching."

"And now?"

"Depends on the pupil. I have no desire to waste my time teaching basics to a marginal student."

Derwen nodded and sat down on a chair across from Ashe's. "These students aren't marginal."

"Students?" Ashe's eyebrow rose again. "I'm certainly not interested in taking healers' sessions. Any competent journeyman or apprentice wizard can do that."

Derwen waved his hand as though brushing something away. "I know it's customary to take one apprentice at a time, but I think that's a mistake. Rand took two girls some ninety years ago, and he says, now he's tried it, he won't do it any other way. They help each other practice and there are other benefits."

Ashe frowned. "I understand the theory. Delanan's been preaching it for years. And the interaction between students was one of the things that made Onchan so successful."

"Precisely," Derwen said.

"But, in practice, I foresee difficulties. The students need to be at the same stage of development and of roughly equal talent or jealousy may arise. At Onchan," Ashe said, "you not only had a large number of children, you also had different wizards, each teaching in an area of particular strength. I think that's the ultimate reason for Onchan's success."

"Unfortunately, there's no way we can duplicate the conditions of Onchan today." Derwen's hand curled into a fist as he brought it down on the arm of his chair. "Jehan knows, I wish we could. Onchan's ratio of achievement in producing qualified wizards was phenomenal compared to what we manage now. Three quarters of the students I've started to train quit before they even made journeyman wizard."

"Wizards are mobile," Ashe said. "There's no reason apprentices couldn't be traded around once they reach a certain level. That way they could learn certain aspects of their training from the best teachers available. Delanan's experimented with various methods on Sussey."

Derwen shook his head. "I've heard of Delanan's work, but most wizards won't accept that. Not sure I would myself, under normal circumstances. Good apprentices are hard to find. When you find one, you feel possessive." He sighed. "But it's no good wishing I could keep mine. They're not old enough for the kind of traveling I'll be doing, and, anyway, my position takes too much of my energy these days. They'll be better off with you."

"Who are they?"

"There's a boy and a girl. They're living in a village called Bria on the west coast. The boy's got the most raw strength I've ever met in a child. Unfortunately, he's undisciplined. It takes more than talent to make a great wizard, as you know."

Ashe shrugged. "What makes you think I might be a suitable teacher?"

Derwen sighed again. "I don't know. Put it down to instinct, or a hunch. Either of these children could become strong enough to be the wizard I've been looking for, the one I'll appoint as my successor. But the boy's hard to judge because his talent doesn't run in the usual channels."

Derwen took a gulp of his wine. "The girl's name is Elise Adun. She's young, and she's unusual because her family want her trained. They sent her to live with relations in Bria four years ago, when they heard I was staying there to train the boy."

"Where's she from?" Ashe's curiosity roused itself.

"The Outer Islands." Derwen shrugged. "An island by the name of Adun to be exact. She's the heir. I suspect it's one of the islands where the sea folk come ashore."

Ashe nodded. "They want to keep her away from temptation and think the study of wizardry's the lesser evil."

"Yes, but they may be too late," Derwen said, frowning. "She's already had dealings with the wigan folk. She learned mind-speech from them; she even learned about mind-links. And one of them visited her this summer in Bria. That worried me. There's nothing like the song of the sea to destroy discipline."

Ashe made a gesture with one hand, part shrug, part acknowledgment. "Most of the population of Sussey survive the lure. I suspect they may be stronger because of it."

"I'd rather not take the chance. We need wizards, not idle hedonists." Derwen set his glass down and rose from his chair to pace the room. "But aside from her connection with the sea folk, the girl should give you no trouble. She's a hard worker. The boy's another story."

"You said he was unusual."

"He has great talent. I've been training him since he was two, but now . . ." Derwen hesitated, then sat back down in his chair. "Actually, I'd been thinking of finding someone else to train Del in any case. We aren't getting along and I'm afraid it's interfering with his training."

"He's difficult?"

"He's stubborn." Derwen waved a hand as though to brush aside his words. "Oh, outwardly he's obedient enough most of the time, but I don't think he ever tries to work at the mental exercises I give him. Half the time he's off in some dreamland where I can't reach him at all."

"His name's Del?"

"Del Maran," Derwen said. "And that's another problem. He's the son and heir of the Lanrai of Luro. With his heritage, he has no reason to care about the study of wizardry."

"But you said he has talent. How can you tell what he's capable of if he doesn't practice?"

Derwen snorted. "Oh, he practices, but not the things I tell him to practice. I think he can communicate with animals."

"How old is he?"

"Ten. I have to warn you though, he's got ingvalarin blood as well. He's even inherited the ability to shape-shift. I don't think he's found that out yet, but he will, and then he'll be even harder to deal with. I only hope he doesn't get involved with the sea folk. Once he hears the song of the sea, we'll never get him back."

"I've often been surprised by who does and who does not become addicted to that music," Ashe said, shaking his head. "It rarely draws the ones I'd most expect it to attract."

Derwen's eyes came up to meet Ashe's. "I hope you're right, but I felt I had to warn you. Del hates staying inside, hates concentrating on anything routine. He's always outside, running across the hills like a wild thing. When he can shift into a dolphin and take to the sea, even if the song doesn't take him, you'll have a hard time finding him to teach him anything."

"He's young. Children like to play outdoors."

"But most human children learn to accept responsibility. You can't say that of the sea folk."

Ashe took a deep breath and let it out slowly. "Aren't you forgetting Sussey?"

Derwen grimaced. "I suppose I am, but I haven't had much contact with the ingvalarin of Sussey, and I've seen too much of the damage the wigan folk do along the coast." He met Ashe's gaze again. "But I apologize. I suppose I am sounding like the worst of racial bigots."

Ashe laughed. "Not quite the worst."

Derwen's eyes narrowed. "Now I'm sure it's a good thing I've had to make this decision. You're what Del needs. If you'll take the job?"

Ashe sobered. "I'll take it. I hope I'll be able to supply what they need. Your children sound intriguing, and it will be interesting to experiment with teaching more than one at a time. I'll have to talk with Rand and Delanan about their methods."

"Thank you, Ashe," Derwen said, "you've relieved my mind. I'm not looking forward to this trip to Cibata, but at least I'll have one less worry."

"I heard about the fall of Nemali, of course. But did we lose so many people when the Mocubatam fell that Balek has real cause for concern?"

"We lost four," Derwen said, "two of them qualified wizards, the other two promising apprentices. But the human foothold in Cibata has been tenuous for years. There's always real cause for concern."

V

4626, 463RD CYCLE OF THE YEAR OF THE MALIK
MONTH OF TORIN

Theocan a Malik ba end a borvajendo,
gabo e ganod.

The Year of the Malik is a time of treachery,
madness and violence.

— FROM THE BOOK OF YEARS

ELISE, AGE TWELVE, SAT WITH THE TWO BOYS who had become her best friends: Del Maran, the son of Orris Maran, the Lanrai of Luro and Commander of the Shore Guard, and Entanu Lesho. They were in their favorite lookout on the point north of Bria, at the top of the highest point of the headland projecting into the bay. Elise had the watch.

She had just spotted a ship slicing through the sapphire waters of the Bay of Luro spread out below her. The sleek, black barkentine sported all its canvas on its course up the bay. Its white sails billowed in the fresh wind, tipping the waves with foam. Elise rarely saw ships that size, ships designed for ocean travel. "Look at that," she called to her friends. "Isn't it beautiful?"

Del and Entanu had been lying on their backs, watching a flock of seagulls soaring overhead. Elise's words brought them to their knees to look over her shoulders through the rocks that surrounded their perch. "Yeah, pretty. Wonder why it's heading this way?" Del Maran's eyes closed.

"I never saw one of the big ships this side of the bay before," Entanu said. "If we see them at all, they're going up to Onchan where there are piers and docks and stuff."

"Even Onchan doesn't get many big ships these days," Elise said. "Uncle Lehar says it's been over a thousand years since all the slips were filled."

"Since the College of Wizards closed." Del's forehead creased as he concentrated on the approaching barkentine, trying to sense it more clearly. "So what's it doing heading for Bria?"

"Ashe gets funny visitors sometimes," Elise suggested.

"They've never come by water before." Del shook his head. He was tall for his age, and lanky, with a shock of unruly chestnut hair. Elise thought that his features looked too big to fit in his face. Although the youngest, his training and strength of will were such that she and Entanu usually deferred to him.

"What can you see, Del?" she asked, suddenly worried by the expression on his face. Del's wizard vision had already surpassed Entanu's were-sight.

Elise's sight was weak in comparison. At that range even her regular eyesight was better. "Can you make them out? You don't think it could be a warship do you? The isklarin didn't give notice when they attacked Ardagh."

Del shrugged, but his eyes stayed shut and he frowned with concentration. "We're not at war with the isklarin, at least not openly. Dad was talking to Mum over breakfast, before he went to Onchan with Ashe. He said they wouldn't want to risk starting an open war now. Anyway, they attacked Ardagh from land. They don't have many ships in the Thallassean."

"Maybe it's a pirate ship." Entanu scowled. "The linlarin raid all the time. My cousins near Dun were raided two years ago. Genua was killed." Although he was the same age as Elise, he was shorter and stockier than Del.

"Are they pirates?" Elise asked.

The ship had come about and had lowered its sails in preparation for anchoring off the shore south of the village. Elise could identify it as a warship now; the sides had gun ports for at least twenty cannon.

"The linlarin mostly attack the east coast," Del protested.

"They raid the Thallassean coast, too, sometimes," Entanu said, watching as the anchor was lowered. "Remember, the raid on Halek down the coast got your father started with the Shore Guard."

The ship was still a long way away. "What do the crewmen look like?" Elise demanded. "I can't make them out from here."

Entanu sighed. "I can't be sure. They could just be wearing tight, dark clothing."

Elise tensed. The strange ship was suddenly not beautiful at all. The linlarin fought naked to facilitate their shape-changing.

"Jehan! They are pirates! They're naked except for harnesses and they have striped hair, I'm sure of it," Del said, turning and starting to climb down the rocks toward the trail.

"What're you going to do?" Elise asked, swallowing hard and following, Entanu right behind her.

"We have to warn Mum." Del reached the trail and started to run. "She'll know what to do. There are only women, children and old people in the village and the ship's anchored where it can't be seen."

"Most of the men are out at sea fishing," Elise gasped, running after Del. She could hear Entanu bringing up the rear, but being steadily left behind.

Before she and Del had completely outdistanced Entanu, they heard the warning bell sound from the Sanctuary of Maera in the village and slowed down.

"What do we do now?" Elise asked, as Del started to run again the minute Entanu caught up. "They've already attacked Bria. The bell means we're supposed to hide."

"Mum's at home. I've got to try and reach her. Dad and Ashe are in Onchan. They won't be back until tomorrow."

"We're supposed to hide," Entanu said, panting.

"No! I've got to reach Mum. They can't have reached Cliff House yet," Del insisted.

Elise had no breath for arguing and followed Del at a reckless speed down the narrow, twisting path, leaping over roots and loose rocks and giving thanks that they were going down hill, not up. It took them some fifteen minutes to reach the place where the trail forked, one branch going back toward the cliffs and Cliff House, Del's home, and the other branch going on down to Bria.

Del took the curve and raced up the path toward his home without pausing. Entanu and Elise followed, but more slowly. Elise felt scared and she thought Entanu was, too. They had heard of the ferocity of linlarin pirates all their lives. She had no desire to see whether the stories were true. The raiders could have reached Cliff House already, if they came this way first, whatever Del wanted to think. Del was being reckless.

To Elise's relief Del did slow down and move off the trail as they neared the crest of the hill where the forest ended and the gardens of Cliff House began. Elise had just taken to the woods herself when Del gestured for them to get down. She and Entanu dove into the nearest clump of bushes.

"When you're threatened, close your mind to everything. Be a mouse," the Wizard Ashe had taught. "Think of individual grains of barley or wheat. Think of piling them in a hole. Don't think of fear or the threat. Thoughts of fear draw an attacker."

She was a mouse, piling treasured grain into a hole in the ground. Her eyes flicked open and she saw fifteen tall, naked linlarin, both males and females, running past her down the trail she and the boys had just come up. Five tigers loped beside them, tigers with domed foreheads. Elise thought of being a mouse and cowered away from the strange, feral smell.

She was still lost in being a mouse when Del shook her minutes later. "They must have come straight to Cliff House." He shook Entanu, too. "Come on, we've got to see what happened."

Elise shook her head to throw off her momentary disorientation and noticed that Del looked pale. "Who else was with your Mum?"

"The maids and gardeners. I don't know how many. Some of them had the day off. Maybe they had time to get away into the woods." Del took Elise and Entanu's hands and led them through the last of the trees to the edge of the lawn where they could see the house.

Cliff House dated back to the Age of Wizards and Elise had always thought it beautiful. Today, despite the bright sunshine, it seemed to loom ominously.

"What if there are still linlarin inside?" Entanu asked, holding back.

"They came to raid. They'll be in a hurry to leave before troops can get here from Onchan," Del said, but Elise sensed that he felt as reluctant to enter the house as she and Entanu.

They walked across the east lawn to where the track coming up from the village met the courtyard set between the main part of the house and the stable block. The front door was broken, hanging drunkenly by one bent hinge. Del pushed it aside and slid through the gap. Elise and Entanu followed.

Inside, she stared, appalled at the wanton destruction left by the raiders. Broken furniture, mirrors and ornaments were strewn about; even the walls had holes through them and the carpets had been shredded. Claw marks scored the polished wooden floor. The trail of devastation led through the front hall and back to the kitchen.

Blood smeared the tiled floor and the air was full of the sweet, coppery scent of it, mingled with a musky tiger smell. Someone had tried to barricade the stairs to the cellar, but there had been too many linlarin. The barricade had been reduced to a pile of bloody sticks.

Elise tried to pull Del back up the stairs when she saw the bodies on the floor of the cellar, but he shrugged her off. Entanu had not followed them past the pool of blood. He stared at it, very pale, his skin covered with beads of sweat.

Elise felt an acrid burning in her throat rising to choke her as she looked down at the cellar. Nothing could have induced her to go closer. She saw the ruined flesh too clearly from where she stood. She thought she might suffocate from the smells of blood and musk. When Entanu broke and ran for the kitchen door, she followed right behind him.

Entanu made it outside before vomiting into the shrubs beside the house. Elise swallowed and tried to breathe deeply, but she could still smell the blood and the feral scent of angry cats. What would she and Entanu find when they reached the village? What if she had to smell that smell in her own house? If one of those bodies had been her aunt or uncle? She felt numb and sank down on the grass beside Entanu.

She was not sure how much time passed before Del found them. He looked pale. Neither she or Entanu had moved from where they had collapsed. She felt cold.

"Come on, El, Tanu, we've got to find out what happened in the village," Del said sharply.

Entanu shook his head. "I can't, Del. I can't."

Del pulled him to his feet and shook him. "We can see what's happening from the bluff. We don't need to go down into the village. Come on, Tanu. We can't stay here."

Elise shuddered, pulled herself together and stood up. At least Del was alive. Following him seemed easier than sitting still.

They crossed the south lawn to the tumbled rocks at the top of the cliff. For a moment the village looked peaceful in the bright sunshine, then Elise noticed smoke coming from one of the houses and a door hanging ajar on another. The body of a woman lay half in and half out of some bushes near the beach. She looked away. She didn't want to see more.

"I'm going down," Del said. "It looks like they've gone. Maybe there's something we can do."

"No! You can't. You'll be killed, too!" Entanu gasped.

"They won't kill me. I've got to go. You don't have to come. You either." Del turned to Elise and she saw rage and defiance burning like hot embers in his eyes.

"If you're going, I'm going." She felt terrified of what his rage might lead him to do.

There was no way down the cliffs to the beach. They were too sheer. Del turned and strode across the lawn toward the path they had come up. Elise followed. They had almost reached it when Entanu called, "Wait for me."

He ran after them. Elise suspected that his courage came from the greater fear of being left alone. When he caught up, Del set off at a run as though to make up for lost time.

"We'll be killed for sure if we run straight into the village," Elise gasped, catching up with Del near the fork in the trail and grabbing his arm to stop him. She had never run so fast in her life. "We were told to hide in the woods if we got raided. That's where everyone else will be, everyone who's still alive."

"I've got to see." Del shook off Elise's hand and continued down the trail. Entanu lagged some distance behind them.

"Not this way," she cried.

Del grunted impatiently but slowed to a walk as they came to the first house set in the woods at the edge of Bria. Its door stood open but no sounds came from within. In fact, the whole village lay silent except for the inevitable susurrus of the waves on the beach. No dogs ran out to greet them. Even the gulls had gone.

They walked down the street. The smoke they had seen from the cliff came from the third house on the right, a neat silver gray shingled cottage with white trim and shingled beehives in the front yard like miniature houses, Katy Armon's place. Del started to run again, heading for the burning building.

Elise followed him, walking through the gate into the small yard and up the path to the doorway, but she couldn't make herself step inside. She smelled blood again. It felt hard to breathe, and a humming sound filled her head. She turned. It took her several moments to realize that the humming came from bees swarming around a hive that had been knocked over.

Entanu stopped just inside the gate. He clung to one of the posts as though he needed it for support, staring down the street. Elise bit her lip and turned in the direction Entanu faced. A tall, naked figure with striped hair stood outside a house at the other end of the village. For a moment she thought the linlar might not look their way. Then the head with its tawny and black striped hair turned and the yellow eyes focused on Entanu.

"Del," Elise whispered. She suddenly understood how a pica felt when it looked into the eyes of a malik. Paralysis. Terror. Inevitability. Entanu clung to his post. The man-like form of the linlar walked down the street. He might have been taking a casual stroll. The insignia on his harness identified him as a Senangan. Elise was surprised when she heard someone scream and realized it was herself.

Entanu didn't scream. He stood there, clinging to the post and staring as the linlar approached. The only sound he made was a choked gurgle as the Senangan's arm swept down, knife in hand, to slit his throat.

Elise sensed Del at her side in the doorway. Then a wave of angry bees rose to block the linlar from her sight. The linlar screamed and thrashed, but the bees formed a living cloak, a hooded cloak covering his head and face as well as his body. He started to run but tripped before he had gone more than a few steps. Then he tried rolling in the dirt of the street. But as fast as he crushed one coating of bees, another swarm with fresh stingers landed on him.

Elise wondered whether he would be missed, if the other Senangans would come back for him. She wondered if he had knocked over the hive, if that was why the bees attacked him, but not Entanu or Del or herself. She wondered if she dared go back down the path, past the hives, to where Entanu lay, the blood from his gaping throat soaking into the dust.

Del shook her to get her attention but she could not respond. She was as frozen as Entanu had been. Finally, Del half carried her down the path, past the hives, Entanu, and the dying linlar, and away from the village to the woods where the other survivors hid.

VI

4626, 463RD CYCLE OF THE YEAR OF THE MALIK
MONTH OF REDRI

Zand jan jathev, gres bat kath
senit la ma jidthe.

When one hears thunder, one knows there was lightning
even if one misses the flash.

— ESLARIN PROVERB

"THE ATTACK ON BRIA AND CLIFF HOUSE was a deliberate attempt to assassinate Orris Maran, the Commander of the Shore Guard. You know it. I know it. Ashe, here, knows it. Jehan, even Vanda knows it," Wizard Derwen protested.

General Braydon snorted, not bothering to answer. Derwen had a tendency to run on, and Braydon was used to letting the wave of words roll over him while he followed his own train of thought. They sat in his small, bare office, and Derwen, in full court dress, pointed up the shabbiness of the surroundings, the plain battered desk and stiff wooden chairs. A different set of maps decorated the walls, but otherwise the room had not changed since Orris had proposed the Shore Guard five years earlier.

"The interesting question is why?" the Wizard Ashe asked, drawing Braydon's attention for the first time. "Orris seems to be doing a good job, but he's no longer irreplaceable. He was thinking of retiring." Ashe met Braydon's eyes. "You couldn't have held him for more than another couple of years. Why would the Senangan navy send one of their fastest, newest ships through Belarrai, taking the risk of losing it, to eliminate him?"

Braydon frowned. Ashe might not look like much, but he had a brain. The general understood now why Derwen had insisted on including him. Neither wizard had hit the key point, though. "Where'd they get their map and timetable?" he said.

"What do you mean?" Derwen asked.

"Map to Cliff House," Braydon snorted. "Not easy to find. Small village. Isolated house. Went right to it. Man's only been home a handful of days in five years. But he should have been there the day they raided. Only a coincidence he decided to go to Onchan with Ashe," he nodded at the wizard, "that morning."

"You're suggesting someone supplied them with the information?" Derwen gasped.

"Anyone in particular?" Ashe asked, and Braydon felt certain that, while Derwen might be surprised by the mention of treason, Ashe had expected it.

"Not yet. Don't know who Orris confided in. Maybe you can help with that. You live at Cliff House," Braydon challenged.

"Yes, but I've lived there less than two years," Ashe said, "and, as you've pointed out, Orris hasn't been there for much of that time. I've no idea who his confidants may be."

"Have to pin Orris down when he comes out of shock." Braydon shook his head. "How's the boy taking his mother's death?"

"Del took the raid badly, and not only because of his mother's death. His best friend was also killed, and he feels responsible," Ashe added with a frown.

"He's not developing as well as I'd hoped," Derwen said.

"You're looking for the wrong things, I've told you so before," Ashe said. "Del has a strong will and his vision is well developed. He just uses them differently than most of us. He's highly advanced along his own path."

"Boy's eleven, isn't he?" Braydon asked. "Think he might be in danger?"

Ashe's eyes narrowed as he turned back to Braydon. "You're implying that someone initiated the raid here in Ilwheirlane. Do you have evidence to support such a supposition?"

Braydon frowned. "Always a possibility when a wealthy man dies, particularly a man in a position of authority."

Ashe shrugged. "I know nothing about the military ramifications, but as to a private motive, I don't think so. After Del, his next heir would be his brother. I know Harrel Maran well and I trust him, as does Orris. I can't think of anyone else who'd benefit from Orris and Del's deaths."

"What about his wife? Might like a title. Women have been known to scheme before," Braydon said. "Any children?"

"I'm not fond of Selicia Maran, but the last thing in the world she'd do is consort with the linlarin, or any of the were-folk. She's a devout Miunist. They have two children." Ashe shook his head. "I'm not sure who inherits after them, but I hardly think anyone would be fool enough to think he could arrange for the deaths of five people without raising suspicions."

Braydon nodded. "Shore Guard or pure chance then. Item of interest enclosed in a report about something else. Linlarin have spies, just as we do. Caught some Senangan's eye. Thought the prestige worth the risk. Possible, but I don't like the smell of it."

"F OR SOMEONE WHO ONLY STUDIES HALF THE YEAR, Errin, you've shown remarkable progress," the Wizard Delanan said.

Errin, fifteen, and the survivor of innumerable family feuds and intrigues, recognized a leading statement. "Thank you, rai," he said, keeping his face blank, his thoughts shielded.

The day's class had let out, but Delanan had called Errin back as he started home. They stood at the top of the flight of steps leading up to the adobe building which Delanan's frequent companion, the Wizard Jao, had dubbed Rakredrem, the House of Knowledge, some three hundred years before, when Delanan first opened the wizard training school and she was only a journeyman wizard. The structure stood on a hill overlooking a rocky beach three kilometers west of the town of Ruffin. Across the road from the school, the hill sloped down to a valley filled with olive orchards and vineyards. The grassy slopes around them were cropped by a breed of long-haired ruminants called metellan.

Errin walked the two kilometers from his grandmother's home outside Ruffin to the Rak, as it was commonly called, every fall and winter day except Jehansday. On Jehansday, as the wizards of the Varfarin were as much priests of Jehan as the ajaren in the temples, no classes were held.

The Wizard Delanan was a dark haired man of medium height. If Errin had not known that Delanan had been born in Kailane of fully human descent, he might have taken his stocky build and brown-gold eyes as a sign of ingvalar blood. The Wizard Jao, who also taught at the Rak three or four months of each year, often teased Delanan that he looked more like an ingvalar than she did, and she had ingvalar blood. But Jao was thin, with small bones.

Errin knew that Delanan and Jao were both senior wizards with hundreds of years of experience, although neither had qualified as a great wizard. They had been students of the Wizard Sura, one of the few human wizards to survive the Wizard's Bane eight hundred years before. He admired them both, but particularly Delanan, who had dedicated his whole life to teaching. He wondered what Delanan wanted, and was afraid to hope that this could be the invitation for which he had waited seemingly half his life.

"Sorry to keep you late if you have something to do at home," the wizard said.

Errin felt Delanan's mind touch his shield and frowned. Maybe this was his chance. "No, rai," he said.

Delanan shook his head. "You never give anything away, do you Errin?"

Errin kept his face immobile. "I don't understand, rai."

"Yes, you do. There's nothing wrong with your understanding. You're just not about to confide in anyone. Can't say I blame you, but I'm not an enemy."

"I never thought you were, rai," Errin said quickly. "I just don't know what you want from me."

"I want your oath. I want you to be my apprentice, formally; I want to train you to become a full wizard. You have the talent. The question is, do you want to use it?"

Errin's eyes widened. "More than anything else in the world, rai. It's what I've always wanted." He deliberately opened his mind and added, *"I will take the oath gladly."*

Delanan's shook his head. *"But in your case, it's not that simple, is it?"*

Errin's eyes met the wizard's. *"Since I turned seven, I've wanted to be one of the Varfarin. I've hoped that you would offer me the chance, and have known what my answer would be."*

"And your family? Will they accept your decision? Will they allow you to become a full wizard? You have an outside chance at a throne. What happens then? Aren't I taking a risk, too, if I train you and then lose you to ancestral duty?"

The images of various of his relatives coming to strange ends and the vast, gilded throne that accompanied the question almost made Errin laugh, especially as the objections Delanan raised were not the one objection he most feared. He thought, *"As I understand the nature of the Varfarin, there would be no conflict. Should not all rulers be dedicated to peace?"*

"The Ahar of Sussey bears Lyskarion. Trained, you could become a great wizard, the equal of Luth himself. What would that do to the balance of power?" An image of the Isle of Sussey swollen to fill the Thallassean Sea accompanied the question.

Errin shook his head, but retreated from the openness of mind-speech. "There are ten people between me and a throne."

"But all the children of the House of Anifi in this generation have been daughters except you. Only five men lie between you and the throne, and Lyskarion links only with a man."

Errin shrugged. "Obviously, I cannot tell you that what you fear is impossible. Stranger things have happened, but two of my cousins have already announced that they intend to have large families. For that matter, my uncle Inebolu is young enough to marry again. If any of my relations felt there was the slightest chance of my succession, they'd go to a wizard to guarantee a male heir ahead of me."

"Because you were born among the wigan folk?"

Faced with that introduction to the subject he most feared, Errin bit his lip. "You took me as your pupil. You know why my relations despise me."

Delanan shook his head. "I've never understood their hostility to you or your mother." He paused, and sighed, "Oh, I understand why the people of Sussey look down on the wigan folk in general, but not why your relations reject you particularly."

"You saw nothing unusual in my genetic patterns?"

Delanan frowned. "I've never examined your genetic patterns. Why should I have done?"

Errin looked down at the ground. "Lothar Yar, my father, is not an ingvalar of Sussey lured away by the song of the sea. He's one of the true wigan folk, from the branch of the ingvalarin who took to the sea millennia ago. By the laws of Kyra they committed the ultimate crime. They bred themselves back to the animals from whom the gods raised them."

"You have a genetic trace of true dolphins?"

Errin looked up, surprised by the tone of Delanan's voice. "You didn't know? It doesn't horrify you?"

"No." Delanan shook his head. "It surprises me, but I'm not that easily horrified. I can understand the ban among the other were-folk. After all, moles aren't very bright. Even bears and tigers wouldn't do much for their offspring's intelligence. But, now you remind me, I'd heard years ago that some of the wigan folk had interbred. I never associated that knowledge with you, I'd forgotten about it, but now I remember that the wizard who studied that particular quirk decided that in the case of dolphins such interbreeding was harmless, perhaps even beneficial to the wigan folk. Dolphins are also a sentient species. There's no loss of brain capacity. Ingvalarin can live with dolphin mates and raise their young together. In many ways, the wigan folk have more in common with true dolphins than they have with humans. And the only trace that usually carries over to the human genome is one that affects hearing and an occasional knack for rhyming. Is your hearing in your human form more than usually acute, Errin?"

Errin stared at Delanan. "I believe it is." He hesitated, then asked, "You'll still accept me, train me to be a wizard?"

"If your family consents, I'll take your oath tomorrow."

Errin felt relief so great he almost staggered. "My mother and my grandmother will consent. Will they be enough?"

"Of course, Errin. Given the circumstances, I won't insist on a royal dispensation," Delanan said wryly.

"WILL HE TAKE THE OATH?" JAO ASKED, eyeing Delanan with concern. She was small and slender with short, seal-brown hair.

"Yes," Delanan said, rubbing his hand across his eyes. "Apparently he's always wanted to do so. And I never knew. He makes me think I'm a failure as a teacher, I read him so badly."

"What do you mean?" Jao frowned.

They were in the bedroom of Delanan's apartment on the second floor of the Rakredrem, quarters they shared whenever Jao visited Sussey. Although they had never formed a linkage, they had been close ever since she helped him start the Rakredrem over three hundred years before, when she had still been a journeyman wizard. It upset her to see him so disturbed.

"Even when he first came to me as a pupil at the age of three, he was hard to read." Delanan said, walking over to the window, but obviously not seeing anything through it, his attention turned inward. "After dealing with the hostility of his relatives, his shields are so strong I can't tell what he thinks. I know now that he wants to be a wizard and join the Varfarin, because he opened his mind and showed me that desire. And it was strong."

"But you never saw any indication before?"

"No." Delanan sighed. "I knew he bottled up a lot of emotion inside, but the cork's always been too tight for me to pry out. I once hoped that his spending spring and summer with his father and the wiga would help, but I gather he's almost as alien to the wigan folk as he is to his mother's relations here. At least I now understand the reason for that a little better."

"His talent's strong. He could become a great wizard," Jao said, her blue eyes intent. "Will his background twist him? If there is that danger, perhaps you should reconsider?"

"No," Delanan was emphatic. "His background is more likely to make him a strong crusader for those he considers persecuted." He turned to face Jao. "He understands better than most of us that there are many forms of discrimination. I'm not worried about his nature turning sour, but he wants to join the Varfarin and, given the circumstances, I don't think that's a good idea."

Jao was startled, then realized what he had to mean. "Lyskarion?"

"Yes. He claims there's no chance of his inheriting, but I think he's wrong. The Wizard Myrriden has been telling everyone who will listen that Lyskarion is active, not dormant, despite a bearer without talent. What purpose could one of the living crystals have but to find a bearer with Errin's potential?"

VII

4627, 463RD CYCLE OF THE YEAR OF THE BEAR
MONTH OF TORIN

> *The inheritance of wizard talent is not a simple matter of a*
> *dominant or recessive gene. In fact, six chromosomes relating in*
> *some manner to such an inheritance have been identified and*
> *researchers suspect that there are others whose roles cannot, at*
> *this point, even be guessed.*

— EXCERPT FROM <u>GENETICS AND WIZARDRY</u>, BY THE WIZARD TORIN

JEREVAN RAYNE, THE SON AND HEIR OF THE HETRI OF LEYBURN, was born early on the third day of the month of Torin, the morning after the summer solstice. The music of a storm heralded his birth: thunder and lightning, howling wind and driving rain, with the roar of the River Eth in spate below. Leyburn House stood high on a hill above the river, and had weathered more than four thousand years of storms. Inside, conditions remained warm and dry, if not calm.

Jerevan's mother, Nadira Comar Rayne, had an easy labor, and he entered the world without undue excitement. His father, the local healer, delivered him. The Wizard Derwen attended the birth, despite Nadira's objections.

Nadira looked pale and tired after the delivery, but her blue eyes still flared with anger whenever they turned to Derwen. Most women would have considered it reassuring to have a wizard in attendance. Nadira thought it blasphemy.

"Well, Derwen? As you insisted on being here, you may as well tell us if the boy's healthy or not," Danor said, holding up the red, wrinkled infant for the wizard's examination. "I only have a healer's talent myself."

Nadira watched as Derwen examined the child, her lips pinched tight. She knew Derwen possessed the high sight, the most powerful level of vision a wizard could achieve, and that with it he could look into the pattern of her child's genetic heritage. She resented her child being the subject of such study. Indeed, had she known before she married Danor that all her children would be exposed to such an examination, she might well have refused him. Her tall, graceful figure and honey-gold hair had made her the reigning beauty of her season. She had not lacked for other offers.

But she had not known, and Danor Rayne, Hetri of Leyburn and close relative of the Estahar, actually third in line for the throne, had been the catch of many seasons.

How could she have known, she thought bitterly, her eyes narrowed and fixed on her child, when her parents had shunned everything to do with wizardry? Danor had never mentioned that all relations of the Estahar were examined at birth. At least, not until she was already pregnant.

She clenched her teeth. Ignorant of some things she might be, but she was no fool. With what she knew of her own genetic patterns and Danor's, she guessed that there was a more than even chance Derwen would find what he sought. But she would never consent to a child of hers being trained in wizardry. She would make Danor's life a torment before she agreed to that.

And she would not stand alone in her objection to having her child so trained. Her father had influence among the followers of Miune, and he shared her fear of wizardry. Any power that could produce destruction of the magnitude of that produced by the Wizards' Bane, with such a lasting effect on the land, deserved to be feared. The wizards had brought about their own fate and deserved what they got. She wished that every one of them had been destroyed.

Nadira stiffened as Derwen finished his examination, her attention fixed on him.

"The child has immense potential," Derwen said, looking up, "more than I've ever seen before. He must be trained."

"I'll never agree to such blasphemy," Nadira said, propping herself up in the bed. The confirmation of her fears came as almost a relief. At least she was prepared. She would not give way. Danor would support her in this or their marriage would be over. This was one issue where she could even appeal to the priests of Miune if he did not.

"Give him to me," she demanded, holding out her arms.

Derwen relinquished the baby reluctantly.

Danor looked from the child Nadira held against her breast to her face, pale but set with determination. He said, "I know I must agree to his being trained as a healer, but the law doesn't allow you to demand that he take further training. And, as further training would violate my wife's religious beliefs, I must forbid it."

"He might be another Cormor," Derwen protested. "He has the strongest potential I've seen in all my years of testing children. I must be allowed to train him. It's the task I've waited all my life to perform."

Nadira stared at Derwen. His intensity made her both angry and afraid. She turned to Danor. "Don't let my child be used by him! Swear it to me!"

Danor shook his head and reassured her. "I can't stop the boy being trained as a healer. I received that training myself; the law requires it. But I won't permit him to be trained as a wizard. You have my word on it."

Nadira nodded. "I trust you."

Month of Redri

Errin rolled the freshly crushed grape juice across his tongue, savoring the flavor. "A good pressing. The grape is strong with plenty of sugar and enough tannin to allow it to age well. I wouldn't keep it more than two years in oak, though." He turned to where the Cellar Master waited with his family, the Wizard Delanan, and the five other wizards Delanan had invited to hear his oath.

They stood on the pressing room floor in the winery at Ruffin, the source, according to experts, of some of the finest red wines made on Tamar. The cup Errin had drunk from had been filled from the huge vat beside him, brim full of the season's pressings. The air of the room was redolent with the aromas of the harvest: the rich, fruity scent of crushed grapes mingling with the mustier odor of yeast.

The Cellar Master nodded. "A good year."

"I wonder who you inherited your palate from?" Pendra, Errin's cousin, mused. "You couldn't have got it from your mother. I don't think she can tell the difference between red wine and white." She looked at Nutena and asked, "Can you, Aunt Nutena?"

Nutena blushed and tried to smile, as though the criticism had not hurt.

Farrell laughed. "A slight exaggeration, Pendra. There's nothing wrong with my sister's eyes. She can tell red from white by the color."

"I think Pendra was thinking in terms of a blind tasting," Aliara said. "I doubt if Nutena could tell the difference without looking. I sometimes wonder if she has any taste buds at all. I used to think you had the worst palate possible, Farrell, until I had Nutena. At least, when I die, you have enough sense to put the winery in Pendra's care. I've taught her all I know, and her palate's nearly as good as mine."

Errin took his mother's hand and squeezed it, receiving a thankful look in return. He knew Aliara did not mean to be cruel. She was fond of Nutena. It never occurred to her that stating the truth would hurt her daughter. Aliara, child of the royal House of Anifi, said what she thought, rarely considering the effect on those around her. And she was dedicated to the winery she had spent her life developing.

With Farrell, Aliara's insensitivity didn't matter – he was equally as insensitive – and Pendra never noticed criticism aimed at herself. Nutena, however, had painfully thin skin. Her mother's unwitting criticism had, over the years, destroyed her confidence in herself and her ability to cope with the world, although, to give Aliara her due, she never called Nutena an embarrassment to the family, nor did she harp on Errin's origins. Those accusations, and worse, came from his cousins, Pendra and Ayana.

Errin sighed. Nutena's elopement with Lothar Yar had been her one attempt to free herself from this environment, and, because of Errin, the attempt had failed. If he had been born with were-sight, she might still be listening to the song of the sea with Lothar. Instead, she had been forced to return to Ruffin so that her son could study wizardry and learn to see with his inner eye. Errin owed her a great deal for that sacrifice.

Delanan interrupted his musings. "Can you tell us, Errin, which elements in the grape juice lead you to infer that it will become a fine wine?"

"The sugar content and the balance of acid primarily," Errin said, "but there's also a rich complex of flavoring elements."

Aliara sniffed. "You can't reduce the art of wine making to a science, Delanan. If wine were just a balance of sugar and acid, we could mix it up in a vat. We wouldn't need the grapes at all."

Delanan laughed. "Thank you, Aliara, for showing us the winery. I found the experience fascinating, but we're here today to take Errin's oath. I think we should get to that now. It's been delayed long enough."

Aliara frowned. "True. But I felt it necessary to have my brother Yambol's permission. He is Ahar of Sussey, and Errin is a potential heir. However, as you know, my family can be difficult. I thought it wise to approach Yambol when I could speak with him alone, and that took time."

Delanan smiled. "No harm was done by the delay, and I admit that I, too, had wanted such permission, but Errin persuaded me of the remoteness of the possibility of his succession."

Aliara arched an eyebrow quizzically. "Did he?" She hesitated, then said, "I understand that taking the oath requires some time. You'll be more comfortable in the library." She led the way out of the winery and up the slope to Pomorry House.

Delanan and Jao followed with the Wizard Elgan and the Wizard Valanta. Errin, trailing behind, could hardly keep his eyes off Elgan. He felt deeply honored that a descendent of Cormor would be present to hear his oath. Elgan even resembled Cormor, it was said, with his chestnut hair and green eyes.

Errin had heard gossip among the other students at the Rakredrem that Elgan was arrogant, that he had quit the Varfarin out of pique when Derwen rather than himself had been named Esalfar after Cormor's death, but Errin knew that other wizards had resigned from the Varfarin at that time. Derwen had not been a popular choice. Certainly Errin saw no sign of arrogance.

And Valanta seemed to be everything her name, which meant 'Essence of Life Giving Rain,' implied. She was tall and slender and full bosomed, with long, black hair and golden skin. Standing near her in the winery he had felt her warmth and kindness. Surely someone with her compassion would not live with Elgan were he truly difficult.

He glanced back at the other two wizards who would hear his oath. The Wizard Melanth, the 'Beekeeper,' tall and blonde, and the Wizard Eldana, short and dark, were both talking intently on their way up the hill. He had never met them before, but he remembered that they had been students of the Wizard Myrriden, another wizard who quit the Varfarin when Derwen became Esalfar.

Errin bit his lip. Had Delanan chosen this group of wizards, or had he just taken advantage of their being in the area? Surely it was strange that the company should include so high a percentage of wizards whose ties to the Varfarin were either weak or non-existent. Maybe it was because Delanan's closest friends in the Varfarin, Rand and his one-time apprentices, the twin wizards Jaoda and Majaoda, were in Cibata. Jao was here, after all.

The form of the oath had been dictated by the Council of Wizards and would not bind Errin to the Varfarin. As Delanan was a member, he would be sworn not to work against the interests of the Varfarin, but that was different from pledging to become a member. Errin had expected to pledge to the Varfarin at the same time he took his oath, but somehow, with this group of witnesses, he did not see that happening.

His musings were interrupted as they arrived at the house and Aliara ushered them into the library. "You should be comfortable here, and I'll see that no one disturbs you," she said. "When you're ready for refreshments ring the bell."

Delanan thanked her and she left.

The library was a large room lined with floor to ceiling bookcases, except for the gaps necessitated by a fireplace, a window, and the two doors, one accessing the entry hall and the other door, made of glass, opening onto the patio.

"Well, Errin, I know you're a worshiper of Jehan. Are you prepared to take your oath in his name?" Delanan asked.

"Yes," Errin said.

Delanan turned to the other assembled wizards. "You've all had time today to meet and talk to Errin Yar and his family. Do any of you here know of any reason why I shouldn't take the oath of this apprentice?"

Errin swallowed, sudden fear almost choking him. One of them would speak now. They all knew of his ancestry. One of them was bound to object.

The silence lengthened, then Delanan thought, *"Then we shall link minds."*

Errin reached out to link with Delanan. Soon he was not simply linked with Delanan, something he had done before, but floating naked in space, his mind wide open, with a multitude of eyes looking into his brain.

"Will you, Errin, honor your oath given to Jehan?"

"Yes."

"Then give your oath, and we shall witness."

Errin took a deep breath and forced himself to remember the word images he had rehearsed so many times. *"I swear that I shall be guided by the laws of the Council of Wizards."*

"And what is the first law?"

"I will not use the knowledge I gain from my training to act against the interests of the Council, the Varfarin, or my master."

"The second law?"

"I will not teach, or transmit in any way, the knowledge I gain from my training to any being who has interests opposed to those of the Council, the Varfarin, or my master."

"The third law?"

The ceremony continued as Errin swore to each of the complex laws with the wizards in rapport to witness both his sincerity and his understanding. When he had sworn to the last law there was silence for a moment. Then Delanan thought, *"You have witnessed this oath?"*

The assembled wizards replied as one, *"We have."*

"Do you accept Errin Yar as an apprentice with all the rights and responsibilities that entails?"

"We do."

Errin felt the linkage dissolve. He was alone again in his own head. He felt exhausted.

Eldana came up and hugged him. Her short cap of dark hair only reached his chin, but her arms were strong. "As the youngest of the wizards here, I'm the one who went through that most recently. You have my condolences. I slept for nearly a week, afterwards."

Errin managed a weak smile, hoping he would soon be able to imitate her and retire. The long period in the multiple linkage had drained his energy. Worse, it had strained the capacity of his will and he could feel a reaction headache forming.

Delanan sensed his discomfort. "You may be excused, Errin. I'm sure Aliara will take care of feeding us and seeing us out. Don't feel embarrassed. Remember, all of us went through the same ordeal; we know exactly how you feel. Go to bed."

Errin nodded. "Thank you, rai," he said, and left the room.

When Errin had retired, Elgan looked at Delanan and said, "So, it's begun."

Delanan nodded and rang the bell. "Errin's the only male child born to the House of Anifi in this generation."

Jao said, "Derwen tested a child in the month of Torin who he swears can be an heir to Cormor. The mother is a Miunist. The child will only be allowed a healer's training."

Aliara came in with two serving maids. One carried a tea tray and the other a tray of sandwiches and hors d'oeuvres. "If tea doesn't suit you, help yourselves to the wine or liquor in the cabinet," Aliara said. She looked at Delanan and added, "There's a bottle of my private reserve."

"Thank you, Aliara," Delanan said sincerely.

Aliara's eyes narrowed. "I realize from your faces that you have more to discuss than Errin's oath. I'll leave you to it." She left.

Elgan asked, "How much does she know?"

"Nothing anyone conversant with current affairs wouldn't guess seeing us here," Delanan said. "Even Errin noticed that you're all, except Jao, presently unaffiliated with the Varfarin."

Valanta sat down by the table next to the tea tray and started to pour. She and Eldana took tea, but Elgan, Melanth, Jao and Delanan opted for wine from the bottle of Ruffin's private reserve.

"I won't pass up the chance for a glass of Ruffin's finest," Melanth said.

When they had all helped themselves to food and drink and found places to sit, Eldana said, "Myrriden reports that Vyrkarion is restless, seeking something. He feels the other karionin waking, becoming more and more aware. What's more, he senses eight of them."

"Cormor knew Cinkarion had survived the Bane," Elgan said, swirling the wine in his glass before sniffing it and then inhaling deeply. "He told me it shut him out. It wanted no contact with another mind after Agnith went mad. Only a mind of fire and ice, he said, could hold the red crystal."

"Kaaremin has also noticed increased activity in Belkarion and its link with the others," Jao said. "He says its awareness is clearer too, but he and Andamin have a strong link. They anticipate no problems."

"Belkarion wasn't present at the Bane," Eldana said. "Perhaps it won't take part in this either."

"No," Elgan said, looking around at the others. "They're all linked. The great wizards may have made them, but Jehan and Maera lent a hand in the fashioning. Cormor saw that clearly, and so far his visions have been frighteningly accurate."

"Is Maera active in this too? Have any of the sibyls prophesied?" Melanth asked, her wide brow furrowed with worry.

"A minor one in Esterias," Valanta said, stirring her tea, her green eyes pensive. "She said that a child would be born with the sign of an eye on his forehead, and that he should be taken to the land where the eye rules."

"The eye is the sign of Rav," Melanth said, her lips compressing. "That means Ninkarion and Ravaar."

"Signs and portents," Delanan said, putting his wine glass down and rising to his feet. "And the isklarin are rebuilding the Road of Masters." He walked over to the glass door to the patio and stared out. "This war will engulf the whole of Tamar."

"We've always known it would come," Jao said, eyeing Delanan with concern.

"Most of us hoped it would wait a few more years, or centuries," Melanth said.

"We still have a long time before it comes to outright war," Valanta said sharply, turning to Delanan. "Perhaps centuries. As of this moment, only Belkarion is fully linked. Cormor said the karionin would all be linked. They're critical. The side that controls the most on the day of the final battle will win."

"But can they be controlled?" Delanan asked, turning back to the others.

"Remember, the bearers will, in the end, be their choices, not ours."

"We must trust in Jehan and Maera," Valanta said, rising and confronting Delanan. "It was their will that the karionin be born. The karionin are their tools. If we worship the gods, we must trust that the karionin will choose wisely."

"The last time the karionin were active produced the Bane," Melanth said.

"Agnith went mad and shocked Cinkarion into seven hundred years of near oblivion," Elgan said with emphasis. "I agree with Valanta. We must prepare as best we can for what we see and know is coming. We must train wizards and hope they qualify, but finally, we must trust the karionin."

"And the gods," Valanta added.

"To Jehan," Melanth and Elgan said, raising their glasses and drinking.

"And Maera," Jao, Delanan and Eldana said, completing the toast.

VIII

MONTH OF ANOR

> *The ability to mentally 'speak' is not true telepathy . . .*
> *To truly communicate mind to mind, all parties to the*
> *communication must comprehend not mere 'words,' but the*
> *actual mental imagery of the others. Such cognitive symbolism*
> *varies from individual to individual, and no two minds ever*
> *naturally interpret such images in precisely the same way . . .*

— EXCERPTS FROM <u>PROBLEMS WITH TELEPATHY</u>, BY THE WIZARD AGNITH

DEL MARAN LAY ON HIS BACK IN THE LONG GRASS underneath a hollow jula tree, chewing a stem of grass and watching the bees. Bees fascinated him. A scout had found a bank of flowers. It danced the direction and coordinates. Soon other bees would go there and harvest the nectar.

The dance took place inside the hive which was inside the hollow tree, but the wood did not impede Del's sight. He could see into the hive, see the queen in her egg chamber, the workers tending the larvae, the combs of honey; he could see them all as easily as he could look inside his own body and see the cells and tissue and bone.

He liked to watch the bees and he understood their dance. Learning it had taken him an entire week, seven lazy summer days when he had been six. He had experimented the rest of that summer, sending patterns directly into the insects' brains, learning the differences in perception of each bee, even determining the range of those differences until he could control the entire hive. Then he had studied different hives until he had learned to make any bee go anywhere he wanted it to go.

He had enjoyed sending them all over the countryside, until some bees had starved because of wasted journeys. After that he had been careful to send them only to where there were flowers. Then they had saved his life. He shied away from the memory of the day his mother and Entanu died, the day he had used the bees to kill and nearly destroyed a hive. He never played with them now, but he still liked to watch them dance.

CHARNA MARAN BEAT HER BROTHER AND ELISE to the top of the hill and stared down into the meadow, arms akimbo and her hands curled into fists, her body language indicating her annoyance. Elise stopped beside Charna and followed her gaze. Del lay in the grass beneath the hollow jula, just where they had expected to find him.

Although she found Charna's frustration amusing, Elise herself found Del's recent policy of isolationism irritating. When she had first arrived in Bria she had been jealous of Del's talent. After a time, though, she had accepted his skill and his leadership. Then the linlarin came and Entanu died. Since then, whenever she turned to Del, he seemed to slip away. She found this doubly hard as, with Entanu dead, she had no other friend to whom she could turn.

Charna yelled, "Hey, Del. Come on, you're wanted."

"Coming." Del unfolded his long, lanky body and crossed the meadow toward them. Elise sensed his reluctance, and suspected Charna did, too.

Charna was the same age as Del, and beautiful. Her small bones, golden ringlets and blue eyes had always attracted male admiration. When she arrived at Cliff House, she expected Del to cater to her whims in the same way her father and brother and a string of other males had done. Elise had been amused, until Charna had turned mean in her disappointment.

"What were you doing?" Ethan Maran demanded as Del climbed the hill. Ethan was sixteen, three years older than Del and Charna, two years older than Elise. It annoyed him that Del had nearly caught up with him in height as well as having wizard talent. Ethan substantially outweighed Del, however, and Elise thought he could still beat Del in a fight. He had done so several times in the months just after the cousins arrived in Bria. Since then, Del had avoided conflict.

"He was sleeping," Charna said. "Del doesn't do anything that requires effort."

"It's too hot to be energetic," Del agreed, eyeing his cousins warily. "If you're going hunting, I won't go with you."

"We don't want you," Ethan said. "Ashe does. The Wizard Derwen's visiting. That's why Elise is with us. You two wizards are supposed to go down to the beach and show off your progress. As there's nothing else going on today, Charna and I decided we'd come along to watch." He turned and started back down the hill.

When Del's mother had been killed during the linlar raid, his father had dedicated himself to the Shore Guard. Unfortunately, that had forced Orris to turn to his brother, Harrel Maran, for help in overseeing his estates, so Harrel, his wife and his two children had moved into Cliff House. Elise had been glad when she heard they were coming. She thought both she and Del needed new friends after Entanu's death. But that was before she met Del's cousins.

"Come on." Charna turned to follow Ethan. "Must you always make him mad?"

"He makes himself mad. I don't have to do anything," Del said, catching up with her. "Why's Derwen here?"

"I don't know. Why don't you ask him?" Charna tossed her head.

Elise said, "He's taking Ashe back with him to court. They leave for Ninkarrak tomorrow."

"How'd you find that out?" Charna demanded.

"I was with Ashe when Derwen arrived."

"Currying favor with the teacher," Charna sneered.

They walked through a thin strip of woods and came out on the edge of the north lawn of Cliff House. The house and garden still looked beautiful. Even Elise's memories of the day of the raid could not destroy her love for Del's home. The original stone building dated back to the time when men first freed themselves from slavery to Gandahar. It had been a walled fortress situated on the top of the bluff overlooking the village. Wooden wings had been added and windows were cut through the stone when the structure had been remodeled during the Age of Wizards. The marinwood shingles were silvered by the effects of time and salt air, and the stone had weathered to a pale gold.

Pink, yellow and red roses climbed trellises up the walls of the house and edged the east and west lawns. Neat hedges of flowering ericala marked the borders and outlined an herb garden between the house and the north lawn. Carefully tended flower beds bloomed all year long, and the air was heavy with their perfume. The perennial beds were vivid with purple and blue iris and golden anathallian, the lower beds brilliant with scarlet meldethin and violet pansies with yellow hearts. Even though the day was calm, Elise could hear the sound of the surf on the rocks at the foot of the cliff.

They crossed the north lawn to the gravel track leading down to the village. They hadn't gone far before they saw a small boy coming up the trail from Bria carrying a bucket of lobsters.

"Oumaroo!" Charna said gleefully.

Elise bit her lip, her steps slowing. Why had Oumaroo Lesho chosen this moment to deliver something to Cliff House? Couldn't he have waited until Ethan and Charna were out of the way on the beach?

"Hey scaly! Is that all you managed to catch today?" Ethan stepped into the middle of the track, blocking Oumaroo's way.

Elise gritted her teeth. The dolphin folk weren't scaly even in their dolphin forms. Dolphins were mammals, after all, but pointing out his stupidity wouldn't stop Ethan.

"This is the number your mother asked for." Oumaroo looked down at the ground and stepped to the side of the trail to get around Ethan. Entanu's younger brother was eleven, but small for his age, with dark hair and eyes and the same stocky build.

"Leave him alone," Elise said.

Charna eyed Del slyly. When Charna and Ethan's mother, Selicia Maran, arrived at Cliff House, she had been shocked to discover that several of the families in Bria were of mixed blood, part human and part ingvalar. Selicia, a devout Miunist, believed that the mixing of human blood with that of the were-races was the greatest sin possible; that the children of such matings were monsters. She had complained to her husband that it was outrageous to expect her to live in the same place with the offspring of such liaisons. He had ignored her bigotry, but she had taught it to her children. Elise had heard Charna and Ethan's parents' fighting about the subject on several occasions.

But Oumaroo was Entanu's brother. If a threat to anyone could prod Del out of his fantasies, it would be a threat to Oumaroo. Elise could see that Charna agreed. The blonde girl had a hungry, expectant look in her eyes.

Elise said, "Leave him alone, or I'll tell your father."

Ethan ignored her. "Aren't you a bit far from water, fish-boy?" He moved to the side, again blocking Oumaroo.

Elise turned to Del. He was frowning but did not move to interfere. "Do something, Del," she whispered.

Del looked at her blankly. "What can I do? Ethan will turn on me if I say anything and you know what will happen then. I'll get knocked out, like I did the last time I fought him. And he'll beat Oumaroo harder because I dared to interfere."

Elise glared at him. "You're older now. You're nearly as tall as he is. Oumaroo is Tanu's brother. You're just spineless."

Del looked away, but she saw the muscles in his jaw clench and a faint flush rose in his cheeks.

Oumaroo had to stop or walk into Ethan. He held the bucket in front of him like a shield and stared at his tormenter, his dark eyes wide.

"Leave him alone, Ethan," Elise said again.

Ethan didn't even glance at her. "Hey, fish-boy! When I talk to you, I want an answer."

Oumaroo's eyes searched from side to side and fixed on Del. "Your uncle wanted lobsters brought to the big house."

"Talk to me, scaly!" Ethan waved his arms in front of Oumaroo. "The gutless wonder won't help you. He's too scared. It's me you have to beg."

"Please let me by," the boy said in a half whisper.

"What if I don't want to let you by, fish-boy? What if I say you don't have any right to go where real people live?"

"He's a better person than you, Ethan," Elise snapped, wishing she were a head taller and at least a hundred pounds heavier and could knock Ethan out herself.

"Your father asked for the lobsters." Oumaroo looked up at Ethan.

Charna examined the green-black crustaceans in the bucket. "Cook ordered them for dinner tonight, Ethan. You'd better be careful or Papa will get angry."

Elise almost smiled. Ethan ignored her, but he listened to Charna. Harrel wasn't a Miunist. He had been brought up on this coast. He would punish his children if Ethan hurt Oumaroo.

Ethan glared at the half-breed, his nostrils flared and his lips curled as though smelling something foul. "Maybe I'll let you by then. But first you have to prove you know your place." He pushed one dirty, sandaled foot in front of the boy. "My foot's dusty. Lick it clean."

Oumaroo clutched the bucket tighter. "No! I won't!"

Ethan stepped forward and grabbed at Oumaroo's shirt but Oumaroo dodged off the edge of the track into the bushes. Ethan started to follow and then screamed as a ground squirrel jumped out of the bushes onto his leg and bit him in the calf. Ethan kicked frantically and the squirrel let go and flew through the air into the middle of the path. Elise saw that its eyes looked wild and foam ringed its mouth. It turned and ran into the bushes on the opposite side of the track just as Oumaroo, seeing Ethan's attention distracted, dodged around him and ran up the trail, the bucket rattling wildly in his arms.

"It bit me!" Ethan yelled. "The bloody thing bit me!" A series of jagged tears marked the fleshy part of his calf and blood ran down his leg.

"It must be sick," Charna said, looking shaken. "They never attack people unless they're sick."

"Here," Del said, "lean on me, Ethan. We'd better get you home. Your mother will want to send for a healer, or maybe Elise could run and get Ashe to look at it. If the animal was diseased, Ashe can take care of the infection."

Elise glanced quickly at Del, suspecting him of mockery, but his face looked sober with concern. Too sober, she thought for a moment, but then was distracted by Ethan's complaints. At least Oumaroo got away.

"So the boy's a coward as well as irresponsible," Derwen said, sitting down heavily on a barrel near where several fishing boats had been pulled up the beach above the high tide line.

Ashe shook his head. "It isn't a matter of cowardice or bravery. Del tried brute force when Ethan first arrived. All it got him was a broken nose and a lot of bruises. And Oumaroo got beaten anyway." Ashe smiled. "Now he's learned subtlety. He put a scare into Ethan and got Oumaroo off without a scratch, and he did it so cleverly that Ethan won't even blame him for it."

Derwen's frown broke into an expression of surprise. "Del was responsible for the squirrel?"

Ashe's eyes widened. "You didn't catch the energy coming from him? The moment he saw Oumaroo he cast about for a creature he could use. When he found the squirrel, he even made the little beast chew soap weed to create the effect of the foam." Ashe laughed. "I thought that a brilliant touch."

Derwen shook his head. "I can't hold my far-seeing vision clearly enough these days to see what you were seeing, but I'll take your word for it. Unfortunately, that still doesn't mean he has the strength needed to be the wizard I must choose to replace me."

Ashe looked down at the sand and turned over a broken shell with his foot. "Your power is failing?"

Derwen snorted. "I've never been a strong wizard, you know that. Now I'm aging, and I don't have enough command of the high sight left to stop the process."

"You can slow it."

"I've slowed it over centuries, but while I'm Esalfar there are calls on my time and energy more important than keeping myself alive." Derwen shook his head. "I must find someone with the potential of another Cormor and I must find him soon."

Ashe sighed and watched a wave curl up and break on the beach. "Del will be a great wizard. He has the potential, and I've never met anyone with better concentration."

Derwen nodded. "That's why I had such hopes for him when he was younger, but an esalfar needs more than that; he needs leadership and other skills. And it's going to take a truly great esalfar to get the human nations through the next few hundred years. Cormor himself said so."

"And Del's more like Ilfarnar than another Cormor or Torin," Ashe said, nodding. "How long do you have?"

"I can keep my carcass breathing another hundred years or so, but what good does that do?" Derwen shook his head. "I won't be able to hang on as Esalfar more than another thirty or forty years, and that's stretching it. After that, I'll be forced to name a successor. Even if I find someone at that point, I'm not likely to live long enough to see that person even halfway trained." He shrugged. "The frustrating thing is that I tested a child last year who could be the wizard I've sought, but his mother is a devout Miunist and his father's the Hetri of Leyburn. There's no way I can get Vanda to overrule their wishes and allow me to train him. And what are my chances of finding anyone else now, when I've been searching for four hundred years?"

"With that background, the law requires he be taught healing," Ashe said. "Find a wizard unknown at court to pose as a healer. Have him throw in as much extra training as he can, short of teaching the child something his parents would notice. Agnith's fires, just have him cram stuff in until they do notice. They may stop the boy's training, but they can't take the learning out of his head. Then, when he's older and can make his own decisions, try persuading him. At least his mind will be open. He'll be able to learn."

Derwen blinked. "Jehan, you're right. Cormor told me that there were ways of forcing someone to learn wizardry. I'd forgotten, it's been so many years, but he said that was why he chose me."

IX

4630, 463RD CYCLE OF THE YEAR OF THE OX
MONTH OF ISKKAAR

There was a time when wizards ruled the world,
And in that Golden Age the wizards made
Eight living crystals to enhance their power
And guarantee their patterns never fade.

Anor and Torin first, the two made one,
Their crystals fused and something more, some part,
Was torn, and so was born Vyrkarion,
The Talisman of Anor, from their hearts.

— EXCERPT FROM "ILKARIONIN, THE LIVING CRYSTALS," FROM LEST WE FORGET: A BOOK OF TEACHING RHYMES, BY WILTON WIRRAMARETH OF ILWHEIRLANE, 4207

FARRELL POMORRY WAS DRUNK. He thought his daughter Pendra had also imbibed too freely at the party held at Ai that afternoon and evening, but she insisted she could still drive. Farrell was too drunk to argue with her. In any event, he thought, the horses knew the way back to the posting inn where they could stay for what was left of the night.

When they left Ai the weather had still been clear, if cool. Now clouds blotted out the moon, and all the stars. The horses wanted to stop. After all, to them everything must appear pitch black.

Farrell could make out the road quite clearly from the heat it had absorbed during the day, and he knew Pendra could too. Horses, however, did not see into the infrared. He doubted whether Pendra considered that with the pace she set. Especially now that they were in the mountains, where the edges of the road frequently dropped off into cliffs.

"Slow down, Pendra, the horses can't see in this murk."

"They don't need to see. All they have to do is pull the carriage," Pendra snapped. "Why don't you keep your horses properly trained?"

Farrell sighed. The wine he had consumed that afternoon had produced a pleasant haze. Unfortunately, as the haze faded, he was left with Pendra for company.

She took after Iddina. Of course, he had left her care in her mother's hands. He supposed that made him ultimately responsible, but he hated arguing.

He had counted on Aliara to control the damage. He snorted to himself. After Pendra turned twelve and Aliara realized that she, unlike the rest of her family, had an extremely sensitive palate, nothing had been too good for the child. Pendra became Aliara's heir. And Aliara refused to see the result and Pendra's ability to recognize subtle nuances between different wines meant she could do no wrong.

Raindrops falling on him startled Farrell out of his musings. He said, "I don't demand of my horses anything that's not in their nature."

"How typical of you, father," Pendra said scornfully. "I, however, demand obedience." She cracked the whip again over the horses' backs.

The right horse shied away from the whip just as a flash of lightning lit up the sky above the mountain to the left. The left horse turned with the right and suddenly the team was headed for the edge of the road. Pendra cracked the whip again, trying to steer the right horse back toward the center, but she miscalculated. The tip of the whip struck the horse on the neck. The startled beast broke into a gallop, still heading full tilt for the cliff.

Pendra yanked back on the reins, but she acted too late. The team galloped off the edge. The drop at that point exceeded one hundred meters.

ALIARA ANIFI FELT THE WEIGHT OF HER SIXTY-FOUR YEARS as she entered the temple of Jehan. She had just returned her only son and favorite grandchild to the sea, scattering their ashes over the waves of the Bay of Aelos. She knew Pendra had been difficult, but she had loved the girl for her shrewdness and the keenness of her palate. Now she had only Nutena, a hopeless incompetent, and the boy, Errin, to succeed her.

Music greeted her as she looked around the austere central chamber of the temple. It appeared deserted. This was not Jehansday. The sun shone outside. The sky was clear. Not a day when she would expect to find many worshipers, which was why she had chosen it. The music, which always filled Jehan's temples, came from behind the screen at the front of the room. She walked toward the source.

As she had expected, Ajare Harmon sat alone in his saffron robe, playing his jalith. He looked up in surprise when she rounded the screen, but nodded toward the chair next to him. Then he interrupted the tune he was playing with a quick trill that Aliara knew would summon another player.

She waited. Harmon's relief appeared with another jalith. Only when the second priest, a woman in a pale green robe, had settled herself and taken up the tune Harmon was playing, did Harmon stop and usher Aliara to join him in one of the private rooms off the end of the central chamber.

"What can I do for you, Your Grace?" he asked, sitting down behind his desk. The small, white-walled room, was simply furnished with a desk, a couch and several well-padded chairs.

She sat in one of the chairs facing him. "I want to know why Jehan determined that my son had to die," she said, her jaw clenched, holding in her pain.

"But your son's death was an accident," Harmon exclaimed, shocked.

Aliara took a deep breath. "Ajare Harmon," she said, addressing him as 'Player Harmon,' the title he was entitled to as a priest of the first branch of the priesthood of Jehan, "you know me. I've been faithful, but my son's death has tried my faith. I can't believe Farrell died by accident, not when so many other strange circumstances plague my house."

Harmon shook his head. "Jehan would not act in such a manner, Your Grace. Truly, none of the gods work so clumsily."

She glared at him. "My niece Ayana had a wizard guarantee her second child be a boy. She bore a daughter. Don't tell me that was an accident."

Harmon looked at her steadily for a moment, then sighed. "There's wizard talent in your blood on your mother's side. The boy, Errin, must have inherited some of his gift from you."

"That may be, but it doesn't answer my question."

"No," Harmon said patiently. "And I cannot answer it with any surety, but I don't believe you need to seek for divine intercession to explain odd circumstances plaguing your house."

"If it isn't Jehan's will," Aliara demanded, "then what can explain it? Psarna, my great niece, is apparently sterile, yet both her parents were healthy and she suffered no major illness in her childhood."

Harmon looked startled. "I had no idea."

"She only recently discovered the fact, and the information has not gone beyond the immediate family," Aliara said sharply. "I trust you'll spread it no farther."

"Of course not," Harmon said, "but I still don't believe you're experiencing divine intervention." He hesitated, then said, "There's a closer agent, with a more powerful motive."

"Who?"

Harmon looked down at his desk and toyed with a pen that sat on the blotter. "The throne of Sussey carries with it a burden," he said finally.

Aliara's eyes narrowed. "Lyskarion! But the living crystals have no volition."

"They're alive," Harmon said, looking up again so his eyes met hers. "Life implies awareness. Lyskarion more so than most. In Luth and Dirga's day, it sang. Was Yambol wearing Lyskarion when he attended the party at Ai?"

"I don't know," Aliara said, feeling shaken. She had wanted the priest to disprove her fears, not identify a possible agent. "But Ayana stayed at the palace several times during both her pregnancies."

"Lyskarion has lived a long time without a bearer who can use its knowledge and its power."

"But Luth and Dirga created Lyskarion to heal, not kill. None of the allies of Rav held it," Aliara protested.

"Who can comprehend the thoughts of a crystalline life form that cannot suffer age or disease?" Harmon said. "Part of my training taught me that the crystals have awareness and powers. There has been concern among my brother priests of the Varfarin regarding them for some time."

"The Wizard Delanan asked my permission before he took my grandson's oath. I got Yambol's permission as well. He wore Lyskarion that day," Aliara said. "He usually wears it."

"Remember, Your Grace. Everything that has happened could be coincidence. There's no possible way to prove that it's anything else," Harmon said anxiously.

Aliara nodded. "I understand that, Harmon. I don't know whether you've relieved my mind or made me more anxious, but I appreciate your being honest with me. I must ponder this."

"The gods deal in dreams and omens. I know of no case in the history of Tamar when they have acted upon the world physically," Harmon said. "I believe they are forbidden by their own laws to do so, except when one may choose to be reborn, an avatar. But even then the god becomes a mortal for his mortal span, and has no more power than any other mortal may have."

X

4630, 463RD CYCLE OF THE YEAR OF THE OX
MONTH OF AGNITH

*Any lar born in Ilwheirlane or in the territories of Kandorra,
Rawi or Fingoe shall enjoy all the rights and responsibilities of
citizenship in those lands. Larin and humans shall enjoy equal
rights and protection under the laws of Ilwheirlane . . .
All larin living within the borders of Ilwheirlane or its
dominions may worship the god or gods of their choice in any
manner they see fit.*

— EXCERPTS FROM THE ACT OF TOLERATION, ENACTED BY VYDARGA V OF ILWHEIRLANE,
IN THE 405TH CYCLE OF THE YEAR OF THE DOLPHIN

ELISE SPIED DEL AS SHE STARTED ACROSS THE SOUTH LAWN with Del's
cousins. He sat with his back against a granite boulder just beyond the
point where the south lawn of Cliff House ended. His perch lay so close to
the edge of the cliff that his feet hung over, but from it he could see most of
the north end of the bay. The bluff did not have as good a view as the lookout
on the headland, but Elise doubted if Del had been back there since the raid.
She had gone once or twice, but it had not been the same without the others.

Del appeared to be asleep sitting up, he sat so still. He was probably
watching ants. Insects fascinated him, although he seemed indifferent to what
went on around him. Sometimes, now, she wanted to hate him, he had
changed so much.

"We want to go riding," Charna said, reaching him first, "and Papa said
we'd have to take you along." Her voice betrayed her irritation.

Elise grinned. Charna did not understand why Harrel Maran would not
trust Ethan to escort them. Ethan was eighteen, an adult, and physically
stronger than Del, but Elise remembered the mare Ethan had foundered last
summer and knew Harrel did too. At least Del could be counted on to look
after the horses. Ethan would not dare challenge Del on that subject, or
Harrel would side with Del, and Ethan would be forbidden to ride at all.

Del climbed to his feet and eyed the clear blue of the sky and the breeze
fingering the treetops in the wood. "Looks like a good day for a ride. Sure, I'll
come."

"How kind of you," Ethan sneered.

Del grinned, throwing away the grass stem he had been chewing and
picking a new one before striding across the lawns toward the stable. "Didn't
think you'd notice." His expression sobered and he said, "The horses are soft
from being grass fed this summer. They can't take much galloping, Ethan."

"A little exercise won't hurt them," Charna snapped. "You'd think they were made of glass the way you treat them."

"It's the way you and Ethan treat them that makes your father insist on you having me along," Del said.

Elise grimaced. Sometimes she did not blame Charna and Ethan for hating Del. Even when he was right, he sounded wrong. He was smarter than any of them, had the strongest wizard talent, and, while only fifteen, had surpassed Ethan in height. Yet he still gave way to his cousins, or poked at them in a snide way that would make anyone want to hit him.

The stables at Cliff House were housed in a long, low stone building built on a courtyard off the east wing of the main house. Clean and well maintained, with roomy box stalls for the inhabitants, the thick stone kept them cool in the summer and warm in the winter.

A groom had saddled four horses. As soon as they were mounted, Ethan set out on the path toward the village. Elise and the others rode after him, down the hill to the fork where Ethan took the northern route leading toward Onchan. It was a beautiful day. Little, oddly shaped fields lined both sides of the road. The villagers had carved them out of the scrub in the narrow strip of land between the shore and the hills. Lambs frisked on the slopes, and the meadows were fragrant with meadowsweet, anathallia and tall wild flags.

The air felt warm in the sunshine but not hot, and their mounts were fresh and eager. They cantered along the grass edge of the road to spare the horses' feet, and for a while Elise thought they might manage to go one day without a fight. Then Ethan left the main trail and started across a meadow toward the forested slopes of Mir Tobin, the highest in the range of worn down mountains along the coast. Del immediately objected.

"We're not supposed to go near the ruins, Ethan. You know that," he called, reining in his own mount.

"You scared, Del?" Charna taunted.

"Your father made you take me along so I'd be responsible. If you go there, he'll blame me," Del said.

Ethan halted. He turned in the saddle and said, "We were told to keep away from the ruins when we were kids, but we're older now. When was the last time they were even mentioned?"

"Just because a command isn't reinforced, that doesn't mean it's lost effect," Del said.

"You can't stop us, can you?" Ethan's lips curled in a sneer.

"Papa won't know if you don't tell him." Charna tossed her head.

"I'll have to tell him if you go there," Del said. "Ruins can be dangerous."

"They're just fallen down stones. You don't believe in haunts, do you?" Charna jibed.

Del stiffened. "I'm not afraid of stones, Charna, or haunts. But lots of things can live among broken stones, real things, and some of them are dangerous."

"You ever been there to know for sure?" Ethan asked. "I bet you never have.

I bet you don't dare."

"Have you, Ethan?"

"We've been planning on it," Charna said. "That's why we didn't want you along."

Del looked at Elise. "Did you know what they were planning?"

Elise looked away from Del's eyes. "No. But I'd like to see the ruins, too. You wouldn't have turned back four years ago."

Charna hooted. "You keep talking about how brave he used to be. But Ethan and I, we've never seen any trace of it." Elise bit her lip, seeing Del's frown. He hated to be reminded of the past.

Del shook his head. "Maybe I learned about responsibility four years ago."

Charna said, "You don't have to come. You can stay here and wait."

"No." Del looked as though he had bitten into something sour. "If Elise is going, I'll go with you. You two may be able to take care of yourselves, but, if something happened, I doubt either of you would think to look out for her."

Elise glared at Del. "I can take care of myself."

Del's eyes narrowed. "I suppose setting out on a harebrained expedition like this is your idea of fun?"

"More fun than mooning around watching you watch ants or bees, or whatever," Elise said.

"Let's go then." Charna kicked her mount into a canter and started across the meadow. Trees edged the far side, the start of the forested slopes of the mountain.

Ethan rode after her. Elise looked at Del. "Coming?"

He scowled but nodded, and, when she started her horse after the others, she heard the hoof beats of his mount behind her.

As she approached the forest, she saw a break in the line of trees, caused by a row of deeply set, flat stones, the end of an ancient road that must once have joined the main road at the point where they had left it. Elise stared in amazement. It must have taken a tremendous amount of work to have unearthed the paving stones across the width of the meadow and to have carted them away. Who would have gone to so much trouble, and why?

Ethan and Charna slowed their horses to a walk when they reached the forest. Huge trees closed in on the old road and some branches hung so low they had to duck underneath to get by. The ancient paving had broken in places, but appeared surprisingly clear of weeds. It almost looked as though it had been used recently. Elise shivered. It was cool in the shade of the forest. They had been riding for more than ten minutes when they reached the end of the road.

Elise stiffened and drew her horse to an abrupt stop, realizing that she had been cleverly set up. There were no ruins, nor was the building at the end of the road deserted.

A chapel stood in a hollow at the foot of the mountain. The symbols above the door indicated that it was dedicated to Kyra, the one humans called 'the

Destroyer,' the mother of the were-folk.

Oumaroo and his mother stood outside the arched doorway. It was plain to Elise that they had just completed some sort of religious observance. She caught her breath in a gasp as Ethan reached into one of his saddle bags and withdrew a coiled leather whip. He rode up to Jumara Lesho, Oumaroo's mother.

"Don't you know, fish-woman, that there's a law against the worship of Kyra in Ilwheirlane?"

Jumara eyed the whip nervously. "There's no such law. The Estahar Vydarga V decreed toleration . . ."

"Yeah, scaly," Ethan said. "Well, the followers of Miune don't recognize laws made by fish lovers too craven to do what's right. And according to the priests of Miune, I have the right to punish anyone found worshiping Kyra." He swung the whip under Jumara's nose.

"How did he know they'd be here now?" Del demanded, pulling up beside Elise.

"I don't know. How can you think I had any idea?" Elise asked, horrified that he thought she had been a party to this.

"You agreed to come here." Del flinched as Ethan snapped the whip, the sound like a musket shot.

"Hear that, fishes? I'm going to slice the cold, scaly hide off your bones," Ethan said, cracking the whip again. The sound echoed off the mountain. "I've been looking forward to this for a long time."

"To see some ruins I'd been curious about," Elise said. "I never thought . . ." She broke off as Ethan brought the whip up again, this time obviously meaning to hit Oumaroo with it. As Ethan brought the whip down, his horse shied violently, nearly unseating him. The leather snapped on empty air.

Charna rode over to join her brother, blocking the Leshos' line of escape. When she was almost on top of them, Oumaroo dodged under her horse and ran toward the edge of the woods. Ethan, regaining control over his mount, turned to pursue, but Charna's horse blocked his way.

"Keep the big fish here. I'll get the sprat," he shouted to Charna, maneuvering around her, and spurring his horse after Oumaroo.

"We've got to do something to stop him," Elise cried.

"What do you suggest?" Del asked. "Have you got a whip, or maybe a pistol?" His attention was glued on the small boy running into the trees.

Ethan had gained on Oumaroo, but he had to pull back to keep his horse from charging right under a large limb that would have unseated him. That gave Oumaroo time to shinny up a tree. Elise could not see what good that would do him; the whip could reach him at any height he could climb to safely. She wanted to yell at him to keep running, but it was too late. Ethan swung his whip as he worked his horse through the trees to the base of the tree Oumaroo had climbed.

Oumaroo had found what he had been looking for. Before Ethan could crack the whip, Oumaroo grabbed a round, irregular mass from a fork in the tree and hurled it right at his pursuer. The hive struck Ethan's chest and exploded into a cloud of angry wasps. Ethan screamed.

Elise stared as the cloud of wasps landed on Ethan and the horse went mad. Ethan was thrown to the ground, still screaming, as the horse bucked and ran, and the swarm expanded out across the courtyard.

Charna abandoned Jumara, spurring her mount toward Ethan at his first scream, but, on seeing the cloud, she reined back and turned her horse, attempting to flee. She was too slow. Elise watched, appalled, as wasps swarmed on Charna and her horse. The horse reared, throwing Charna to the ground, then bolted. Jumara reentered the temple and Oumaroo seemed to have disappeared.

Elise had a sudden memory of a linlar cloaked in bees, then Del grabbed the reins of her horse and turned it back the way they had come. He struck her horse on its rump, with his crop and she felt it start, then she was galloping back down the ancient road toward home, with Del behind her. She tried to pull up, but her horse had the bit in its teeth and would not obey. She had to flatten herself and ride bent over her horse's neck for fear of being swept off by overhanging branches.

She screamed over her shoulder at Del, "We've got to go back for them. The stings will kill them."

"We'll fetch Ashe," he yelled. "It won't do them any good if we get stung too."

Elise tried to check her horse again, but the mare refused to obey her. It seemed cowardly to abandon Ethan and Charna, even if they did deserve punishment for what they had planned, but what Del said was true. Ashe would be able to help them, and she and Del could do almost nothing but get stung themselves, but it felt wrong and she remembered that Del had not tried to help the Leshos either.

She was still angry when they rode back down the ancient road with Ashe, less than an hour later. They had not gone far when they met Ethan and Charna. Both of Del's cousins were covered with bright red lumps. Ethan's eyes were swollen shut and his hands looked like mittens; his fingers so swollen he could not separate them. Charna was not in much better shape. At least they were alive. Maybe, Elise thought, if a few stings were all that was wrong with them, they deserved what they got.

The Wizard Ashe seemed to agree, for he smiled at their condition and refused to heal them. "You'll survive," he said. "It'll be good practice for you in learning to heal yourselves. If it takes you a while before you can stop the pain, the experience may teach you to mind your own business and not bother others who mind theirs."

"I command you to heal us," Charna said through her swollen lips. Her whole face was red and distorted, her eyes narrow slits.

"No," Ashe said.

Elise grinned at the consternation on Charna and Ethan's faces. They often sneered at Ashe behind his back, mocking the self-effacement he practiced so effectively. It amazed her that they never sensed the power behind his facade. Elise had recognized that Ashe's sand-colored hair and forgettable face in no way reflected his nature from the day Derwen introduced him.

"Worshipers of Kyra the Destroyer are enemies to all humankind." Charna's voice was shrill and she glared at Ashe through her slitted eyes. "In Ninkarrak they'd be stoned to death if we reported them to a priest of Miune."

"Not true," Ashe said, shaking his head, his expression one of mild disgust. "No matter what the priests of Miune may have taught you and your mother. There's a chapel dedicated to Kyra in the Great Temple District and larin are permitted its use. Only humans are forbidden inside, and that's by the laws of Kyra, not those of Ilwheirlane."

"The worship of Kyra the Destroyer is illegal," Ethan insisted.

Ashe sighed. "No. Humans are discouraged from such worship, but there's no law against it. All such laws were repealed when Vydarga V ratified the Act of Toleration for Ilwheirlane and all its territories. But even before then, the penalty for such worship wasn't death, or whipping," he added, nodding at the leather whip Ethan still carried.

"The Act of Toleration?" Del questioned.

Ashe frowned. "I take it Selicia chose the school's teacher. I'll have to remedy that." He stared at them and Elise shivered. "None of you will take this road again. Is that understood?"

Elise nodded and watched as the others also submitted. Ethan was last, his acknowledgment only a brief jerk of his head.

Ashe studied them. "Most of those in Ilwheirlane with larin blood who still pray to Kyra worship her in her ancient form as Kyra the Chronicler. But even if they did worship her as the Destroyer, none of you would have a right to interfere. Do you understand that?" He waited until they all nodded, even Ethan, although again Ethan's nod was perfunctory.

When they returned to Cliff House, Elise was relieved to find that the horses had made it back to the stable and that they had escaped with only a couple of bites each. Perhaps their hair had protected them, but that explanation did not entirely satisfy her. In fact, she had a strong suspicion that she had missed some vital element in the events of the day. The feeling bothered her. She kept remembering the bees that had killed the linlar four years before. Still, it wasn't until she was nearly asleep that night that the solution came to her.

Del! Del, who was fascinated by insects. Del, who loved all living things. Del, who might have learned to control any creature he wanted to control. She shivered, remembering dozens of incidents when animals had behaved strangely. Every time Del had been there.

But if Del did exercise such control, and she could no longer doubt it now that she had reviewed all the evidence, then all the times she had blamed him for his lack of action, she had been wrong. She laughed. Del did still care about Oumaroo. Maybe he still cared for her a little, too.

Then why hadn't he told her? Why had he been getting more and more difficult to reach? She thought about his impatience, the flashes of anger she had sensed in him when she had criticized him, then she bit her lip and buried her head in the pillow. Maybe he had expected her to understand. Maybe her lack of faith in him had hurt him as much as his seeming indifference had hurt her. She felt like a fool, and wondered how she would face him in the morning.

THE NEXT MORNING, HOWEVER, SHE DETERMINED that she had to face him, no matter how painful the confrontation might be. She owed him an apology.

Fortunately Ethan and Charna were keeping to their rooms, the stings still causing them a good deal of pain. They had tried to get their father to order Ashe to heal them, but Harrel had only laughed. "I'm not about to try ordering a wizard to do anything. What's more, if you weren't in a good deal of pain already, I'd be tempted to take a whip to you both myself for what you planned. The Leshos have as much right to worship Kyra as you do to worship Miune. If I ever hear of you causing any of them any trouble again, I'll take a whip to both of you."

Elise found Del where she had expected him to be, lying on the grass next to the hollow jula tree in the meadow. "I realized something last night," she said, sitting next to him.

"Really."

"I realized I owed you an apology."

Del turned to look at her. "Why would you think that?"

"Because I've blamed you for not doing anything a lot of times when you've really been acting very efficiently and I just haven't understood," she said.

He chuckled. "I figured you wouldn't miss the wasps. After all, you were there when I killed the Senangan with the bees."

"But I had to figure out what you were doing for myself. You weren't ever going to tell me, were you?" Elise asked.

Del looked away. "At first I felt so guilty I just couldn't talk about it. Then, I guess, I got mad at you because you thought I'd let Ethan get away with picking on Oumaroo. It became a matter of pride that I could inflict twice the damage on him that he'd ever inflicted on me or anyone else, and he wouldn't even know I was doing it."

"You certainly got both of them yesterday. Jehan's aspect of Arrun, the Jester, with all his tricks, couldn't have done it any better. They'll be in pain for days," Elise agreed.

"Yes," Del said. Then he turned back to Elise. "But Ethan wouldn't hate animals as much as he does if it weren't for me. That horse he foundered last summer, he wouldn't have done that if I hadn't made the horse throw him several times. It was my fault the horse suffered."

She met his eyes and saw the pain he was no longer trying to hide. "No,

Del," she said. "You can't take the responsibility for Ethan's evil nature. He pulled wings off flies before he ever met you."

He sighed. "I guess you're right about that. Until Ethan came here, I never really understood that there was such a thing as evil. I mean, I knew people could be misguided and do harm, but someone who did harm intentionally for the pleasure of it? No, I never imagined someone like that until I met Ethan."

"What will become of him?" Elise asked. "Both Ashe and your uncle have tried to reach him, but . . ."

"I heard them discussing the problem once," Del said, then looked shamefaced. "Actually, I was riding the mind of a mouse and it ducked through the paneling into Uncle's office."

"But the mouse couldn't understand them, could it?" Elise asked.

"No," Del said, "but I could hear the things it heard. Anyway, Ashe said there had to be something wrong or missing in Ethan's brain. He told my uncle that there are wizards who specialize in mental healing. He was trying to arrange for one to come here." They both looked down at where a honeybee was taking pollen from a clover flower in the grass between them.

"Will you accept my apology then?" she said.

"If you'll accept mine."

"Of course, Arrun," she said, grinning. "I think I'll call you that from now on."

"And, maybe, when I qualify as a wizard, I'll take the name for real," Del said, and Elise thought the words sounded like a vow.

XI

MONTH OF ANOR

> *And thus imbued with life the crystal did*
> *Their patterns hold, as many as they knew,*
> *And magnified their will beyond their dreams,*
> *And so, despite their loss, their power grew.*
>
> *Iskkaar and Minneth linking in the north,*
> *Brought forth Belkarion, the Heart of Snow,*
> *And found it thought, like other living things,*
> *Except its thoughts were adamantine and slow.*

— EXCERPT FROM "ILKARIONIN, THE LIVING CRYSTALS," FROM LEST WE FORGET: A BOOK
OF TEACHING RHYMES, BY WILTON WIRRAMARETH OF ILWHEIRLANE, 4207

THE MORNING OF THE DAY SET for the second wedding of Aliara's
nephew, Inebolu Anifi, heir to the Aharion of Sussey, dawned clear and
dry. There had been no rain for weeks, and the fields and vineyards of
Sussey were parched with the heat. Even the park surrounding the Palace
in Krydani looked dusty, the once green grass dried out to pale gold.

Aliara, walking with her brother, Bilsen Anifi, eyed the clear sky with
disgust. "We need rain, Billy," she said. "I can't think of a better day for it."

Bilsen grunted. "I can. A little rain isn't going to stop the festivities, and
if it rains today, I'll have to stand around in it and get soaked. I'm too old
for a wetting, unless it's in the sea."

Aliara laughed. "But wouldn't you like to see that horror Ayana's foisted
off on poor Ebby standing in the rain with all her finery sopping wet?
How did Ayana and his daughters ever get him to agree to marry Imelda
Atygan?"

Bilsen stopped where the walk joined the path beside the stone wall that
lined the cliffs overlooking the beach. "Ganged up on him, nagging him
day and night. He finally decided he'd get more peace if he married, no
matter who they chose." He rested his arms on the top of the wall and
looked out over the clear blue water of the Bay of Kryma.

"He couldn't tell the servants he wasn't to be disturbed?" Aliara asked,
leaning against the wall next to him.

"Servants couldn't tell Psarna and Ikaria they couldn't see their father.
Ayana rode their wakes." Bilsen shrugged. "Ebby's never been a great one
for evasive tactics, as you know, Ali. You took advantage of that a time or
two yourself."

Aliara sighed, then eyed him curiously. "They didn't try to work on you?"

"Ayana visited me once," Bilsen grinned. "I served in the navy, know all about repelling hostile boarders." He turned away and started walking along the path next to the wall.

"What about Antram?" Aliara asked, catching up.

"She tried." Bilsen chuckled. "Wish I'd been present. According to Hexam, his valet, Antram told her off the same way he did when she was nine and used crayons on his school notes. He called her, 'an obnoxious, noisy, little brat.' When she persisted, he took her by the scruff of the neck and escorted her to the door."

Aliara laughed. "I wish I'd been there, too."

"But it isn't really funny, Ali," Bilsen said, stopping again and turning to face her. "Since Cardessa converted to Kyra, that side of the family has gotten twisted. They're all acting as though the end of the world would come if Errin inherits. What's it doing to him? And to Nutena?"

"Errin's fine. He's expected something of the sort since Farrell died, but Nutena . . ." Aliara shook her head and looked away. "I know I've handled her badly. I don't mean to hurt her, but somehow everything I say comes out wrong when she's around."

Bilsen turned to look back out over the bay. "Needs another husband. Someone who'll take care of her, coddle her a bit, make her feel needed. She's insecure. It's not all your fault, Ali; you're just too rough edged for her. You're used to strong people who stand up to you and hit back."

Aliara shook her head. "I know she needs another husband. I've been working on that for some time, but she has so little confidence in herself." She shrugged. "She makes it difficult."

"The guest in your party," Bilsen said, nodding. "Typical of you Ali, to pick a wine merchant."

Aliara glared at him. "He's not just a merchant. He's a noted connoisseur and a very nice man. What's more, he's in love with her, has been for years. And he'd take care of her, and coddle her, if she'd let him."

Bilsen raised his hands as though warding her off. "Easy, Ali. I wasn't criticizing him. I'm sure he's all you say, but you have to admit it's convenient that he's also qualified to take over the winery."

"I really didn't pick him for that. If she'd liked someone else, I could have found a manager for the winery, but she's as attracted to Galen as he is to her; she's just afraid of another relationship." Aliara put her arms on top of the wall and looked out over the bay. "She wasn't happy with Lothar Yar, whatever she says to Errin."

Bilsen nodded. "Not surprising. Living in the sea requires daily life and death decisions. That must have been a constant strain on Nutena, whatever her relationship with Errin's father, and the one time I met him he didn't appear to be particularly patient. I'm surprised she stayed as long as she did." He watched a seagull floating in a warm updraft over the cliffs. "But that isn't what I brought you out here to talk about."

"No. I didn't think it was," Aliara said, her voice flat. "You want to talk about the boy Ayana didn't have."

Bilsen turned to stare at her. "How did you know?"

"Come now, Billy, given the circumstances, didn't you think I'd have a spy in Ayana's household, too, not to mention the palace?"

"Then you know we're living in dangerous times."

"Of course. Cardessa's son and mine are both dead. I don't grieve much for my nephew, Izaren. He's been dead seventeen years and I never liked him much anyway. But, believe me, I grieve for Farrell. And they were the only men born to this family in their generation, other than Antram."

"You think their deaths are part of it?"

"Yes," she said, "I do. Errin will be a wizard, a powerful one, or so Delanan says. He took his oath as Delanan's apprentice four years ago, but I noticed that the wizards present to hear that oath were mostly those who aren't current members of the Varfarin."

"But Delanan's a member of the Varfarin. I don't understand what that has to do with what's been happening."

"Delanan expects Errin to hold Lyskarion," Aliara said. "I think Lyskarion itself has decided Errin would make a suitable bearer, and Delanan knows it. I was taught as a child that the great wizards created the living crystals at the inspiration of Jehan and Maera. I didn't think they had volition, but after Farrell and Pendra's deaths, Ajare Harmon, the head priest of my local temple, told me that the crystals do think and act. I believe Lyskarion wants to wield power again."

Bilsen nodded. "I'll keep the wretched thing locked away during my period of custody and I'll warn Antram to do the same, but why would that prevent Delanan taking Errin into the Varfarin? I'd think they'd want him even more."

"If Errin links with Lyskarion, he'll be the first wizard to do so since Luth. Delanan and the other wizards want to preserve his right to independent action. The current head of the Varfarin isn't overly popular."

Bilsen shrugged. "Well, you've obviously been keeping up with what's happening. Let me know if you learn more that might help me when my time comes. I don't think old Ebby's going to last long."

Later, when Aliara entered the sitting room of the suite she occupied whenever she stayed at the palace, she found Errin waiting for her.

"Why did you invite Galen?" he demanded. "You know he makes Mother nervous. She's upset enough about Inebolu's marriage without something else to disturb her."

Aliara shook her head. "I know that I haven't always been kind to Nutena, even when I've done my best. But in this case, Errin, I know what I'm doing. Galen makes Nutena nervous because he's attracted to her and she's attracted to him. I'm hoping that eventually he'll get through her lack of confidence and convince her to marry him."

"Mother is supposed to marry so that Galen Tarenta can manage the winery for you?"

Aliara stiffened. "That will be an added benefit. They might even produce an heir to the kulharion."

Errin froze. "Does that mean you intend to disinherit me?"

Aliara stared at him. "For Jehan's sake, boy, don't be a fool. It isn't even in my power to disinherit you. Only your mother can do that now, and she wouldn't think of it any more than I would. But you can't inherit Ruffin if you're the Ahar of Sussey."

"Ahar of Sussey," Errin said, stunned.

"Come now, don't tell me you've never thought of it. I won't believe you. And it's become more and more apparent lately that you will bear Lyskarion, the first trained wizard to do so since Luth and Dirga."

"There are still eight people between me and the throne of Sussey. Are you saying you think they're all going to die?"

Aliara laughed. "Only three men, all of them much older than you. And I'm willing to bet this ridiculous marriage of Inebolu's will fail to produce a son."

"You're mad."

Aliara shook her head. "No. I just see the pattern. I've thought about it often since Farrell died. Ask Delanan, if you don't believe me. Tamar is moving closer and closer to outright war between the races. Kyra and Tarat work to inflame their worshipers and increase the tensions. The human god, Miune, does the same. Jehan and Maera want power in the hands of those who won't be carried away by racial or religious hatred. A living crystal, in the hands of a trained wizard, represents a major focus of power. You'll bear Lyskarion. I've felt it for several years now. It will come to be."

AFTER HIS INTERVIEW WITH ALIARA, Errin hardly saw Inebolu's wedding ceremony. He truly had not thought of becoming ahar. He had been too aware of the hatred Ayana, Psarna and Ikaria felt toward him to think they would ever allow him to take the throne. It had never occurred to him before that it might be beyond their power to prevent.

He watched absently as Inebolu and Imelda swam together, two dolphins dancing in the clear waters of the bay, changing to human form at the same moment as they came ashore. Errin noticed that Imelda looked clumsy in the water and fell down in the surf trying to stand, causing him to think that it might be the first time she had swum as a dolphin since her childhood.

The palace orchestra played the traditional wedding music as the royal couple climbed the long staircase from the beach to the courtyard before the palace. At each landing they paused to be clothed in another item of apparel, symbolizing their acceptance of Sussey's land-based society. By the time they reached the top of the stairs and took their oaths to each other, they wore full court dress and Imelda looked less flustered.

Errin wondered if the full-length, traditional wedding ceremony, uncommon these days, had been Inebolu's vengeance for being driven to remarry. If so, he had certainly succeeded in making Imelda uncomfortable. She would not be able to look back on the wedding itself with triumph.

When the ceremony was complete Errin tracked down Delanan, finding him in an antechamber of the palace with Jao and two other wizards he did not know. "May I speak with you privately?" he asked.

Delanan frowned, but signaled to Jao, who said, "We'll leave. It will be private here. I'll see that you're not disturbed." Then she and the others left.

"I'm sorry if I broke up something I shouldn't have," Errin said. "But I had to speak to you." He poured out all Aliara had said, finishing with, "She said I'd bear Lyskarion."

"What do you want me to tell you?" Delanan asked. "Should I confirm that you will? Or cry out, 'Oh, no, that could never happen?'"

Errin shook his head. "I don't know. I think something closer to the second."

"But I believe it will happen," Delanan said. "Aliara's right. Why do you think I've avoided taking your oath to the Varfarin these past four years?"

Errin stared. "I don't know, but that explanation never occurred to me."

"When you come to bear Lyskarion, you must not be pledged to obey any will but your own. At present, if you pledge to the Varfarin you pledge yourself to obey the Wizard Derwen. While I feel nothing against him personally, and believe he's done his best as Esalfar, I'd never put the kind of power one of the karionin command within his reach. Nor would Cormor have wished it so."

"They say the Wizard Elgan quit the Varfarin out of jealousy when Derwen succeeded Cormor as Esalfar," Errin said, "but that wasn't the real reason, was it?"

Delanan shook his head. "No. Cormor had other tasks for Elgan, and for Myrriden, and for most of the wizards who left the Varfarin after Cormor's death. Jehan granted Cormor the ability to foresee many things, and we've prepared as best we could for the events he envisioned. There's a crisis coming, a time beyond which nothing could be predicted even by Cormor, but he saw that the outcome of the crisis will depend on the karionin."

"And I'm to be the bearer of Lyskarion?"

"Study hard, Errin. Be the strongest wizard you can be, for the karionin have volition, they are aware, and the triple linkage is the greatest power on Tamar. A linked couple joined with one of the karionin wield virtually the power of a god. But you must rule Lyskarion, not allow it to rule you."

XII

4631, 464TH CYCLE OF THE YEAR OF THE DRAGON
MONTH OF TORIN

"Our ancestors drove the isklarin from the shores of the Inland Sea. To our shame, not only have we let them return, we are allowing them to rebuild their Road of Masters, our Road of Shame. Construction began six years ago and this year, for the first time since the beginning of the Age of Wizards, human slaves will again be dragged in chains from the shores of the Thallassean Sea to Gandahar. We must act now to stop them! We will not be safe to live our lives freely until we have driven the were-peoples from our shores."

— EXCERPT FROM A CONTEMPORARY EDITORIAL IN "THE SPECTATOR", ONE OF THE PRINCIPAL NEWSPAPERS OF NINKARRAK, ILWHEIRLANE

A BRISK WIND WHIPPED AT THE WATERS OF THE BAY OF LURO. Spray burst over the bow whenever the sailboat plunged into one of the larger waves. Ashe sat near the bow with Charna, Del, and Elise, while Ethan controlled the rudder and sail from the stern.

Ashe eyed his students and Del's cousins carefully, aware that Del's thoughts were not on the subject he had been discussing, but concentrated down in the sea with the schools of fish: inglings and rock cod, debarran, and the rare deep-sea bass.

The minds of the sea creatures were as open to the boy as the minds of the creatures of the shore. Del could change the direction of a whole school of fish with a moment's concentration. Of course, Ashe thought watching him, his influence did not last. Some other stimulus would come along and instinct would take them on another path. But for the boy to have even that degree of control at his age was impressive. Ashe knew himself to be a powerful wizard, but he could not have made even one fish in that school change its direction, not without mentally reaching out and moving the fish by the force of his will. Del just inserted the correct images into the fishes' minds and they turned the way he wished.

It sounded easy. But learning the precise imagery that would turn each fish seemed to Ashe an almost overwhelming task. The conceptual symbolism, the internal code that controlled such movements, differed, not simply for each species, but for every single living organism. Yet Del controlled them all. The sheer volume of the data involved awed Ashe. And Del had not yet been given a crystal to augment his phenomenal memory.

Still, Del needed to practice other skills as well. *"What talents define a great wizard?"*

Del looked up and then around at the blank faces of the others, realizing that Ashe had asked the question only of him. *"A great wizard is a wizard who can hold the high sight for twelve hours without pause, transport himself to any place he can see or knows well within the range of telepathy, and raise or manipulate a mass of at least a thousand pounds."*

"How many great wizards are there today?"

"None. Cormor was the last, and he died several hundred years ago."

"Why do you think there are no others?"

Del frowned. *"I guess because it takes so long, so many years of study,"* he thought finally.

Ashe nodded. *"What does one need to do to qualify as a wizard?"*

This time Del didn't hesitate. *"Be able to change one's shape, be able to lift one's own body weight, be able to communicate by telepathy to any place within one hundred and thirty kilometers or direct line of vision, and be able to hold the high sight for ten minutes without pause."*

"Very good," Ashe thought, indicating with a wave of his hand that Del could go back to what he had been doing. The boy's word imagery was clear.

"Duck," Ethan yelled from the stern, swinging the rudder to the port side.

The boat swung about and a wave caught them broadside. The wind blew from the southwest off the Thallassean, and Ethan had been tacking back and forth across it and as close into it as he could manage, maneuvering the boat toward the mouth of the Bay. This time he made the turn clumsily, allowing the sail to luff too much. Ashe sighed, but did not try to correct him. Ethan was unteachable, and would need serious help before long, but if the wretched youth were not here with the others he would be getting into trouble. At least sailing kept Ethan out of the village, and it was a good day for him to practice.

Ashe turned his attention to Elise. It was nearly time for her annual return to Adun. He suspected that her grandmother would not want her to return to Bria after this visit. Elise would be eighteen this winter, old enough to marry. He sighed. He had not spent enough of his time with her. She had always been quiet and obedient. She tended to slip into the background, but he was sure that was not her true nature. Still, after seven years of being her teacher, he was no closer to discovering what lay behind her quiet surface than he had been the day he met her. Nor did he know what decision she would make when her grandmother tried to marry her off.

"What skills do you need to qualify as a journeyman wizard?" he asked her.

Elise blinked, then thought, *"You must be able to heal down to the chromosome level, you must be able to lift a weight of twenty pounds, you must be able to hold the high sight for ten seconds and the were-sight for a full day without pause, and you must be able to communicate mind to mind over a distance of thirty kilometers."*

"How about an apprentice wizard?"

"An apprentice wizard must be able to hold the were-sight for twelve hours without pause, must be able to lift a weight of five pounds, must be able to project mind to mind for a distance over a kilometer, and must have attained the high sight, if only for a second at a time," Elise supplied promptly.

"What about the wizards who never attain the high sight?"

"Some of them call themselves wizards among the laity, but they're not entitled to use the term according to the laws issued by the Council of Wizards. The highest rank such a person can attain is that of journeyman."

Ashe smiled. Her word imagery was also clear and precise. She had potential, a great deal of it. Except for Del, she was the strongest student he had helped to train. She might well, if she continued her studies, become a great wizard.

"Why do you think there are no great wizards today?" he asked her impulsively.

"There are wizards who have the potential," she thought, *"but it takes so many years of concentration, such dedication, that, with all the other duties wizards have, that level of skill is nearly impossible to achieve."*

Ashe nodded, but his mind supplied the exception. Even that level of skill would come easily for Del, to whom concentration came naturally, like breathing. Del was born to be a great wizard, but Derwen might be right about his not being the best choice for esalfar. He could have been, if there had never been a raid, or if his cousins had not come to live with him, but the linlarin had raided, and Ethan and Charna had finished the damage the raid had begun. Del was not apt to step forth and take a leadership role again. The Del of today preferred trickery and sleight of hand to achieve his goals, like Arrun, the Jester, as Elise had started calling him, and that was not what the Varfarin needed in its leader. But, Ashe thought, I'll back him against anyone in an undercover operation. He might well become the best agent the Varfarin's ever seen.

He sighed and looked over at Charna, wondering why she had appeared so excited earlier. She still had an air of expectancy about her. She had been taunting Del about something, too. He would have to find out what she was up to. Strictly speaking, she was no more his responsibility than Ethan was, but Harrel had asked for his help with her, and after she was separated from her brother, she might make a passable journeyman. Not a healer, however; she lacked the temperament.

"What are the requirements for a journeyman?" he asked her.

Charna looked confused. "What did you say?"

Ashe sighed. At least she had known she was being addressed. "I asked you to tell me the requirements for a journeyman. Tell me with your mind."

Her face screwed up into a mask of concentration. *"Heal,"* she thought. Then there was a long pause. Finally, she said, "I can't remember the images for the rest of it."

"Duck," Ethan yelled, turning the rudder to starboard so the boat swung about again. He performed the maneuver with more skill this time, and the sail came around smoothly.

When Ashe looked back at Charna, she said, "Excuse me, can I ask a question?" There was a calculating expression on her face.

"Of course. What do you want to know?"

"When we went to Onchan last week I heard some women talking in the market," Charna said. "One of them had a cousin who had borne a baby in the month of Ingvash and the baby was supposed to have died two months later. They said she must have gone down to the sea. What did they mean?"

Ashe looked at her, trying to penetrate her shield. She was a clever child; she could never have reached the age of seventeen living on this coast without knowing the meaning of the phrase 'gone down to the sea.' What was she up to? He sensed that her question disturbed Del. "Why don't you tell us all what you think it means?"

Charna tossed her head. Her blonde hair caught the wind like a banner. "The ingvalarin, the dolphin folk, come to these shores in the spring and early summer. If a baby's born eight months later, in Ingvash or Cerdana, doesn't that imply the mother lay with one of the fish folk?"

"No husband beds his wife in the spring? Don't be silly," Ashe said, annoyed by the girl's bigotry. "It's true that some of the women of the islands and along the coast have 'gone down to the sea,' as they say, or mated with ingvalarin. But it doesn't happen often. Once or twice a generation, if that."

"Not even when the parents say the baby died in the spring, when the fish folk come ashore?"

"Some babies die," Elise said.

"And some babies are left on the beach," Charna said, "babies that have the were-sight and the ability to change. Isn't it true that those babies are left on the beach?"

Ashe nodded reluctantly. "Sometimes it's true. But rarely when they're that young. And for every child left on the beach, gossip would make it a hundred."

"It works the other way, too, doesn't it, Ashe?" Elise asked, glaring at Charna. "Some of the parents who go down to the sea come back with a child, don't they? Only it isn't the same child."

Charna looked puzzled. "What do you mean?"

Ashe sighed. "She means that as humans are said to 'go down to the sea,' so some ingvalarin could be said to 'swim for the shore.' The kindred of Maera watch certain beaches in the spring, just as the ingvalarin do, and sometimes a baby is put ashore, a baby born without the ability to change. The families who've lost a child are always given the first chance to adopt when that happens."

Ashe watched Charna as the meaning of his words sank in. He didn't understand where this conversation was going. Elise seemed to be trying to shock Charna, perhaps to distract her, but the lesson was one that Charna needed to learn. She had absorbed too much of her mother's teachings. And why had she picked today for this conversation? Her shields were too good for him to look into her mind as he would have done when she was younger.

"You mean human families adopt the offspring of fish?" Charna gasped. "They must be sick."

"Mind your language, Charna. You should know better than to express such an opinion in front of me," Ashe said.

"Duck," Ethan yelled from the stern, swinging the rudder to port, and they just had time to bend down before the boom swept over their heads.

Del's attention was distracted from the schools of fish beneath them by the sail sweeping over him. He must have been aware of what they had been talking about all along, though, Ashe thought, for he turned to Charna and said, "You may as well get it over with, Charna. Say it straight out."

Charna glared at Del, her eyes bright with malice. She asked, "When a woman's been down to the sea and her child has the shape-changer talent but not the were-sight, what does the mother do then? Does she leave her child on the beach, or does she raise it like a human child?"

"She raises it, of course," Ashe said, angered by her insensitivity. "What else would she do with her own child? Without the were-sight, the child couldn't change even if he had the genetic ability. The ingvalarin wouldn't take such a child."

Charna smiled. "That's what I thought."

One of the gulls flying overhead swooped, nearly colliding with Charna's head. She screamed and the gull swerved up into the sky, cawing as though to answer her.

"Hateful birds," Charna said.

"He must have thought you were a fish," Del said, but there was no humor in his face. In fact, Ashe was shocked by the bleakness in his eyes.

Charna glared at Del and said, "No one would mistake me for a fish, but they might mistake you for one. Except it wouldn't be a mistake, would it?" She turned to Ashe. "Has Del told you how well he can swim? That he turns into a fish in the water?"

Ashe turned to Del, surprised that the boy had not told him about discovering his changer skill himself. "So, you've heard the song of the sea?" he asked, wishing he could read from Del's expression what went on in his mind. Of course, he never could. Even scanning the boy's mind never told him anything. Del's shields were better than Charna's, as remarkable as his vision.

"I have the shape-change talent. Why shouldn't I use it?" Del asked.

Ashe frowned, wondering what to say. What made Del so secretive? "There's no reason for you not to use any of your talents. My purpose is to help you develop them, not hinder you. I merely wondered why you hadn't told me yourself, why it was Charna," he nodded to the blonde girl who smiled smugly, "who informed me of your discovery?"

"Why should I brand myself a bastard before I had to?" Del asked.

"What do you mean?" Ashe asked, shocked by the words and more shocked by the anger he sensed behind them, a crack in the boy's normally impenetrable shield.

"I have the shape-change talent. I was born in Ingvash. What do you think Charna's been getting at?" Del asked, his voice acid with bitterness. "That's why she's so pleased. If I'm proved a bastard, her father will inherit Cliff House and the lanrion and Ethan after him. I'd have spared my people that."

Ashe was stunned. "You think your mother went down to the sea?"

"What else can I think?"

Ashe shut his eyes and fought for control. The boy obviously believed what he was saying, however misguided he might be, and apparently had believed it for some time. Ashe searched for the right words. "Del, why do you think Derwen tested you for wizard potential at birth?"

"I don't know," Del said, surprised by the change of subject.

"Charna, why were you and your brother tested?"

Charna's smug expression wavered. "Because we have noble blood?"

Ashe enjoyed her hesitation. She deserved a spanking, had done so for years. But he nodded. "In a sense. Who was Dai Maran?"

"The Wizard Agnith," Del said automatically, looking bewildered.

"All the known descendants of the great wizards are tested for wizard potential, as are all members of the House of Cinnac. There aren't wizards enough to test every child as we would wish, even if parents would allow such testing, but certain lines are always checked and your line is one. You are Orris Maran's son, Del, a true descendent of the Wizards Agnith and Ilfarnar, two of the greatest of the great wizards. There's never been any question of that and there won't be. It's printed in your genes for any one with the high sight to read."

"But he can shape-change," Charna said.

Ashe looked at her and sighed. "Your mother came from inland and your father protected her from certain things because of her religious beliefs. But you're seventeen, Charna, and you have some talent of your own. It's time you knew the truth."

"What truth?" Del asked.

Ashe turned to the boy. "The people who live on the islands and along the coast, their women don't need to go down to the sea to bear children with the changer talent. There's hardly a child born along this coast who doesn't have a trace, or more than a trace, of the sea folks' blood."

"You said it didn't happen often," Charna accused.

Ashe shook his head. "It doesn't, not in any single generation. But it's been going on since men first came to these shores more than five thousand years ago." He turned to Del. "Both your parents had mixed blood. Derwen told them you'd be able to shape-change right after your birth. I've been expecting you to discover the ability since I took over your training. I was beginning to worry about you."

Ashe looked back to Charna, who had paled and was staring at him with shocked eyes. "Your father has mixed blood too, Charna, and so do you and Ethan."

"No," she shouted, jumping to her feet, "that's not true. You're lying. Mother would never have married him."

Ethan, in the stern, yelled, "What's the matter, Charna? Get down before you capsize the boat."

"He never told her," Ashe said. "I told him it was wrong, what he did, when he first came here. But he loves her. He's kept it from her for longer than I'd have thought possible, but, as Del has learned to change, she'll have to learn the truth or she'll come up with the same foolish notion you did."

"I don't believe it," Charna shouted.

"Get down," Ethan yelled.

"Ethan!" She staggered toward the stern. "Ashe says that Papa's got mixed blood, that we've got the blood of fish."

Ethan rose, letting go of the rudder which promptly swung to starboard. The small boat swung about in the wind, catching a large wave broadside. It rocked wildly and water poured over the side. The boom swung back, striking Charna and knocking her overboard before Ethan could grab it. He swung it away from him and yelled at Ashe, "Take care of the boat," before jumping in after his sister.

Ashe, still shocked by Charna's violent reaction, reached out with his mind and brought the boom and the rudder under control. He looked at Del and Elise, thinking to tell them to take over the rudder and sail, but they were laughing too hard to hear him.

Ashe felt himself grin. How long, he wondered, had it been since Del had discovered his shape-change ability? How long could the boy have hidden such a deep-seated fear?

"*Heads up,*" he thought, projecting a mild mental reprimand with the words. "*We have passengers to pick up.*"

XIII

MONTH OF ILFARNAR

The ability to communicate mind to mind is more difficult than it might seem. Almost anyone can perceive another being's emotions. Even those without sight often pick up such powerful emanations, but an emotion is not a complete thought . . .

The transference of visual images can be taught in the early stages of a wizard's training, but a visual image may have more than one meaning . . .

The most common form of telepathic communication is really only an extension of speech. This is the transfer of agreed upon word images . . .

— EXCERPTS FROM PROBLEMS WITH TELEPATHY, BY THE WIZARD AGNITH

THE WIZARD KINDRIC PUT A CANDLE IN THE CANDELABRA on the table. "Watch closely now, Jerevan. It's important that you learn to see what I'm going to show you." He took the boy's hands.

Jerevan Rayne, heir to the Hetri of Leyburn, looked at the candle. Then Kindric's vision took over and he no longer saw a candle, but a grainy network of forces, dense where the candle was, much looser around it. The whole world became a network of interacting forces. As he watched, the forces around the candle coalesced and flared into a new kind of force that ate at the dense network and accelerated the movements of the looser forces in the air. Jerevan blinked, but the vision persisted even with his eyes shut. Then Kindric released him and the world returned to normal.

"Can you see the candle that way by yourself?" Kindric asked, extinguishing the candle.

Jerevan stared at the candle, remembering the feeling of seeing through Kindric's eyes. Kindric had focused like so. Jerevan tried to focus that way on the candle again. For a moment he thought he had it, but it was hard to focus that way. He blinked.

"Try again, Jerevan," Kindric said.

Jerevan looked up at him. "It's hard. It hurts."

"You mean you saw the candle, as I did?"

"For a moment, but it hurts to look that way," Jerevan said. "I don't want to do it any more."

"All right, Jerevan. I think we've done enough for now anyway. You can try again tomorrow."

The next day, Jerevan focused on the candle with the were-sight.

A week later Kindric gazed out the window while his pupil lit a candle with the power of his will. The boy had only turned five a few months before, yet he absorbed training like a sponge. The power of his will dwarfed any potential Kindric had ever seen before. Jerevan had already learned more than most healers could learn. He could even receive and send mental images. Of course, it would take a lot longer to train him in the correct forms of mind-speech.

"I did it," Jerevan said.

Kindric turned back to the boy and looked at the candles. "Very good." He walked over to the boy. "Do you understand why you're able to light the candle, Jerevan?"

"'Cause I can see it with my inner eye," Jerevan said. "If I can see something, I can change it."

"That's right," Kindric said. "Now you must learn to look at your own flesh. After all, the purpose of your training is not to light candles, but to heal."

"I don't like looking inside me," Jerevan protested. "I look all gooey and there're nasty things."

"You've already observed your own body then?" Kindric had thought he was accustomed to Jerevan's speed in absorbing new things, but Jerevan continued to astonish him. Even older students rarely took the step of examining their own bodies without instruction.

Jerevan looked up at him, wide-eyed, "Wasn't I supposed to? You didn't tell me not to?"

"No, I'm not angry with you, Jerevan." Kindric smiled and reassured the boy with his mind, but he had to resort to verbal speech for more complex concepts. "I was merely surprised. With most students I have to persuade them to try new things. With you, I can hardly keep up."

"Why do I have to look inside me?"

"You have to learn how to fix things if they go wrong, don't you?" Kindric asked. "Isn't that what being a healer means?"

Jerevan thought for a moment. "I guess so."

"Then don't you first have to know how things look when they're right?" Kindric asked.

Jerevan considered that and sighed. "Yes." He looked up at Kindric and cocked his head. "Why do you make my mother mad?"

Kindric frowned. "What do you mean?"

"Whenever my mother sees you she purses her lips and glares at you. Then she gets mad at me too."

Kindric sighed. He wished Jerevan were less observant, but that was part of what made the boy so phenomenal. "Your mother doesn't approve of wizardry," he said carefully. "She associates healers with wizards."

"Why doesn't she approve of healers? My father's a healer, isn't he?"

"Yes, Jerevan. Your father's a healer, but I don't think your mother considered that when she married him." He shook his head. "In any event, your mother knows that your father doesn't have the ability to go beyond being a healer. You do have that potential."

"How do you know?"

"A wizard attended your birth. He told your parents that you have a great gift. He wanted to train you to be a wizard. The idea terrifies your mother."

"Are wizards bad?"

Kindric bit his lip. "Some wizards have done bad things. That doesn't mean all wizards are bad."

In the following weeks Kindric alternated teaching Jerevan word images with getting the boy to learn his body and manipulate the flesh. Jerevan learned so quickly it was a pleasure to teach him, but Kindric knew his time was now limited. While technically most of what he was teaching the boy could still be considered healing, as it was necessary to reach the level of Advanced Healer, he knew the boy's parents had not wanted the boy to learn anything more than basic healing, and Jerevan had passed that level some time before.

The only reason he had been able to teach Jerevan as much as he had was that Danor, Jerevan's father, had taken three years to absorb basic healing, and had never learned to alter the flesh at all. As Jerevan had only been studying for a year, it had not yet occurred to Danor or Nadira that he could have already surpassed his father's ability.

Kindric knew when he opened the door to Danor that his time with Jerevan had run out.

"Yes, what is it?" Kindric asked. The hour was still early, the sun just over the horizon.

"I've come to tell you to pack," Danor said. "I suggest you get out quickly before my wife gets up. She'd like to claw your eyes out."

"I see."

"I notice you aren't asking why we want you to leave." Danor said. He had not yet shaved and his jaw thrust out aggressively.

"I've known I was here against the wishes of your wife from the beginning," Kindric said. "I assume you feel the boy has learned enough."

"Just how far above a healer's skill have you taken him?" Danor demanded.

"He hasn't reached above a healer's skill," Kindric said.

"I'm ranked a healer," Danor said, "but I can't light a candle as Jerevan did at the dinner table last night."

"Then you can't work with the flesh," Kindric said, smiling wryly at what had given him away. "All you are is a skilled diagnostician and therapist. All advanced healers must be able to heal the body. The candle is the first step in that learning process."

"The candle is a wizard's trick," Danor said.

"The earliest stages of wizard training are the same as a healer's," Kindric said. "You know that."

"The law does not require Jerevan to become an advanced healer, just a healer," Danor said. "You knew our wishes. Why did you disregard them?"

Kindric looked at Danor. The hetri was still a good looking man, but signs of dissipation had begun to show. He said, "I don't work for you, but for the good of the people Jerevan may heal. Despite your objections, Jerevan's skill will save lives, perhaps even the lives of people you care about."

Danor stiffened. "Leave quickly, or I'll see that you're thrown out." He turned and walked off.

Kindric shrugged and started to pack his bags. He had managed to teach Jerevan more than he had expected when he first started. He just hoped it would be enough to help the boy later on. He had grown fond of him.

XIV

4631, 464TH CYCLE OF THE YEAR OF THE DRAGON
MONTH OF MINNETH

A place of shingle, rock and slimy weed
Where waves wash in to suck the sand away.
Avoid that shore.

And tho', 'tis true, the young may little heed
Old women's warnings, yet you'll rue the day
You walk that shore.

For there's a fish who'll swim out of the sea
And come to walk upon that shore with thee.

— EXCERPT FROM "THE MAIDEN WHO WALKED BY THE SEA," AN ANONYMOUS FOLK SONG
FROM THE OUTER ISLES OF ILWHEIRLANE

"YOU'RE NOT GOING BACK TO BRIA THIS YEAR after the mathendin, Elise," Mother Adun said. "You're eighteen now. It's time we started making arrangements for your wedding."

Elise stared at her grandmother, hardly believing what she had just heard. The old woman, sitting enthroned in her high backed chair in the parlor, stared back. Mother Adun's hands, gripping the antimacassars, looked like claws.

"My wedding?"

"Aye, child. Your grandmother and I, we think it's time you settled down," Brennan said. He stood at the side of the fireplace, his usual place during all the confrontations she could remember having with her grandmother. It occurred to Elise that, except at the dining table, she had never seen him sit in Mother Adun's presence.

"I'm not getting any younger, and I want to see my heirs before I hand over the tiller," Mother Adun said, her voice rising as though she sensed Elise's opposition to her will. "It isn't as though we're expecting you to marry a stranger. You like Timmon Skane, and you've known him since you were ten."

"Timmon Skane?" Elise repeated, feeling like one of the birds the carnivals kept that echoed the words said to them. She did like Timmon, but she had never thought of marrying him. She remembered being home when he had come to Adun to train as her grandmother's agent. She thought he must have been about seventeen, the son of a friend of her grandmother's on the mainland. Elise had shown him around the island. "I can't marry Timmon," she said. "And what about my training?"

"You have enough training now to take my place as Healer for the islands," Mother Adun said. "We sent you to Bria more to give you a normal childhood with other children, than have you trained for wizardry, but you're not a child anymore."

"No, I'm not," Elise said, "and you can't treat me like a child. You can't force me to marry Timmon, or make me give up my training."

Brennan's fist struck the mantle. "They've twisted you, tha wizards. I knew it would happen. You never wanted ta leave Adun when you were little. You never wanted tha training. Yet now, you'd turn down a good man, an honest man, ta go back ta what? What will wizard training bring you?"

Elise flinched at the pain in her father's face. She had not meant to hurt him. "I'm sorry, Da, but I hardly know Timmon. I never thought of marrying him."

"I promised his father he'd be your consort when I brought him here from the mainland," Mother Adun said, her eyes bright and hard like brown agates. "It's not easy to get good workers out here. Most people won't come, or they turn right around and leave. They can't take the isolation, the lack of amenities. If you don't like Timmon, I'll take you to the mainland, to Ninkarrak, and give you a season to pick a husband. But you'll have to find one who can live here, and that won't be easy."

"I don't want to marry at all."

Elise watched Mother Adun's chest inflate. She didn't want to hear what her grandmother was going to say next. She wasn't skilled at receiving thoughts from those without proper mind-speech, but she knew she was going to hate what her grandmother had to say.

"You've always been Adun of Adun. You've always been my heir. But unless you marry a man I can accept within the next year, I'll name a new heir and you'll never set foot on Adun again." Moira leaned back in her chair, and Elise realized, with the kind of shock that overturns one's world, that her grandmother really was very old, and weary; that the autocrat of her childhood who had just threatened her with permanent exile was a tired old woman whose time had nearly run out.

Still, Adun was her home, and her grandmother's threat of exile was real. Instead of feeling angry, as she would have done even ten minutes earlier, Elise felt sad. "Very well, Mother Adun, I'll think about marriage, and I'll talk to Timmon. But, if I decide against it, and want to return to the mainland to finish my training," she turned to include her father in what she had to say, "then you must accept that neither of you has the authority to force me against my will."

Did she truly want to be a wizard?

Elise stood at the top of the cliff where her mother had fallen so many years before. She understood now why her mother had sought that place. Standing on the top of the highest part of one's world gave one a feeling of power. And there was another element. If you could see everything, then shouldn't you also be able to understand everything? Wasn't that what the wizards taught? She sighed. Her father had been right when he said that she had never wanted to be a wizard as a child. But was that true now? How did she feel about the abilities she could feel developing inside her?

She liked being able to see into the structure of things. She liked being able to communicate across distances. She liked being able to heal and change things. If she stayed home this year, she could talk to the sea folk again in the spring. Perhaps Errin Yar would still be with the wiga, and she could show him what she had learned.

She took a deep breath of the cold wind. The day was clear, but clouds were gathering to the northwest. There might be snow by evening.

Her knowledge could not be taken away from her. With what she had already learned she was the equal of any of the larin. Did she truly want to continue her training? Hadn't she had doubts even before she came home this time?

And that was another point. Whatever she might think of her grandmother, Adun was her home. She had always been Adun of Adun, destined to take her grandmother's place. Could she give that up? It was a part of her own image of herself?

She shook her head, feeling her braids swing against her cheeks. Suddenly she could not stand any sort of restraint. She tore the ties off the bottom of her braids and loosened her hair so it could blow free in the wind.

If she went back to Bria she would have to swear an oath to the Varfarin, now that she was eighteen and ready for training beyond that of advanced healer. She knew what kind of obligation that entailed: a lifetime of service, and wizards lived for a long time. If she stayed on Adun, she would take her grandmother's place when her grandmother died, and that time would not be so far in the future. Wasn't that what she had always wanted?

Timmon Skane wasn't a bad looking man. He had big hands and feet. She remembered him stepping on her toes at a dance in the village on the other side of the island. She had been what? Fourteen. He had been twenty. He had done better the past year. He had filled out, and she had been pleased to be his partner.

She should have realized years ago that her grandmother had been pushing them together, but it had never occurred to her. He had just been there, handy as an escort whenever she had been home and wanted to go somewhere.

"You'll have a time untangling that mop."

Elise spun round to see Timmon on the path, about three meters below her. "What are you doing here?"

"I followed you." His eyes shied away from Elise's, down to his feet.

"I wanted to do my own proposing. I figure I can't do a worse job than your grandmother."

"Then you want to marry me?" She realized that she had not even thought about what Timmon might want. She had been too caught up in her own concerns.

He climbed the rest of the way up the path, stopping about a meter away from her. His eyes met hers. He had brown eyes. They reminded her of the eyes of the dog Joady, the handyman, had owned. The dog had been old and lame, and his eyes had been that same liquid brown, had held that same beseeching look.

"I've wanted to marry you since you were fourteen and we went to that village dance. You looked so pretty. I stepped on your foot; you made me feel so big and clumsy. But you were too young." He looked down at his feet and poked a pebble with his toe. "I guess your grandmother always knew how I felt about you, but I never expected her to demand that you marry me. I don't understand why she did that, why she'd even want you to marry me. I've been to school. I can read and write and keep figures." He looked back up at her. "I can manage your farms and deal with your tenants. I know the islands and the people here, but I don't have any wizard talent and I'm my family's third child, so I don't have any prospects either."

Elise stared at him. She had no idea what to say. She liked him, had always liked him, but she had never thought of him as a lover. A big brother, perhaps. The idea of kissing him seemed wrong, like incest, yet he wasn't related to her. He wasn't even unattractive. In fact, if she had to have a husband chosen for her, Moira had done a fine job. Timmon did seem to care for her, and he loved her home as much as she did. He would be happy here.

She shook her head. "I don't know, Timmon. I just don't know. I never thought of you that way. You and my grandmother will have to give me time, to see if I can get used to the idea."

XV

4632, 464TH CYCLE OF THE YEAR OF THE EAGLE
MONTH OF INGVASH

In spring the sky is blue, not sullen gray,
And even seagulls cry in harmony,
Along that shore.

In spring bright flowers bloom amid the rocks
And every curling wave is capped with cream.
I walk that shore.

I will defy the harshest words, the looks
From father, friends and others for I dream
About that shore.

And of the man who swam out of that sea
To laugh and love upon that shore with me.

— EXCERPT FROM "THE MAIDEN WHO WALKED BY THE SEA," AN ANONYMOUS FOLK SONG FROM THE OUTER ISLES OF ILWHEIRLANE

ELISE, CARRYING A BUCKET AND CROWBAR, picked her way across the shingle to where the waves lapped her bare feet. The water felt icy cold. The gray sky and northwest wind showed no sign of spring although Ingvash was nearly over. Cold and gray, that was winter in the Outer Islands. She sighed, thinking of the rich soil of the farms and meadows around Bria where everything would be turning green. She had missed the islands all the time she had been away, and now, back on Adun, she missed the green of the mainland. How fickle.

Yet she might soon be married. She thought of Timmon with his sober, steady face and sighed. She liked him, but he did not excite her, and she feared that he lacked a capacity for joy. At least, he had never demonstrated such an emotion in her presence. She had worried the subject for months, but today she had decided to escape from it and gather mussels.

The tide was all the way out, as low as she had ever seen it. Great, kelpy boulders were drying in the sun. Elise gripped the wooden bucket and started out over the rocks. She had lost none of her agility in the years she

5TH

had been away. When she reached the farthest group of drying boulders, more than thirty meters from shore, she crowed at the sight of the harvest to be gathered. The tide rarely exposed the rocks so far out, and the mussels had grown huge.

She used the crowbar to pry loose the big, black mollusks, larger than her hands, that clung to the boulders, their shells sharp and encrusted with barnacles. Without the iron bar she could not have moved even one of them, so tightly did they attach themselves to the stone. She worked quickly. While she had not had many opportunities to practice in recent years, she had gone musseling at least once every time she came home.

She had always looked forward to her visits home, but did she really want to live on Adun the rest of her life? And be married? She pried up another mussel almost viciously and tossed it in the bucket.

As though her thoughts had summoned him, she heard Timmon's voice hail her from the shore. "Elise, come in. It's too dangerous out there. You'll get caught when the tide turns."

"I'm all right," Elise yelled back. "My bucket's nearly full. The mussels are bigger out here."

Timmon worried about everything. She had been picking mussels from these boulders since she was four. Even he couldn't seriously think she was in danger, could he?

"Come on back, Elise," he called again. "Those rocks are treacherous."

Elise bit her lip to keep back the, "Leave me alone!" that was her first response. Timmon came from the mainland. He didn't understand the sea. The tide would turn soon and then, he was right, she would have to leave, but she would have warning. She knew the sea.

Still, there was some justification for Timmon's fear. Even her father and grandmother did not understand Elise's instinctive feel for the sea. The currents flowed fiercely in the cove. Climbing the rocks with their coating of razor sharp shells and spiny sea urchins could be dangerous. Swimming among them was worse. Even Elise would not try it alone, only when the sea folk were there to look out for her. As a child she had loved playing with the sea folk in their dolphin forms, clinging to them as they swam through the rocks like great, silver fish. She wondered what Timmon's reaction would be to seeing her do that and shook her head. He would be appalled.

She had half expected to feel the ingvalarin when she woke this morning. They were due any day. She pried loose one last mussel, filling the bucket. Then she rose and started back to shore. She made the climb look like a dance.

MOIRA ADUN STRAINED HER RHEUMY EYES looking out over the dunes to where the gray waves curled against the shore. Soon the sea folk would come. How many times had she seen it happen in her eighty years? Sixty? Closer to seventy, she thought. Then, for a while those waves would be a scene of joyous life. And some of that life and joyousness would come ashore.

She felt her aged hands with their liver marks and arthritic fingers clench into fists, and relaxed them. She was too old to feel her blood quicken in the spring. If she was too old for love, surely she should be too old for hate as well. But she wasn't.

Perhaps this year they would take another route, miss the islands altogether. But they hadn't come last year and they almost never missed two years running. One more year and her granddaughter would be safely married and maybe carrying a child. Elise was so pretty and ripe and rebellious. She would never be able to resist the lure.

Moira sighed. The sky was gray. Even the dune grass was a dull gray-green. It was sharp, that grass. It could draw blood if you walked through it carelessly. Like the sea folk. They were handsome and fun loving, and as oblivious to the hurt they caused as the saw grass.

The shore looked beautiful in the summer when the sun shone down and warmed the sands beneath a bright blue sky, but to Moira its beauty was a lie. She thought it more honest now, with its cold, gray waters and the mourning cries of the gulls.

IN THE LAST WEEK OF INGVASH, when Elise went down to the shore, one of the sea folk stood on the smooth stones at the edge of the high tide line. He was tall, broad-shouldered and naked, as Elise could not help but notice when she was halfway down the path to the beach.

She hesitated. Her grandmother had again forbidden her to go near the cove if the sea folk were there. Elise thought the warning ridiculous, as ridiculous as she had thought it that last summer she had spent on Adun when she had been seven. But there was a new intensity to her grandmother's warning, and Elise had grown wary enough to suspect some reason behind her grandmother's prejudice. Still, she had looked forward to seeing the sea folk again after so long.

The ingvalar had been looking out to sea, but, as Elise paused, he sensed her presence and turned. He was magnificent. He stood at least a head taller than she. He had the broad shoulders and deep chest of the sea folk, but he wasn't the least bit heavy like most of the adult ingvalarin she remembered. He wasn't even stocky. His waist was lean and hard. His long, dark hair was wet, and lay in strands like black snakes down the golden skin of his back.

"Dathend," he said in Eskh, meaning, "Good day."

Elise felt the blood rise beneath her skin, flooding her cheeks with red, "I'd f-forgotten," she stammered, "that your people rarely wear clothes."

He laughed. "Clumsy things. Such a nuisance for shape-changers." He eyed her with amusement and a trace of some other emotion.

She felt his eyes on her body like a physical touch, and she knew he saw more than the surface of her clothes and skin. She withheld her own vision, though, remembering her reactions as a child. "Before I was sent to school on the mainland, I used to play with the children of the wiga that summered here." She smiled at the memories, and finished climbing down the path to the shingle beach.

He bowed. *"Errin of the wiga of Tarle Farswimmer, at your service, Elise Adun. Has it really been so long that you've forgotten me?"* His muscles rippled under his skin.

Elise felt as though her breath had been knocked out of her. Errin! She had thought of him so often in the early years of her training, especially after he visited her. But he had never come again, and he had changed. She remembered a skinny boy, not a man with the most perfectly structured physique she had ever seen. It wasn't just nudity that brought the color to her cheeks; it was *his* nudity. And to discover that this was Errin! She had never felt so aware of another body before. Never felt so aware of her own. *"Errin? But why are you here alone?"*

Errin's smile widened. *"Your wizard training has strengthened you. I wondered when you didn't look back at me."*

"You taught me to mind-link." Her thought accused him.

"And now you know why I wouldn't link with you that last summer." He shrugged. *"You taught me the danger of it."*

She looked around desperately to hide her embarrassment. *"Where are the rest of the wiga?"*

Errin smiled. His smile spoke of his knowledge of what she was feeling, and she wasn't surprised when he crossed the shingle to where he could reach out and touch her. *"The seas are restless this year. The wiga needed a scout. I volunteered. Now I'm glad."* He extended a hand to her hair. *"I don't remember your hair so red, like fading embers. Is it as warm?"*

Elise's scalp tingled at the feel of his fingers. His eyes were still the blue-green-gold of a stormy sea brushed by the sun. She wanted to touch him back, but she was afraid of the power of her own feelings, the gladness she felt at meeting him again, seeing how handsome he had become. *"Aren't they expecting you to return?"*

"Only if I find some reason for them not to come here. You don't look like a threat."

She started to giggle but choked the sound off, chagrined. Errin's hand moved down from her scalp to her back, bringing their bodies closer together. She wondered if he could hear her heart beating. *"When will they get here?"*

"Tomorrow." His hand stroked her back and she sensed the heat of his fingers through the fabric of her dress. She felt as though she were caught in a powerful current and it was sweeping her away from everything familiar. *"No,"* she thought.

"Why not?" he thought. *"You're grown now, almost an apprentice wizard, not just a young island girl."*

Elise swallowed. The sensual pull radiating from him had lessened with his question, but it was still there, just banked. *"I've learned some things, but I'm not an apprentice. I've taken no oath."*

"*But you can join our company,*" he thought, and for a moment she sensed the network of minds that made up his wiga, all of them connected by a tenuous link though they might be spread out over hundreds of kilometers of ocean.

She drew back, closing her mind to him, frightened again but in a different way. "No," she said, speaking aloud, deliberately rejecting the intimacy of the mind touch. "I'm human, not ingvalar."

His smile faded and he released her, stepping back. "You are untouched," he said, "and I've frightened you. I'm sorry."

Elise felt cold with the loss of contact, though the day was still warm. "I'm not afraid of you."

He laughed. "Not of me, but of yourself and what I made you feel. You're full of fire inside. That's why, when I saw you just now, I never thought you could still be untouched. Among my people your fires would burn often and fiercely."

She felt the shock of his words and her body ached in strange places. "They say the nomads of the sea are so caught up with their senses that they think of nothing else," she said. "They neither build nor create, but float with the current from one pleasure to the next, leaving nothing behind them but pain."

He stiffened and she thought he was angry, but then he nodded. "There's truth in what you say, but not all my people are nomads."

"The folk of the wigan are."

He nodded again, his expression sad. "Open your mind."

"*Why?*"

"*So that I can remind you that I'm not solely of the wigan folk. My mother lives on Sussey and she only gave up her home for a short time before returning to it.*"

Elise relaxed her mental barricades. "*Are the folk of Sussey so different from the wigan folk?*"

"*They are not vagabonds, Lise. Not all my people follow the currents of the sea, building nothing and leaving nothing behind. On Sussey, we have towns and cities, we plant crops and stay to harvest them. We even go to sea in ships.*"

"But you are of the wigan folk," she said, drawing away.

"*I am of both,*" he thought. "*Look into my heart.*"

"*Why show me your pain?*"

"*Because the fire that could grow between us would be both bright and strong. You feel it as well.*" His eyes were green-gold fires, and she felt herself melting in their flame.

She shook her head and turned to put her back to him. "No," she said. "If I decide to stay on Adun, I'm to be married to a man of my grandmother's choice." Her hands clenched into fists. It took all her will not to turn back and walk into his arms.

She sighed when he made no response and turned her head to see what he was doing, but he was no longer there. She saw a flash of brown skin as he dove into a wave, but when he surfaced again it was the smooth gray flesh of a dolphin that broke through the sea. He leaped once, as though to salute her, and then he was gone.

After that Elise meant to stay away from the cove while the wiga camped there. Her meeting with Errin made clear to her why her grandmother had insisted on her going away to school. She understood many things that had been incomprehensible before.

She had not been aware of the sensuality of the ingvalarin when she played with them as a child; her own sensual nature had not then surfaced. The sea folk did not molest children. Nor, she thought wryly, did they molest women. They didn't need to when they could seduce so easily. But, despite her wariness, she could not resist the lure of the shore.

She rose early on the morning of the fourth day after meeting Errin and, bracing herself for her grandmother's displeasure, did what she had done as a child, slipping out of the house with her basket full of pots of butter, jugs of milk and packages of honey candy. It was a cold, clear day, and ardethin and crocuses bloomed amid the roots of the sparse, wind-twisted trees on the inland slopes of the hills, just as she remembered. The barren cove had blossomed, too, into the same village of neat, round, sharkskin cauraks she recalled from her childhood.

She watched for a time from the top of the hill but saw no sign of Errin. In fact, few of the ingvalarin could be seen, only those tending small children or those who appeared old or infirm in some way. She decided that the rest were out hunting, and walked down into the village.

She went first to the largest and most beautifully decorated caurak, which she guessed would be the home of Tarle Farswimmer, although it was no longer painted like a debarra. When she called out a greeting, it was answered by a tall, dark-haired woman of majestic size and bearing who greeted her politely, "Good day, youngling. How may I help you?"

Elise had expected Renala, but while this woman resembled Renala slightly, she was younger than Renala would have been, and taller. Elise concealed her confusion and bowed formally. "I'm Elise Adun from the farm over the hill. I've brought gifts. You may remember me from when I was a child. I've been away for many years, but I used to play with Tarle's daughter Pela."

The woman nodded. "I recognize you now. I'm Manata, second wife to Tarle, but I was a free swimmer the last year you came here, when Incal Sharkbiter was still arrage."

"What happened to Incal? And Renala? Is Pela still with you?" Elise asked, pausing as she realized that her tongue was running away with her. "That is, if I have your permission to visit?"

Manata laughed and said, "Incal was killed by a kanakar in the waters of the south three years ago, but Renala is still first wife to Tarle. She'd be here, but, now that I'm here to share the household duties, she often swims with her younger children on the children's hunt. And Pela's still with us, though she has a caurak of her own now, and, of course, you may visit, for as long as you please. Only, when you are ready to leave, you must stop back here and let me give you a gift for yourself and your grandmother."

Elise smiled. "Gladly, if you'll take some of these pots of butter and milk off my hands, so that I have room to carry other things." She reached into the basket and pulled out two tubs of butter and a jug of milk. "Unless she's changed beyond recognition, Pela will only be interested in the candy."

"I don't think she's changed too much, then," Manata said, smiling and taking the tubs, "but I thank you for these. I grew up on a farm in Sussey, and butter is one of the things I miss most now that I live in the sea."

"Like Errin's mother," Elise said, startled into speaking before she thought. She looked down in embarrassment and fished another jug of milk out of the basket, handing it to Manata. "That's all I have now," she said, "but I'll bring more butter and more milk while you're here. I remember how much Tarle likes milk with egastin."

"You're very kind," Manata said, balancing the tubs of butter and the jugs of milk against her massive bosom. "I don't remember Errin's mother. She left Lothar before I joined the wiga, but there are always land-born among the wigan. Some, like Nutena, stay a few years and then return to land. The song of the sea isn't as strong for them. Others, like me, make our homes with the wigan folk for life." She shrugged. "The song of the sea becomes a drug we can't resist and we give up the civilized amenities of land, and sometimes even family and friends, to be able to hear it whenever we want. It's both a blessing and a curse." The tone of her voice changed and Elise looked up and met her dark blue eyes. "You land-born should remember that, before you judge us."

"I wouldn't think of judging you."

Manata's lips curved in a half smile. "But you've met Errin, so there'll come a time when you'll judge us. Ask your grandmother, if you doubt me." She shook her head. "But you're young and unlikely to heed warnings. Pela's caurak is the third on the left, the one spotted like a leopard shark. I don't think she swam with the hunt today, so you'll probably find her there."

The skin flap closed over the doorway and Elise turned away, spotting the caurak with the leopard spots without difficulty. But she was still pondering Manata's words when she called out to Pela.

"Hello, Pela, do you still like honey candies?"

"Elise! Is that you, Elise?" The flap flew open and Pela burst out and hugged Elise to her now generous bosom. She had been a plump, boisterous child, and, Elise reflected, she did not appear to have changed, except to have grown bigger and even more enthusiastic. "It's been so long since I've seen you. What have you been doing? Tell me about your boyfriends. I've always wondered what it's like for shore folk."

"I'm due to be married soon," Elise said, a little overwhelmed.

"Really?" Pela said. "I won't be ready to marry for years yet. Your man must be special, if you're marrying so young. What's it like with him? How did you meet him? Does he have his own farm?"

"He works for my grandmother. He's her agent, handling her business affairs," Elise said, embarrassed by the bluntness of Pela's questions. "His father and my grandmother are old friends. He's nice, but a little earnest sometimes."

Pela looked shocked. "The son of a friend of your grandmother's and all you can say about him is that he's nice." Her eyes widened. "Why, you haven't even had him fill you yet. What if you don't fit together? I knew the customs of the shore folk were strange, but Elise, that's crazy."

Elise flushed. "My people value different things than your people," she said, conscious of the vastness of the cultural gap separating her from Pela. She hadn't noticed it as a child, but perhaps the gap had not been as great in the matters important to children. "But what about you? What have you been doing?"

"I can tell you better this way," Pela thought. *"You're a wizard now. We can exchange more than just a few words."*

Reluctantly, Elise nodded. *"We were close as children."*

"Let me tell you about . . ." Pela began, and somehow in the hours that followed, despite Elise's new awareness of their differences, they recovered something of their earlier friendship. Elise also came to understand far more about the ingvalarin way of life.

It was early afternoon when Elise left Pela's caurak. The sun felt hot in the sky overhead. The rocks on the headland south of the cove threw up splashes of foam as the waves rolled in against them. Errin came out of the sea to walk with her before she had covered half the distance to the path over the hill.

"I've thought about you," he told her. *"Have you thought of me?"*

She sensed the way he had thought of her and flushed. "Yes," she admitted reluctantly.

"Walk with me?"

"I should go home. My father and grandmother will worry." She felt a prick of conscience at the truth of her words.

"But you'll walk with me anyway," he thought. *"You don't love the man you're supposed to marry."*

"Do you of the wigan marry always for love?" she demanded, knowing the answer from her talk with Pela.

"You know we don't." Impatience colored his thought. *"Love is not common among my people. I doubt it's common among yours. Still, we believe it's wrong to ignore love when it does exist."*

"How would you recognize love?"

He hesitated, then admitted, *"I don't know. I only know I want you differently from the way I've wanted other women. I felt the difference from the moment your mind touched mine."* He reached out and pulled her body against his. *"You felt something, too."*

She tried to pull away but his grip was too strong. She sighed and let her forehead rest against his shoulder, smelling of salt and cool from the sea. He felt so good, his arms close around her. *"Yes,"* she admitted, *"I felt it too, but I'll not lie with you. Not now, not like this."*

"Then we can talk and play in the waves as we did when we were children. You can tell me about your training and the years you spent on the mainland. The time I visited you is the only time I've set foot in Ilwheirlane."

Somehow hours passed in what seemed like moments, and it was evening before Elise left the beach to go back to her grandmother's house, her clothes as damp and sandy from being used as towels as they had often been when she had been a child.

Her grandmother was waiting in the parlor in her high-backed chair. She called out as Elise entered the house. "I know what you've been doing, girl. You've been gone all day."

Elise, faced with the inevitable, confronted the old woman defiantly, but it shook her to see her father there as well.

"Yes," Moira said, "I see it in your eyes, despite the way you're using your talent to hide it. You've been down to the shore for a roll in the sand with one of the sea folk." The old woman paused and her hard brown eyes narrowed, sharpening the lines of the wrinkles that covered her parchment face. "Them with their cold, fishy blood and slimy hides."

"They aren't slimy," Elise protested.

The old woman nodded. "And you've felt one to make sure, haven't you, child?"

Elise flushed, but she faced her grandmother sitting in the winged armchair as though it were a throne. "Their blood isn't cold either."

"No, it's their hearts are cold, not their blood. Why do you think I warned you, from the time you turned seven, to stay away from the sea in the spring and never talk to the sea folk?" The old woman's gnarled hands clutched the antimacassars on the arms of the chair until her knuckles were white.

"You're old and prejudiced. You don't know them. What fun they are to be with. You can't imagine."

Moira laughed a shrill, cackling laugh. The sound held no humor. She stopped abruptly and glared at Elise. "You talk as if you thought I was born old and wrinkled. You're a selfish child and blind despite your wizard training," she shook her head and continued reluctantly, "but I suppose you're no worse than I was at the same age, or your mother."

Elise turned to her father. "I haven't done anything, Da. I spent most of the day with Pela. We were childhood friends. And if I spent some time with one of the men after that, I knew him too. We rode the surf together. I like him and I haven't had much to do, since my training stopped. It isn't as though there are many people around to talk to with Timmon working most of the day. And the sea folk travel so far, see so much."

"Timmon spends as much time with you as he can. He's taking care of your inheritance," her grandmother said.

"He's your choice, not mine," Elise said, then turned again to Brennan. "I'm sorry, Da, but I don't love Timmon. I'm fond of him. I thought it would be all right, that love might grow between us, but now I don't know. I don't think love's a thing that grows when there's no seed to start with."

Moira also turned to her son-in-law. "You see. It's time she heard the truth, Brennan. She'll not understand otherwise, and she's willful. She'll make the same mistakes her mother and I made, and we'll have no one but ourselves to blame."

Brennan frowned. "She's too young. She won't understand."

"If she's old enough to walk the shore with one of the sea folk, she's old enough to lie with him. Enough members of this family have gone down to the sea with their children. I'll not have it happen again without trying to stop it."

Elise stared. "Gone down to the sea? But I don't know anyone who's gone down to the sea."

"You had a brother, child," Moira said. "A pretty babe. It broke your mother's heart to lose him. And the boy's father never came back. The rest of the wiga came, but Voisan Whalesinger was no longer with them, and no one would say what had happened to him or the boy. She waited five years. It wasn't a fall that killed her. She spent hours on that cliff, watching the sea. In the end, she didn't want to go on living, waiting, knowing she'd never see your brother or his father again."

"But Da," Elise turned to her father, "you were her husband."

Brennan frowned and looked away from her. "I could nay have children, Elise. Your mother married me so there'd be a man ta take care of tha farm. She never pretended ta love me. Her heart was always out there." He nodded toward the distant sound of the surf.

"You're not my father?"

"I raised you," he said. "I care what happens ta you."

"But you're not my father," Elise said, facing the truth of her grandmother's words.

He shook his head, defeated. "Not by blood."

Moira broke in between them. "Don't look so shocked, child. Your mother wasn't the first in our line to go down to the sea. You said I didn't know what the sea folk are like, that I can't imagine what it's like to lie with them. Was I never young? I don't have to imagine; I remember too clearly. Your grandfather was one."

Elise gasped. "My grandfather was Anther Crowel."

"No, child. I married Anther for the same reason your mother married Brennan, for the sake of the land, to supply a father figure for the children we could keep. Your aunt Tessa was Anther's daughter but your mother and my son, the one they say died, they had another father."

"What do you mean, 'say died?'"

Moira glared. "Barra was a shape-changer like his father, so I had to carry him down to the sea for his father to take. The sea folk insist on that. He was only four. Levian told me he'd bring the boy back to see me, but it was three years before I saw either of them again, and by then Barra didn't remember me. The only time in all the years of my life that the sea folk missed coming to these islands two years running. Oh, their blood runs hot in the spring but their hearts are cold, child, cold and cruel like the sea itself. But at least Levian came back and Barra knows who I am. I even see him every few years. Voisan never did return, not even after Anitra's death."

"Errin wouldn't do that to me," Elise cried. "He cares for me. His customs are different, but he cares."

"He lives in the sea. He won't leave it for you. How long will love last when you only see him two or three months of the year, and not every year at that? You'll hate him in the end. I know. The hate lasts longer than the loving."

XVI

4632, 464th Cycle of the Year of the Eagle
Month of Cerdana

Oh, he had eyes the color of the deep,
The changing sea, but he changed, too, like tides
Upon that shore.

The heat of summer killed the flowers bright,
The rocky shingle cuts and burns my feet.
I walk that shore.

I weep, for all the warnings they were right,
Oh, how I wish I'd never looked or loved
Upon that shore.

There was a fish who swam out of the sea
But he swam back and far away from me.

— excerpt from "The Maiden Who Walked By the Sea," an anonymous folk song
from the Outer Isles of Ilwheirlane

Mother Adun kept Elise busy on the farm the day after the scene in the parlor, but the following day she slipped out at dawn. Errin waited at the top of the slope leading down to the cove. The sun had crested the horizon to the east, but the cove still lay in the shadow of the hill. The mist that had risen off the sea in the night lapped at their feet.

"*I would have walked all the way to your house, if you hadn't come today,*" he thought.

"I said I'd come when I could," she said, avoiding his eyes and starting down the path toward the beach. The rays of the sun caught the top layer of the mist and turned it to silver haze.

"*They've upset you.*" Errin took her arm to stop her and turned her to face him. "*Something your family said, it's upset you. I can feel anger. What is it?*"

Elise nodded. "Anger; is that all you feel in me?"

"*Confusion, too,*" he added, frowning.

"Is it true," Elise said, closing him out of her mind and staring at the silvery fingers of mist at her feet, "that if I have a child by you and that child has sight and is a shape-changer, as you are, you'd demand I give that child up to you?"

Errin sighed and looked away from her. "That's the law of the wigan," he said. "If the child is of the sea, he needs to swim in the sea, learn the songs. Otherwise, he can't grow as he should."

"What about the children of your people who grow up on Sussey? How do they learn the songs of the sea?" Elise mocked, pulling away from him and continuing down the path.

"Most of the children of Sussey spend large parts of their childhood in the sea. All of them spend at least a part of one year," Errin said quietly, following her. "It's true they may spend the rest of their lives on land, as human children do, but they all spend enough time in the sea to learn its songs. And most of the people of Sussey share the mind-speech and can be reminded of the songs even without going back to the sea. That's why the music of Sussey is the most beautiful on Tamar." He caught up with her and she felt his mental touch. "How can our insistence on our children knowing their heritage anger you so? Why are you closing me out?"

Elise shrugged. "What right do I have to criticize the sea folk? But for a minor genetic accident, I might be one of you."

"What do you mean?"

She negotiated a tricky part of the trail in silence and stopped on a ledge halfway down the hill to the beach. The sea mist dissolved where the sunlight hit it, but the cove itself still lay in shadow, filled with an opaque mass of fog. She turned to face Errin as he, too, reached the ledge. "My grandmother told me something when I got home the other night," she said. "She told me that my father wasn't my real father and that my grandfather, whom I remember dandling me on his knee, wasn't my real grandfather. She told me about a brother I've never seen and an uncle, whom I may have seen but never knew. She said that if I was old enough to walk on the shore with you, I should know the consequences. So now I know them."

Errin stared at her. "You'd never had a hint of any of that before?"

"No," Elise said. "Isn't that funny? I never knew a thing about my own family. I hardly remember my mother, but I've always depended on Da and he isn't even related to me."

"I'm sure you can still depend on him," Errin said. "Love doesn't follow bloodlines, you know."

"I don't seem to know much of anything anymore."

"Why are you still headed toward the shore? Why did you come, if you don't want to see me?"

"But I do want to see you," she said, shaking her head. "Even after having my whole life turned upside down, part of me won't stop thinking about you, wanting to see you again."

He pulled her back into his arms. She was limp, unresisting. "*Hear me, Lise,*" he demanded, and her eyes flickered up to meet his. "*The things your grandmother told you, they didn't change the way you feel because they don't matter. They don't make any difference to what happens between you* and me. *I'm not your father, or your grandfather, just as you're not your mother or your grandmother. Could your mother, or your grandmother, speak with the mind-speech of my people?"*

"No." She allowed his arms to draw her closer.

"Then what we feel is different." His mind opened to hers and she saw that he believed what he told her. *"I couldn't feel this way about you, if you couldn't be close to me mind to mind. Neither your mother, nor your grandmother, could mate with an ingvalar. Such a mating would not be valid by our laws. They could only couple. But I can mate with you and it will be valid, even though you can't change your shape. You have the mind sense and that is what matters."*

Elise shuddered, pulling away. *"You mean, to your people, my mother and grandmother are mere beasts. I'm only a person to you because I learned mind-speech. If I hadn't learned, you might have coupled with me, but that's all it would have meant, the casting of your seed before a beast."*

"I didn't mean it that way."

"But that's the essence of what you thought, isn't it?"

"You make it sound twisted." He shook his head. *"But how can love exist without the contact of mind to mind?"*

The sun rose higher and the cove filled with pearly, opalescent light. *"I don't know,"* Elise thought, *"but if they felt no love then there shouldn't have been the physical coupling either. My mother may have died of loss and loneliness. Yet you've just told me my father couldn't have felt anything for her at all. Your disregard for the feelings of my people is so basic you didn't even think about how that might sound to me."*

"I'm sorry," he thought. *"Your thoughts are true. They shame me, but I can't change the past. I can only affect what is now. I feel for you. I desire you."*

"Even now you aren't saying you love me."

"How can I, when I hardly know you? We've had no time to forge a bond that strong. What I feel for you is stronger than anything I've felt before. I believe it's the beginning of love."

Elise saw an image of a sprouting seed in his mind and felt the warmth of the flower that might bloom from it. She shivered because, despite every reason against it, including her revulsion to the attitude his people had for hers, she still wanted nothing more than to be with him, lie with him, love him.

She turned away and continued down the path to the beach. Her mind was filled with confusion, but she no longer tried to close him out. She wanted him to share the chaos of her thoughts.

When Elise reached the strip of shingle at the foot of the path, she stared at the waves curling in brokenly around the boulders thrusting up through the sea. She heard music in the crash of the surf against the shore. She swallowed, and turned back to Errin, *"How much does love mean to you?"*

"What do you mean?"

A flock of birds rose from the headland, their cries mingling with the roar of the sea. *"In the history of my family's relations with your people, the women of my family have made the sacrifices. Your people have given nothing in return,"* she thought, her mind full of images of pain.

She saw him wince, but he nodded. *"That's true. Perhaps not the only truth, but still true."*

She turned away from him and looked out at the sea where gulls and keriarin dived for fish. "If I lie with you and give what's between us a chance to grow," she said aloud, "then I'll come to love you, if I don't already, but you'll still leave in a few weeks time. That way, I'll have followed the pattern of all the women of my family and I'll have given up much, and you nothing." She wasn't blocking her thoughts from him, but she needed the precision of words without the overlay of emotion the mind-speech gave them. "Am I wrong?" She faced him.

He sighed and shook his head. "No. What you say is true, but it's a cold truth and you and I together could be warmth and fire. I'd come back to you."

"I don't need a man who must come back to me," she said, pride and anger in both her voice and her thoughts. "I'm Elise Adun of Adun, my grandmother's heir. This island and all those around it will belong to me when she dies: more than two hundred square kilometers of land and two dozen tenant farms. I need a man to farm it with me."

Errin stiffened.

She nodded. "You know what I'm asking. Is it so much? Your mother came from Sussey. I know you spent part of your youth with her people there. You said yourself you aren't wholly a nomad. If I lie with you, you must swear by Jehan, a god of your people as well as mine, to give up the sea for at least a year and come and live in my home and work the farm with me. I won't ask that you marry me. I won't ask for any bond beyond the period of one year." She looked away from him to the sea that had turned from misty gray to blue, with whitecaps sparkling like jewels in the sunlight.

"Even you find Taelessa, the Sea of Tears, beautiful," he said bitterly, "and you are not a part of it, as I can be." He sighed, and she sensed his regret. "What you ask is much."

"There'd be nothing to stop you from swimming in the sea," she said. "You could swim every day, as long as you'd done your work first."

"You want me to be your pensioner, the kept man of your household," he said, bending down and picking up one of the smooth, flat stones that covered the shore. "What would your grandmother say to having one of the sea folk living in her home?" He threw the stone hard sideways along the line of the surf. It hit a patch of slack water and skipped three times before being swallowed by a wave.

"What can she say? What she told me two days ago gave me the right to make my own decisions," Elise said and then hesitated. "But I didn't mean for it to sound as though you'd be dependent on me. You'd be treated as my husband with the same status as my father. You'd be my partner, not a pensioner."

"At the end of the year, what would happen then?" His sea green eyes with their flecks of gold darkened. "If you continued your training and became a wizard, then I could demand the same of you, that you turn your back on the land and spend a year in the sea."

His black hair curled around his shoulders in loose waves and Elise realized suddenly that she had never seen it dry before, at least not since they were children. She swallowed at the anguish she felt at the thought of never seeing it dry again. "I doubt that I'll continue my training now," she said, "and I don't know what would happen after the end of the year. You could swim away and never see me again, if that's what you want, and if I had a child, and the child had sight and proved to be a shape-changer, I'd carry it down to the sea when you asked, as my mother and my grandmother did before me."

"Then what would you have gained by keeping me here for a year?" He stared at her, his expression puzzled.

She sighed. "I'm not sure I'd gain anything. I might simply be increasing my own risk of pain. On the other hand, if you stay, you would be sacrificing something at least for my sake." She paused and bit her lip. "And there's the chance that you might find that life on the shore isn't as bad as you fear. You might decide at the end of the year that you'd be willing to stay again. Not every year, but maybe every other one. I could live with that. Sailors' wives see their husbands even less often."

Errin stared at her and Elise felt color rise in her cheeks. She turned away from him and started to walk back to the path. "I'm sorry. It was a stupid thing to ask. Of course, you can't give up the sea, the life of a nomad, for the day to day work on an island farm, not even for a single year."

He stopped her before she had gone three steps. "I wish I could stay," he said. "Believe me, I would give up many things to be able to live with you now."

She swallowed, glaring at him. *"But not a year of your life, of course not,"* she thought, *"when you've already admitted you don't love me."*

"I think, perhaps, I was too hasty," he thought. *"Your fires have been burning me since we first met."* He hesitated, and then added, *"But I cannot stay with you now, however much I might love you. I have other obligations in this coming year that I cannot set aside."*

She turned away from him, pulling out of his arms and closing her eyes to keep the tears in. "No is no. Don't try to put a sugar coating on it."

"I cannot stay with you this year," he said, "but I will make a time for us. Give me a year, and I'll return and stay for you. I wish I could stay now, but I will come back."

She laughed, but her laughter had a harsh sound and tears welled from her eyes. "'I wish I could.' How pathetic that sounds. Have you no control over your own destiny?"

"I am not one of the wigan folk. I have obligations on Sussey. It's not the pull of the sea that takes me from you, but my duty to my family. My grandfather is ill, perhaps dying, and my mother is fragile. And I have other responsibilities. I must notify people and prepare them before I can spend an entire year living with you. It was hard for me, even making time for this visit. I can't lie with my mind. Feel that what I say is true."

And it was true. She felt the truth in him with the same deep sense that told her of the tides and movements of the sea. He cared for her. It would hurt him to leave and he would try to come back to her, but that changed nothing. He would leave.

The reality was a knife stabbing her. She took slow deep breaths to control the pain, and she knew, suddenly, that she would complete her training, would become a wizard. And, if she was going to be a wizard, she could not let pain rule her. She must not. She summoned all the control she had ever learned. Then she sought out the love and pain inside herself and put a shell around them, forcing them down to a place in her mind where she would not have to look at them again. The tears dried on her cheeks and she turned to him. *"Then, if you cannot stay, go. I don't want to see you again."*

Errin bowed his head. *"You will be a strong wizard some day, Elise. I see that nothing I can say will change your mind now. So be it. But you'll see me again. I'll return in a year. And when I do, I will have time and there'll be no more duties or obligations standing between us. You may bury your love now, but it will still be there inside you. I will dig it out."*

XVII

4633, 464TH CYCLE OF THE YEAR OF THE LIZARD
MONTH OF ISKKAAR

Mend larin dubarem inifla.

The old forget to dream.

— ESLARIN PROVERB

NUTENA POMORRY LOOKED OUT OVER THE PATIO BALCONY at the Bay of Aelos. She had a decision to make, but she did not know how to make it. All her life, people had wanted her to decide things, but when she did decide something it always turned out wrong.

The sky was gray. The sea was gray and almost flat. The air felt heavy. It would rain soon, she could feel it. Then she would have to go in and deal with her mother and Galen and Errin. Even her son was bound to ask for her assurance that she wouldn't need him during the next whole year, so he could go off and live with some woman on the islands he had visited as a child.

"Mother," Errin said. "Are you all right?"

Nutena whirled to see Errin standing in the doorway to the study. Maybe her thoughts had drawn him.

"I don't know, Errin. I don't know if I've ever been all right."

Errin crossed the patio and took her in his arms. Her cheek rested against his shoulder. She sighed.

"You'll be all right, Mother. Grandfather was old and ill. It was time for him to die."

"But what if Mother dies, too?" she cried. "Who will take care of this place?"

Errin chuckled. "Granny Aliara is as tough as the metellan they raise in the hills," he said. "I don't think you need to worry about her dying for years."

"My brother died, and there was nothing wrong with him," Nutena said. "Mother could die. Any one of us could die. And what would I do then? I can't run the winery. I can't even direct the servants to prepare a formal dinner. Look what happened when I tried last year. Ayana complained about everything and told me I was a hopeless fool."

Errin put his hand under her chin and forced her to look up at him. "Mother, Ayana complains about everything anyone does. Don't you remember how Granny Aliara tore into her? You did a fine job of arranging that dinner. There was nothing wrong with it. Just Ayana behaving like the fathik she is."

"Oh, no," Nutena said, burying her face again in Errin's shoulder. "Ayana was right. I arranged everything badly. I always do."

Errin sighed. "Then if you ever have to be hostess for a dinner again, tell Mistress Ryuna to make the arrangements. She's perfectly competent to do so, and she wouldn't mind at all."

Nutena looked up at him with tear drenched eyes. "But Mother always tells her what to do."

"That doesn't mean Mistress Ryuna isn't competent," Errin said gently. "It just means Granny Aliara likes to do everything her way. She enjoys arranging every detail, but if you don't enjoy doing it, there's no reason you need to do anything. Just tell the servants to take care of it, whatever it may be." He stepped back so that she stood by herself but he still supported her by her shoulders. "Now, come on inside. It's going to rain soon and you'll get soaked."

She twisted out of his hands and went back to the railing, looking out over the bay. "I don't want to go in there yet."

"Why not?"

"I don't know," she said sharply. "I just don't want to."

Not for the first time, Errin wondered why he always ended up being the care giver when it came to his relationship with his mother. He took a deep breath and asked, "Is it because of Galen?"

Nutena turned back to glare at him. "He wants me to marry him."

"Do you want me to tell him that you don't want to see him anymore? That his advances aren't welcome?" Errin demanded.

"Oh, no," Nutena gasped. "I couldn't bear it if I didn't see him any more."

Errin gaped at her. "I thought he upset you."

Nutena looked away. "Only when he asks me to marry him. I don't ever want to get married again."

She could feel her son's eyes on her. She had encouraged him to believe that she still loved his father. She had thought that would be comforting for him, and it had been easier for her than explaining her own shortcomings.

"If you married him, he could run the winery for you," Errin said carefully.

Nutena braced herself and turned to face her son. "But then he'd find out how deficient I am as a wife and as a woman. I couldn't bear it if Galen said the things that Lothar used to say to me."

"So Granny Aliara was right. You do care about Galen?"

"Yes. But I don't want to marry him."

"You just want to keep him dangling," Errin said flatly.

Nutena bit her lip. "I want things to stay as they are."

Errin shook his head. "All things change, Mother. I don't think Galen is anything like my father. I don't believe that he'll get angry if you ask him to help you with things. And, if you marry Galen, you wouldn't have to leave your home where things are familiar to you. He would move in with you here."

Nutena stared at him, surprised by how much his words reassured her. Errin did understand her. Maybe he was right, and she shouldn't be so afraid of marrying Galen. Maybe Galen was different than Lothar.

ALIARA TOOK ERRIN AWAY TO HER STUDY after dinner, leaving Nutena with Galen. "That was clever, what you said to Nutena before dinner. I think you actually managed to calm some of her fears. I think, given a little more time and encouragement, she may even marry Galen now."

Errin sighed. "I sincerely hope so. I owe you an apology. I thought you'd picked Galen for his palate."

Aliara chuckled. "Jehan, no. I can hire a wine master. Getting someone who'll actually support Nutena was always more important to me. I can't do it. I can see what's wrong, but every time I try to talk to her I just make things worse."

Errin smiled. "I'll be glad to see someone else supporting her myself."

"Yes," Aliara said. "Will I like this girl from Adun?"

Errin looked at her. "I think you will, but quite frankly Granny, I don't really care."

Aliara laughed. "Good for you, boy."

MONTH OF INGVASH

ERRIN POMORRY SWAM UP OUT OF THE SEA and rode a wave to shore on Adun in the middle of the first week of Ingvash. Then he dressed and walked to Elise's grandmother's home and knocked.

Moira Adun opened the door herself.

"I've come to see Elise."

"You're a year too late," Moira said, her smile bright with malice. "She left for the mainland last summer. She's gone to join the Varfarin. And in any event she wouldn't want to see you again. She's carrying Timmon Skane's child."

BOOK II

THE HEIR TO CORMOR

Taga a nalor ba qua karad, puat nithewe e wanewe e lokanwe sen bara gao. Nik ba dales nith e malacab ba dales lokamdem. Ilnalor ue me grest non dalne boruna gao irhe amvalod.

The will of a wizard is like a sword, it must be fired and tempered and sharpened if it is to have strength. Pain is the finest fire and despair the best of whetstones. A wizard who has known these well will have the power to change the universe.

— FROM THE WRITINGS OF THE WIZARD RAV

XVIII

MONTH OF CERDANA

> *Can the end justify the means? Surely the answer to that*
> *question depends on both the desired end and the means*
> *utilized. An unworthy goal cannot justify any measure taken to*
> *accomplish it. A worthy goal must at least justify the expenditure*
> *of time and energy.*
>
> *Can a worthy goal justify an unworthy act? That is a more*
> *difficult question. Again, all things are relative. If the goal is*
> *extremely worthy, and the act, while wrong, specific and limited*
> *in its damage . . .*

— EXCERPT FROM <u>MORAL DILEMMAS OF WIZARDRY,</u> BY THE WIZARD TORIN, ILWHEIRLANE, 2039

JEREVAN RAYNE, THE HETRI OF LEYBURN, strode into the Inn of the Spotted Hog at Onchan late in the afternoon. Having ridden straight from Leyburn, stopping only to change horses, he was tired and irritable.

"Meyer," he greeted the landlord, "my servant, Otto, reserved me a room." He shrugged off his multi-caped riding coat and handed it to a waiting servant. He was a tall, broad-shouldered young man, his jacket and breeches of a fashionable but conservative cut.

"Of course, Your Grace, your usual room's prepared," Meyer said. "Otto's waiting for you in the private parlor." The landlord hesitated. "There's a gentleman with him."

Jerevan nodded, his expression grim. "Yes, I'm aware of the gentleman," he said, with sarcastic stress. "He's the reason I'm here."

Meyer looked pale. "He's the Varfarin's chief wizard."

"I know who he is." Jerevan ran a hand through his disheveled golden hair. "Has he been here long?"

"He's been in Onchan for about a week, I believe," Meyer said.

"He's not putting up here?"

The landlord shook his head and swallowed. "No, thanks be to Jehan. He's patronizing the Bel Ingling down by the docks."

"Witness the marvelous effect he's had on our shipping," Jerevan said bitterly.

"Beg pardon, Your Grace?"

Jerevan waved his arm, as though brushing aside the landlord's bewilderment. "No matter, Meyer. I'm tired. I'd better bathe and change before I make my appearance in the parlor." He grinned. "Otherwise, I might speak out of turn and we can't have that now, can we?"

Meyer swallowed. "No, Your Grace. I'll see that hot water is sent up immediately."

"And tell Otto I require his presence upstairs. The wizard can put up with his own company for a few minutes."

The landlord's eyes bulged. "Y-yes, Your Grace."

Jerevan slapped Meyer lightly on the back and bounded up the stairs. "Good man. I know I can depend on you."

He came back downstairs half an hour later, immaculate in dress shoes, stockings and pantaloons, as though he were on his way to court or a formal ball. His expression was preoccupied, however, and he was unconscious of the admiration he evoked from the waitresses as he passed through the public bar.

"Will you wish dinner served immediately, Your Grace?" the landlord asked.

"Give us an hour, Meyer. The size of my party may be reduced by then," Jerevan said. "But bring a bottle of that red wine you have from Ruffin."

"Certainly, Your Grace. Right away."

Jerevan nodded and entered the parlor. It was not a large room. The man he had come to see stood before the fire.

The Wizard Derwen looked both heavier and grayer than Jerevan remembered him. His once brown hair was a salt and pepper grey, and his skin was weathered like old leather. Jerevan thought his eyes too close together above his bulbous nose. Still, while Derwen had never been handsome, Jerevan had to grant him an air of dignity.

"I thought the delay of your seedlings would bring you here, Your Grace," Derwen greeted him, smiling in a satisfied manner and rocking back on his heels as he stood with his back to the fire.

"If those seedlings are damaged, I'll take my complaint to Vanda," Jerevan said. "You have no authority to interfere with peaceful shipping."

Derwen shook his head. "But I do, Your Grace. I have the authority of power. There's no greater authority than that." He sat down in one of the two chairs in front of the fire.

"You're mad," Jerevan said. "Abuse of power can be punished, even in a wizard."

"No," Derwen said. "My peers would only censure me for something major, and then, only if I couldn't justify my acts."

"How do you justify delaying the arrival of my seedlings?" Jerevan asked, crossing the room to seat himself in the chair opposite the wizard's. "Genetically tailored plants may be expensive, but I've never heard of anything from Isin posing a threat."

Derwen frowned. "I needed to capture your attention in a way you couldn't ignore."

Jerevan laughed but there was little humor in the sound. "And now that you have my attention?"

For the first time Derwen looked less sure of himself. He hesitated, then said, "You have great potential. It must be developed."

Jerevan stiffened. "I told you three years ago, after my father died, that I had neither time for, nor interest in, the study of wizardry. If that's the reason you wanted my attention, you're wasting your time."

Derwen sighed. "Your mother was still alive then. Her religious beliefs kept you from receiving training as a child. But I don't believe you're a follower of Miune?"

"No," Jerevan said, "I'm not, much to my mother's disappointment. But I agree with her regarding wizardry."

Derwen toyed with the large, clear crystal that hung from a chain around his neck. "I'm sorry, Your Grace, but I'm no longer willing to give you a choice."

"What do you mean?"

Derwen sighed. "Twenty-one years ago, when I tested you for wizard talent, I could hardly believe the results. I'd never seen a child with potential like yours. Yet, because of Nadira's beliefs, your father would only permit you to receive a healer's training."

"My father wasn't any fonder of wizards than my mother," Jerevan said. "I'm also well aware that more was crammed into me during my training than was necessary to make me a healer." He paused, closing his eyes for a moment, controlling his temper. "But that's old history. Get to the point."

"Three years ago, Your Grace, when you came to court, I examined you again. Your potential is greater even than I estimated at your birth, or than Kindric, who taught you healing, indicated. In all my five hundred years, I've only seen one man your equal, and that was my master, the Wizard Cormor, the greatest of the Great Wizards. I told you then that you had to take training, that Ilwheirlane and the human lands need you."

Jerevan sighed. "We've been over this before. What did you mean when you said you were no longer willing to give me a choice?"

"Just that, Your Grace. Three years ago, I understood your desire for time to reorganize the hetrion after your father's death. He wasn't, after all, the most notable manager. And your mother was still alive, with all her prejudices. I told you, however, that the matter was not settled, that I would insist on training you."

"How can you accomplish that?" Jerevan demanded. "You can't push knowledge into my mind. You can't teach a man who doesn't want to learn."

Derwen sighed and nodded. "True, to a point. In fact, I said something of the sort to the Wizard Cormor. He told me to think again. So, while it's true I can't teach you if you don't want to learn, it may be possible for me to change your attitude."

Jerevan rose abruptly and strode across the room to the window, opening it as though he had a sudden need for air. "How do you expect to achieve such an alteration?"

There was a knock on the door and Otto entered, bearing a tray with a decanter of wine and two glasses. "The wine you requested, Your Grace." He walked over to the table by the window, put down the tray, poured a small amount into one of the glasses and offered it to Jerevan. "It needs longer to breathe, but I think you'll find it tolerable."

Jerevan tasted the wine and nodded, handing the glass back. "What happened to Meyer?"

Otto said, without a trace of emotion, "He found it necessary to serve in the public bar this evening. I assured him there'd be no problem."

One of Jerevan's eyebrows rose and a glint of humor flashed in his blue-gray eyes. "Of course."

Otto poured wine into both glasses, giving one to his master and carrying the other to the wizard who had risen and was again standing with his back to the fire.

"Now, Derwen," Jerevan said, sipping the wine, "You were about to answer my question."

Derwen took his glass and swirled the wine, staring at it while Otto took up his station by the door. "Won't you be reasonable, Your Grace?" he asked. "The training will only take one or two hours a day. I'm willing to accommodate my schedule to meet yours."

"Forgive me," Jerevan masked his anger in politeness, "but I'm afraid I don't think that I'm the unreasonable one here. I'm an independent adult, responsible for lands and property. You have no right to impose your will on me."

Derwen nodded. "Precisely, Your Grace, I have no right but the right of power. Which was what prompted the demonstration which brought you here. Do you deny that I have power?"

Jerevan frowned. "How can I? It's obvious. Even the landlord's tiptoeing about like a frightened mouse. You're head of the Varfarin, the pre-eminent wizard in the human lands."

"Haven't you ever desired such power, Your Grace?" Derwen asked. "The great wizards wielded more power than any hetri, more than an estahar, for that matter. You could be equally as powerful, with training."

Jerevan laughed and walked back to the chair he had abandoned earlier. "No, Derwen, you missed your mark with that arrow," he said, sitting down again. "Power's a two-edged sword. It entails responsibility. I have enough of that now."

Derwen nodded, resuming his seat in the opposite chair. "But you handle it well," he said. "In just three years, you have your lands on the way back to prosperity, despite your father's neglect. Ilwheirlane and the other human nations are under siege, and the situation is only going to get worse. The were-folk want to see an end to our power. They've grown bolder every year since Cormor's death. Think what your contribution could mean; think of the good you could do given a wider challenge."

"I told you," Jerevan said, "I have all the challenge I want. I'll do my duty in the Privy Council as advisor to Vanda, but I'm not interested in a wider scope."

Derwen sighed, but persevered, "If you're so happy with your life, what objection can you have to extending it? You're twenty-one. Even with your training as a healer, you can only expect fifty or sixty more years, seventy at most, before your strength starts to dwindle and you become prey to all the diseases of old age. A wizard with your potential can live millennia."

Jerevan leaned back. He was tired from the long ride, and angry about the need for it. The wizard's persistence increased his irritation. "I prefer quality to quantity," he said. "Show me a wizard who enjoys his extended life. Look at you, for instance. They say wizards can take any form, but every time I've seen you, you've been the same grey pudding of a man. Where's the passion in your life, Derwen? Or did it all run out centuries ago, leaving only the fatty shell?"

Derwen flushed. "You're narrowing your own choices, Your Grace. I'd prefer persuasion, but as I've pointed out, I can use force."

Jerevan's eyes narrowed. "I thought we'd established that a man can't be forced to learn something."

"No," Derwen said, "we established that knowledge can't be crammed into someone's head from the outside, that a man has to want to assimilate it. On the other hand, a man's wants can change. No malik wants to carry a rider, but a good trainer gets around that. He may simply bribe the malik with meat. But if that doesn't work, and sometimes it doesn't - if the malik isn't hungry - then he tries something else."

Jerevan swirled the wine in his glass. "So what comes next, now that you've established that I'm not hungry."

Derwen's eyes widened, as though he were startled. He hesitated, then took a gulp of his wine. "You know the answer to that – the trainer uses a goad. The principle's the same with a man. Only, a man requires a special kind of goad."

"So what kind of goad have you decided to use?"

"I hadn't decided. I'd still hoped you could be persuaded by rational argument."

"Which means," Jerevan observed, stiffening, "that you have decided now. What's it going to be, this goad? What threat are you going to hang over me?"

Derwen shook his head. "No, it's too late for threats. Even I can see that." He took up his crystal and stared into it before turning back to Jerevan. "We both know I could devise one great enough to drive you to say you'd study, but your heart wouldn't be in it. You really don't want to be a wizard."

Jerevan straightened in the chair, watching as Derwen turned his attention to the crystal which had started to glow with a faint radiance. "If not a threat, then what form of persuasion can you use?"

Derwen looked up. "You're worried now, aren't you, Your Grace." The wizard's eyes narrowed and Jerevan thought he looked like nothing so much as a mean tempered pig with his close-set eyes brilliant with triumph.

"Yes," Jerevan admitted, "I am worried. I've suddenly realized that you have no conscience, and that there may be no power on Tamar willing or able to thwart you."

The wizard frowned and rose, standing over Jerevan, still seated in the chair. "I have something better than a conscience. I have loyalty to the human lands and a purpose that was drilled into me by my master, an overriding purpose."

"And what is this overriding purpose?"

"To find a wizard with potential to equal my master's and see that he's trained to serve." Derwen glared at Jerevan. "You're the only one I've found in more than four hundred years. I'm getting old, as you observed, though not politely. I've never had the power of one of the great wizards and what I had is failing. I can't keep myself young forever, so I can't wait another four hundred years for a new candidate. You're it."

Jerevan rose. "I still don't see why you have to have me. Three people in five have some level of wizard talent, or so I've been told. What percentage of the children of Ilwheirlane have you tested? One percent? Or less? It seems to me only relatives of the royal family and known descendants of the Great Wizards are even looked at. I doubt it would take you long to find someone else, if you really searched."

Derwen turned to face the fire. "The few wizards left in the human lands have too much to do now. We don't have the time or energy to examine every child. We check those we can, and it's closer to fifteen percent here in Ilwheirlane, but your level of potential was considered miraculous even in the Age of Wizards. Only one or two of the greatest came close to Cormor."

"So what are you going to do?"

Derwen hesitated, then turned to face Jerevan and said, "I've cursed you."

"You've what?"

"I've placed a curse on you, a compulsion. I couldn't make it anything painful. Pain would interfere with your concentration. Nor could I make it anything truly debilitating, like crippling you or blinding you. I thought of simply spoiling your good looks, but I was afraid being ugly might not be a sufficient goad. Also, ugliness would increase your tendency to distance yourself from others, and I need your leadership skills as well as your wizard talent." He paused.

Jerevan swallowed. "Well, go on."

"Actually," Derwen continued, "it was something you said that put the idea in my mind. Well, two things."

"How helpful of me."

"Yes. It was," Derwen agreed. "You made a rude comment about my girth," he continued, patting his paunch, "and you said of yourself that you weren't hungry. I decided that you deserved to be hungry. Very hungry. Of course, if you eat enough to satisfy your new appetite, you may grow a little excess flesh of your own, but then, if you don't, I'm afraid your condition may actually get painful. The goad, you might say."

Jerevan stared at him with dawning horror. "You've already placed this curse?"

"Yes," Derwen said. "I willed certain changes in your metabolism while we talked. I must warn you, if you don't eat, the pain will continue to increase until you lapse into a coma."

"I thought you said pain would interfere with my concentration."

"But you won't need to feel pain," Derwen said. "Your condition will be perfectly manageable. All you have to do is remember to eat regularly."

Jerevan turned and went to the open window, staring out. "And for you to remove this curse, I have to agree to study wizardry?"

"No." Derwen sighed. "I told you I wouldn't threaten you. I've placed the curse. To break it, you must become a wizard. Otherwise, you'll have to live with your new metabolism for the rest of your life."

Jerevan turned from the window to face Derwen again. "But the study of wizardry can take centuries."

"However long it takes, you must study until your mind develops strong enough pathways for your will to exceed mine. At that point, naturally, you'll be able to free yourself. As you're potentially far more powerful than I, it shouldn't take you long: forty to sixty years, seventy at most."

"Seventy years!"

"That's the longest estimate. You can develop your potential much more rapidly, if you concentrate and apply yourself." Derwen hesitated, then added, "Oh, and while earlier I said I'd adjust myself to your schedule, that was before I had to go to such lengths. Now, I think you can do your studying in Ninkarrak, at my convenience."

Jerevan stared at him. "Don't hold your breath."

Derwen smiled. "I'm afraid you'll soon find you don't have a choice." The wizard walked to the door of the parlor, which Otto opened for him. He bowed to Jerevan from the doorway and said, "I'll be waiting." Then he was gone.

Jerevan went back to the chair before the fire and sank down in it. "You heard all that, Otto?"

"Yes, Your Grace."

"I had to lose my temper, didn't I?"

"He gave you some provocation, Your Grace."

Jerevan snorted. "I hope that's not my epitaph."

XIX

Malputo: Has he had enough to eat?

Landlord: Enough? The man's a glutton.
He would eat me out of business.

Malputo: Be silent man. You're being paid.
Even gluttons have to eat.

— ACT I, SCENE 3, LINES 14 - 18, THE CORPULENT SUITOR, BY HAROL GLADEN OF
ILWHEIRLANE, 4619

JEREVAN WOKE IN THE DARK, ACHING WITH EMPTINESS. Food. He had to eat; he was starving. He rolled over and sat up, swallowing the rush of saliva that filled his mouth at the thought of eating. Still half asleep, he groped for a match to light the lamp by his bed. What was the time? Why was it so dark? He must have slept for hours, missed several meals, to feel so ravenous. He had never been so hungry before.

He found the matches and had just lit the lamp when the aching void in his stomach gave way to a violent cramp. He dropped the match and doubled over. "Otto," he called, his voice reduced to a croak.

He strove to control his breathing, then tried again. "Otto," he cried and folded up on the bed as the cramping intensified. He hurt too much to stand or sit up. At least Otto was a light sleeper and had the room next door. He ought to have heard the last cry. Jerevan concentrated on riding out the pain, but it did not fluctuate. It just rose higher and higher.

When Otto found him he was rocking in agony.

"Your Grace, what's the matter?"

"F-food," Jerevan gasped. "I have to eat."

Otto's eyes widened with appalled comprehension. "I'll be right back." He ran from the room.

It seemed hours before Otto returned. From moment to moment Jerevan thought the pain could grow no worse, but it did. His sheets were soaked with sweat and saliva that dribbled from his mouth no matter how often he swallowed.

Otto had to prop him up with pillows and help him to drink from a mug filled with milk; Jerevan's hands shook too badly for him to manage on his own.

The milk helped. The violence of the cramping decreased as Jerevan finished the mug and was able to sit up. Otto put the tray with the remaining food on the table by the bed. "The cook is fixing a proper breakfast, Your Grace, but I thought you'd need something right away," he said, as though it were normal for his master to demand food at three o'clock in the morning.

Jerevan took the roasted sulcath in his hands and ate, only answering when he had picked every morsel off the bones. "You're right, Otto." He paused and his hand went down to his stomach which was sore but no longer cramping. Then he met Otto's concerned eyes. "The wizard's curse seems to be effective. I'll need a large meal to satisfy my new appetite."

Otto nodded. "I feared that might be the case. The cook should have your breakfast ready. I'll fetch it, Your Grace."

Jerevan sighed. "Thank you, Otto."

The breakfast Otto brought bore little resemblance to those Jerevan had eaten in the past, being more than sufficient for breakfast and lunch. Yet Jerevan's hunger did not subside until he had eaten it all and felt uncomfortably full.

Dressed and ready to leave, Jerevan took a long look at himself in the mirror on the wall. He did not consider himself a vain man, yet he realized he had taken for granted the knowledge that his appearance was pleasing to others, particularly women.

The figure in the mirror was tall, with broad shoulders and a slender waist. Athletic pursuits came easily to him. He felt almost nostalgic looking at himself. This was what he had been until he argued with a wizard. What would he become? He turned away.

They left the inn at dawn and rode hard all morning. At ten, Otto suggested they stop at a posting inn, "Just for a bite, my lord. The wizard said you'd need to eat regularly."

Jerevan shook his head, despite his growing hunger. He had eaten enough that morning. He wanted to go home, to reevaluate his options on his own ground. The night before he had hoped the wizard's curse might be ineffective or something he could live with. Now he knew it was not. He had to make new plans.

As he rode his hunger grew to a physical ache. By eleven, that ache became acute. At first Jerevan tried to ignore the pain, but his stomach muscles were still sore from the early morning cramps. He ceased to be able to think of anything but food and his mouth flooded with saliva.

"There's an inn ahead, Your Grace," Otto said.

Jerevan glanced at his servant, wishing he could deny the exigency of his condition. "Is my need so obvious?"

Otto nodded. "I can tell by the way your throat works. The curse's riding you hard. Better feed it, so you don't repeat what happened this morning."

"I'll turn into a walking balloon, a freak fit only for a carnival."

"Then study wizardry, defeat his curse with his own weapons."

"Tarat's furies," Jerevan swore, "you sound like him." He reined his horse into the courtyard of the inn. Two ostlers ran out as Jerevan dismounted. "Cool them down and water them," he commanded, flipping the men some coins, "but just loosen the girths, don't unsaddle them. We'll need them again soon." He strode into the inn.

"The wizard said you had a talent for it," Otto said, when they were both seated at a table in the common room and the host had taken their orders, looking only mildly surprised when they ordered dinners while it was still morning.

"I'm a healer," Jerevan said. "That's all the wizard training I ever thought to need. The Age of Wizards is dead and good riddance!"

"He's right about the human lands needing leadership, the way the were-folk have been pushing our borders," Otto said.

"I don't question his politics," Jerevan admitted. "He's head of the Varfarin. He ought to know more about the international situation than anyone else in Ilwheirlane. I just don't see why he has to pick me. He'd do better to find someone who wanted the job."

Otto shrugged. "Wanting a skill doesn't mean you'll have it, Your Grace."

Jerevan grimaced. "Yes, Otto, you don't need to continue. I'm not that much of a fool. I was converted in the early hours of this morning. I know I have no choice but to study wizardry. But I'll slit my throat before I study under Derwen and, if I ever do become a wizard, I'll see that he regrets what he's done."

Their food arrived and for a time Jerevan was capable of nothing but easing the emptiness inside him. He ate his own portion of roast seral and Otto's as well.

When Jerevan had nearly finished and his appetite appeared less compulsive, Otto asked, "Then what will you do?"

Jerevan shrugged. "Make arrangements at Leyburn to be away for a time. Cherwell's a good bailiff. He'll just have to take over a few years earlier than I planned."

"And then?"

"Then we board a ship sailing to Lara," Jerevan said, voicing aloud the plans he had formed during the ride. "From there we travel up the Aodh to the Ranaodh and then to Belkova."

"Why so far?"

Jerevan's eyes narrowed. "Because the White City is the home of Myrriden, one of the few wizards surviving from the Age of Wizards. If he can't, or won't, break the curse, I hope at least to persuade him to train me. He's no friend of Derwen's; he resigned from the Varfarin when Derwen became Esalfar. The Wizard Elgan did too, but I don't know where to find him." Jerevan rose and dropped some coins on the table. "I hope you enjoy sailing."

Otto grinned and followed his master out into the courtyard where their horses awaited them. "I get seasick in heavy weather, but I'll manage."

Jerevan laughed. "Yes. I'm depending on that."

The rest of the day they stopped every three hours at some inn or tavern for Jerevan to eat. The constant interruptions slowed their progress, but relieved him of discomfort. More importantly, he found that the amount of food he ate could be quite small, as long as he ate regularly. With darkness, however, Jerevan's impatience increased and he insisted on pressing on to Leyburn.

By the time he arrived home, it had been five hours since he had eaten and he was again in pain. He requested that his housekeeper serve dinner immediately.

Mistress Saffin looked startled. "Certainly, Your Grace. I'm sure cook can find something tasty for your supper. I'll have to wake her, though. You usually stop on the road when you're going to get in late."

Jerevan shrugged. "I was in a hurry to get here, but now I'm hungry." He swallowed to control the saliva filling his mouth. He had not realized how humiliated he would feel, having to explain his condition to his household.

"Of course, Your Grace." Mistress Saffin curtsied. "I'll see to it immediately." She bustled out of the room.

Otto said, "There's no need to explain to them, Your Grace. I'll see you get enough."

"Thank you, Otto." Jerevan shook his head. "I'm glad now that I'll need to be away for some time. I only hope I can manage to eat like a gentleman rather than a starving beast for the rest of our stay."

The roast sulcath and braised caulis that the cook prepared would not have been sufficient to ease his hunger, but Otto saw to it that Jerevan had a bowl of fruit, part of a wheel of cheese and half a loaf of marin nut bread to accompany it, not to mention a bottle of wine.

It was close to midnight and he was very full when he finished off the last lommas fruit and burped. Otto looked pleased and said, "That should hold you to morning, Your Grace."

Jerevan burped again. "I hope so. At this moment I feel as though I don't ever want to see food again."

Yet, despite his enormous dinner, he woke before six in the same condition as he had been in the previous morning. Otto, who had insisted on sleeping on a cot in his room, woke at his first groan, took one look at him, threw on his clothes and ran to the kitchen.

When he returned he helped Jerevan swallow a jug of milk to stop the cramping. "The kitchen maids are still abed, Your Grace, but this should hold you until breakfast." He set down a tray of food.

Jerevan ate as voraciously as if he had been starved for a month. Worse, his hunger was not satisfied when he finished, and saliva still flooded his mouth.

He swallowed as Otto cleared the plates away, turning his head to keep Otto from seeing his discomfort.

But Otto noticed the telltale movements of his throat. He said, "It's worse than yesterday. You stretch your stomach every time you wait too long before eating and then have to gorge to stop the pain. You'll have to plan on waking up for meals in the night, and you can't afford to skip any more during the day. Every two or three hours it'll have to be, regular as clockwork." He frowned at the empty plates in his hands. "I'll get you something more now, to hold you till breakfast."

Jerevan flushed but nodded. "I'm afraid you're right."

In the days that followed the kitchen staff was amazed by Jerevan's appetite, despite the fact that Otto smuggled him nearly half the food he needed. One kitchen maid, who had not been at Leyburn long enough to know that Jerevan had not always eaten so much, commented within his hearing, "And thin as he is, too. I don't see how he does it." The remark stung as Jerevan had already detected a rounding of his stomach and other physical changes. He hurried his arrangements, deciding that he would prefer the mockery of strangers.

In the end it took him three days to outline contingency plans for an absence of several years with both his bailiff and man of business. He also left addresses where couriers could reach him or discover his current address at various dates. While an international mail service existed, Jerevan feared it would be too slow and unreliable in an emergency.

His appetite continued to be large, but Derwen had been right. If he ate small meals regularly, every three hours so that his stomach was never empty, he did not need to gorge in the ravenous manner of his first two mornings. Eating regularly entailed, however, the necessity of waking up at three hour intervals throughout the night. Jerevan, unused to such a schedule, felt tired as well as uncomfortable from overeating by the time he completed his arrangements.

"Is everything packed?" Jerevan asked, as Otto assisted him to dress the morning of their departure.

Otto hesitated, then asked, "How long will the trip to Lara take, Your Grace?"

"I'm not sure. I don't know what vessels go that way this time of year. Two to three weeks, I should imagine, depending on the weather. Why?"

"It occurred to me, Your Grace, that you may need additions to your wardrobe."

Jerevan looked in the mirror. Where his stomach had been flat a week earlier, soft flesh now showed above and below the waistband of his breeches. "Quite. I'll need looser clothes."

"Yes, Your Grace. I thought we might obtain apparel in several sizes in Onchan," Otto said, assisting him on with his jacket, which also felt tight.

Jerevan sighed. "I'll leave that to your discretion, Otto. I have to arrange for money and letters of credit to banking institutions in both Lara and Belkova. I don't want to be in Onchan more than a few days, though."

"No problem, your grace. I can obtain what's needed in one, if necessary, and make alterations myself."

Stopping as frequently as they were forced to do by Jerevan's condition, the return to Onchan took two days. And occupying his usual room at the Spotted Hog, Jerevan was embarrassed by the looks his late night and early morning meals attracted. He made it a point to eat at different places during the day so that no one could tell how much food he consumed.

On the afternoon of the second day, when he finished his sixth meal, the button on his breeches popped as he stood up, forcing him to return to his room at the inn.

Meyer's wife was passing as he reached for the key and his jacket swung wide. "Oh, Your Grace," she said, "your button's come off. I could sew it for you, if you've saved it." Then, seeing the strain on the material, she added, "You'll have to watch those late night meals or you'll grow out of all your beautiful clothes."

Jerevan cringed but thanked her for the offer and reassured her that his valet would take care of his clothes. Then, safely in his room, he removed the unwearable pants and examined himself in the mirror. Only ten days had passed since he had been cursed, but the concavity below his rib cage had already partially filled with soft flesh. He still looked slender, but he could see the difference. How much weight had he gained? Seven pounds? Eight? Not that much, but it was frightening when put in the context of ten days.

When Otto returned, he found Jerevan doing exercises on the floor. "I have to keep my muscle tone up, or I'll turn into a mound of jelly," Jerevan explained.

"Yes, Your Grace," Otto said. "I understand from a comment made by the landlady that you . . ."

"Burst my breeches," Jerevan supplied when Otto hesitated.

"Yes, Your Grace. I thought that pair was a little tight this morning. I have some things which should fit better, if you need to go out again."

Jerevan sighed. "Thank you, Otto. I do need to go out. I'm having trouble finding a vessel sailing for Lara. Wool doesn't start being shipped that way until next month, and the last of the grain ships sailed three months ago."

The new breeches and jacket fit, and Jerevan returned to the Harbor Master's office, but that evening, when he passed through the public bar, he noticed that the waitresses, who had flirted in the past, were suppressing giggles. A glutton was a figure of fun even when he was not fat. Jerevan was glad he would be leaving soon. He did not want to see their reaction when he started to look fat as well.

Unfortunately, they could not leave directly for Lara. Onchan was not a major port. The only ships available were small coastal traders which made too many stops. The Harbor Master advised him that taking the mail packet to Ninkarrak and sailing from there on one of the early wool ships would be his fastest route.

XX

MONTH OF ANOR

Tolu ba majenalad, ganesh ba tan.

Peace is an illusion, war is reality.

— A SAYING OF THE FOLLOWERS OF KYRA THE DESTROYER

THE EIGHTH LEGION OF THE ESTAHARIAL ARMY of Gandahar marched into Nadrum in the afternoon of the fifteenth day of Anor. The populace mounted no resistance to the invasion. Most of the able bodied were out fishing. Those working in the poor, hard scrabble farm lands around the city stood and gaped as the front guard of malik cavalry loped past. One of the final regiments of foot soldiers sent out a detachment to round the farm people up and herd them into the temporary slave pens errected outside the town.

Errin Pomorry, examining a rotting pier on the waterfront, had more notice than most of the population. He saw the malik cavalry and officers with their banners crest the hill on the other side of the Siwara River north of the town. He ran to notify the wizards Rand and Jao, who were operating a clinic in a crumbling mansion a few blocks away.

"The army of Gandahar is on its way into town. We have about twenty minutes before the advance guard gets here," Errin said, panting from his run.

"How many units?" Rand asked, straightening up from the patient he had been examining. He was a tall, dark man, his skin tanned from long exposure to the sun.

"A full legion, from the banners. I didn't wait to see more. We need to get out of here. The boat's provisioned. I'll notify the kindred while you pack."

"I have to finish treating this patient, or she'll die," Jao said, bending over a cot at the other end of the room. "Nadrum can't be a major objective. Maybe they'll march past."

"There's nothing to the south but lands poisoned by the Bane," Errin said impatiently. "Even if they're foolish enough to march through the Bane to another target, they'll secure Nadrum on the way. If we don't leave soon, we'll be caught."

"What can they want here?" Rand demanded.

"I don't know, but a legion will have officers with the high sight," Errin said.

"True." Rand frowned. "Jao, Errin's right. Finish as quickly as you can. We'll have to leave."

"I'll be back in two minutes," Errin said and ran down the street to the Sanctuary of Maera.

"A legion of the army of Gandahar just crested the ridge north of town," he told Arnella, the member of the kindred on duty. "I suggest you at least take off your robes and mingle with the people, if you can't get out of Nadrum. The kindred were put to death when Gandahar took Ardagh."

Arnella paled, but said, "That would mean abandoning our duty. I'll notify the others, but I must remain here."

"Just remember that you won't be able to help anyone if you're dead," Errin said, and ran back to Rand and Jao.

Rand was packing his things, his shoulder length black hair disheveled. "I'll need the rest of my papers from upstairs. I won't leave my research."

"I'll get them," Errin said, "You finish up here."

Errin climbed the stairs to the rooms they had used during their stay two at a time, knowing he would be much quicker than Rand. He was tired of Nadrum and the heat, dust, insects and rats, which appeared to be the only healthy life forms left in the region, but he understood Rand's reluctance to leave.

Prior to the Wizard's Bane, Nadrum and its sister city, Ardagh, a hundred and thirty kilometers northwest, had been the two major ports of the Aharion of Arduin, one of the most fertile regions on Tamar. Nadrum had been the capitol. The Bane, however, had destroyed Arduin. More than half the population had died, and much of the fertile farmland been destroyed.

Ardagh had turned to piracy to survive until the isklarin had captured it three quarters of a century earlier and changed its name to Kavarna.

Nadrum lacked the energy for piracy. From a wealthy populace of many thousands, its inhabitants had dwindled to less than a thousand. It was a city of rotting piers, crumbling buildings, and worn and defeated people.

Rand, Jao and Errin had worked there for the past two months, and Rand had become more and more fascinated with the effects of the Bane.

He believed Nadrum's proximity to contaminated land was poisoning the people and animals living there. A symptom he found of particular concern was the percentage of deformed children, which was certainly higher in Nadrum than anywhere else around the Thallassean Sea. Residents were also prone to strange growths and often suffered from a disease of the blood, both rare conditions elsewhere on Tamar, except in Cibata, near the Wizard's Peace, which Rand had also visited.

No. Rand would not leave his research notes. Errin filled a carrying case and shoved the rest in his own backpack on top of his things, then hurried back down the stairs. He calculated that no more than fifteen minutes had passed since he saw the army crest the hill. There should still be enough time to reach the docks.

Jao had finished the treatment she had been performing, given instructions to the girl she had trained as a nurse and gathered her things. She looked out the window. "I don't see anything unusual."

"Good," Rand said, doing a final check of his desk. "I think we've got everything."

They slipped out of the building and started toward the waterfront. Almost immediately, however, Errin saw that they were too late. A troop of malik cavalry had already cut off their escape route to the sea. The dock area swarmed with the huge, deadly lizard-birds and their riders.

"Agnith's fires," Rand swore, ducking into a gap between buildings, out of sight of the waterfront. "We can't reach the boat that way. We'll have to go south and slip around them."

"If we can get to an unguarded beach, we can change to dolphins," Jao said, starting down the narrow alley which fortunately ran parallel to the shore. She turned to Errin, "You didn't see naval support, did you?"

Errin shook his head. "No. And one of us can probably slip back and steal the boat tonight."

"One of you will have to carry me in human form. We don't have a waterproof pack and I won't leave my notes behind," Rand said. "Particularly as we won't be able to come back here any time soon."

Errin said, "I'll carry you. I've done it before and I'm more used to being a dolphin than Jao."

Jao nodded. "But we have to find an unguarded beach first."

They paused as they reached a place where they had to cross a road in full view of the waterfront. Rand ducked low and looked around the corner, then said, "We'll need to strip and use camouflage across here and probably for a good part of the rest of the trip." He looked at Errin. "You know how to match your background, don't you?"

Errin nodded. "I can control my body temperature, too, if necessary."

Rand shook his head. "Not yet. Their attention is still on the boats and buildings facing the water. They're not looking this way. We just don't want to catch their attention."

They took off their clothes and stuck them into their bags. Rand lay down and took on the appearance of the ground. His skin, backpack and even the carrying cases turned the color of dust and dry, beaten earth. Jao joined him and Errin imitated them. His illusion was not quite as smooth, particularly with regard to his backpack, but this was the first time he had practiced the technique outside of the Rakredrem.

Rand and Jao looked at him. "*Good,*" Rand thought and started across the street. Jao and Errin followed.

They used camouflage for each street they crossed. As they approached the outskirts of the ruined city, however, the buildings degraded, supplying less cover, and they had to use it more frequently.

Finally, they reached a place where there were no more standing buildings at all, just bare ground and lumps of stone overgrown with scrub brush. They continued south, but having to crawl slowed their progress and they could still see mounted troops between them and the shore.

The shadows from the stones and scrub lengthened as the sun set. They were still less than two kilometers from Nadrum, and malik riders passed regularly between them and the sea.

"How far south are they patrolling?" Rand wondered as the last edge of the sun disappeared behind the western hills.

"They must have discovered there are wizards in the town," Jao said. "We made no secret of our presence."

Errin sighed, knowing their danger increased with dark as the isklarin, having were-sight, could see them by the heat given out by their bodies. Controlling body heat was more difficult than holding a visual illusion.

He focused on his skin being cold, holding all his body heat deep in his body. His skin took on the temperature of the ground. Fortunately, it was summer and the sun had been hot. The ground was not much cooler than his body temperature, but it would grow colder over the course of the night and Errin was not sure how long he could hold his heat inside. It was not a skill he had practiced often.

"If we live through this," he thought to Jao, "remind me to keep up my camouflage training."

They flattened against the ground as a malik troop rode past, heading for the beach, the closest maliks treading less than three meters from where they lay.

"Close," Rand thought. "We have to angle toward the beach soon, or we'll be too tired to hold an illusion next time they pass."

Jao agreed and they resumed their slow progress on an angle approaching the shore. Time passed. Errin felt his body heat starting to slip through his guard. "I can't hold it any longer," he thought. His head ached in a way he had not experienced since early in his training.

Rand sighed. "You've done well to last this long. I'll cover you for a while. We're almost at the beach."

"They still have guards every twenty meters," Jao protested. "I'll have to drop the illusion to shift. So will Errin."

"But we'll be in the water then," Rand thought. "If they don't detect us before you shift, we should be able to get away."

Jao swallowed. "I guess we don't have any choice."

They crawled down the beach to where the waves lapped the shore. "We'll have to risk standing from here," Jao said.

They started wading out to sea. The water was colder than the sand of the beach. Errin hoped Rand's shield covered him. He felt his heat radiating like a beacon.

Unfortunately, this portion of the beach had no quick drop to deep water. The seabed sloped gradually. They were thirty meters from shore before the waves reached their chests. Jao stopped. "I can shift here."

"So can I," Errin thought.

"Go ahead," Rand thought. *"I'll shield you as best I can. We should be far enough out now to get away, even if one of the guards spots us."*

Errin handed his pack to Rand and shifted. As his body stretched and contracted, the skin changing texture, even his organs moving and altering, he felt the same pain-pleasure that shape-changing always caused him. Then he felt himself a dolphin lying in uncomfortably shallow water. It took a effort to control his instinct to dive.

He sensed Jao doing just that in front of him, but he waited while Rand juggled his carry cases and the backpacks around enough to enable him to grip Errin's dorsal fin. When he was sure Rand was secure Errin started to swim.

Rand's adjustments had taken too long. There was a cry from the beach behind them.

Errin tried to increase his speed, but Rand's weight was unwieldy with the luggage. Errin instinctively wanted to dive, but could not with Rand on his back.

Still, the malik riders on the beach could not catch him. Maliks hated water and would refuse to chase him once the water rose past the second joint of their legs.

Errin had just started to feel safe when he sensed two ships setting out from Nadrum's harbor: small, fast yachts. Still, he had a two kilometer lead on them. He swam harder.

There were wizards aboard the yachts. That was the only explanation for their unnatural speed. *"We're being chased,"* Errin thought to Rand.

"I sense them," Rand said. *"The wizard in the lead boat is strong."*

"Shift and leave the luggage," Errin thought.

"Too late," Rand thought. *"He's already attacking me. I'd have to drop my shields to shift and I don't dare do that now."*

"Do you need help?" Jao's thought reached them from a distance well out to sea.

"Don't come back for us," Rand projected. *"We'll get away or not. If we don't make it, tell Myrriden."*

Errin tried to swim harder, but a weight other than Rand's dragged him backward. He felt a mind probe his shields. It grew harder and harder to swim against the backward pull and still hold his own shield tight. His mind and will had already been strained from holding the illusion so long. His head ached, but he fought on. At least Jao had escaped.

The boats drew ever closer no matter how hard Errin swam. When their lead dwindled to less than fifty meters, Errin sensed Rand gather himself for a duel. A great, globe of light formed in one of the boats and Errin felt Rand struggle to answer, but his globe did not glow as brightly. When spears of light lanced out from the globes and met in a coruscating flash over the water, Rand's was the spear that flickered and faded and was driven back.

The isklar wizard stopped short of killing Rand, however. His lance withdrew before Rand's collapsed.

"Stop." The demand came from the lead boat, the one bearing the wizard who had fought Rand. *"You cannot escape."*

Errin tried to keep swimming. Yet with Rand's defeat, the wizard he had fought added his strength to that of the lesser wizard attacking Errin. Errin felt the drag on him more than double and the pressure on his mind increased. He fought, but the pain in his head grew and grew. He blacked out.

XXI

MONTH OF TORIN

> *Malputo:* *He is a man of wealth and means,*
> *a substantial man.*
>
> *Beltrana:* *Indeed, there is substantially more*
> *of him than there is of other men.*
>
> — ACT II, SCENE 7, LINES 52 - 55, THE CORPULENT SUITOR, BY HAROL GLADEN OF
> ILWHEIRLANE, 4619

JEREVAN'S STOMACH GROWLED. He pulled open his saddlebag and grabbed a handful of assorted grains and dried fruits, crammed the mixture into his mouth and chewed, washing the stuff down with a swallow of water from the canteen slung over his shoulder. He could see Belkova in the distance, but there was no point trying to wait until he could reach an inn.

It took him only minutes to finish the food in the saddlebags. Even then, his stomach felt uncomfortably empty, but the town gates were less than a kilometer away. He would be all right if he found a place to eat quickly in Belkova. He took a last swallow of water and examined his body. As a healer, he had managed to cope with most of the painful side effects of his condition.

He healed a sore area where the pressure of the pommel chafed the tender new flesh of his growing belly. Healing the skin of his inner thighs, where with their unaccustomed layer of fat, they were rubbed raw from the constant riding took longer. After that, he lacked the strength to fully repair his strained stomach muscles. He massaged them, exerting his remaining energy to heal as much as he could.

While the routine of healing tired him, it also calmed him. But he was afraid. The fear shortened his breath and made his palms sweat. He was entering Belkova, the home of the Wizard Myrriden. Would his gamble pay off? Or would he be stranded in this isolated town with no choice left but to suffocate in his own swelling flesh? Even that fate still seemed better to him than kowtowing to Derwen. In fact, the only hopeful direction his thoughts had taken recently had been imagining the sort of revenge he might take were he ever to become the wizard Derwen wanted him to be. But he knew he would have to suppress such images when he was dealing with Myrriden.

He belched and sighed, turning to the guide. "Which inn do you recommend? I'd prefer one close to the gates."

THE WIZARD MARION WATCHED THE THREE RIDERS as they entered Belkova. The big blond in the middle had to be the Hetri of Leyburn, she decided. He was a handsome man, just a bit stocky. Derwen's curse must not have had much effect as yet.

She followed the men to the courtyard of the Inn of the Red Dragon where the guide parted from the others, and slipped inside while the hetri and his servant saw to their horses.

She found the landlord in the public bar. "Do you know who I am?" she asked.

The innkeeper was dark-haired, dark-eyed, and as round and hard as one of his barrels of ale. He stared at Marion a moment, then nodded, his eyes narrowing. "Aye, the new wizard. What do you want from me?"

"A job as a waitress, without comments about my being new." She looked him in the eye. "I'll only need the job for a day, but I want to start immediately."

His jaw clenched. "I want no one dead on my premises."

Marion laughed. "You're a brave man, but I don't mean to kill anyone. Just meet someone."

"Aye, then." He nodded grudgingly and yelled across the room to a heavy set woman, "Hey, Bella, got a new girl. She's starting right away. Valerie needs a break."

"Does she know what she's doing?" Bella yelled back. "We've got enough broken crockery now."

The innkeeper snorted. "Don't worry, Bella. This one won't be clumsy. But you're not to comment on her being new, you hear."

Bella's head came up and she stared over at the bar, seeing Marion for the first time. She stiffened, then nodded, frowning. "Aye, I don't like it, but I hear."

OTTO WENT TO THE MARKET while Jerevan paid for their rooms, then Jerevan headed for the public bar. He needed a full meal.

After he had eaten, he approached the innkeeper. "Could you tell me where to find Wizard Myrriden?"

The innkeeper's eyes widened. "Sane folk avoid wizards, but if you're crazy enough to seek one out, take the north gate. His tower's about an hour's ride out of town. You can't miss it, but he isn't much for company."

Jerevan shrugged. "I'll have to take my chances."

He met Otto in the courtyard. It was late in the afternoon. When told the wizard lived outside the town, Otto said, "Your Grace, this country is not of a configuration I'd enjoy exploring by night."

Jerevan sighed. "No. And I never trust the phrase, 'You can't miss it.' We'll wait until morning. In the meantime, I'll bathe and take a walk around the town. I need the exercise."

"Yes, Your Grace." Otto held up the package of clothing he carried. "I'll be in my room."

"Get some rest, too. I'm sure I'll find a few bars that serve food all night. I should be used to waiting. All I've done lately is wait, or eat." He was tired, but too tense to sleep.

Later, after he had bathed, he set out to explore the town. At least he would find out soon whether the journey had been worth the effort, he thought, as his steps took him toward the north gate. He paused and leaned against the side of a building, watching the traffic, mostly peasants from nearby farms. Then he realized that his hands had reached automatically to massage his stomach when he stopped moving.

How quickly habits form, he thought. He could hardly remember what it had felt like not to worry about where or when he would get his next meal. What it had felt like to be neither hungry, nor stuffed like a sulcath ready to roast.

He pushed off from the wall and started walking again, taking a direction at random. He had tried to exercise during the voyage, but the ship had been a small freighter not intended for passengers. Their quarters had been cramped; there had been no way to exercise enough. The trip from Ninkarrak to Lara had taken over three weeks, but he couldn't recall the weather or the sights of the ocean. He remembered the smell of wool, and sitting at a table in his cabin and eating.

The stay in Lara had taken longer than planned. His letters of credit took three days to be examined and approved. Then he discovered that overland caravans reached Belkova more rapidly than the river route he had anticipated. While pole boats made better time on the journey up the Aodh to its junction with the Ranaodh at Camuz, much of the Ranaodh wasn't navigable, and overland routes starting from Camuz were long and poorly maintained.

They had just missed a caravan, however, and there was more than a week's wait before the next. When Jerevan suggested that he and his servant might travel alone and try to catch up to the recently departed caravan, he was told that would be unwise without a knowledgeable guide. The caravan routes were unmarked. They might get lost. Finding a guide took another four days. In all, they had spent a week in Lara.

Jerevan paused to catch his breath, only then realizing that he had been climbing a hill. Not a steep rise, he thought ruefully. He wouldn't have noticed it two months before, but now he felt winded.

He looked around, trying to orient himself. Belkova lay on the north shore of the Ranaodh. He made out the river ahead of him. He must have walked halfway across the town. He sighed and started back the way he had come. At least this way was down hill.

After a time he heard music coming from the street to his right and turned that way. His hunger was not urgent, but he thought it wise to find a tavern. Fortunately, there was one on the corner of the next block. He entered a smoke filled room crowded with the fans of a local musical group, and sat down at a vacant table near the back.

He ate at two more taverns in the course of the evening, not returning to the Inn of the Red Dragon until the early hours of the morning. Even nights were hot so far south, and he was tired and sweaty by the time he sat down to order, feeling grim.

The heat from the soft flesh of his paunch resting against the top of his thighs added to his depression, all the worse for being a new sensation, and he looked down at the bulge of his belly. He had left Lara three weeks ago. What else could he expect after twenty-one days of riding and no other exercise? He had been trying to pull in his stomach all afternoon, but it would no longer pull in enough to lift off his thighs, and his attempts put further stress on his strained muscles.

The barmaid came over to his booth, leaning her hip against the side of the table. "Back again, lesska," she said, vulgarly referring to the size of his manhood.

Jerevan was disconcerted to recognize the woman who had served him that afternoon. That had been nearly twelve hours ago. She shouldn't find it strange that he was hungry again. That was why he ate in different places.

She grinned. "You must have liked the food, or was it the service?" She expanded her chest to display her bosom. "You want the same again?"

He blinked, disconcerted. She was a beautiful woman, generously endowed, and he was suddenly very aware that he hadn't been close to a woman in months. He said, "Yes. I'll have the stew and another flagon of your best ale," and tried to look away, but his eyes wouldn't cooperate. She had a tiny waist, despite the fullness of her breasts. Her eyes tilted upwards, giving her a feline look, and her hair was a glossy black mane. She didn't look frazzled like barmaids he had seen in the past at the end of a long shift. Furthermore, she eyed him as though the sight of him aroused her, an expression he had not expected to see again.

"Back in a moment." She grinned, looking as though his response pleased her, and returned promptly with his ale, a heaping bowl of stew and a loaf of bread. She bent over as she set down the food, giving him an unobstructed view of her cleavage. She wore nothing under the thin blouse and her breasts thrust up firmly, without support. "Eat up, lesska; you never know when you'll need your strength."

The view absorbed him. He was hardly aware that he was literally licking his lips until she laughed. Then he swallowed and blushed, his eyes rising to her face. Her eyes danced, and she put out her tongue and ran it around her lips. Jerevan found the gesture intensely provocative. She tossed her head and walked away to attend another customer.

After that, he ate automatically, but could not stop his eyes from following the barmaid.

When she came to take his empty plate, she placed her hands on his shoulders, again bending over in such a way that he could look straight down the bodice of her blouse. "I bet you need a lot to keep your strength up."

Jerevan stiffened, feeling his body react to the sight and scent of her. Two months before he might have taken her attention for granted and ignored it. He would not have seriously considered bedding a tavern wench, but today he felt ashamed of his appearance. While the barmaid's interest made him doubly conscious of the sagging weight of his belly, it also stimulated a surge of desire. He breathed in her aroma, heady with the scent of flowers and musk. Then, before he could stop himself, he put out a hand and caressed one of her breasts. It felt firm and pliant, filling his hand. She wriggled and pressed against him. "That's right, feel me."

Jerevan inhaled. Her scent was like a drug, intoxicating. He pulled a coin out of his pocket and tucked it between the round globes of her breasts. "What's your name?"

"Marion." She took the coin and transferred it to the purse hanging from her belt.

He blinked. Her name meant 'Chaos' in the high tongue. Perhaps her mother had liked the sound. He caressed her soft flesh, feeling the heat of her gaze. "You'll get two more, Marion, if you want to check on my strength upstairs. The second room on the left."

She smiled. "Just let me get Bella to relieve me out here, lesska, and I'll be right up."

Jerevan went to his room still feeling more than halfway intoxicated. He could not remember feeling such an instantaneous reaction to a woman. Only when he saw the mirror on the wall did he begin to have second thoughts.

He crossed the room and looked at himself full length for the first time since leaving Lara. Then he shut his eyes. The whole outline of his body had changed. Every part of him looked rounded, swollen with a layer of fat. And his belly bulged above and below the too tight waistband of the largest pants Otto had bought in Lara.

When Marion knocked moments later, his first instinct was to send her away. Then he thought of the coins he had promised her and decided she deserved that much.

He opened the door and handed her the coins, starting to apologize, but she slipped through before he found the right words. She put her arms around his neck and reached up to kiss him, leaning her body against his. The musky floral scent and the heat of her body drove all other thoughts from his head.

"Hadn't I better know your name, lesska?"

He shook his head, trying to clear it. "Jerevan Rayne, at your service," he said. Had he really been going to tell her he no longer needed her services? The response of his body made that a lie.

"Oh, I hope so." She ran her hands up his chest. "Come on, Jerevan, we've both got too many clothes on." She started unbuttoning his shirt.

Jerevan shuddered at the feel of her hands against his skin and reached for her blouse, freeing it from the waistband of her skirt. As he had observed earlier, she wore nothing underneath and her large, firm breasts filled his hands.

Her fingers probed the too tight waistband of his breeches. As she released the top button, she said, "You'll have to watch yourself, big boy, or there'll soon be too much of you to turn a girl on."

He swallowed, the reminder cutting through the sensual power she wielded over him. He started to pull away. "Don't you mean there's too much already?"

"Hey," Marion protested, reaching out to caress him. "I didn't mean to hurt your feelings. I think you have a fine figure." She ran her fingers down from his collarbone to his navel and he felt a twinge of pain as his stomach muscles tried to contract. "I like my men with meat on their bones." She bent over and nipped his chest, running her tongue between his nipples, which, with his weight gain, were now raised on pads of fat. He shivered and reached for her.

She helped him pull off her blouse and undid her skirt, letting it fall to the floor. "Look at me," she said. She was generously built, with wide hips and large, full breasts. Her waist was small and her breasts thrust upward with almost no sag.

Jerevan's breath sucked in as she pressed her naked body against him, her hands moving down to finish undoing the buttons of his pants. "What's the matter, Jerevan," she asked. "Don't you want me?"

His body answered for him as her fingers found his errect manhood. He groaned.

"Ah," Marion said. "I knew a big man like you would have a big sticker, too."

Jerevan shut his eyes and allowed her to finish undressing him while he in turn caressed her. The feel of her was so good he forgot to be self-conscious when she removed his clothes, and Marion did not seem to find his altered figure repulsive. At least, she never stopped touching him, running her hands over him, until he was so aroused he could not think at all.

He was not sure how they found the bed, only that he lay on it beside her, tasting her with his tongue and lips. Her hands drove him higher and higher, and he begged for her to slow down. Despite the heat and the smokiness of the taproom, her skin smelt fresh and sweet like wildflowers, with only that tantalizing hint of musk. He kissed a circle around each of her high firm breasts, while his hand stoked her hips and thighs and found the soft hair where her legs met.

Then his mouth moved up to suckle on the pebbled peak of her right breast as his hand found the nub of flesh between her legs. She cried out and her hands, which had given him no respite, suddenly lost their grip.

He massaged the nub as he nibbled her breast, then ran his tongue down the slope of her right breast and up the left to suckle again on the peak. Her back arched and her body writhed, her hands rising to grip his shoulders so tightly he felt the bite of her nails. He continued until her body convulsed and his finger on her nub felt the moisture of her dew.

He mounted her and sheathed himself in her, grimacing as he felt his belly compress between them. He leaned back to ease his weight off her. She moaned and her legs wrapped around his as her hips rose to meet him. He thrust and filled her, but the mound of his stomach pressed her down into the bed. He angled his upper body farther back, easing the pressure, and carefully brought them both to climax. Yet, even when he felt her body contract around him and let himself experience his own relief, he could not completely let go. Where once he could have lost himself in the pleasure she gave him, now he needed to adjust every movement to allow for the mound of his belly jiggling between them.

Yet she was not content to let him pull away. When he would have withdrawn, her hands explored his body, clever hands, finding pleasure points he had not known he had. Then she pushed him over on his back, mounted him, and rode him so he had no need to think about anything but the spiraling tension between them that exploded into bliss.

She was fire and heat, her passion insatiable. He lost himself in her sensuous thrall. Only when he saw the light of morning coming through the window did he realize he had missed a meal. He lay on his back, exhausted from their last bout of lovemaking, and stared at the light, hardly believing what he saw. That was not the light of early morning but of full day. Even as realization came, hunger clenched his stomach.

He sat up and swung his legs over the side of the bed, as saliva filled his mouth. He swallowed and bent over to pick up his pants, but a stomach cramp struck and he sat back down on the bed. He was not going to have time to dress and get downstairs.

Marion sat up, staring at him. "What's the matter? You look ill."

"Just hungry," he said, pressing his stomach. "Would you call my servant and ask him to bring me something to eat?"

Then he saw an expression of horror cross her face as the cramping took over and he doubled up. He was hardly aware of her departure. "Otto," he cried, only then remembering that his servant's room was on the other side of the inn from him. He had not thought it would matter; the regular meals had been controlling his condition so well.

The next minutes felt like part of a nightmare as he tried to dress despite the cramps. He succeeded in getting his breeches on and was trying to fasten them when Marion returned, carrying a tray of food.

"Here," she said, holding out a mug of milk. "Drink this."

He took it, but his hands shook and she had to help him hold it to his mouth while he drank. The cramps eased but did not stop and he turned to the food. She had brought a large breakfast, but it would not be enough this morning.

He started to eat, but doubled over as another cramp gripped him. Marion rolled him on his back and spooned food into him until the cramping eased and he was able to sit up. He ate everything on the tray, but even as he finished it he felt his stomach cramp again.

Marion said, "I'll get some more. I'll be right back."

Jerevan was doubled up on the bed with yet another cramp when she returned.

This time she had brought a whole pitcher of milk and another of ale, a platter of half a dozen scrambled eggs, a ham steak and a bowl of assorted fruits. She had to help him to eat half of it before the cramping ceased and he was able to eat on his own. But even after he had eaten it all, his stomach still ached with emptiness.

"That wasn't enough, was it?" Marion asked, staring at him.

Jerevan said, "Enough to stop the cramping. I'll be all right now. But I'd appreciate it if you'd tell my servant that I need him." He could not bear to look at her.

"I'll call your servant, but I'll also bring you something else to eat," Marion said, piling the dirty plates back on the tray. "I don't think you're going to get far before the cramping starts again."

Jerevan tried to think of some protest but all he could concentrate on was the ache in his belly and the new rush of saliva that filled his mouth at the thought of more food. He watched helplessly as she turned and left.

Otto arrived a few minutes later with two servants carrying a copper tub for Jerevan's bath. He looked appalled when he saw his master's condition. "What happened?" he demanded. "You were controlling it so well, Your Grace." He helped Jerevan to remove the clothes he had pulled on and assisted him to the bath.

Jerevan allowed Otto to bathe him while he healed and massaged his sore stomach muscles, easing the pain. "I was distracted. There was a woman, a barmaid. She was beautiful and she wanted me, belly and all." He shook his head. "I've never felt such a sudden attraction. I lost track of the time. I woke and it was morning and my stomach was starting to cramp."

"How did you get food? You've eaten, or you'd be in worse shape," Otto said, helping Jerevan out of the tub.

"Yes. Marion was still here when the cramping started," Jerevan said, flushing at the memory. "I asked her to fetch you, but she brought me food instead, two trays full," he added, grimacing. "She said she was going to get more, too."

"And so I did," Marion announced from the doorway.

Jerevan grabbed the towel to shield his body, but Marion winked at him. "I've seen it all. Don't you remember?"

She carried the replenished tray over to the table by the bed and put it down. It held another full meal.

Otto looked from her to the tray and said, "Yes, that ought to be sufficient."

Jerevan stared at her, but as soon as Otto had helped him into his robe he could not stop himself from reaching for the food. After all, he could hardly put on a more disgusting performance than what she had already witnessed. So he ate.

His hunger was stubborn this morning, however, and the ache only left when he had eaten every bite and his belly felt as tight as a drum. He sighed and rubbed his stomach, causing an enormous belch. Then he flushed as he realized that Marion had not left, but watched him eat every bite.

She grinned. "I'm glad to know it's possible to fill you. I was beginning to wonder." She gathered the empty plates and shouldered the tray as though that were the reason she had waited. Then she said, "I get off early tonight. I have a big bed and I'll make sure there's plenty of food, even for you. Come any time after ten. Third house on the right on Spinners Lane, west of Market. It has a green door."

When she had gone, Jerevan turned to Otto. "Why would she want to see me again, after what she witnessed?"

Otto shrugged. "You're a handsome man, Your Grace."

Jerevan shook his head. "No. After what she saw this morning, she should still be running. There must be a reason."

He shook his head and allowed Otto to finish dressing him, noting with relief that Otto had finished tailoring one of the new garments purchased the previous afternoon. At least his clothes would fit when he went to meet Myrriden.

XXII

MONTH OF TORIN

Malputo: You say he cannot rule himself? Which of us can?
Your noble suitor may be subject to his appetite, but
we are all subject to something greater than ourselves.

— ACT II, SCENE 7, LINES 77-81, THE CORPULENT SUITOR, BY HAROL GLADEN OF
ILWHEIRLANE, 4619

MYRRIDEN'S TOWER SAT IN THE MIDDLE of a swiftly running stream, its base an upthrust of granite in the center of a narrow canyon, the channel of a feeder of the Ranaodh. The structure, built of huge blocks of the same granite, looked menacing. The only access zigzagged down the steep side of the canyon wall to a narrow stone bridge.

Jerevan ate before approaching, hoping to get though his meeting with the wizard without having to beg for a meal. Then he told Otto to wait for him and started down the trail. Both the appearance and isolation of Myrriden's home confirmed that the wizard would be as opposed to visitors as the innkeeper had indicated.

Nevertheless, after crossing the bridge, Jerevan rode up to the huge, ironbound, wooden door of the tower, dismounted, and struck the gong positioned on one side of the entrance.

There was no response. He hit the gong again.

Still no reaction from the tower. Jerevan took a deep breath, trying to calm both his fear and his anger. Then he gripped the mallet that hung beside the gong and beat it again and again. The noise echoed off the canyon walls.

"All right, all right, I'll let you in!" The thought emerged in Jerevan's mind, flavored with testy iritation.

Jerevan dropped the mallet and waited, shaken by the feeling of someone else's thoughts in his head. He had not experienced mind-speech since he had been a child. The door swung open. He stepped inside.

And paused in amazement. The inside of Myrriden's tower bore no resemblance to its forbidding exterior. A deep pile carpet covered the floor. The walls, lined with a substance softer than stone, were white. A high ceiling gave the entry hall a feeling of space and airiness, while colorful paintings decorated strategic areas and objects of art filled a series of display cases.

"Up the stairs. Second floor, first door on your right," the mental voice directed.

A spiral staircase curved up one side of the entryway. The steps were wide on their outer edge but steep. Jerevan was panting by the time he reached the second landing, conscious of the drag of every pound he had gained. A hall cut straight across the diameter of the tower. He hesitated outside the first door on the right, catching his breath. Then he opened it and went in.

He felt a tingling sensation as he entered the room and his eyes met Myrriden's. He stopped and shook his head, disoriented.

"So you're the Hetri of Leyburn," Myrriden said aloud. "Not quite what I expected." He was a small man, almost a dwarf. He looked old, with dark, wrinkled skin and snow white hair that grew in cottony tufts.

"You've heard of me?" Jerevan asked, startled.

Myrriden laughed, a surprisingly mirthful sound. "Of course I've heard of you, Your Grace. Kindric has talked of little else since he gave you healer's training. I may live a retired life here in Belkova, but I'm not totally isolated." He paused and grinned, deepening his wrinkles, "As your arrival proves."

Jerevan looked around the opulently appointed chamber. "My problem is understanding why you should find the subject interesting," he said.

"If you can still ask that after the trouble Derwen's taken to get you as an apprentice," Myrriden snorted, "you're not as bright as I was told."

"You know about Derwen's curse?" Jerevan demanded.

Myrriden chuckled. "Now you think that, because I'm aware of your condition, I must be in league with Derwen. Nonsense! Every human wizard on Tamar knows who you are, and half of them know what Derwen did to you. The other half are in Cibata or Kandorra, or somewhere else equally distant, and they'll know soon enough. And if you haven't figured out why, you're a fool."

Jerevan flushed. "Then you know why I'm here."

"Ah, there I'm not sure, and you're guarding your thoughts now. Your shield is quite good, incidentally, considering how little practice you've had." Myrriden cocked his head at an angle. "Of course, two possibilities come immediately to mind."

He turned and walked over to a table against the wall laden with bottles and glasses. He poured something for himself from one of the bottles and turned back to Jerevan. "Have a seat, man." He waved at a grouping of two chairs near the table. "And speaking of your, um, appetite, can I offer you some refreshment? I have a wide selection of drinks here, and food, too, if you need it."

"Can you cure me of Derwen's curse?"

"No."

Until that moment Jerevan thought he had prepared himself for a negative answer. He had told himself to expect it. But he had not been prepared. He sat down in one of the chairs Myrriden had indicated and shut his eyes, swallowing the bile that rose in his throat.

"I'm sorry," Myrriden said, and Jerevan looked up into bright blue eyes that stared through him. He felt a moment of dizziness.

Myrriden said, "The effect the curse has on you, the reason it's so strong, is your own potential. I doubt Derwen took that into account. He's a fathik, but I don't think he meant to do you as much harm as he's done. After all, he wants you free to study. Are you sure you wouldn't like a drink?"

Jerevan sighed. "Thank you, I would like one." His stomach felt empty already, despite the meal he had just eaten. He closed his eyes, trying to control his fear of that too rapid return of hunger. Myrriden knew of the curse. There was no point in trying to conceal his condition. "And something to eat as well."

Myrriden poured a glass full of a deep ruby liquid and handed it to Jerevan. A young man appeared bearing a tray laden with food: fruits, different meats and cheeses, slices of bread and several sauces and spreads. He set the tray down on a table between the chairs and left as silently as he had entered. Myrriden said, "Help yourself."

Jerevan sipped the wine, swallowing the saliva that flooded his mouth at the sight of food. How could he be this hungry so quickly? Less than half an hour had passed since he ate.

Still, he was hungry. He only hoped he could avoid bolting the food in front of the wizard. He nibbled a piece of fruit and said bitterly, "I suppose you're going to tell me that no one can help me."

Myrriden shook his head, sitting down opposite him. "I didn't say that. I could have broken the curse a few hundred years back. But Derwen's younger. He's not as strong as I was, but he's stronger than I am today. Still, his own power is failing. There are stronger wizards about."

"Where?"

"I didn't say those stronger wizards would help you," Myrriden protested. "Some of them could. But that's a different matter."

"Where?" Jerevan repeated.

"Most of the wizards in the Varfarin are stronger than Derwen is now," Myrriden said, "but they won't aid you. They're pledged to obey him, whatever their personal feelings might be."

Jerevan swallowed a slice of bread smeared with sauce and folded around slices of meat. "Isn't there anyone who both can and would aid me?"

Myrriden shook his head, regretfully. "No one who could be relied upon. Most of the strong wizards left today, those that aren't pledged to the Varfarin, are old. Half of them are raving mad, so caught up in their own concerns that reality rarely touches them. While a few might be capable of helping you, I doubt any of them would." He paused, then said, "That's why you're important to us."

"What do you mean?"

Myrriden smiled. "You're the one capable of being what you're looking for. Your potential is equal to the most powerful ever seen, and you owe no allegiance to anyone."

Jerevan realized that the tray of food was half empty. He forced himself to stop eating. "If you're trying to persuade me to study wizardry, don't bother," he said. "Derwen succeeded in that. I'd simply prefer to live normally while I study. My present condition is distracting." The saliva flowing into his mouth forced him to swallow. He sighed and fixed another pile of bread, meat and cheese, but tried to eat more slowly.

"You could ask Derwen for relief," Myrriden said. "As I indicated earlier, I don't think he meant to make your condition so severe."

"He wouldn't grant it."

Myrriden nodded. "You're probably right. He has a long memory for any slight. He might well make the most of your humility, and then refuse."

"Precisely."

Myrriden took a sip of wine and watched as Jerevan emptied the tray. He said suddenly, "Your meal isn't as untimely as you think. You were unconscious for over two hours while I examined you."

Jerevan looked up, startled. "How could you do that without my being aware of it?"

"Tricks of the trade. I wouldn't have told you, either, but the time factor bothered you." Myrriden shrugged. "You have enough to cope with without my adding to your worries."

Jerevan hated the note of pity in the wizard's voice. "Why did you want to examine me?"

"To see precisely what Derwen did," Myrriden said. "Metabolic alterations are fascinating. I wouldn't have thought Derwen capable of something so clever. He's usually less imaginative."

Jerevan finished the last of the food on the tray with a sigh. Myrriden had known the exact amount he needed. He looked straight at the wizard. "Will you train me?"

Myrriden smiled. "Derwen will be furious with us both."

Jerevan shrugged, suppressing a stab of anger. An emotional display would not help him now. He needed to use logic but, as he had said, his physical condition was distracting. Now that the pain of emptiness was gone, he felt the strain on his abused stomach muscles. He shifted, trying to ease them without massaging them. He refused to sit rubbing his belly in front of Myrriden.

The wizard's eyes weighed him. "Do you really want to be a wizard, or do you plan to learn just enough to remove the curse?"

Jerevan hesitated, knowing his answer was crucial.

He met Myrriden's eyes. "You're right, of course, my first intention was to learn enough to break the curse, if I couldn't break it any other way. But

I've had time to contemplate what Derwen did to me. I don't like being a victim. I never realized until two months ago how vulnerable I, or any normal person, could be before the power of a wizard. Now I'll never feel secure until I can face anyone on Tamar and know I'm their equal. I can only do that if I become a wizard."

Myrriden nodded. "You know it won't be easy?"

"I remember the training I took in healing as a child. I understand what I'm facing."

"No, you don't," Myrriden said, frowning. "The younger you are, the easier the training. The mind sets into patterns as it gets older. It's harder to shift. Fortunately, Kindric slipped a little more training into you than just healing, witness the fact that you can receive my thoughts, at least when I project them hard enough."

"However difficult it may be," Jerevan said, "look at my alternative." He patted his belly. "At this rate I'll drown in my own flesh."

"True." Myrriden nodded. "However rapidly you learn, you have some uncomfortable years ahead of you. You must understand from the beginning that there isn't much I can do to make them less unpleasant."

"Be assured," Jerevan said, "I know who to blame."

Myrriden shook his head. "Derwen isn't solely responsible, not in this case. Cormor set him a task. The times we live in called for such an answer. I've never liked Derwen, but given your potential and the circumstances that led to your refusal of training, something like your present condition was inevitable."

"So being born with talent is justification for being denied personal liberty?"

Myrriden sighed and looked away.

Jerevan cursed his temper. "I realize you aren't responsible," he said, in a milder tone.

"Perhaps not directly," Myrriden said sadly, "but to some extent every human wizard on Tamar is responsible. I'll accept you as an apprentice." He rose from his chair and crossed the room to a large lammaswood desk. "But there are conditions. You'll have to swear to all the normal oaths. I presume you're prepared to do that?"

"I took the healer's oath as a child," Jerevan said. "I expected wizards to have something of the sort, but given Derwen's behavior, I have doubts regarding their value."

"Understandable, but you'll have to swear to them." Myrriden took a book from the desk and brought it back to Jerevan. "This is a copy of The Laws as dictated by the Council of Wizards. Study them. Your training can't start until you've taken the oath. That oath must be taken in mind link with at least three other wizards so they can testify to your sincerity."

"I can't take it now?" Jerevan asked.

"No. These oaths are more complicated than the one required to become a healer. You need to understand them, and there must be other wizards present to witness." Myrriden went back to the desk. "Fortunately, there are other wizards in the area. That shouldn't cause more than a day's delay."

"What else might cause delay?"

"Nothing," Myrriden said, turning to face him, "if you're willing to assist the Varfarin."

"The Varfarin!"

Myrriden sighed. "This has nothing to do with Derwen."

"I came to you because I understood you weren't a member."

"I'm not," Myrriden said. "But some of the wizards I've trained are. One of my best students and a promising apprentice were recently taken prisoner by the isklarin. If you're going to be my apprentice, you'll have to accompany the rescue party. The journey won't delay your training. As you'll be working with three wizards and other apprentices, it should advance it."

Jerevan stared at Myrriden, then took a deep breath and let it go. "I'll do anything within my power, but I don't see how, presently, I can be of assistance to anyone."

Myrriden smiled wryly. "By yourself, you couldn't, but it's the power of your will that makes you unique. The first thing I'll teach you is how to link minds. When you're linked to a wizard, that wizard will be able to use some part of your will, thus increasing his or her own power."

"Then I agree," Jerevan said, rising. "I have no choice."

Myrriden nodded and took a candle out of one of the desk drawers. "Then I need to give you a quick test, to see how much you remember of what Kindric taught you."

He put the candle into a holder at the edge of the desk. "Can you light it?"

"I could have when I was a child," Jerevan said, frowning. "I think I still can. I stopped because my mother got so angry when she caught me at it. Let me see." He concentrated, remembering the nature of flame. Then he duplicated it. The candle caught and burned.

Myrriden said, "Very good. You're an advanced healer, then, able to work with the flesh?"

"Of course," Jerevan said. "How else could I heal wounds? I'd be in worse shape now, if I hadn't been able to heal my sores and chafed places."

"How long can you maintain your sight?"

"Ten minutes," Jerevan said. "We had a fire at Leyburn last year and I treated a number of severe burns. I held ten minute sessions. I had to rest for nearly two hours between sessions, but I treated everyone by the end of the day."

"Excellent," Myrriden said. "You're more advanced than I expected. You need to work on your mind-speech. Still, I won't be stretching the rules much if I start you off with the rank of apprentice journeyman." He paused, "That way you'll be on the same footing as my present apprentice."

Myrriden pulled open another of the desk drawers. "His name is Balen. He shows some promise. He'll never have your power, but his training is more advanced. I just elevated him to apprentice journeyman, but it wouldn't be good for either of you if he thinks of you as his inferior."

"Isn't he bound to think that, if his skill is greater?"

"No," Myrriden said, disturbing the pile of small boxes in the drawer. "Wizards have a rigid hierarchy. Those of a given rank are allotted the same entitlements despite wide disparities in skill, as long as they meet the base requirements."

"That doesn't seem practical." Standing up increased the strain on Jerevan's abused stomach muscles. He massaged them absently while he watched the wizard sort through the boxes.

"It works out," Myrriden said. "It's usually the difference between someone who's just qualified for a rank, and someone who's almost ready to qualify for the next rank up. At any rate, I'll make you Balen's equal in rank, if not quite yet in skill, by giving you a crystal." He selected a box from near the bottom of the drawer. "Here's the one I was looking for." He turned around to face Jerevan, holding the box.

Jerevan let go of his belly, embarrassed to be caught massaging it, but Myrriden did not appear to notice. He opened the box and pulled out a clear crystal the size and shape of a hen's egg, attached at the pointed end to a silver chain.

"What is it?"

"A focus," Myrriden said. "They're called wizard stones or power crystals, lots of names. What they do for a beginning wizard is help you focus your will, the part of your mind that controls the world around you, once you can see it properly. And they retain information."

"Derwen wore one. He played with it while we talked."

"That would have been when he imposed the curse," Myrriden said.

"What does it do for an advanced wizard?"

Myrriden eyed him wryly. "Many things. You won't need to learn them all for years, but the simplest is to form linkages. Two wizards can link to the same crystal, making both stronger."

"What do I do with it?"

"Wear it. See if you can imprint information on it. Once you learn to do that, practice retrieving the information. Just having it gives you the rank of apprentice journeyman. But when you get back to Belkova, for the time being, it's more urgent that you practice your mind-speech."

"I can't stay here?"

"Not now. You need to memorize the laws and practice mind-speech so you can take the oath before I can train you further."

Jerevan swallowed the lump in his throat. "I'll practice, if I have someone to practice with. That's something I can't do on my own."

"My colleague will contact you."

Jerevan frowned. "About this rescue party. Won't the isklarin have killed wizard prisoners by now?"

"Improbable," Myrriden said, turning back to the drawers. He put the candles back and restored the boxes to their original order. "Rand and Errin have strong potentials. The isklarin will have capped them and taken them somewhere they can be used for breeding. But you'd better leave now," Myrriden added. "If you don't, I'll have to feed you again, and I haven't had time to lay in enough supplies."

Jerevan flushed, but asked, "Should I come back tomorrow?"

"No." Myrriden shook his head. "Study the laws. I'll send for you when I'm ready to take your oath, but my colleague will contact you before then."

XXIII

4648, 465TH CYCLE OF THE YEAR OF THE MOLE
MONTH OF TORIN

> Beltrana: I want to marry a man of taste. A man of discrimination.
>
> Malputo: But your noble suitor has great wealth. And he is
> certainly a man of taste.
>
> Beltrana: Yes. He tastes everything that comes his way.
>
> — ACT II, SCENE 7, LINES 25 - 31, THE CORPULENT SUITOR, BY HAROL GLADEN
> OF ILWHEIRLANE, 4619

JEREVAN SPENT THE LATE AFTERNOON AND EVENING after he got back
from Myrriden's tower in his room. Otto brought food to him at regular
intervals, but he devoted the time to studying the laws of the Council of
Wizards. When he had read through the book Myrriden had given him
twice, he took a long walk and then spent several hours examining the
crystal Myrriden had given him.

He could, with some effort, imprint an image onto the crystal, leave it,
and then find the image again. The image was fuzzy, however, and he knew
he would have to get much better at the process before the crystal would
be useful to him.

As the hour approached ten o'clock, he found it more and more difficult
to concentrate. Finally, when Otto was about to go out and fetch another
meal, he said, "No, don't bother. I have to get out and exercise anyway. I'll
eat at a tavern somewhere."

Otto nodded. "I won't worry about you then, Your Grace. Have a good
evening and give the lady my best."

Jerevan laughed. "Am I so obvious?"

"Not always, Your Grace. And only ever to those who know you well."

"It's the puzzle she represents," Jerevan said.

"Yes, Your Grace. You've never left a problem unsolved. Not even the
dangerous ones. Not since I've known you, at any rate." Otto went out the
door and shut it behind him.

Jerevan walked for more than an hour though the cooling streets of
Belkova before stopping at the tavern located on the corner of Spinners
Lane and Market. When he had eaten, he walked down the block to the
house with the green door. Spinners Lane looked more respectable than he
had expected a barmaid to be able to afford. The house was large and well

kept. He decided that either Marion had another source of income, or she was the mistress of a wealthy man.

The latter solution was the most likely, given her exotic beauty. He almost turned back, but he needed to know why she had helped him that morning. The experience could not have been pleasant for her. Why had she stayed?

MARION PACED THE HALL OF HER HOUSE and tried to decide what approach she should take to explain the previous evening. Jerevan was not the person Derwen had described. Not at all. None of his reactions had been predictable. Even this evening, she had expected him to come promptly. It was now after eleven and she had to face the fact that he might not come at all.

She was relieved when Jerevan knocked. She opened the door immediately and hugged him. "I knew you'd come."

She smiled up at him, then hesitated when she realized his expression was wary rather than passionate. He was examining her clothes and she remembered that she no longer wore the dress of a barmaid but her own, richer, apparel.

"I came to find out why you helped me this morning," he said, "but now I realize that's only half the puzzle."

"Why? Wouldn't any woman have done the same?" Marion asked, wondering how suspicious he was. And what he suspected.

He shook his head. "I don't believe for a moment that it was an act of good will, or motivated by my physical appeal." He snorted. "You wanted to find out something about me and you studied me like a specimen in a laboratory."

Marion's full lips twisted in acknowledgement. "You'd better come in and sit down, so you can be rude to me in comfort. When did you last eat?"

"I just left the tavern on the corner." He followed her into her living room.

A fireplace occupied the center of the opposite wall and a divan had been set close to it on one side. Soft wool carpeting similar to that in Myrriden's tower covered the floor and animal skins further cushioned the area before the hearth. A low table next to the couch held platters piled with food and tall carafes of various colored liquids.

"You didn't trust me to provide for you?" she asked, trying to gauge his mood.

"I don't trust you at all." He crossed the room to sit on the couch. "I've done a lot of stupid things, particularly recently, but I don't believe I'm notorious yet as a fool."

"No." Marion sat down next to him. It could have been worse. He could have been hostile, instead of curious and wary. "I don't think you're a fool. I underestimated you, but only because I'd been told certain things about you that weren't true."

Jerevan leaned back in the couch, positioning the cushions to support his back. "You were told I was vain of my appearance. That may have been true, but no one who has to eat like a pig day in and day out for two months until he develops a belly like this," he patted his stomach, "can stay vain about what he looks like." He paused, studying her. "You also expected me to be an absolute toad in bed. You were surprised when I gave you any pleasure at all to begin with. No, not just surprised, shocked."

She took a deep breath, shaken by the accuracy of his guesses. Either Derwen was a very bad judge of character, or he had deliberately misled her. "I enjoyed having that preconception corrected," she admitted, deciding that honesty was the only approach left to her at this point.

"Who are you? And why did you stay this morning?"

"I stayed this morning out of concern, because I did enjoy last night very much." She sighed and pulled her feet up on the couch so that she sat cross-legged facing him. "And out of guilt, because it was my fault you missed your meals. I deliberately distracted you and damped down your awareness of the early signs of your problem."

"I knew you had to be a wizard the moment you opened the door," he said. "Were you examining the effects of the curse out of morbid curiosity, or did you have some other reason?"

Marion bit her lip and looked away. "I wanted to see what would happen. I had no idea the effect would be so violent."

"Well, at least you helped alleviate that effect," Jerevan acknowledged. "You wouldn't happen to be Myrriden's 'colleague,' would you?"

"Is that what he called me?" Marion asked, relieved by the change in the tone of his voice. She smiled tentatively. "I told him not to refer to me by name, but I suppose he thought that mentioning my sex might be as big a clue."

"Why the games?"

She shrugged. "I'd heard a lot about you from Derwen, mostly uncomplimentary. I was worried. A linkage is an intimate thing. If it's prolonged for any length of time the interaction can change the parties. They can come to rely on it; the effects may even become permanent." She hesitated, then said, "I know Myrriden isn't contemplating anything like that. Just a one shot use of your raw potential. But no linkage can be taken lightly. I had to find out if I could work with you before I agreed to help train you." She looked at him anxiously.

"Sex does tend to further an acquaintance," he agreed.

"It's also very revealing," she said.

"Myrriden didn't go into detail about the nature of linkages," Jerevan said.

She was disconcerted by the sudden intensity of his gaze. "He should have explained the risks to you," she said. "Perhaps he knew I'd do that for him."

For the first time since his early childhood, Jerevan strove to project in mind-speech *"Myrriden said I must practice this before I can take my oath. I hope you did find us compatible."*

"*Yes,*" she thought.

Jerevan smiled at the emotion carried with her thought, but shied away from the intimacy of mind-speech regarding the rest of what he had to say. "I have no objection to linking mind to mind with you. However, you're likely to find my very presence embarrassing soon."

"What do you mean?"

"You're a beautiful woman, and I'm rapidly turning into a freak."

"You're not that heavy," Marion protested, and he sensed her surprise at his attitude. *"I meant it when I said I liked a full-figured man."*

Jerevan stared at her and then realized she had no way of knowing how much weight he had gained. She had never seen him before the previous day. For all she knew, he might have gained only a few pounds. "I might find that reassuring," he said, "if I hadn't been considerably thinner two months ago."

Marion suddenly comprehended a great many things. "How much weight have you gained?" she asked aloud.

"I don't know precisely, but over forty pounds. I haven't weighed myself since I left Lara."

"No." She was shocked.

"Are you going to tell Myrriden that you withdraw?"

Marion was startled by the question, even though she now understood why he asked. *"Certainly not. What gave you that idea?"*

"The expression on your face. You looked appalled."

"I am," Marion thought, her mind open to him, *"but not by you. I'd never realized what a monster Derwen could be."*

Jerevan looked skeptical. *"But there's nothing you can do to break the curse?"*

Marion shook her head. *"No. I know you have reason to doubt me, but I'd help you if I could, now that Myrriden has confirmed that you're committed to the study of wizardry. But I no longer have the strength to overcome Derwen's will. I used to be stronger than he is now, but I was captured by the linlarin and capped some years ago. I haven't recovered the full use of my will."* She looked away.

Jerevan sighed. *"I believe you. My understanding is that it's almost impossible to lie with this form of communication. And Myrriden has already convinced me that none of those able to help, would, and that those who might be willing, lack the ability."*

She looked at him, disturbed by the expression on his face. *"You realize that what Derwen did to you,"* she thought, *"the wizards of the Varfarin, we wouldn't ordinarily tolerate such a perversion of power."*

Jerevan's jaw clenched. "My main mistake in dealing with Derwen was my belief that even wizards were answerable for their abuses. You can't tell me now that they are, when I'm experiencing the exception."

Marion bit her lip. "I know it's hard for you to understand, but you're a special case. Cormor was favored by Jehan. He denied foreseeing the future, but we know he saw possibilities. And one of those possibilities was someone like you. There's no wizard alive today with even a fraction of Cormor's power, but we understand it in theory."

Jerevan stiffened. "What did Cormor foresee that could justify Derwen's action?"

"Cormor told Derwen that a time would come when the Varfarin and the human lands would need a leader. He said that Derwen needed to be both ruthless and single-minded in finding a successor to be Esalfar, and when he found such a person, he was not to accept refusal." She shook her head. "Derwen has never been the strongest, or the wisest, wizard in the Varfarin. Cormor picked him on the basis of his stubbornness. Given that background, on this one issue, there's no one who'd argue with whatever means Derwen chose to use."

Jerevan brought his hands up to his face and rubbed his temples. "So law and justice mean nothing when set against the visions of a man dead four hundred years."

She looked away from him into the fire. "I realize there's no way you can understand that now." She hesitated, then turned back to him, forcing the intimacy of mind-speech once again, *"But someday, when you can see the way Cormor saw, you'll understand. When that day comes, you may forgive us."*

Jerevan looked down at his altered figure. "I imagine my forgiveness will depend a great deal on what I have to go through in the process of becoming a wizard. So far I've suffered embarrassment and discomfort, but my condition is bound to get worse before I can learn enough to be able to remedy it." He looked back at her face. *"Isn't that true?"*

She looked at his body and remembered how much he had eaten that morning, the pain he described as discomfort. *"I'm afraid so,"* she admitted. She looked back at his face and found him watching her.

"Then I want you now," he thought, *"while I'm still capable of giving you pleasure in return."*

She smiled, feeling her body respond to the images he projected. She also wanted a repeat of the previous night. And tonight her pleasure would be heightened by the fact that everything she had learned about him made her like him better. She rose and went to him.

Sometime later, when they were both spent and satisfied, their clothes scattered about the floor, Marion noticed the crystal hanging around his neck. "I see Myrriden gave you a crystal. Have you started recording your body on it?"

"I'm not good enough to imprint things clearly yet," Jerevan said.

"But you have to learn your organs and the structure of your body as it is now, or you won't be able to restore yourself to the way you were before Derwen cursed you," she said. "You need to record every cell on your crystal as soon as possible."

"I figured that out," Jerevan said. "And I have become familiar with my inner workings over the past two months. I've had to, or I wouldn't have been able to repair myself. I plan on working on the recording every day until I get it right."

"Have you had much damage to repair?"

"Just the odd chafed spot and sore muscle," he said, noting her expression. "Not enough to require assistance, Marion."

She studied him carefully, but changed the subject. "Did you have anyone special before all this happened?"

"No. Several friends, but no one special."

Marion sat up and poured two glasses of a pale, straw-colored liquid full of tiny bubbles. "This comes from Khorat." She handed him a glass. "I want you to taste it before you have to worry about filling yourself up. It's a delicacy that needs to be savored."

He grimaced. "When you have to consume as much as I do, you cease to worry about taste."

"I know." She bit her lip. "I saw you this morning. But that's why I thought it might be nice if sometimes you made a point of savoring something. So you don't forget how." She looked away from him.

He took her hand and kissed it. "Thank you," he said. "You're quite right. I used to be proud of my palate. If I don't at least occasionally remember that and use it, then Derwen will have won no matter how quickly I break his curse."

Marion turned back to him, surprised to feel herself smiling like a child given a treat. *"That's what I meant. I was afraid you wouldn't understand and you'd be angry."*

He grinned. *"I'm not that sensitive yet. I hope I won't get that sensitive."*

After that she fed him tidbits and tastes until they were both aroused, and they made love again. The pattern was repeated throughout the night. They slept very little, but neither Jerevan nor Marion minded the loss of sleep.

XXIV

4648, 465TH CYCLE OF THE YEAR OF THE MOLE
MONTH OF AGNITH

*Wizards may be taught the correct 'image' of each word as soon as
they are capable of transferring any image at all . . .
The advantage of 'speaking' mind to mind is such communication's
range and privacy . . .*

— EXCERPTS FROM <u>PROBLEMS WITH TELEPATHY</u>, BY THE WIZARD AGNITH

E LISE RAN THROUGH A CALMING EXERCISE as Ashe led Del and herself
through the hot, crowded streets of Darenje. She was a qualified
journeyman wizard. She and Del, or Arrun as she usually thought of him
now, had stayed with Ashe longer than was common for apprentices. She
should not be nervous about meeting a new mentor, yet she had spent most
of her life as Ashe's student with Arrun her closest companion. Tomorrow
they would leave for Cibata without her, to fight Senangans. Aside from the
danger they would face, the journey took months. If she did not get along
with the Wizard Marion, she would not be able to rejoin Ashe, and it would
be months before she could get back to Ilwheirlane and be reassigned.

She had refused the assignment in Cibata because of Jorum, her son.
While he lived now with his father and grandmother on Adun, he was only
fifteen, and she could not leave the Thallassean region while he might have
need of her. So, when Ashe knew he would be leaving for the southern
hemisphere, he arranged for Marion to become her mentor.

Ashe had assured her that she would like Marion and the others working
Massif's Carnival of Wonders, the Varfarin's main recruiting operation in the
southwest Thallassean region, but it still took all the self control mechanisms
learned over years of study to keep her heartbeat from increasing and her
palms from sweating more than could be accounted for by the heat.

The Rusty Anchor had a blue adobe front and a real, rusty anchor
hanging over the door. Inside, the main hall of the inn was dim, with dark
wooden paneling. The air felt cool after the heat outside.

The private parlor, where the innkeeper directed them, was lit by two large
windows. A beautiful, black-haired woman stood by one of them, talking to
a small, elderly man with short white hair. Two younger men, one blond and
one dark-haired, sat at a table on the other side of the room, playing some
sort of dice game with a small woman with a cap of short brown hair.

The brown-haired woman jumped up as soon as she saw Ashe and came across
the room to embrace him. "Ashe," she said, "how many years has it been?"

"Too many, Jao. One visit to Sussey is never enough. How is Delanan doing these days?"

"Wishing he didn't have to keep school this season," Jao said, then turned and studied Elise with intent blue eyes. "So you're the young journeyman wizard who'll be joining our carnival. I'm Jao, and I'm sure Marion will want to teach you to dance. With that hair you'll be a sensation."

Elise smiled tentatively. "I've never performed before. It may take a lot of teaching."

"I doubt that," the black-haired woman said, coming to join them. "I'm Marion. I hope we'll be friends. As Ashe may have told you, I was a prisoner in Senanga after the fall of Nemali. I still haven't fully recovered from the experience, so I feel strongly about this mission."

Elise looked quickly at Ashe, then back to Marion. "No, he didn't tell me anything," she said, her eyes shifting to circle the entire group, "about any of you."

"I thought she could form her own opinions," Ashe said. "May I introduce to the company Journeyman Wizards Del Maran and Elise Adun. For those of you who haven't met me before, I'm Ashe. Del and Elise, may I also present the Wizard Myrriden." He gestured toward the elderly man.

"And these two," Jao said, indicating the young men at the table, "are Myrriden's apprentice journeymen, Jerevan Rayne and Balen Scurek."

"The formalities being complete," Ashe said, "as we've had a long journey, may we now relax and have something to eat?"

"An excellent idea," Myrriden agreed. "Balen, tell the landlord we're ready for him to serve."

Elise watched as the tall, dark-haired apprentice went to the door. That meant the heavy set blond was Jerevan Rayne. She fixed the names and faces in her memory.

Later that evening, she and Del escaped to a table in the public room of the inn.

"How does it feel to be going out on your first real assignment?" Del asked, taking a swig from his mug of ale.

"Strange," Elise said, toying with a puddle of liquid on the table where the serving maid had slopped some while filling their mugs. "But at least I'll still be within a few weeks' voyage of home. It'll take you almost half a year to get to Cassinga."

"Yes," Del said, "but I'll be fighting Senangans. I've wanted to do that since the raid, and now I'll get my chance. I've read military reports and analyses going back over a thousand years. I know there are things others have missed about fighting linlarin. I think I can make a difference."

"I hope you can. From what Ashe has said, the situation there is pretty bad," Elise said, envying him his enthusiasm.

"But you're not so sure how happy you'll be, are you?" Del asked.

"Marion's a bit intimidating," Elise admitted, avoiding his too knowledgeable eyes. "I've never seen a more beautiful woman. I don't know if I'll ever feel comfortable with her, and the mission sounds dangerous."

"You're not bad looking yourself, Elise and from what I've heard about being capped, Marion must have gone through a lot. I think you'll find there's more to her than looks, and I know you keep your head in a crisis."

Elise looked up to meet his eyes. "I hope so. I didn't mean to criticize Marion, just my ability to relate to her. I'm so used to Ashe. I can ask him anything."

"Ashe has been chaste since I've known him," Del said, taking another drink of ale. "I'd say advice from Marion would be more pertinent. Unfortunately, the apprentices looked too young for you."

"The last thing I need is a man in my life," Elise snapped, remembering her return to Bria after her disastrous reacquaintance with Errin Yar. She had taken her oath and pledged to the Varfarin, but she had been sick with memories and regrets. Finally, she had decided to wipe out the regrets and fulfill her obligation to her grandmother in one stroke. She had gone back to Adun and lain with Timmon Skane. She had not married him, and had stayed with him only long enough to conceive a child to be her grandmother's heir. But lying with Timmon had not erased her memories of Errin.

Her son, Jorum, grew up in Bria, visiting Adun every fall. When Jorum had turned fourteen the year before, she had left him with her grandmother and Timmon so they could teach him the ways of the islands he would inherit. She missed him terribly, however, and without him to love and care for, her thoughts turned too often to the past.

Del eyed her with concern. "Elise, you can't keep dwelling on a relationship that ended when you were eighteen. Let it go."

"I've tried, Arrun," Elise protested, taking a drink of ale and trying to banish the memories. "And it isn't as though I still desire Errin. I couldn't have had Jorum if I hadn't been with Timmon."

"Who was your first and did nothing for you but supply his seed," Del said with disgust. "Just do yourself a favor and look around for someone you can care about."

"What about you?" Elise demanded. "I haven't seen you diving into any long term relationships."

"But plenty of short ones," Del responded. "I'll find the one I'm looking for some day. I just haven't met her yet."

"I wish it were that easy for me," Elise said wistfully, "but I wish you success, Arrun. In everything."

"Thanks, Lise. I wish you well, too. We probably won't see each other again for years, but I'll think about you and pray for your success as well."

WHEN THE BUSINESS OF THE EVENING had been completed and Myrriden and the other wizards started in on the 'do you remember' routine, Balen nudged Jerevan and whispered, "I've got family and friends here I'd like to see before we leave tomorrow. You want to come?" He nodded toward the wizards. "They'll be reminiscing about old times for hours yet. They won't even notice we've gone."

"I'd have to tell Otto," Jerevan said, and hesitated.

"Yeah, and you'll need to eat," Balen said. "I understand the routine, but Ma'll be glad to feed you. She and Pa haven't seen me since the kindred of Maera decided I had enough potential to study with Myrriden."

"You come from Darenje?"

"Yeah," Balen said, his round face stretching in a broad grin. "The kindred recognized my talent when Ma brought me in for some sickness when I was about four. I trained here until they decided they couldn't teach me any more. That was two years ago. I haven't been home since."

"Then, if my presence won't interfere with your reunion, I'd love to see more of the town," Jerevan said.

"Come on then." Balen jumped up, his blue eyes eager.

Jerevan left a message with the landlord for Otto not to wait up for him and followed Balen. When Myrriden told Jerevan that he already had an apprentice, and one with more experience, Jerevan had worried that Balen would resent him, or ridicule him, but Balen had only been pleased to have company his own age, and someone with whom he could practice.

When Jerevan explained the curse, Balen just said, "Got Niolo's luck, didn't you?" referring to a legendary eslar who offended the god Tarat and went from being the gardener of his grove to being a crippled beggar, losing his family in the process. Since then, Jerevan had grown continually more grateful for Balen's presence, assistance and almost unfailing good nature. He had also realized that Balen's round face, snub nose and ingenuous blue eyes concealed a surprising intelligence and a quirky sense of humor.

The streets were cooler with the sun down, and busier than they had been during the day. Street vendors and musicians played at populous intersections, but Jerevan didn't see any beggars. Most of the crowd seemed to be merchants or wealthy farmers, in town to trade or to enjoy the food in the many cafes.

"Does Darenje hide its beggars, or does it really not have any?" Jerevan asked after a time.

Balen shrugged. "Darenje has its poor, but they don't have to beg. Anyone who wants a free meal, a place to sleep, or a change of clothes can get what they need from the Sanctuary of Maera or the Temple of Jehan. The merchants put money in a fund to pay for stuff and the Sanctuary and the Temple handle the rest. The merchants say it's good for business. More people come to town when they're not harassed or made to feel guilty."

Balen's home was a medium sized building amid a row of similar buildings in a quiet neighborhood on the north side of town. Balen's parents welcomed Jerevan as eagerly as he had said they would. Jerevan joined Balen, his father, mother, and sister, tossing horseshoes in the backyard, and afterward, Balen's mother supplied him with a bowl of soup and a large mixed salad, as Marion had told him he would be better off eating foods with a high fiber content.

From Balen's home they went to visit the Sanctuary of Maera, passing through the hospital area to the private living quarters at the rear. Again Jerevan was welcomed, the white-robed kindred happy to entertain any friend of Balen's. They turned the occasion into an informal party, setting up a table loaded with food and drink so that they and their guests could help themselves. Notice was sent to some of the priests of Jehan Balen had known from the nearby Temple, and within twenty minutes there were pastel robes mingling with the white.

Jerevan noticed immediately, however, that one of the kindred, a young woman with a cap of curly black hair whom Balen introduced as Jula Morec, was more to Balen than a friend. They went off in a corner together and talked earnestly until it was time to return to the inn.

BALEN COULD HARDLY BELIEVE HIS EYES WHEN HE SAW JULA. When he had left Darenje she had been only sixteen and he had thought of her as a child. Now, while she was still small, the dark curls on top of her head coming only to his chin, there was no way any man could mistake her for a child. Her breasts were full and upright, pushing against the drape of her white robe.

As soon as he could manage it without being rude, he drew her apart from the others to a quiet corner. Again he was grateful for the ability to mind-speak which allowed him to speak to her intimately even in the middle of the crowd. *"You've grown,"* he thought.

"I'm eighteen," Jula answered, her hazel eyes flashing with green glints. *"Did you expect me to stay a child?"*

Balen shook his head, baffled by the anger he sensed from her. *"No, but it doesn't seem like it's been that long. You didn't sound different in your letters."*

"You wanted to be a wizard," she thought, her disapproval plain. *"You must be having fun, if time passes so quickly for you."*

"I've told you how good I feel about what I'm learning. I want to do more than heal," he answered. *"I always did. You know that. I wanted you to come, too."* He tried to project how much he missed her.

Her head came up, her pointed chin angled aggressively. *"The wizard wouldn't have taken two apprentices, and I don't want to learn more wizardry. What I've learned already is enough."*

"You don't know he wouldn't," Balen thought, his mental imagery showed him brushing aside her excuses like smoke. He admired the graceful line of her throat, the delicacy of the bones of her face. *"He has two now anyway. He's a good old guy, and with Marion living with us he has plenty of help. The Wizard Delanan teaches a whole school of apprentices at the same time."*

"But I don't want the training," she responded, an angry edge to her thoughts.

"It's the Bane, isn't it?" Balen asked, with a sudden sense of insight. *"You changed after that trip. Lydia told me you had nightmares."*

"Lydia had no right to tell you anything about me," Jula protested, her full lips compressed and her eyes stormy, glinting green and gold.

"But I'm right, aren't I? The Bane scared you."

Jula shut her eyes and her shoulders slumped. *"Very well, the Bane did frighten me."* She stiffened, and added, *"It should terrify any sane person."*

"Yeah, it's scary," Balen admitted. *"But that's no reason to turn your back on everything to do with wizardry. The wizards of the Varfarin, hey, they're dedicated to stopping wars, not fighting them."*

"Myrriden isn't a member," she pointed out.

"He works with them. He just doesn't harmonize with Derwen," Balen thought.

"Major conflicts like wars often start with little things like disharmony."

He argued with her for the rest of the evening, resenting the fact that the friendship he had thought of as an anchor in his life was shifting away from him. Yet the longer they communicated, the more he felt separated from the woman she was becoming.

Finally, when it was time to leave, he broke from the intimacy of mind-speech and said, "Jere and I have got to be going. I guess I shouldn't bother writing any more."

"No," she agreed. "I think we've said all we have to say to each other."

JEREVAN FELT EMBARRASSED AT FIRST TO BE LEFT ALONE with so many strangers, but they were eager to hear about Ilwheirlane, and he was curious about Darenje. Eventually, one of the kindred, who introduced himself as Petrel Quanat, brought out a jalith, the only instrument Jerevan could play. Several of the ajaren of Jehan immediately brought out their own instruments and they traded popular songs for the rest of the evening.

When it was time to leave, a tall, thin woman with a silver streak through her hair and the open eye insignia of a sibyl on her robe came up to Jerevan. She studied him intently and said, "My name is Zenobia. I've seen you in a vision. You bear a cloud on your soul which casts a dark shadow over your near future, but you must not despair, for beyond the shadow I see brightness and joy."

Jerevan thanked her and went back to the inn with Balen feeling optimistic about the future for the first time since his meeting with Derwen. He noticed, however, that Balen did not seem as cheerful as he had been at the beginning of the evening.

XXV

MONTH OF MINNETH

> *Of were-folk there are races six;*
> *Be careful now, don't get them mixed.*
>
> *. . . An isklar, when he changes shape,*
> *Can raise a frill around his nape.*
> *A lizard, he sheds hair for mail,*
> *And waves his long, reptilian tail.*

> — EXCERPTS FROM "THE WERE-FOLK," PUBLISHED IN A CHILD'S GUIDE TO THE LARIN AND
> OTHER BEASTLY TAILS, BY ENOGEN VARASH OF ELEVTHERAI, 4557

ELISE STARED IN AWE AT THE MAGNIFICENT SNOW WHITE PEAKS of the Serak Fokai, looming ever higher above her as she approached the upper reaches of the Vale of the Gwatar. Mount Bektor and Mount Umalat to the north and Mount Aydak and Mount Eranal to the south were, she knew, among the highest mountains on Tamar. The view was breathtaking.

Still, she wished that she was not riding steadily closer to those peaks. That afternoon, the carnival would camp outside the Gandaharan city of Sydyk. Sydyk of the Silver Falls. Elise grimaced. The waterfall at the upper end of the Vale of the Gwatar was said to be the highest in the world. She felt sure it would be as impressive as the mountains. But Sydyk, sitting on a ledge at the foot of the north face of Mount Aydak overlooking the falls, was also the gateway to the heartland of Gandahar.

Elise had no desire to go any farther into the isklarin empire, however beautiful the scenery might be. Hopefully, this time they would find the prisoners they sought.

In the past three months they had traveled from Darenje, over the mountains to Lamash, then up to the headwaters of the River Dariel and across a spur of the Serak Fokai into land held by Gandahar for hundreds of years. Three times the carnival had arrived at towns where the wizards thought the prisoners might be imprisoned, only to discover that they were days or weeks too late. Moreover, since entering Gandahar they had been forced to stop in each town and city to perform, in order to maintain their cover. Myrriden's original estimate that the entire mission would take only a month or two now seemed absurdly naive. They had been on the road for three months already.

Still, Sydyk was a major military installation, a likely place for prisoners the isklarin meant to keep for some time.

Marion had explained to Elise that wizard prisoners were rarely slain out of hand by the were-folk, especially if they had strong potential. Both Gandahar and the mixed-blood linlarin nations in Cibata used such captives for breeding purposes. To do so safely, they put a specially treated metal cap over the wizard's brain, blocking all vision and rendering even the most powerful wizard helpless.

Elise shuddered at the thought. Being capped was a wizard's worst nightmare. Marion had worn one for a year, and that experience had damaged her brain so much that she was only now, after twenty-four years, beginning to recover what she had lost.

Elise wondered how the prisoners they were trying to rescue were faring, and remembered her shock when she learned that one of them was named Errin and that he came from Sussey. What would she do if the Errin Pomorry captured with the Wizard Rand was the Errin she remembered from her childhood? They couldn't be the same; the last name was different. Her Errin was a member of a wiga, a primitive savage, yet she recalled he had once mentioned the Wizard Delanan, and she had never known his mother's name. The possibility that they might be the same frightened her more than the journey into Gandahar.

She looked around at the colorful wagons of the carnival. Although she had been a member of the Varfarin for sixteen years, this was her first experience traveling with one of the circuses that were often used as covers for Varfarin activities. She had been amazed to see how skillfully Marion danced and walked a tightrope. Even more surprising had been Myrriden's aptitude as a carnival wizard, when he had not been a member of the Varfarin for hundreds of years.

JEREVAN SHIFTED IN THE SADDLE, conscious of the pressure of the pommel against his growing paunch. He was hungry. He took a bag of mixed vegetable sticks out of his saddlebag and started chewing. At least three hours had passed since his last meal and the hunger wasn't severe as yet. Marion's idea of having him eat as much roughage as they could find seemed to be working. High fiber foods filled his stomach faster and took longer to digest. Since he had shifted to eating a high percentage of caulis shoots and other fibrous vegetables and fruits, his weight gain had slowed.

Of course, on the road such foods were not always available, and the curse would not allow him to eat only fiber. If he did not include some fat and carbohydrates, he found himself hungry even when his stomach was full.

He estimated that he had gained about forty pounds in the four months since he left Belkova, but that represented a much slower rate of gain than what he had suffered before his arrival there, despite his already enlarged stomach. He could now imagine a time when he might be able to stabilize his weight.

On the other hand, his progress in learning wizardry seemed abysmally slow. He had given his oath to Myrriden on his third day in Belkova, with Marion, Jao, and Balen as witnesses. Since then he had spent time every day practicing mind-speech with one or another of them, and had succeeded in imprinting a complete cellular pattern of his body on his crystal. His body gave him plenty to practice on in the way of manipulating matter with his will. He constantly had to heal broken capillaries, chafed skin and sore muscles. He even occasionally managed to break down a few ounces of fat.

Still, his mind could only stand so many minutes of using his vision and will before he developed a headache. Myrriden assured him that the fifteen minutes he had managed five times the day before represented a remarkable achievement, considering he had only been practicing for four months, but Jerevan felt frustrated at his lack of progress.

A disturbance passed through the procession ahead, and word came back that the town of Sydyk was in sight. Otto joined him as they crested the lowest slope of Aydak to the rocky shelf that supported both the town and the fortress.

The first thing Jerevan registered was green. The upper end of the Vale of the Gwatar had been golden with the dried grasses of winter. The slopes on either side of the trail going up to Sydyk had been scrub and barren rock. Yet ahead there grew a great multitude of trees, a mass of foliage that blotted out the lower face of a nearly sheer cliff. At first he could make out nothing else, as he had not yet learned to focus his wizard sense over distances longer than a few meters. Then he realized that the trees were of two varieties, with a rigid pattern in their growth. The tall, thin trees were date palms, their naked boles stretching up to huge feathery crests. The other trees were short and round, some variety of citrus by their appearance, planted between the stately rows of the palms.

The wagons reached the area where the wizards planned to camp, beyond the orchards, between the Fortress of Sydyk and the town, late in the afternoon. This space, like the trail leading up the mountain, was mostly bare rock. Jerevan unsaddled his horse, brushed it down, staked it out with the other riding beasts, and carried the saddle to the camp area where Otto was unpacking their things. He helped Otto set up their tent, then fixed himself a meal.

After he had eaten, he went out and joined the carnival roustabouts who were setting up the main tent for the evening show. It was hard work, but he enjoyed it. It provided exercise and proved that he was still capable of useful physical labor. He could hammer in a stake, and had become adept at putting his weight into tightening a rope.

Aside from his frustration at his lack of progress as a wizard, he often felt a supernumerary on this journey. He had no entertainment skills that would enable him to perform, and though he had been brought along for his wizard talent, he was only expected to use that in a linkage. The ability to get out and help to construct something made him feel better. Also, the exercise converted some of his new weight to muscle.

When the tent was up, Jerevan joined the wizards at their campfire. "Has Massif discovered anything?" he asked.

"Not yet," Marion said. "But we know the division stationed at Fethi was transferred to Sydyk. Myrriden expects a number of soldiers to attend tonight's performance. He's hoping we'll be able to learn more then."

"I hope so, too," Jerevan said. "Being this far into Gandahar makes me nervous."

THAT NIGHT'S SHOW DID DRAW SOLDIERS FROM THE CITADEL which sat across the narrow end of the shelf of the mountain, blocking the entrance to the gorge of the Gwatar above the falls. Some of the soldiers also patronized the midway. Elise, performing the dance Marion had taught her, succeeded in getting one appreciative member of the audience to discuss his duties, which included tending prisoners, during her break.

"Isn't that dangerous work?" she asked, looking up at him wide-eyed, projecting admiration and desire.

"Nah," he said. "We've got a couple of wizards that might be dangerous if they weren't capped, but capping 'em takes all the fight out of 'em."

She looked wistful. "Are you allowed to have visitors in the fortress?"

He eyed her body, displayed to advantage in the skimpy dancing costume. "Wish I could, but only officers get to bring in guests. Wouldn't do me much good if I could get you in. I sleep in a dormitory with twenty other men. No privacy. But I don't have to be back until midnight."

Elise radiated regret. "I have to dance in all the shows between now and two in the morning. Can you get time off during the day tomorrow?"

He shook his head. "I won't get off again until next week. How long will the carnival stay in Sydyk?"

"I don't know. We'll give another show tomorrow night and see if attendance is as good as tonight's. If it is, we'll probably stay another day or so." She eyed his muscular physique and remembered what Myrriden had told her to ask. "The fortress looks so big and scary. I've heard there are ghosts. Have you ever seen them?"

The young soldier's chest expanded. "Nah. We hear noises sometimes, especially in the lowermost levels where the prisoners are kept, but I've never seen anything."

"But someone you know has?" she prodded, sensing something about his reaction when she mentioned ghosts and shielding her glee at the information already acquired. How had Myrriden known what to ask about?

"Well, not exactly. But we've all heard stories about the old days. One of the human Great Wizards used to live in the caverns under the mountain, or so they say. There are passages that are blocked."

A whistle blew from behind the stage and Elise managed to appear sad. "That means I have to go." She looked regretful, then ran away before he could grab her.

But after the next show at eleven she left another of the carnival people to take her place among the dancers and joined the wizards back at their camp.

"So Rand and Errin are here and they're being kept on one of the lower levels. What's more, there are blocked passages to some sort of cavern system under the mountain," she concluded, giving her report to the others. "If we can find a way into the caverns, we might be able to get them out without even meeting the guards."

Myrriden nodded. "The Wizard Lovar spent his life building an immense complex under Aydak and Bektor to the north. There are hundreds of kilometers of tunnels and caverns. Vyrkarion has a map of it as it existed two thousand years ago, when Anor and Torin visited Lovar there, but he undoubtedly made changes after that. He disappeared sometime around 3100, but that still gave him centuries to shift things around."

"You have a map of the system, though?" Jao demanded.

"Yes," Myrriden said, "but as I said, its accuracy is suspect. We can't depend on it for more than a broad outline. Also, the isklarin are aware of the existence of the caverns. They blocked all the access points to the fortress ages ago, but they still guard the entrances to the cavern system as well. And they'll have a way of sensing if we break through one of the blocks. We'll have to get in and out quickly."

"How do you know that?" Marion demanded.

"I explored parts of the caverns with Cormor once, centuries ago," Myrriden said, "when the Wizard Sura got herself captured."

Jao said. "She was my mentor. I knew she'd been captured once, but I never knew she'd been a prisoner here. The rest of you wouldn't know her. She died three hundred years ago."

"She wasn't a prisoner long," Myrriden said. "Cormor only brought me along because he knew Vyrkarion contained a map. He didn't need me for anything else. He whisked her out of there within days of her capture."

"How do we get in?" Marion asked.

"There's an access point about three kilometers from here. It used to be just a cave entrance, but the isklarin built a small guard tower in front of it to seal it off. I doubt if they keep many guards on duty there, though."

"We'll find out in the morning," said Marion.

THE NEXT MORNING THEY APPROACHED THE TOWER at the foot of the cliff warily, waiting until the sun had warmed the sand and rocks to nearly the heat of a human body. Myrriden went first, with Jao and Balen behind him, then Jerevan, with Marion and Elise behind him. The three wizards were responsible for shielding the others and themselves from view.

Jerevan had expected the climb up the tower would be grueling, but he had not worried about the hike across the desert. Three kilometers on level ground would have meant nothing to him six months before, but after only half that distance he was sweating heavily and gasping for breath. The new layer of fat around his thighs shortened his stride, and the sand shifted under his weight so that he sank to the ankle with every step. Fortunately his boots were high enough the sand did not spill over, but by the time they had covered two kilometers the muscles of his legs quivered like jelly and he had to rest.

"Wait," he thought. *"I can't make it without a break."*

He felt Myrriden evaluate his condition. *"He's right. He's exhausted. We should have taken his physical state into account."*

"We'll give him a break," Marion agreed.

As a result, they didn't reach the base of the tower until nearly ten o'clock. Jao had gone ahead when they stopped to allow Jerevan to rest. She had taken care of the guards and signaled from the top as they approached.

Unfortunately, the tower had no entry from ground level. The guards entered from a stairway on the cliff face that connected the fortress to a trail chipped out of solid rock.

"Can you make it up the wall?" Elise asked, eyeing him critically.

"Don't know. Could have before," Jerevan thought. The rest had been too short, and the last kilometer had seemed to be almost all sand.

"Try," Marion thought.

Jerevan examined the wall, which was constructed of rough stones. A few months earlier he could have climbed it with ease. There were plenty of hand and foot holds. He got a grip on a stone above his head and stepped up on one of the projecting ledges, squashing the bulge of his belly against the wall. Then he reached for a higher hold and pulled himself up, searching for another foot hold while uncomfortably aware of the drag of the rough stones against his stomach. He found a foot hold and reached for a higher stone, cursing the increased strain on his arms caused by his inability to flatten his body against the wall. Still, he was off the ground and managing to cling to the wall. *"I think I can make it,"* he thought, *"but it's going to take a while."*

"Take your time," Marion thought. *"I'm behind you."*

Jerevan found a grip and then another, slowly moving up. He reflected that climbing while fat was like climbing with a cushion tied to his chest. He had to be constantly aware of his stomach's tendency to push him away from the wall. Everyone but Marion climbed past him with no difficulty, and his arms started quivering from the strain when he was only halfway up. After that, the climb was a nightmare. When he finally made it to the top, the others had to drag him over and his arm muscles immediately started to cramp.

"Be all right in a minute," he thought. He focused on his arms and forced himself to see into the overstrained muscles, to relax them. He was dizzy with fatigue when he finished, but the cramps were gone. He managed to make it back to his feet.

"The guards are asleep," Jao thought. *"I've made sure they'll stay that way for a while. There were only two of them."*

"Good. The steps are over here," Myrriden thought, gesturing to the right. Jerevan followed.

The walk through the dark passages and strange, vaulted caverns seemed endless. Near the entry he noticed traces of guano and other signs of bats, but as they went deeper the signs disappeared. Still, Jerevan occasionally sensed movement in the darkness.

The rock fall blocking the passage into the dungeons under the fortress looked like a natural collapse of the ceiling. Myrriden and the others spent over an hour moving the boulders out of the way, one at a time, setting them down gently so that no noise could be heard on the other side.

Once they were through the blockage, the dungeons of the fortress looked little different from the passages they had already gone through.

"How do we find the prisoners?" Jerevan asked Marion.

"Myrriden knows the area of the dungeon used in the past for keeping wizards. Once we're there we should be able to sense the guards," Marion answered. *"We won't be able to sense Rand and Errin through the caps, but we're sure they'll be guarded, and probably by wizards."*

A few minutes later Myrriden signaled he had found what they sought. *"Three wizards guarding them,"* he thought.

Jerevan closed his eyes. His helplessness terrified him.

"We knew we'd have to face wizards," Marion thought, reassuring him. *"Remember, almost all the isklarin of Gandahar have mixed blood, so most of them are journeymen, even without training. But they have good training techniques as well. Wizards aren't rare in Gandahar as they are in the human lands, and, anyway, they need good wizards to take the prisoners' sperm and process it. That's why we needed you. I know the techniques of wizard battle, but I don't have the strength, not since I was capped. Myrriden and Jao have never been strong in dueling with wizards. Even all together we couldn't win against more than two wizards by ourselves, but linked to you we can. You don't need to do anything but let the energy I draw from you flow freely. Don't try to hold anything back. Are you ready?"*

Jerevan drew a deep breath and nodded. What choice did he have? He felt her mind reach out and link with him, just as they had done in practice. Then he felt Elise being pulled into the linkage. Then Myrriden, Jao and, finally, Balen.

Marion opened the door.

One half of the room was outfitted like a small laboratory, and the other half was furnished with a couch and chairs. The isklarin rose from their seats where they had apparently been resting. The tallest one said, "So, the bait has lured some fish. I'd hoped for bigger ones, but you six will do for a start."

Three glowing globes of light appeared in the Gandaharans' hands.

Jerevan shut his eyes, but he could still sense the wizard lights. Three more appeared, one in Marion's hand, one in Jao's, and one in Myrriden's, but this second set of globes were all linked with tenuous streamers of force. The globes flared simultaneously, giving birth to shafts of light that met in three coruscating flashes.

Jerevan felt a current of energy flow out from his body into the linkage. It drew and drew. At first there was no pain, just a feeling of being drained. Then there was less of him left to draw from and the lines the current flowed through began to burn.

The light in the hands of the isklarin opposite Marion and Jao started to flicker. There was a flash and the two isklarin fell to the floor.

Jerevan felt part of the current of energy that had been flowing out snap back like a bowstring. The burning sensation became a hot flash of pain. He passed out.

ELISE WATCHED AS THE THIRD ISKLAR FELL, automatically checking the surge of energy that came back at her. She felt numb. She had never killed before.

Marion shook her head, then turned to examine Jerevan, who had fallen with the first two isklarin. Elise assumed he was suffering from backlash. She had felt Marion try to shield him, but they had all still been fighting. Being so inexperienced, he was bound to have been hurt being hit with two backlashes at the same time.

Myrriden went over to the fallen isklarin and searched their bodies, taking the crystals that hung from chains about their necks. "One of them's still alive, but he's burned badly enough he won't be a threat for some time, and maybe never again without his crystal," he said. He also found two other crystals in a chest by the rear door. "These must be Rand's and Errin's."

Jao went to the door at the back of the room and examined the locking mechanism. Elise saw her concentrate. The door swung open.

The cell was dark, but Elise made out the forms of two men lying on the floor with silver caps on their heads.

She moved to the doorway, staring at them, as Myrriden and Jao sank down beside them and shook their shoulders. They stirred and sat up. The taller one turned his face toward the light and Elise gasped. "Errin," she said, unaware she spoke aloud.

His head turned toward her and his eyes blinked from the glare of the light behind her. He squinted, but she realized he would not be able to make out her face against the light. She went into the room and sank down beside him.

His eyes widened when they focused on her face. "Elise," he croaked.

She stared at the silver cap, realizing that what she had thought was the edge was only the point where it sank into his flesh. She looked at it with the were-sight and saw that it was embedded in the bones of his skull and bonded to them.

Myrriden and Jao helped Rand to his feet. *"Help him get up, Elise,"* he thought. *"They're both weak and we haven't much time. A whole troop of isklarin will be down here soon."*

Numbly, Elise put her arm under Errin's elbow and helped him to stand. He swayed when he reached his feet, so she pulled his left arm around her shoulders and started for the door.

Myrriden supported Rand ahead of her.

Jao came to help her with Errin, pulling his right arm over her shoulders. Marion and Balen lifted Jerevan between them. He appeared to be still unconscious.

Myrriden looked out the door. *"All clear for the moment,"* he thought and stepped out into the corridor half carrying Rand. Marion and Balen followed with Jerevan, and Elise and Jao followed with Errin. In the distance she could hear the sound of voices, and metal grating against stone.

They half ran back down the corridors they had traversed on the way in, hearing the voices of the Gandaharan soldiers getting closer and closer behind them.

A sudden increase in the noise behind them told Elise that the fallen wizards had been found. Errin stumbled, almost pulling her down. She caught herself and saw that Jao had caught her balance also.

Errin got his feet back under him and they started forward again. The others had gained on them, however. Elise pulled at Errin, but he was too weak to run.

Then they were back at the passage to the caverns. Elise and Jao half carried Errin through after the others. Myrriden had let go of Rand who sat with his back to the tunnel wall.

Elise left Jao to support Errin and turned to see Myrriden face the entrance to the tunnel and the pile of stones they had moved to break into the fortress. There was a grating noise, and suddenly the whole roof fell down across the entryway.

Elise gasped as dust from the falling rocks flew up, choking her.

"That will take them some time to move," Myrriden thought with satisfaction. *"We should be well away by then."*

JEREVAN REGAINED CONSCIOUSNESS TO Marion shaking him. *"Wake up. We've got to get out of here. Get up."*

He felt himself being pulled to his feet. He had the worst headache he had ever had in his life and dazzle spots blocked his vision.

"Can't see," he said, no longer capable of mind speech.

"Just hold on and follow me," Marion said, thrusting one end of her belt into his hand.

They were apparently back in the tunnels. Jerevan clung to the strap and followed her. His head pounded in agony with every step, and he could see almost nothing. After a time, however, he realized that they were back at the tower. "Can't climb like this," he said.

"*Quiet! We'll lower you in a sling. Myrriden's at the bottom to get you.*"

Jerevan didn't know if he nodded an acknowledgment. Time had ceased to have meaning, except that he could feel the hunger starting again. Then he was shoved into a sling and he felt himself swing through the air. The pain in his head surged, and he almost blacked out. Myrriden pulled at him.

"*Get up. We've got to hurry. The isklarin will send guards to all the known entrances.*"

Somehow Jerevan got himself to his feet. "Can't see," he whispered.

"*Backlash,*" Myrriden thought. "*Drink this.*" A canteen was thrust in his hand. He drank. It was soup. He drank it all and Myrriden gave him another canteen. He could hear the others moving about, but he still couldn't see and his head felt full of molten lava.

He finished the second canteen and a rope was thrust in his hand. When it jerked tight he followed it, struggling through the sand. He fell down several times, but someone always helped him back up; he couldn't tell who. When the rope was thrust back in his hand he went on. When they reached the horses, someone helped him into the saddle and still another canteen was handed to him. He drank it, and then passed out.

He woke to stomach cramps as well as the headache, unabated, and Otto shaking him. He didn't seem to be sitting on a horse anymore, but he still couldn't see. "Hungry," he said. "Head hurts, too. Can't see."

Otto thrust a glass into his hand and he drank from it. Then Otto put food in his hands and he ate. After a while the stomach cramps went away. With that pain eliminated, he allowed the blackness to swallow him.

"WILL HE BE ALL RIGHT?" ELISE ASKED, looking down at Jerevan.

They had made it back to the carnival's campground by mid-afternoon. Myrriden and Jao were removing the caps from Rand and Errin in the next tent, and Balen had gone to inform Massif, the carnival's general manager and ring master, that Gandaharan soldiers were likely to invade the camp at any moment.

Marion looked up from her position beside Jerevan. "He should recover in a few days, but he'll have to ride in the wagon with Rand and Errin. It'll be a while before he'll see well enough to ride a horse cross country."

Marion stood up and faced Elise. "But Jerevan's not the one you're really concerned about, is he?"

Elise looked away and shook her head.

"Why didn't you tell me you knew Errin Pomorry?"

"Because I didn't." She faced Marion. "I've never heard of Errin Pomorry. I knew an ingvalar of the wigan called Errin Yar. I had a childhood crush on him sixteen years ago. How was I to know they were the same person?" Elise sighed.

Marion snorted. "But you thought they might be. That's what's bothered you since you joined this expedition. Something must have given you a clue they might be the same person."

"Just that Errin Yar once mentioned the Wizard Delanan and Myrriden said that Errin Pomorry was trained by Delanan. That's all, but I admit the thought did disturb me." Elise stared at the tent wall, wishing Marion would stop pursuing the subject.

"Why should that disturb you?"

Elise swallowed. "The spring when I last saw Errin wasn't a happy time for me. Seeing him again is bound to bring it all back."

"You know, Elise, you'll never make a top rank wizard until you learn to stop lying to yourself," Marion said blandly. "I'll leave you to watch Jere while I see if I can help Myrriden with Rand and Errin."

XXVI

MONTH OF MINNETH

And if you think their ways are strange,
Or that it's bestial to change,
Remember that the larin call
Us humans only animals.

— EXCERPT FROM "THE WERE-FOLK," PUBLISHED IN A CHILD'S GUIDE TO THE LARIN AND OTHER BEASTLY TAILS, BY ENOGEN VARASH OF ELEVTHERAI, 4557

GANDAHARAN TROOPS SEARCHED THE CARNIVAL GROUNDS thoroughly before the evening performance. They were expected, however. Rand and Errin were packed in wardrobe trunks that appeared to hold only clothes, even to wizards' eyes. Cormor had created the prototypes of those trunks and their use was as old as the use of carnivals in the Varfarin's business.

The next morning, after the troops had scoured the camp for a second time, the trunks and Jerevan were loaded on a wagon and Myrriden's group left the rest of the carnival. When roving units of malik cavalry stopped them, Myrriden claimed Jerevan was the owner of the carnival who had thought to take this year's tour with them. However, as he had fallen ill, they were returning him to his home.

That night they made camp on the banks of the Gwatar, some fifty kilometers east of Sydyk. Errin sought out Elise as soon as he was released from the trunk. He found her alone in the tent she shared with Marion. She was not surprised when she saw him, and he knew he had been expected.

"May I come in?" he asked.

"You may as well."

The tent was small. The sloping ceiling closed him in, and being so near her disturbed him. "I went back to Adun the year after we last spoke," he said, staring at her. She looked more beautiful than he remembered. Her hair had mellowed to the color of polished copper. Her figure had filled out. Her waist was still as slim, but her breasts were fuller, her hips more rounded. Her hazel eyes still looked huge in her narrow, fine-boned face, but lines of character marked her cheeks.

He felt a stab of pain at the years between them, the changes in them both. "I would have stayed the year you asked, if you'd still been there."

Elise stiffened and turned away from him. "It wouldn't have worked," she said. "My grandmother would never have accepted a child with your blood as her heir."

"So you had a child by Timmon Skane." Errin remembered the betrayal he had felt when he learned that, not only had she not waited for him, she had conceived a child by another man.

Elise's chin rose, but she did not turn to face him. "I gave my grandmother the heir she wanted. That freed me to live the rest of my life the way I wanted."

Errin ran his hand over his newly shaved skull. His head ached fiercely from the removal of the cap and from Myrriden's reconstruction of his cranium. He had trouble organizing his thoughts, but he knew that the sight of Elise still moved him. That knowledge did not help him know what to say, how to explain his feelings, or if they would matter to her. "When I heard you had conceived a child by another man, I understood that what I thought was between us didn't matter to you."

She turned and glared at him. "There's nothing between us."

"You asked me to stay," Errin said. "I would have stayed, if I could. I told you I'd come back. I arranged to spend a year with you. I thought your asking that of me meant that I meant something to you."

"A child's foolish fancy," she said, but her eyes evaded his.

Errin shook his head. "I'm the foolish one. I linked with you when I was nine, and allowed the linkage to penetrate too deeply, at least on my part. Hardly a day of my life has passed since, without my thinking of you."

"Sixteen years have passed," Elise said, looking back at him. "If you've thought about me so much, why didn't you seek me out?"

"I did," he said, remembering the pain. "Twice. The first time, as I said, I went back to Adun to find that you had lain with Timmon and formed a child. So I told myself to forget you. And I tried, but you haunted me. Then seven years ago I went to Ilwheirlane to find you. You were no longer living in Bria, but in Ninkarrak. I followed, determined to see you again, to talk to you. I found your address and called on you there. The Wizard Hulvar opened the door. He told me you were away but that he'd tell you I'd called. So I went back to Sussey."

"He never told me," Elise said, but again she was looking at the floor.

"Do you still live with him?" Errin asked.

"No," she said.

"I've tried to find someone else," Errin said, "but there's been no one else for me but you."

Elise snorted and glared at him again. "I find it impossible to believe that one of the sea folk has gone without sex for so many years."

Errin frowned and met her eyes. "There's a difference between sex for the purpose of physical relief, and the intimacy between two people who care for each other. I may have had sex many times since I saw you last, but I haven't shared my life with another woman, or left my seed in one. I care for you Elise, but I'm not one to seek out pain."

"Then leave me alone," she said, turning away from him again. "I didn't know it was you I was helping to rescue. If I'd known, I'd have tried to find someone to replace me. I never wanted to see you again."

Errin nodded. "I'm ill from the cap. I have no strength to argue with you now. If you wish to be left alone on this journey, I won't seek you out again. But this is not the end between us, Elise. I don't think there will ever be an end between us while we both live."

"No, Errin. There was an end sixteen years ago," Elise said, but she did not turn back to face him.

He smiled wryly. "I watched you lock your heart away, but I warned you then that I would pry it out again. Goodbye for now." He turned and ducked out of the tent, aware that she watched him leave, but she made no gesture to stop him.

THE FOLLOWING EVENING, when Elise was preparing for bed, Marion brought Jao back to their tent. Elise braced herself, recognizing their manner. She was in for a grilling. Well, she had expected it. She had nothing to hide but a childhood indiscretion. After all, she had never even lain with him.

Nevertheless, when the two wizards sat down on Marion's cot and demanded the story of her relationship with Errin, she found herself feeling defensive. "So I asked him to stay for just one year and he refused," she concluded.

"But he told you he'd return, didn't he?" Marion asked, her green eyes narrowed in puzzlement.

"The sea folk often tell lies to seduce women," Elise said. "The truth was that he wouldn't stay then."

Marion shook her head. "Aren't you the one who talks so much about family obligations? Didn't it occur to you that he might have obligations that he couldn't break?"

"The wigan folk have no obligations," Elise said flatly.

Jao shook her head, her blue eyes snapping. "When he spent that last spring with the wiga, Errin had already taken his oath as Delanan's apprentice. He would have had to arrange for a year's absence with Delanan as well as with his family. What's more, Errin Pomorry may have lived part of his life with a wiga, but he is not, and never has been, one of the wigan folk, Elise."

"Then what is he?" Elise demanded, glaring at Jao. "He swam with them, he talked of the song of the sea. He's one of them in every way that counts, whether he spends a few months of the year on land or not."

Jao sighed and met her eyes. "To my knowledge the only times Errin has spent more than a few days in the sea since his fifteenth year, when he took his oath as Delanan's apprentice, were when he traveled to Adun to see you. When he left on the second trip, he had arranged to spend a year away from Sussey, although that was not an easy thing for him to do at the time given his family responsibilities."

"What responsibilities?" Elise demanded. "I've never known one of the wigan folk to worry about responsibilities."

Jao stared at Elise. "Both Jehan and the Varfarin teach us not to judge how other people live, Elise. I hadn't realized your mind held such hostility toward the ingvalarin."

Elise flushed. "It's not that I dislike them all. I was fond of Pela as a child. I know that for the most part their way of life hurts no one. But the way the wigan folk lie with the people of the isles, even while they think of those people as no more than beasts, that I cannot accept or condone."

"Do you really believe Errin considered you no more than a beast, Elise? When he would have given up a year of his life for you?" Jao asked.

"When it was convenient for him," she snapped. "And if what you say is true. But, in any event, what is a year in the life of a nomadic wanderer?"

"How can you speak of Errin that way, Elise, when you know he's no such thing; that, in fact, he's been a journeyman wizard for years," Marion said.

"Yes, Elise, listen to yourself," Jao said. "You're so full of bitterness, you can't hear your own lack of logic. I understand that the wigan folk hurt your family in the past, but you personally have no claim to injury."

"I never knew he was studying wizardry," Elise said.

"That may be, but I've often heard you speak proudly of your heritage as Heir to Adun," Jao said. "It's time you realized that Errin Pomorry is heir to the Kulharion of Ruffin, a title greater than your own, and that, as things presently stand, he may well become the Ahar of Sussey and bearer of Lyskarion. His claim to family obligations is better than your own." She rose and left the tent.

Elise stared after her, stunned. Errin had a title? Heir to the Kulharion of Ruffin? She had heard of the wines of Ruffin. She looked at Marion, perceiving from her expression that she also felt Elise was in the wrong. She bit her lip, realizing that, whenever she thought about Errin's family, she thought of them as peasants like her grandmother's tenant farmers. She had never considered Errin a social equal.

Was that why she had been so quick to dismiss the attraction between them? Was she as big a snob as Marion and Jao thought?

XXVII

4650, 465th Cycle of the Year of the Ox
Month of Redri

> *"Sen ua lordom ya, bal abwin larin e he lomcaul ean. Jao quen ean; bajal quen ean. Va resriontwe quen tonod.*
>
> *"Sen ua ba nalor e lordom ya, ua puat mit nik itne he lomcaul. Bal abwin mawhen e ean hedal, senit ilmekod boril uase va. Nalorin bores papailin a lorin."*
>
> *"If you worship me, go out among the people and give them pleasure. Sing to them; dance for them. Life is meant to be enjoyed.*
>
> *"If you are a wizard and you worship me, you must stop pain as well as bring pleasure. Go among the oppressed and rescue them, even at the cost of your own life. Wizards bear the responsibilities of the gods."*

— FROM LESSONS TAUGHT TO WIZARDS, ATTRIBUTED TO JEHAN THE PLAYER

ERRIN RODE OUT TO MYRRIDEN'S TOWER AS THE SUN SET. He had arranged for someone else to take his part in the night's performance. A year and eight months had passed since he last saw Elise, and he could not wait any longer. No matter how many times he told himself he would be better off forgetting her, he always came back to the fact that he loved her. The time had come to actively pursue her.

He felt a little strange being in human form after spending a year and a half as a dolphin, but at least his head felt clear and his sight focused easily, without pain. His headaches had been so constant right after the escape from Sydik he had feared the cap had caused permanent brain damage. Seeking relief, he had taken dolphin form and sought out his father's wiga, swimming in the sea until the headaches had nearly ceased.

When he emerged from the sea he had felt obliged to seek out Rand, but fortunately his obligation then agreed with his desire, and he volunteered to join the carnival setting up in Belkova.

Myrriden welcomed him with a wry smile. "Don't tell me you came to visit me, Errin. I won't believe it."

"I owe you thanks for helping to rescue me. With the carnival in Belkova, I assure you, that would have been enough of a reason by itself."

"But you have another, much stronger, motivation," Myrriden concluded.

Errin laughed. "Well, yes. More than one, actually. But I didn't realize my primary motive was public knowledge."

"When a major symptom of wizard potential is the ability to sense emotion? We don't even need training to manage that, and you and Elise both broadcast a lot of emotion the last time you were together. I'm surprised it's taken you this long."

Errin shrugged. "I wanted to recover from being capped. Elise will give me a hard time. I wanted to be able to take the punishment."

Myrriden laughed. "The punishment may be greater for keeping her waiting."

Errin shrugged. "Will you tell me where to find her?"

"She and Marion are working with Jerevan in the library," Myrriden said. "If you go down a level, it's the second door on the right."

Errin hesitated, then said, "Afterward, I need to talk to you. I have messages and we've never discussed the implications of Gandahar's takeover of Nadrum."

Myrriden's eyes narrowed, but he nodded. "Very well."

Errin went downstairs but paused outside the door for a moment, trying to think what to say. Nothing came to mind, so he braced himself and went in.

Elise and Marion stood on either side of a large library table watching Jerevan play pickupsticks. Errin remembered the game in his own early training. The idea was to pick up each stick from the pile without moving the other sticks. Of course, the sticks had to be moved by the wizard's will rather than with his fingers.

Elise and Marion faced the door as Errin entered and Elise stiffened. Jerevan did not lose his concentration until the last stick floated up and joined the others in a neat pile. Then he, too, looked at Errin and expressed surprise. "Errin Pomorry, isn't it? What brings you here?"

"My excuse is to thank you all again for rescuing me, as I was in the area," Errin said, "but actually I came to see Elise."

Jerevan braced his hands on the desk and stood up. "Marion and I will be happy to give you some privacy," he said.

Errin was startled by the weight Jerevan had gained. He had been told about the curse, but he had not expected it to have such a rapid effect. Jerevan appeared to have almost doubled in size since Errin last saw him.

Elise redirected his attention by saying, "That won't be necessary, Jere. Errin and I don't have anything important to say to each other."

Errin turned to Elise and said, "Yes we do, Elise, if only to talk over old times and old friends. Don't you want to hear how Pela is doing? Or is the fate of one of the primitive wigan folk beyond your sphere of interest?"

Elise drew in her breath. "I wouldn't have thought a possible heir to the throne of Sussey had much time for keeping track of wigan folk, either."

Errin studied her. "But I find the time, Elise. Even before I was capped, I spent a few days or a week every few years with the wiga. They're my family. And I went back to the sea to recover from the cap. But if you don't care about them, any more than you cared about me, then I suppose we don't have much to say to each other."

Elise dropped her eyes. "I don't want to talk to you."

Errin sighed. "No. I see that, but we will talk. If not now, then some other day. There are things between us that need to be straightened out."

"I have to go," Elise said, and pushed past him and out the door.

Errin watched her go then shook his head and turned to Jerevan. "How's your training coming?"

Jerevan shrugged. "I should make journeyman soon. I was already a decent healer and I've had no trouble learning to work with a crystal. I can't quite lift a pound yet, and my record with the sight is fifty-five minutes, but I should make both marks before the end of the year."

"You haven't attained the high sight?"

"No. Myrriden says it will come. He only showed it to me six months ago."

Jerevan shifted on his feet and Errin realized that his weight now made him uncomfortable just standing. "You've gained more than I'd expected," Errin said.

Jerevan flushed. "I can't seem to gain less than a few pounds a month," he said. "They add up." He moved back behind the desk and sat down.

Errin frowned, watching Jerevan lower himself carefully into the chair. "You might be more comfortable living in Sussey when you get really heavy. It's not so hot there, and the ingvalarin are accustomed to obesity because of the wigan folk."

Jerevan's eyes narrowed. "I'm hoping that, as I get more skilled, I'll find a way to reduce the gain, if not stop it altogether."

Errin smiled. "I hope you succeed. But it's hot here in Belkova and I know my friends in the wiga hate the heat when they have to go ashore. That's why the wigan folk generally go north in the spring. And Sussey is much cooler than Belkova."

"Myrriden is my teacher," Jerevan said, pushing himself to his feet again. "I must live where he lives until I can break the curse." He walked over to the door. "Please excuse me, Marion, I'm tired."

"Of course, Jere," Marion said, her voice subdued.

Errin nodded but looked at Marion as Jerevan left the room. "My fatal charm," he said.

Marion frowned. "Jerevan's too sensitive, and Elise is hurting herself as much as you."

"I should have kept after her when we got out of Sydik, but I was in pain from the damned cap and could barely manage mind-speech. I swam with the wiga for over a year before the headaches eased up," he said, passing a hand over his eyes.

Marion studied him. "Not to mention the methods the Gandaharan wizards used to collect your sperm."

He looked up at Marion, stunned.

She smiled wryly. "I was a prisoner once too, remember, and the male prisoners weren't kept seperately from the women. In fact, they tortured us in front of each other deliberately. I doubt that Gandaharan techniques are much different than the Senangan. Did the wiga help with those problems, too?"

Errin sighed. "Pretty much. But you're right. That's another reason I left Elise as abruptly as I did. I couldn't have been a man for her then even if she'd wanted me."

"Do you love Elise?" she asked.

Errin shrugged. "She's haunted me since I was seven. I've never cared for another woman. I doubt now if I ever will, and I've never even had sex with her. Is that love, or obsession?"

"I don't know," Marion said. "Will the carnival be in Belkova long?"

"Two days. We plan on doing the basic outfitting for the whole tour before starting down the valley, and there are things I need to discuss with Myrriden."

When he joined the others for their evening meal, Elise was conspicuously absent. After the meal, though, he managed to get Myrriden alone again in the old wizard's rooms on the third floor. "Jerevan's gaining weight awfully rapidly, isn't he?" he asked.

Myrriden sat down behind his desk and eyed Errin shrewdly. "I doubt it's concern for Jerevan that brought you up here."

Errin studied the old wizard, then said, "Perhaps, again it's not my sole motivation, but I still am concerned. He helped save my life and I owe him. Wizard training takes decades, not years. At the rate he's going, he'll be close to the size of the largest of the ingvalarin before he can hope to challenge Derwen. Am I wrong?"

Myrriden shook his head. "No. You're right, and it worries all of us. Derwen was diabolical in the way he designed that curse. We can't reduce the size of his stomach. We can't do anything that will really slow his weight gain without breaking the curse, and none of us have the strength to do that."

"I suggested to Jerevan that he might be more comfortable living in Sussey," Errin said, sitting down in a chair facing the desk.

Myrriden's eyes sharpened. "He probably would be, but he's touchy about the subject."

Errin shrugged. "His weight is a reality. He has to learn to cope with it. One reason he's sensitive is undoubtedly the reaction he gets from the local population whenever he leaves this tower. Am I wrong?"

"No," Myrriden said, "but it would be worse to keep him locked up in here for the next twenty years. He has to go out and deal with the community he lives in, or he'll get too reclusive to ever become the esalfar we need."

"On Sussey, people would hardly remark on his weight," Errin said. "Chairs in public places are wide and sturdy. More than half the people of Sussey are overweight by mainland standards. He wouldn't become remarkable there for years. He probably won't ever get as big as the biggest of the wigan folk."

Myrriden frowned and tapped a pen absently against the desk. "You're right. I should have thought of that myself. Aside from the fact that I know you have an ulterior motive, you've solved a major problem for us." His eyes narrowed on Errin. "Could we all live at the Rakredrem?"

"I'm sure Delanan would love to have you, but it might get a little cramped with your whole entourage," Errin said, smiling. "On the other hand, Aliara would enjoy having you at Pomorry House. It's a great barn of a place that could hold three times your number without noticing."

Myrriden snorted. "And Elise would be particularly welcome."

"What's more," Errin continued, ignoring the interruption, "you could travel with the carnival. We're headed down the Ranaodh this fall, then up to Lara. We'll hit the towns along the coasts of Sardom and Lamash and end up in Darenje in the spring. My tour of duty will be over then. I'll sail with you to Sussey and help you get settled. It would be good experience for Jerevan and Elise to travel with one of the carnivals during a recruiting tour. You couldn't have done much recruiting on your way through Gandahar."

Myrriden stared at him. "The fiendish part of your plan is that it makes sense. As you say, it would be good for everyone, particularly Jerevan. Except traveling with the carnival will be uncomfortable for him."

"He's almost five hundred pounds now, isn't he?"

Myrriden nodded.

"Then everything is going to become increasingly uncomfortable for him," Errin said. "I've known a lot of the wigan folk and the trouble they have on land. Annais Tidewatcher is our carnival's fat lady this year. She can help him adjust as well as anyone. She chose to be the size she is because she likes life in the sea and weight is an advantage there. Carnival folk take people as they are, you know that. It's the best experience Jerevan can have right now."

Myrriden nodded. "You're right again. I can't fault anything you've said. You've obviously thought it out well."

"Then you'll travel with me?" Errin asked.

Myrriden nodded. "It's the least you deserve, I suppose, for solving a problem that's been worrying me for months."

"Elise won't be happy," Errin warned.

"No, but I'm fairly sure she'll stay with us, despite your presence. You've won yourself the time you wanted with her."

Errin grinned. "Now I just have to persuade her to talk to me. Do you suppose five months will give me enough time?"

Myrriden shook his head. "I don't know. I don't understand the woman at all. All of us think she cares for you. Emotion radiates from her whenever your name comes up, but she won't admit it. I don't think she even admits it to herself."

"Elise always exercised too much control over herself, even as a child. But, believe it or not, Elise and Jerevan's welfare aren't the only reasons I want extra wizards along on this carnival tour."

Myrriden frowned. "What do you mean?"

"Haven't you ever wondered why Gandahar took Nadrum?"

Myrriden shrugged. "Gandahar's always trying for new territory. I just wanted to get you and Rand back."

"For which you have our thanks, but Aavik sent an entire legion into Nadrum. And most of that legion is still quartered there, despite the fact that they have to bring in their provisions. Why?"

"I have no idea. I suppose they could be planning an assault." His eyes went to a map of the Thallassean Sea that hung on the wall to the left of his desk. "But where to? It would be stupid to try marching an army across the Bane."

"True," Errin said, following the line of Myrriden's eyes and looking at the map as well. "But Nadrum has an extremely fine port and most of the piers still stood, only needing minor repair, when Rand, Jao and I were there. Rand and I discussed it while we were prisoners and he's been investigating since then."

"Investigating what?"

Errin met Myrriden's eyes, and said, "The isklarin have completely repaired Nadrum's port facilities. Rand thinks Aavik's planning to use them to launch an invasion of Darenje."

"Darenje!"

"Yes. It may be a small target, but it's a wealthy one, and the valley inland is a rich agricultural resource. Rand believes Aavik plans on taking Darenje to establish a base so he can move against Lamash and all the city states of the south Thallassean."

"They don't have enough ships," Myrriden said. "Gandahar only has half a dozen ships in the whole Thallassean large enough to be used as troop carriers. They couldn't take Darenje with that small an army."

"They could if they had Senangan naval cooperation," Errin said. "Linlarin traffic in the Thallassean has increased steadily over recent years. Kavarna has become a major source of supplies for them. Recently Senangan ships have been sailing into Nadrum, too. Rand thinks Aavik's been negotiating with Senanga. He believes they'll bring an entire linlarin fleet through the strait at Belarrai to lend naval support for the attack."

Myrriden nodded slowly. "Great Jehan, it makes sense. In fact, it's exactly the sort of thing Aavik would plan." He looked up at Errin again.

"So the carnival breaking up in Darenje is part of your investigation?"

"Yes. I'd like more wizards examining the Gandaharan presence along the whole coast. Also, you're well known in this region. If you decide that the danger is imminent enough to warrant warning anyone, you might be listened to, where Rand and I probably wouldn't be."

"Darenje's a nice little place. If Aavik wants it, they don't stand a chance against the Gandaharan army even without linlarin naval support. Aavik could just march overland through the foothills," Myrriden said, looking back at the map.

"He could," Errin said, "but it would be a much more difficult problem in terms of supply lines. Most of the area to the east is near desert. He'd have to cart water and food for the whole army over hundreds of kilometers of rough terrain. The sea route, on the other hand, is quick and efficient, once he's arranged for transport."

Myrriden sighed. "What does Rand think we can do about Aavik's plans?"

"Do you think Ilwheirlane's navy would be willing to help block the strait?"

"I don't know, but the person you should ask about that is Jerevan. He knows Vanda Cinnac personally, and would have taken up a position on her Privy Council if Derwen hadn't put the curse on him."

JEREVAN HAD TO PAUSE TO REST FOUR TIMES on his way up the stairs leading to Myrriden's private suite and, having reached the landing, it took him several minutes to get his breath under control enough to approach Myrriden's door. He was nervous enough without arriving panting like a grampus. The old wizard had not summoned Jerevan to his private quarters since they returned to Belkova. After the exertion of the climb, he thought he understood why. Which made the current summons more mystifying, but he felt sure whatever Myrriden wanted had something to do with Errin's arrival. Errin's arrival and Errin's shock at Jerevan's increase in girth. Perhaps Myrriden had chosen to force Jerevan to make the climb to point out his growing physical disabilities? The idea mortified him.

"Come in," Myrriden thought before Jerevan had a chance to knock.

Jerevan entered, appreciating Myrriden's love of comfort more now than on the occasion of his first visit. When Myrriden gestured for him to sit, he sank down gratefully on the padded couch. *"Thank you, rai."*

"When was the last time you rode into town, Jere?" Myrriden asked.

Jerevan blinked. The question was so different from what he expected it took him a moment to comprehend. It took another to remember. *"Two months ago. I went to buy a new horse, to make sure he'd be up to my weight."* He shifted slightly, adjusting the mass of his belly to relieve the drag on his back.

Myrriden nodded. *"How often have you ridden since you got him?"*

Jerevan hesitated, realizing where the conversation was heading and not feeling happy about it. *"Five times."*

"About once every other week?"

"I've only ridden once in the last month, if that's what you want to know," Jerevan thought, letting Myrriden feel his resentment as his hands automatically massaged the chronically abused muscles of his abdomen. *"Sitting astride a horse is becoming difficult for me."*

"As all of us should have known it would, if we'd considered your problem on a long range basis."

"I take it Errin has done just that," Jerevan thought angrily.

Myrriden sighed. *"Errin has lived among the wigan folk, Jerevan. That makes him more familiar with the problems of obesity than the rest of us."*

"What do you mean?" Jerevan frowned. Again the conversation had taken an unexpected turn.

"What do you know about the ingvalarin?"

"Nothing, except that they can change shape to dolphins."

"That's right," Myrriden thought. *"Your mother was a Miunist."* He hesitated. *"Do you personally dislike were-folk? Is that why I sense hostility on your part toward Errin?"*

"No," Jerevan thought. *"I wasn't even aware Errin was an ingvalar. I just know he did something to Elise, and he's been overly curious about my personal affairs."* His left leg was going numb from lack of circulation. He shifted again, trying to ease some of the weight of his belly off his left thigh.

"His curiosity was prompted by concern," Myrriden thought. *"Obesity by human standards is common among the ingvalarin who spend most of their lives in the sea."*

"I've heard of the sea folk, but more about their amorous proclivities than about any weight problem they might have."

"Nevertheless, it's not uncommon for the older wigan members to weigh over a ton. The weight's an advantage in their dolphin form and, as they rarely come ashore, they don't mind it handicapping them on land."

Jerevan gaped. "Over a ton?"

Myrriden nodded. *"Yes."*

Jerevan closed his eyes. His present weight appalled him, but he still only weighed about a quarter of a ton. He had spoken of being a prisoner of his own flesh; he had never believed his condition would come to that.

After a moment of total denial, Jerevan forced himself to do a mathematical calculation of the weight he could expect to achieve at his current rate of progress in both wizardry and poundage. His first reaction was rage, but he forced himself back from that threshold. Myrriden was not responsible. Myrriden was trying to help, and so, apparently, was Errin. Derwen was the source of his problem. One more notch in the list of things that he would see Derwen suffered for in turn. When he had himself under control, he thought, *"What does Errin suggest I do about my weight problem?"*

"He suggests we move to Sussey. Your weight won't be an embarrassment to you there for many years, making it easier for you to go out in public."

"Something that's already difficult for me to do here," Jerevan admitted. His right leg was losing circulation. He shifted on the couch again, trying to lean back farther, realizing that the seat was too shallow for his present size.

"Pomorry House is on the coast," Myrriden said. "Swimming will be a good exercise for you until you learn to shape shift."

"How long will that take at my present rate of progress?"

"Twenty to thirty years."

Jerevan sighed then looked at Myrriden. *"What will this solution to my problem do to Elise?"*

Myrriden chuckled. *"She'll be furious for a time, but in the end I'll wager she'll be glad. Don't try to take sides in the relationship between those two. You'll only end up with both of them at your throat."*

Jerevan studied Myrriden's expression. *"I thought he'd hurt her."*

"No more than she's hurt him. They linked too deeply when they were both too young to understand the danger, but I have faith in them. They'll work their problems out. In the meantime, what's between them is their business. The rest of us should keep out of it."

"And how do you feel about being uprooted from your home for an unknown length of time?" Jerevan asked.

Myrriden laughed. *"You mean, will I be upset about spending a few years in a virtual paradise? I think I can manage to endure it. For your sake, of course."*

"Sussey is that beautiful?"

"In more ways than one, Jerevan, as you'll see. And as an added bonus, we'll be living in Ruffin where the finest wines in the world are made."

Jerevan shrugged. *"I seem to remember enjoying wine from Ruffin, but that was in another life entirely."*

Myrriden frowned. *"I know you're suffering, Jerevan. We all know that. You'll suffer more before you can hope to break the curse, but you have to remember that your condition is temporary. You aren't doomed to spend the rest of your life this way, just maybe twenty or thirty years."*

"I might find that reassuring," Jerevan thought, staring Myrriden straight in the eyes, *"if I weren't only twenty-three. Thirty years is more than a lifetime to me."*

XXVIII

MONTH OF REDRI

Have you been to the circus yet today,
Where elephants and lions play?
Come see the man who swallows fire,
The woman who skips across a wire,
And watch the horses dance and prance,
The silly clowns who play their pranks,
The acrobats who dare to chance
Their lives to fly above the ranks
Of lesser folk like you or me.
Oh, the circus is a sight to see.

— "THE CIRCUS," PUBLISHED IN A CHILD'S GUIDE TO THE LARIN AND OTHER BEASTLY TAILS,
BY ENOGEN VARASH OF ELEVTHERAI, 4557

ON THE THIRD DAY AFTER ERRIN'S ARRIVAL, in the early morning, Massif's Carnival of Wonders rolled out of Belkova with the full company of wizards and apprentices from Myrriden's tower outfitted and assigned to wagons or mounts. Elise sat stiffly in the wagon she shared with Marion. She was not sure what Errin had said to persuade Myrriden to go along with this crazy trip. Surely the last thing Jerevan needed was to be paraded around as a carnival freak, but even Marion, who was closest to Jerevan, had voiced no objection to Errin's plan.

It had happened so rapidly she had not had a chance to muster her own objections. One evening Errin arrived; two days later they were packed and moving out. She did not remember Errin having that sort of effect on people when she had known him before. Obviously, he had changed. More than she had.

She was still the quiet one. The one who was constantly having her life rearranged for her, whether she liked the new arrangements or not. She clenched her jaw. She would not descend into self pity.

She looked over at the gentle flow of the Ranaodh to the right of the road. It was late fall. The once green grass had dried to gold. The occasional jaod pines dotting the hills to either side and the clumps of fantyr trees along the bank looked dusty. There had not been much rain in the recent weeks. There never was in Sardom in the summer. The level of the river was at its seasonal low.

They didn't have far to go today, from what she understood. Mekar was only thirty kilometers east of Belkova, along the north bank of the Ranaodh. They had already passed beyond the heavily farmed plain around Belkova. Here the northern and southern hills edging the valley of the Ranaodh reached almost to the banks of the river, and the land was sparsely populated.

She wished Errin would try and talk to her so she could get rid of her tension and yell at him. It did not matter what she tried to think about. All her thoughts came back to him.

She saw Jerevan riding beside a wagon ahead of her. He looked miserably uncomfortable perched on top of his plow horse. The size of the horse might be necessary for it to bear his weight, but she thought it must make it even more difficult for him to straddle the animal.

JEREVAN'S ROLLS OF FAT and the distended mound of his belly jiggled with the motion of the horse. Looking at the motion, he felt nauseous. Before the curse, he had thought nothing of spending a day on horseback. Now his thighs were too fat to grip the saddle and he jounced like a pudding.

He sighed. At least he had chosen a draft horse when he last purchased a riding animal. No normal horse could carry his present weight all day, but Borespail, the Load Bearer, as he had named the gray gelding, bore him with seeming ease.

He was sure his size and constant consumption amused the carnival folk, but they were more politic about it than the general public. In any event, there was nothing he could do about either his appetite or his expanding rolls of fat. Before the curse, he would have been among the mockers if he had seen someone else of his proportions.

Since Derwen had cursed him he had gained almost four hundred pounds, twice his original weight. He looked around at the carnival wagons and remembered saying after the curse took effect that he would soon only be fit to be a carnival freak. Well, he was with a carnival now. That had not bothered him on the trip to Gandahar. He had not been really fat then. But now he actually weighed enough that Massif, the Ring Master, had said he would work out a comedy act for Jerevan to perform with Annais, the fat lady, in the larger towns. His jaw clenched and he promised himself that, if he did survive this to become a wizard, he would see that Derwen experienced the same pain and humiliation he had inflicted, and more.

They arrived outside Mekar just before dusk. By the time Jerevan had dismounted, unsaddled Borespail, staked the horse out, and got back to the camping area, Otto had finished all the other chores that Jerevan had shared with him on their last journey. Jerevan regretted that his increasing physical disability put a greater load on Otto, but even simple chores were getting to be too much for him.

He joined the wizards sitting around the campfire, positioning himself with his back against a water barrel, and concentrated on healing the sores and listening to the others while he ate.

Bokal Massif, the manager of the Carnival of Wonders, came into the circle and looked around at the wizards and apprentices. A small, wiry man with black hair and swarthy skin, he came from Jamnagar and spoke with strongly idiomatic speech patterns. "Attention, please," he said, interrupting the various personal conversations. "You should know agent had trouble negotiating with Mekar for use of site."

"In Jehan's name, why?" Myrriden asked, sitting up in the padded chair Balen had supplied for him. "We've been using this same field every few years for centuries."

Massif nodded. "True, but trouble grows among city states of Sardom. Mekaran officials fear we spies from Girohi. Let us stay because come from west and have no trouble with Belkova, but there be more difficulty when reach Girohi."

"I've never heard of fighting between the city states along the Ranaodh before and I've lived here for centuries," Myrriden said, frowning. "What started the dispute?"

"Don't know," Massif said, "but told us look for unusual we see on journey. Hostilities unusual, and impediment to future operations."

"Thank you, Massif," Errin said. He was squatting, as most of the carnival folk did, at the edge of the fire between Myrriden and Marion. "This is the sort of action we should have expected. How better to defeat an enemy made up of many small parts than to divide those parts so they can't unite against a threat? We need to seek for agents of Gandahar earlier than we expected."

"Agents of Gandahar," Elise snorted. She sat cross-legged almost opposite Errin, between Balen and Otto. "What interest would Aavik have in Sardom? Your imprisonment must have made you paranoid."

Errin turned his head toward Myrriden. The flickering of the fire made his expression difficult to determine. "You didn't tell them the other purpose of this journey?"

Myrriden shrugged. "I thought there'd be plenty of time before we needed to discuss the subject. I didn't expect to find evidence of Gandaharan activity before we reached Lara."

"You mean Errin may be right? There may be agents of Gandahar this far south?" Elise exclaimed, leaning forward so the fire illuminated her shock.

Myrriden nodded. "Possibly. He and Rand have been looking into the reasons for the taking of Nadrum. They came to a rather disturbing conclusion, which is proving more probable with this latest turn of events."

"What conclusion?" Marion demanded.

"That Aavik plans a major assault on Darenje in the near future," Errin said, turning from Myrriden to look at her. "Gandahar is holding a full legion in Nadrum, and they've repaired all the piers and harbor facilities."

"Darenje!" Balen exclaimed, horrified, from his position between Marion and Elise.

"Yes, Darenje," Errin said. "Which he'll then use as a base of operations against Lamash and all the human ruled city-states of the south Thallassean region."

Marion nodded, her grim expression made harsher by the fire's uneven light. "The Varfarin should have expected some such move. Cormor's been dead a long time. Gandahar under Aavik has been growing in strength. He trades with the linlarin of Cibata. He knows about the steady gains Senanga has made against Cassinga. It would be incredible if he weren't tempted to take advantage of our present weakness."

"But my family live in Darenje," Balen said. "There's got to be a way to stop them."

"We should notify the kovarain of the various towns and cities as we pass through them," Marion said. "Tell them we believe their current problems are due to Gandaharan interference rather than the iniquity of their neighbors."

"But will the headmen listen?" Jerevan asked, speaking for the first time. He sat back from the circle where the fire's light barely reached.

"Probably not," Myrriden conceded. "But we'll have to make the effort, no matter how they respond."

"You could try to arrange for them each to send a messenger to their representatives at the Council of Kovarain in Lara," Jerevan said. "I realize the Council only meets every ten years and the last meeting was two years ago, but there must be administrative personnel in existence full time. I'm sure I've heard that there's both a mechanism and precedents for setting special sessions."

"During the plague and after the Wizard's Bane," Myrriden said, nodding. "I don't think they'll see rumors of Gandaharan activity as a crisis of the same order, not unless we can back up our words with solid evidence, but the idea's sound. We'll have to try."

THE CARNIVAL PERFORMED THE NEXT DAY. In her free time, when she wasn't working the midway, Elise wandered around, watching the performances as though she were one of the villagers. Most of the acts were different from those which had accompanied the carnival into Gandahar. The acrobats were a different group, performing different stunts. Instead of the weight lifters who had formed a human pyramid, there was a troop of six hailarin dancers whose soaring leaps made them appear to fly. The tightrope walkers had been replaced by a group that climbed poles and spun around them holding on only with their teeth.

Even many of the animals were different. Instead of tigers, they had jidlinin, or fast cats, from Kandorra, who not only leapt through hoops of fire, but also ran down pakinin, the coursing hares from Aarma Es, the high desert west of ancient Arduin. And the cats not only caught the pakinin, they carried them back to the trainer unharmed.

Finally, Elise watched Errin perform as the carnival wizard. It was the first time she had seen a full carnival wizard's performance. In the journey through Gandahar, where all the audiences had were-sight, the part of the performance designed to stimulate human children with the potential for sight had been eliminated.

Elise watched as Errin produced illusion after illusion, and then gave them a clairvoyant vision of an ancient dragon who located missing items. Finally, at the end of the performance, he invited all the children who had not been born with were-sight to bring up an object of their choice and look at it through his eyes.

Children born without sight could not learn to see unless the sight was demonstrated to them while they were still young. However, if a child possessed potential, even one demonstration could stimulate the development of sight. The younger the child, the greater the chance. The greater the talent, the older a child could be and still learn. Once any level of sight had been achieved, further development was possible, no matter the age.

Elsie wondered how many of the swarm of children lining up to see would develop sight. With only one demonstration, Errin would be lucky to reach even one. The more often the exposure, the greater the chance of success. If stimulated from birth, three out of five human children could achieve some level of sight. Still, Errin performed well. She realized with chagrin that she had hoped to catch him out in some flagrant lapse of technique.

The following day the carnival moved on to Girohi. There, as Massif predicted, they were refused permission to camp on the site they had used in the past, and were forced to continue on and camp in open country.

In Jalora and Kotaj, the next two towns on their itinerary, they met no problems or hostility, but Hisar was on the verge of war with Duna further down their route and they were forced again to push on to more welcoming locations.

Errin waited to approach Elise until they camped outside Baksan, the first real city on their route since Belkova.

"Dathend, Elise."

She was on her way back to her wagon to go to bed, but she spun around when she heard his voice. "So, you finally got around to talking to me. How long has it been now? Twelve days? We've been on the road twelve days and you've just now gotten around to greeting me."

"I waited until you stopped glaring, Elise. I knew I couldn't reach you when you looked at me as though you wished I were dead."

"So that's my fault, too," she said. "You shouldn't have bothered talking to me at all. I didn't want to come on this journey, and I don't want to talk to you. And maybe I do wish I could hurt you."

"You have," Errin said, "many times, and if that's your attitude, then Dathend, 'Good day,' and Bal a danat, 'Go with good fortune,' are all I can say." He turned away.

"No. Stop."

He stopped, but he didn't turn around to face her again.

She stared at his back and said, "I'm sorry."

He turned back to her. "So am I. Sorrier than I have any words to express. I wish all our past history could just go away, and I could meet you for the first time today and tell you how lovely I think you look."

She inhaled, struck by how much she wished the same thing. "I wish that too."

His eyes brightened. "Then why can't it? Let's just say as of this moment that we've never met before, but you're someone I'd like to know better, and I'm someone you'd like to know better."

Elise stared at him. The idea stunned her. Was he someone she would like to know better? Of course he was. She said, "Then maybe someday we'd be good enough friends that we could discuss all our ancient history."

"Maybe," he said, "but right now we hardly know each other, and how can we learn what we both need to know when we're constantly dragging up the past?"

"What past?" She smiled.

XXIX

MONTH OF MINNETH

A leader takes responsibility for more actions than his own.

— EXCERPT FROM THE ART OF GOVERNMENT, BY VYDARGA V OF ILWHEIRLANE

BY THE TIME THE CARNIVAL REACHED CAMUZ, at the confluence of the Ranaodh and the Aodh, they had encountered half a dozen cases of extreme hostility between neighboring city states. No one had been able to identify the parties guilty of inciting the problems. Myrriden or Marion met with the kovarai or council governing every city or town they passed and notified them of what they believed with regard to Aavik's intentions and the probability of Gandaharan agents in the region. Most of the kovarain dismissed the warnings.

Camuz was a large city, and the carnival stayed there five days, doing two shows a day on alternate days. Myrriden decided that he, Marion and their apprentices would stay at an inn, rather than camp on the carnival grounds with Errin as they had been doing. "I'm too old to put up with all the racket of the carnival at night when I don't have to," he stated. "We'll all be better off for a few nights in a proper bed."

Jerevan agreed, as the ground seemed to grow harder as he grew larger. He also needed to escape the carnival atmosphere. Due to participate in his first clown routine the third day after their arrival, he suffered from both stage fright and humiliation.

When the time came for Jerevan's performance, Otto assisted him into the clothes provided by Massif. Costumed as a clown, Jerevan looked in the full-length mirror of the dressing tent and flinched. Except for the bright colors, the looseness of the costume and the oversized shoes, what he wore was little different from his regular dress. Jerevan understood that Massif did not feel his size needed emphasis to be funny. The knowledge was painful. His constant gain would soon put him over six hundred pounds, undoubtedly also the reason why the costume was loose. Massif would not want the expense of having to change it too often.

Annais came up beside him and clapped him on the back. "Don't worry. You'll do fine. Just remember to relax completely when the bridge drops out from under you. The net will hold you. If it holds me, it will have no trouble with you."

Jerevan turned to Annais. She had been generous with her help since the beginning of the trip, teaching him things that made coping with his weight easier. And she was always cheerful despite the fact that she weighed a good deal more than he did. He did not understand how she kept her good nature with the problems her weight had to cause her.

"Don't you feel humiliated when your appearance is enough to make the audience laugh?" he asked.

She smiled. "I don't mind their laughter. I live my life the way I wish, in the sea. This year I needed to earn money, however, for my son to start a business on land. He isn't happy in the sea and I can't earn money there, so for him I live on land and let the land people pay to laugh at me. If they came to the sea they wouldn't laugh, for there my size means power."

She studied him for a moment. "But for you I see it's different. You've never lived in the sea. To you the weight means inconvenience and embarrassment. More, it's something that's been done to you, rather than something you've chosen. Still, you must learn to accept what fate gives you and find the lessons in even what you consider cruel injustice. If you don't seek out those lessons and learn from them, you'll waste your life in frustration and bitterness."

Jerevan bowed his head. What she said might well be true, but his anger and the desire for vengeance that he had to suppress from his companions sometimes seemed like all that was left of him.

When the signal came for him to perform he strode out into the ring with his shoes flopping and went through the pantomime of courting an attractive woman who mimed great horror at receiving his attentions. Annais was brought on stage in a litter, playing his mother, urging him on in his courtship. When his intended bride ran away from him, Annais encouraged him to chase her. His quarry ran between two stage prop trees. Predictably, where she ran through, he got stuck between the trees and the litter bearers had to put the litter down and pull him free. After that there was a wall she jumped over and he fell over and other obstacles of an equivalent nature. The grand finale was a series of ramps leading up to a bridge. She ran up and across while he had obvious difficulty climbing and when he tried to cross the bridge, it collapsed in the middle. The audience could see the start of his fall, but the net he fell into was obscured by various stage settings.

The spectators shrieked with laughter, and Jerevan was smuggled out of the ring area between pieces of scenery. He was exhausted, but at least he had survived the ordeal without falling down anywhere but where he was supposed to fall.

Annais congratulated him. "You may have hated it, Jerevan, but you did very well. You have a natural sense of timing, and the audience loved you. I'm sure Massif will make it one of our regular skits."

Jerevan was surprised at how much her praise meant to him. At least he would contribute to the business of the carnival for the rest of the trip.

ERRIN AND ELISE TOOK A RARE FREE DAY during their stay in Camuz. Over the past weeks they had lived day to day, discussing issues of the moment and never bringing up the past. They were friends, but they both understood that their friendship was precarious, like a building without a foundation. While traveling and performing, they had little time to explore their relationship further, so they both looked forward to an entire day with no outside distractions.

They did not plan anything special, but wandered through the market district and explored the shops in the narrow lanes nearby. Errin bought her a necklace and earrings of amethyst beads, and later they ate at a restaurant situated on the bluff north of the Ranaodh and west of the Aodh, where the rivers met.

"You never talked about your family when we were young," Elise said, using her finger to form a pattern in the condensation on her glass of chilled lommas juice. "Yet now I understand that you're the heir to a great estate."

Errin shrugged and his eyes avoided hers, turning to the rush of swirling brown waters below them. "When I knew you on Adun I was only Errin Yar. I'm the heir to Ruffin because my uncle and his daughter died in a carriage accident. I liked Uncle Farrell. He was one of the nicest of my relatives. The inheritance brought me no pleasure."

"But you were the heir when we met that last spring. Why didn't you tell me?" Elise asked.

"We didn't have much time for exchanging family histories, but I did tell you that I wasn't one of the wigan folk, Elise. I tried to tell you more that last day, but you didn't want to listen. Would my being the heir to Ruffin really have made a difference?" Errin asked, turning back to meet her eyes. "I told you that my grandfather was ill, that I had an obligation to my family. He died that fall, and my mother was frail. She relied on me for support."

Elise looked away, her eyes drawn, as his had been, to the churning waters where the rivers joined. "I don't know. The things my grandmother told me that spring, they changed my whole way of looking at who I am. And then you told me that my father and my grandfather could have felt nothing for my family. You're right. Once you said you couldn't stay, I didn't want to hear any more. It wasn't just because I saw you as one of the wigan folk, although that was true too, and I was afraid I'd end up like my mother and my grandmother."

Errin sighed, his eyes intent on her face. "There is much that is good about the wigan folk. Still, it's true they aren't known for responsibility, but I would never have approached you if all I'd wanted from you was a tumble in the sand."

"But you lived with the wigan folk, even if you were different from them," Elise said quietly, turning back to him. "And I was hurting and afraid. I wanted you to share my hurt. When you said you couldn't stay, the reasons didn't matter to me then."

He took her hand in his and raised it to his lips. Then he said, "I felt your pain, and wished that I could soothe it, Elise. I wanted to stay with you, and I made sure that you felt that desire in me. I even understood why you sent me away. What hurt me was returning to find that you'd left and bore another man's child."

"Jorum," she said, her eyes intent on his. "My son's name is Jorum."

"Jorum," he said, testing the sound, acknowledging her concern. "I'm sure he's a fine boy, but why was he conceived, Elise?"

She shut her eyes and drew her hand back from him, clenching it. "He was the price I paid to my grandmother to be free to leave Adun, yet still be allowed to return."

He stared at her rigid pose for a moment. Then he rose from the table, tossed money down to more than cover their bill and said, "There's a theater here in Camuz with quite a good troop of players. I think we need to go back to being new acquaintances for a while."

She swallowed, but nodded and rose to accompany him.

THREE WEEKS LATER, AT THE END OF MINNETH, the carnival arrived in Lara. Located around the mouth of the Aodh, the city stretched for kilometers but was divided into two halves with only one great bridge connecting them near the southern edge. There were grand public buildings and vast tenements, quiet neighborhoods and clamorous markets. Lara was the most populous city on Tamar, and humans and larin came there from all over the world to trade.

Lara was also the capitol of the loosely federated city states of Sardom. Myrriden arranged a meeting with Kennar Larkin, the Kovarai of Lara, the hereditary Chairman of the Council of Kovarai, and a direct descendant of Emil Larkin who had led the rebellion against isklarin rule in Lara almost three thousand years before. The meeting took place the morning after they arrived in the city.

"I've been expecting you for weeks now," Kennar said when Myrriden was ushered into his office in Government House on the west bank of the Aodh. The room had high ceilings and white stucco walls. The windows looked out at the vast, crowded expanse of the Aodh, the view of the far bank almost blocked by ships.

"Then some of the kovarain we talked to on our way did listen," Myrriden said with satisfaction, examining the books and art objects filling the shelves than lined the wall opposite the windows.

"Yes," Kennar said dryly, gesturing to a chair in front of his large marinwood desk. "Please sit down. It appears that, between your party and Aavik's agents, the Valley of the Ranaodh is buzzing like a hornet's nest."

"The nest was disturbed before we prodded it," Myrriden said, sitting down in the offered seat. He leaned forward across the desk and his eyes sought Kennar's. "Darenje will fall to Gandahar if no effort is made to prevent it."

Kennar met his eyes, but shook his head. "I can imagine no action that we in Sardom could make at this time that would prevent the taking of Darenje, if that is indeed Aavik's intent. We have no standing army, only militia local to each of our separate cities. For the Council of Kovarain to call out that militia to form a standing army would require the approval of over half the population of each city. There's no way to win that approval at this time, when Gandahar has taken no overt hostile action."

"Gandahar did conquer Nadrum," Myrriden protested.

"Nadrum!" Kennar snorted. "At least as slaves of Gandahar the beggars of Nadrum will be fed. Aavik could make a valid claim that he took Nadrum out of charity."

Myrriden rose and paced the room. "Is it out of charity that he's maintaining an entire legion there?"

Kennar stiffened. "Make no mistake. I believe your claim. If I had absolute power, I would order that the militias be mustered. But I don't have that power."

"I'm sorry," Myrriden said, turning back to face Kennar. "I know you're right. But Aavik and Gandahar will be more difficult to fight with the resources of Darenje behind them."

"True," Kennar said. "And I'll do what I can to prevent that happening, but I'm afraid, against the armies of Gandahar, that isn't much." He turned to study a map of the southern Thallassean covering a large part of the wall opposite his desk. "I suggest that you take your appeal to Erna Gojani, the Ahar of Lamash. Her country will be even more at risk than the cities of Sardom if Darenje falls."

"We intend to do that."

"You must also remember that Sardom and all the countries and city states of the south coast of the Thallassean, even Darenje, have a large permanent isklarin population. This cannot be made a matter of race."

Myrriden grimaced. "No, that's the last thing anyone associated with the Varfarin would want."

Kennar nodded. "Then I'll do what I can. I'll call out part of the local militia here in Lara and start to train a cadre of officers. I have the authority to do that on my own. I'll also send investigators and mediators to put an end to the unrest on the Ranaodh and anywhere else in Sardom that may be affected. If any of them find proof of Gandaharan interference or if you bring me hard evidence of such activity, I'll call a special session of the Council."

"Thank you, Kennar," Myrriden said earnestly. "That's as much as we could hope for, all things considered."

THE CARNIVAL TRADITIONALLY SPENT TWO WEEKS IN LARA, doing two days of double performances in each of the five major districts. Errin, however, gave everyone a day off for their first day in the city. He and Elise went sightseeing through the southwest market and ended up at a small cafe featuring a local musical group. The building housing the restaurant opened on a small plaza and the tables extended out under the trees. Each table had a brightly colored umbrella over it, and the tablecloths matched the colors of the umbrellas. The musical group played to both the patrons of the cafe and the general public from the center of the park.

"Jao said that you're in line for the throne of Sussey," Elise said suddenly, putting down her wine glass, after they had finished their meal. Their table had a bright blue cloth.

"My grandmother was the fourth child of Civreel Anifi who was Ahar of Sussey. However, there are nine other descendants of Civreel between me and the throne. Believe me, my cousins would be horrified if they thought there was any chance of my inheriting Lyskarion," Errin said, looking up to meet Elise's eyes. "Being born in a wiga makes me no more popular with my mother's relations than I am with your grandmother."

"Oh," Elise said, startled. "That must have been difficult for you as a child."

Errin shrugged. "Granny Aliara and Uncle Farrell were all right, and great uncle Bilsen and his son. My cousin Pendra, Farrell's daughter, could be a trial, but Aliara kept her in line pretty well. My other cousins were the problem. Cardessa, Aliara's older sister, converted to the worship of Kyra the Destroyer, and she had a hand in arranging her brother Yambol's marriage and Inebolu's. Her granddaughter Ayana and Inebolu's daughters all hate me and despise my mother."

"The Ahar of Sussey is a worshiper of Kyra the Destroyer?" Elise exclaimed.

"While Inebolu was ahar, yes, but now that Bilsen has inherited, no," Errin said. "Bilsen was an admiral, in Sussey's navy and his son is a noted scholar. Cardessa never controlled them the way she did Yambol and his children. Fortunately for Sussey, Inebolu and Ayana, Cardessa's only grandchild, have only given birth to daughters, although I'm sure Ayana will go to a wizard to guarantee a son if she thinks there's a chance of my inheriting."

Elise laughed. "I'll never be able to remember them all."

"Don't worry about it," Errin said. "Now that my mother's remarried and doesn't need me to supply emotional support, I rarely go home. In fact, this trip will be my first visit in over five years." He paused as the musical group, a trio of a jalith player, a lomkas player and a percussionist, started to play a new number.

When the number was over, the waiter arrived to clear their plates. Errin stopped him from taking the glasses. "We'll have another half carafe of the wine," Errin told him. "We want to listen to the music."

When the waiter had gone, Errin asked abruptly, "How long did you live with Wizard Hulvar?"

"One month," Elise said, biting her lip. "Our relationship was a mistake from the start."

"Did you love him?"

She shook her head. "I was dazzled by him. He was a full wizard. When we started dating, I thought we shared similar ideas." She looked away from him and added, "He looked a little like you. He had ingvalar blood, but he despised the wigan folk. I was lonely."

She fell silent and the band started another number. It was a sad song of unrequited love. The jalith player had a soft, velvety tenor. When the number ended, Elise waited for Errin to say something, but he just watched the musicians.

Finally, he said, "I like the jalith player."

Elise sighed. "The percussionist isn't bad either, but I don't think much of the lomkas player."

Errin grimaced. "He has hit a few sour notes."

The musicians started another number.

> Oh, good folk of the cities of Sardom,
> Where the sun is so warm and so bright,
> Listen close to our words, for our tale
> Is the tale of a man of great wisdom,
> One who knew what was just, what was right,
> With such strength that he never did fail.
>
> Now his name is not strange to our ears,
> For all Tamar has heard of his fame,
> And the battles he fought long ago,
> Though we may have forgot, since the years
> When we bowed to the sound of his name
> Are long gone, and a time of great woe.
>
> For the story we've come to recite
> Is the tale of the Kovarai Larkin,
> Who led all the people of Sardom
> When we rose and began the great fight
> That set free all our cities and kin,
> Though he won for himself a sad doom.

Errin asked suddenly, "The music they're playing, didn't we hear that tune in several towns we visited along the Ranaodh?"

"It does sound familiar, but you have a better ear than I do," Elise said, frowning. "Does it matter?"

"I don't know," Errin said. "But it's given me an idea. I want to talk to those musicians when they finish the set."

THAT EVENING, MYRRIDEN MET WITH THE OTHER WIZARDS and apprentices in the public room of the Molting Griffin.

"A better response than I expected," Marion said after hearing Myrriden's report of his meeting with Kennar Larkin, "given that we have no solid evidence that the unrest we encountered is related to Gandahar."

"Have we got any leads at all?" Balen asked. "I mean, are there any new merchants traveling through, or old ones changing their routes?"

"I haven't heard of any new merchants," Errin said, "but there's a musical group touring Sardom. I've heard local musicians in several towns singing their songs. The music reminds me of some old Gandaharan ballads. What's more, I've also heard some controversial parodies of one song. For instance, I heard this version in Camuz:

> *Oh, good folk of the city of Camuz,*
> *Where the sun is so warm and so bright,*
> *Listen close to our words, for our tale*
> *Is the tale of a man so obtuse*
> *He could hardly tell left from his right,*
> *And his acts have made all of us quail.*
>
> *Now his name is not strange to our ears,*
> *Pray all Tamar does not hear of his fame,*
> *He went out for a ride with his wife,*
> *While addled with just a few beers.*
> *Do not laugh at the sound of his name,*
> *He was addled, not up to the strife,*
>
> *When his wife took the time to recite*
> *All the faults of the Kovarai Graid*
> *He fell off of his horse with a wail.*
> *So his wife, in disgust, left the fight.*
> *When he tried to remount without aid,*
> *Poor old Graid ended up face to tail.*

Balen said, "Hey, I heard another variation, back at out first stop in:

> *Oh, good folk of the city of Girohi,*
> *Where the sun is so warm and so bright,*
> *Listen close to our words, for our tale*
> *Is the tale of a man of stupidity,*
> *Who could not tell a wrong from a right,*
> *And such weakness he should be in jail.*
>
> *Now his name is not strange to our ears,*
> *Soon all Tamar will hear of his fame,*
> *As you've heard of his acts ere this day.*
> *Though you'll try to forget due to fears*
> *Of the power that goes with his name,*
> *As his family still says, "You'll obey."*

Balen looked at Errin. "Same tune, isn't it? I thought when I heard it, hey, they're feuding, what can you expect? It didn't occur to me it could be a reason for all the ruckus. I never heard the original."

Jerevan nodded. "It never occurred to me, either. But the piece I heard came from farther along our route. I think it went something like:

> *Oh, good folk of the great Tarouat,*
> *Where the sun is so warm and so bright,*
> *Listen close to our words, for our tale*
> *Is the tale of the Kovarai Farat,*
> *Who has said that his might makes all right,*
> *And selected his bride from a jail.*

Myrriden smiled. "Clever. Both the conception and Errin for detecting it. They all do sound as if they come from the same source. If Errin's right, and it seems likely, the information will give Kennar's investigators a strong lead. I'll pass it on to him tomorrow."

XXX

MONTH OF ISKKAAR

Malputo: It's true your noble suitor is a trifle large.

Beltrana: The word is fat, Malputo, fat. A simple word. Even you should be able to comprehend it.

— ACT II, SCENE 4, LINES 21-25, THE CORPULENT SUITOR, BY HAROL GLADEN OF ILWHEIRLANE, 4619

THE CARNIVAL REACHED LAMASH near the end of Iskkaar. Kappar, the capitol, located at the mouth of the River Dariel, while half the size of Lara, was still one of the major ports on the southern Thallassean Sea. Most of the buildings were constructed of adobe brick with red tile roofs. The avenues were wide and well planned with tall palms and elanda trees lining the sidewalks. More trees and flowering shrubs grew in islands down the center of the major thoroughfares. Three bridges spanned the river, connecting the northern and southern parts of the city.

The carnival traditionally occupied a large park in the northeast section. As Kappar was another major stop, the wizards again took lodging in one of the numerous inns, the Green Dragon.

Myrriden went to the palace the morning after their arrival to make an appointment to see the ahar and was told to come back the next day. When he returned, he was kept waiting all morning, and then was ushered in to meet a minor official.

"I made an appointment to meet with Erna Gojani," Myrriden said. "I thought my request was clear."

"The Ahar doesn't meet with just anyone," the official said. "I'll need to establish your reason for taking up her time."

"I have information relating to the security of Lamash," Myrriden said, controlling his temper. "I can't think of a better reason for her to meet with me."

"I'll be the judge of that when I've heard the information," the official said.

"I have no intention of giving you information," Myrriden replied. "I requested a meeting with Erna. The information is for her ears only."

"Then you won't meet with her," the official said. "Anyone can make a claim to bear important information."

"I'm a wizard," Myrriden said. "I don't make claims that aren't true."

"But I have only your word for that. I don't know you or your reputation," the official said blandly. "If you find someone known to me to vouch for you, then, perhaps, I could ask if the Ahar would be willing to see you. Without either the information or such a reference, I won't disturb her."

"There are days I regret I swore an oath not to use my power frivolously on people who annoy me," Myrriden said. "But for that, I'd turn you into a large toad, which, come to think of it, wouldn't be a major transformation." He turned and stalked out.

He reported his frustration to Marion and Errin in the taproom of the inn that afternoon. Jerevan, Balen and Elise were working the evening shift at the carnival. He finished by saying, "So I'm not sure how to arrange a meeting."

"Erna Gojani, the Ahar of Lamash," Marion said. "I've heard that name in some other connection." She grimaced with the effort to remember, then an expression of enlightenment suffused her face. "I remember. She sent a ship to Cassinga to bring back rare and exotic birds. That must have been over twenty-five years ago. Does she still collect them?"

"Yes," Jao said. "Her aviaries are known all around the Thallassean, but I don't see how that can help us."

"But it will," Errin said, grinning. "We've got three mated pairs of karatuin and several young single birds in the menagerie. You all must have seen the act Massif's boy, Niko, does with the older birds. But the young ones, they've just started training. If he's willing to part with one, I'll bet Marion gets in to see Erna tomorrow."

Marion, with a young cock karatu on her shoulder, was admitted to the presence of Erna Gojani the next morning. The audience took place in the palace gardens where Erna sat on a throne-like chair set on a lawn area surrounded by flight cages full of exotic birds.

Erna, Marion noted, bore a strong resemblance to a bird herself. She had a sharp, pointed chin, a beak of a nose, thin lips, amber eyes and black hair only lightly sprinkled with white despite her more than sixty years.

"You've gone to some expense," Erna said, nodding at the bird on Marion's shoulder, "to gain an interview with me."

Marion blinked. "You're aware that another member of my party sought an interview?"

"I'm aware of everything that goes on in Lamash," the Ahar said, her pale, amber eyes full of amusement. "A suitable bribe to the official would have served the same purpose as the bird, but I must admit it wouldn't have pleased me as much." She held out her arm. "Bring him to me."

Marion stepped up to the informal throne and transferred the karatu to the pad on the Ahar's arm. Erna scratched the back of the young cock's neck, and he chirped his approval.

"He's young," Erna said, "does he speak yet?"

"No. He should start soon." Marion hesitated, then said, "Are you aware that Aavik of Gandahar plans to annex Darenje?"

The old woman looked up at Marion and her pale eyes narrowed. "Does he, indeed?"

"He's stationed a legion in Nadrum. We believe he's negotiating with the Senangans for transport of his troops."

Erna's eyes went back to the bird on her arm. "He has beautiful markings. I have several hens for him to choose from, but I'm short of cocks."

"So we discovered when we asked one of the cleaning boys working in your aviary which you'd prefer," Marion said. "But don't you care about the fate of Darenje?"

"Why should I?" Erna asked.

"Because if Gandahar takes Darenje, it will be to use it as a base of operations from which to attack Lamash and all the human ruled city states of the southern Thallassean," Marion said, her eyes searching for any break in Erna's implacable calm. "We've already detected agents of Gandahar in Sardom sowing unrest. It's likely that there are similar agents here in Lamash."

"No," Erna said. "My people would have noticed and informed me."

"Then you won't do anything to help Darenje?"

"Darenje's merchants are major rivals of the merchants of Lamash," Erna said. "Even if Gandahar takes Darenje, and I don't believe for one moment that they will, the only effect I can see for Lamash will be to increase our prosperity. That's not something I'd care to prevent."

"If Darenje falls, look for Lamash to be next on Aavik's agenda," Marion said.

"No," Erna said, stroking the karatu. "Aavik may pick on the Ardaghs and Nadrums of the Thallassean. Perhaps, he may even aspire to swallow Darenje, or a few of the city states of Sardom, but Lamash is a major power. He wouldn't dare attack us here."

DURING JEREVAN'S PERFORMANCE THAT AFTERNOON two of the buttons of the once loose costume popped off when he started to breathe heavily, and his jacket flapped for the rest of the skit. While the audience thought it part of the show, Jerevan was reminded again of how rapidly his weight was growing. Otto altered Jerevan's clothes so frequently he no longer noticed.

Mounting Borespail for the ride back to the Green Dragon seemed more difficult even than usual and, by the time he entered the taproom where he was to meet Marion and the other wizards, he felt extremely depressed.

He paused inside the entrance of the taproom, waiting until his eyes adjusted to the dimmer light before maneuvering between the tables. Clumsiness was another problem he had. His growing bulk unbalanced him. His muscles didn't adjust rapidly enough to keep up with his weight gain. Moreover, his eyes tended to judge the space between objects by the amount of room he had required in the past.

He eased his way across the room but, despite his care, he brushed against a chair here, nudged a table there, attracting the attention he most wanted to avoid. Marion had said they would meet at a corner table at the back, so he had most of the room to traverse.

"Hey, fatso, can't you see where you're going?"

"Bet he hasn't seen his feet in years."

"Yeah. If he's near sighted he'd never see anything around that paunch."

Jerevan sighed with relief when he spotted the booth where Marion, Balen and Myrriden were sitting, but then, as he approached, he realized that the table and bench formed a single unit and could not be pushed apart. There was no way he could squeeze his present bulk into the seat.

Balen recognized the problem at once and said, "I'll get a chair."

Jerevan stood, feet widespread, conscious of the amused attention of the company in the taproom, while Balen fetched a chair from a nearby table.

When the chair was positioned in front of the booth Jerevan lowered himself into it, forgetting in his embarrassment the care his condition demanded he exercise when sitting down on unfamiliar furniture. The chair gave way with a loud splintering of wood, depositing him onto the floor.

A roar of laughter went round the room.

Jerevan lay still for a moment, trying to recover the breath knocked out of him by the fall. Insults washed over him like a wave.

"Can you get up?" Marion asked.

"Minute," Jerevan gasped.

The noise from the crowd brought the landlord into the bar. "What's the trouble here?"

"A mountain just crushed one of your chairs, Virek. Looks like you'll need a cargo hoist to get him up," one customer responded, louder than the rest.

Virek came over to where Jerevan lay and asked, "You hurt?"

"No," Jerevan managed.

"You owe me for a chair," the landlord said.

"I'll be happy to pay you." Jerevan allowed Balen to help him to his feet amid the catcalls of the audience. "But could you find a sturdy bench for me to sit on?"

Virek stared for a moment, then said, "There's a bench out by the stable. I'll get a couple of the boys to bring it in. After all, with you here the lads won't need to go see the carnival." He chuckled at his own wit.

Jerevan stood silently, ignoring the comments from the spectators. Even when the bench arrived, still adorned with wisps of straw, and he could sit down, he said nothing but what was necessary to order his meal. When Marion reported her own frustration regarding her interview with Erna Gojani, the mood around the table lapsed into a general state of gloom.

Thus, when Jerevan ordered a bottle of dalnith, the date liquor common to the region, after he had eaten, no one saw fit to argue with him about it. Myrriden retired early, and Jerevan drank the whole bottle and another one after it. When Balen and Marion protested the second bottle, he said, "This will be the first time I've gotten drunk in years. I think I'm entitled to a binge today, don't you?"

In the end, they all had too much to drink, finishing off a third bottle before Jerevan passed out. Marion got two ostlers to help him up to his room.

As a result, Marion herself was too drunk to think to warn Otto to wake Jerevan, and he slept until the cramps woke him.

Fortunately, Otto had the next room, and heard Jerevan cry out. He had to bring vast quantities of food before the cramping could be controlled. Jerevan's capacity had grown along with his girth and the pains did not let up completely until he felt so full he could barely move.

Otto then helped him to bathe, but the hunger pangs attacked again the moment the tight, stuffed feeling eased, and he had to eat even more.

After such a massive orgy, the clothes Otto had set out for him proved too tight and Otto had to find another outfit, the first time that had happened in over a year.

When the ostler brought Jerevan's horse for him to mount, Jerevan's engorged stomach prevented him from raising his leg high enough to get his foot in the stirrup. When he lowered the stirrup as far as the strap would allow and stood sideways to the horse, he could just manage to get his foot in, but he could not pull himself up into the saddle from that position. All his struggles accomplished was the entertainment of the grinning audience of stable boys and travelers. Mounting a horse from the ground was no longer difficult, it had become impossible. Finally, he had the ostler lead the horse around to the wagon loading platform while he climbed the stairs and lowered himself into the saddle from above.

When he reached the carnival just in time for his performance, Jerevan asked Massif, "Do you think the roustabouts could construct a portable platform and steps to enable me to mount each day?"

Massif grunted. "You growing fast. Won't need platform long. Need to ride in wagon."

"Nevertheless," Jerevan said, "I'd prefer to ride as long as I can."

"You can't now, if you can't get on by self," Massif said, "but acrobats' platform may work for while. I'll see if they let you borrow."

THE FOLLOWING DAY, ERRIN AND ELISE TOURED the cafes of Kappar with Errin listening for any trace of the music he had identified in Sardom, but they heard only the traditional folk music of the region and some classical pieces from cultural centers such as Kailane, Esterias, Mahran and Ilwheirlane.

They finally gave up and dined in a restaurant on the north shore waterfront, the Jolly Angler.

"I don't see what else we can do here, do you?" Elise asked when their meal had been served.

"No," Errin said. "Perhaps Rand or one of the other members of the Varfarin may know someone of influence here, or someone who can leak information to Erna's people. Maybe if her own system supplies the information, she'll take it more seriously."

"Maybe," Elise said doubtfully. She toyed with her food, but she was not hungry. She looked out through the window at the boats going up and down the river. "Why haven't you ever joined the Varfarin?"

Errin shrugged. "Delanan doesn't want to take my oath until he's sure I won't inherit Lyskarion," he said. He sighed. "Don't ask me why, because I really don't know the answer."

Elise frowned, stirring the food on her plate. "He must believe that there's a real chance you'll inherit it."

"Then he knows something I don't," Errin said, chuckling at the thought. "As I've told you, my relations would do anything to keep me from inheriting, including having a wizard guarantee that one of them bears a son." He ate some more of the fish he had ordered and washed it down with a swig of ale.

"Then why haven't they done that already?" Elise asked.

"I don't know," Errin said, "Probably, knowing Ayana, she thought she was bound to have a son on her own and her daughters are only just reaching child bearing age. One of them will bear a son any day now."

Some of the tenseness went out of Elise's shoulders, and she ate a little more of her meal. Then she said, "Have you forgiven me for Hulvar yet?"

Errin stiffened, then sighed. "It isn't a matter of forgiving you. You had a right to lead your life as you saw fit. I was just jealous, I suppose." He looked up and met her eyes, "And still dreaming the dream I had that spring that I would be the first one to stoke your fires and burn in them."

She swallowed. "I don't think my fires have ever really burned."

His eyes lit. "Then don't you think it's time they did?"

"Yes," she whispered.

SOMETIME LATER, WHEN THEY BOTH LAY RELAXED in Elise's bed at the inn, Errin thought, *"You wouldn't link with me?"*

She turned to him, her eyes wide, "I thought we burned quite hot enough without that. If I had linked with you through that, would we have ever really been separate again?"

"That is how wizards marry, Elise. You know that."

"I think I love you," she said, looking away from his too intent gaze and shielding her mind, "but I'm not ready yet to link with you for a lifetime. Can't we just be lovers for a while?"

He put a finger under her chin and turned her face back to him. "No, Elise, not for a while. We'll be lovers for the rest of our lives, but I can wait for the linkage until you're ready."

MONTH OF DIRGA

THREE WEEKS LATER THE CARNIVAL CROSSED the low range of hills that divided Darenje from Lamash. While passing a forrested area with thick brush, a small animal darted out between Borespail's hooves. Jerevan had chosen the gelding for his temperament as well as his size. He did not bolt as many horses would have done, but he did sidestep suddenly. As Jerevan's legs no longer had any grip on the saddle, even that was enough to dislodge him.

He fell on his back. The shock drove all the air from his lungs and he passed out. When he regained consciousness, he ached in every joint and could not rise without assistance.

"You can't ride any longer, Jere," Marion said, her expression anxious. "You're lucky the ground here is soft, not rocky. If the horse had shied somewhere else, you might have been killed."

Jerevan sighed. He knew she was right, but giving up his horse to ride in one of the wagons was one more defeat, one more freedom lost to the prison of his swelling flesh.

BOOK III

THE KARIONIN

There was a time when wizards ruled the world,
And in that Golden Age the wizards made
Eight living crystals. So, while wizards die,
The karionin live and never fade.

— EXCERPT FROM "ILKARIONIN, THE LIVING CRYSTALS" FROM <u>LEST</u>
<u>WE FORGET: A BOOK OF TEACHING RHYMES,</u> BY WILTON WIRRAMARETH
OF ILWHEIRLANE, 4207

XXXI

MONTH OF DIRGA

> *Then Redri and Cerdana joined to bear*
> *Golden Kaikarion, the Harvest Stone,*
> *And Rav and Sugra copulated to*
> *Create the Eye of Rav, Ninkarion.*
>
> *Yet as the karionin waxed in might,*
> *So did the strength of those who gave them birth*
> *As slowly wane. Thus did the wizards learn*
> *The price of power and creation's worth.*

> — EXCERPT FROM "ILKARIONIN, THE LIVING CRYSTALS," FROM LEST WE FORGET: A BOOK OF TEACHING RHYMES, BY WILTON WIRRAMARETH OF ILWHEIRLANE, 4207

A STEADY, PENETRATING RAIN TURNED THE WORLD GRAY the day Bilsen Anifi, Ahar of Sussey, was returned to the sea. Errin stood with his mother, his stepfather Galen, and Aliara, among the dripping trees of the Royal Park, listening to a stream of people mourn the passing of the deceased monarch.

Errin would still have been with the carnival if Antram's summons had not accompanied the notice of Bilsen's death. Fortunately, the carnival had reached Darenje and had been ready to disband. Myrriden promised to take care of the final details of the dissolution. He assured Errin that he could deal with notifying the Council of Darenje of the threat from Gandahar, and that he, Balen, Marion and Elise would bring Jerevan to Sussey as scheduled.

With those assurances, Errin had packed his waterproof sharkskin backpack and had dived into the sea, arriving the night before the funeral ceremonies. He had swum direct to Krydani, however. If Nutena had not brought appropriate clothes for him from Ruffin, he would have been forced to attend in the informal garb he wore while with the carnival. He grinned.

"What do you find so amusing?" Aliara asked sharply.

"Imagining Ayana's expression if she'd caught me sneaking into the palace last night in my carnival clothes," Errin said, glancing pointedly down at his green satin pantaloons and coat.

Aliara smiled. "I told Nutena to pack for you. I knew you wouldn't have anything with you appropriate for the occasion."

"Then I thank you, Grandmama, but in a way I might have enjoyed luffing Ayana's sails. She couldn't have had me thrown out, not after Antram insisted so forcibly on my attendance," Errin said, surprising himself. When he had been a child, Ayana and Inebolu's daughters' contempt had bothered him. Now that he was accepted by his fellow wizards, he realized he had lost that insecurity. These days, Ayana's attitude amused him.

"Speaking of Antram," Errin said, looking around for his great uncle, "where is our new Ahar?"

"I don't know," Aliara said. "I haven't been able to get near him today."

Errin decided that the crowd was too large to try and search through it. The number of people that had come to honor Bilsen, despite the inclement weather, impressed him. The old man had only lived five years after taking the throne, but even in so short a time his wisdom and greatness of heart had been felt. When Inebolu returned to the sea, the attendees had been sparse and the emotion quite different.

Still, where was Antram? Twice Errin thought he had located the new Ahar and had started through the crowd to reach him, but each time Antram disappeared, as though he were deliberately avoiding Errin. Yet Antram had insisted he attend. 'While I understand you may be occupied with important affairs of your own, it is imperative you make an effort to return to Sussey immediately. I have great need of your personal presence,' the summons had read.

Delanan approached, and Errin felt himself being minutely examined. Delanan hadn't seen him since he had gone to swim with the wiga after being capped. "How are you feeling?" the wizard asked. "I was surprised to hear you were present. I thought you were still with the carnival?"

"I was," Errin said, "but Antram wanted me here. I gather he sent a ship or swimmers to every place the carnival was due to stop this month. I arrived last night."

Delanan frowned. "Was that wise? Did you have to swim far?"

"Peace," Errin thought. *"I'm fine. The headaches have ceased, and my sight is as good as it was before I was capped. I'm back to better than I was before, in fact. I should be able to qualify as a full wizard within another three years, before I reach forty-three."*

Delanan's frown eased. *"That's good news. We worried about you."*

Errin smiled, returning to ordinary speech for the sake of his mother and Aliara. "I worried, too, right after the cap came off, but the sea is a great healer, and the carnival tour was interesting as well."

One of the ubiquitous palace servants came up to Errin carrying a silver tray with a sealed envelope on it. "His Majesty asked me to bring this to you. I'm to wait and guide you to him," the man said.

Errin opened the envelope and read the letter. "Errin, please follow the man who brings you this. I need to talk to you privately," signed "Antram," in Antram's unmistakable scrawl.

"It seems I've been summoned again. This time to a private meeting," Errin said. "Please excuse me. I can't imagine what Antram wants, but I'm sure I won't be long."

He nodded to the servant, "Lead on."

The servant bowed and led him around the crowd to the far wing of the palace. They entered by a small service door off the kitchens and went up a back staircase, arriving at the royal suite by a route that avoided all public areas of the palace.

The servant ushered Errin into what appeared to be an office and closed the door behind him, leaving him alone with Antram.

Antram rose. "Thank you for coming so quickly. I know my urgency must seem strange to you." He took something wrapped in cloth out of his pocket and unwrapped it. Then he walked up to Errin, took Errin's hand and placed the object on Errin's palm without touching it himself. Errin tried to pull back his hand, but Antram held it there.

"I'm sorry," Antram said, "but I felt I had no other choice than to give this to you now."

Errin brought up his hand and stared at the large oval crystal Antram had pressed upon him. His eyes widened. "Lyskarion!"

The crystal had been cold when it first touched his hand, but it warmed rapidly, and Errin saw a pulse of light rising in its opalescent core, a pulse that beat with the same rhythm as his heart. He looked up at Antram. "Why?"

Antram sighed. "Because I don't want to die as rapidly as my father did."

"What do you mean?"

"Lyskarion wants you to be its bearer. Now it has you," Antram said. "Hopefully, now that it's linked to you, you'll be able to control it. No non-wizard can."

"What do you mean it wants me to be its bearer? The living crystals have no volition."

"Perhaps most of them don't," Antram said, "I don't know anything about the others, but Lyskarion certainly does. All three of Inebolu's daughters are sterile. Ayana has borne only daughters, despite having a wizard guarantee her sons with both her last two children. And my father was healthy for his age until he took up that thing."

Errin stared at Antram. "You think Lyskarion is responsible for all of that?"

"Perhaps even more," Antram said, meeting Errin's eyes with a steady gaze. "At any rate, I considered my alternatives and decided I wouldn't touch it. I had a stone made to look like it to wear on ceremonial occasions."

"Nothing can look like Lyskarion," Errin said, staring at the pulsing jewel in his hand. The size and shape of a goose egg, the nacreous crystal looked like a huge, translucent pearl with a light at its heart. An intricately wrought platinum starfish gripped the narrower end and attached to the chain that enabled it to be worn around the bearer's neck.

"It looks like Lyskarion looked after my father died. Surely you can put some illusion on it to fake the pulsing core when I have to wear the wretched thing," Antram said impatiently.

Errin tore his eyes from the crystal and looked at his cousin. "Delanan might be able to do so. My training isn't . . ." he began, but as he started to speak a picture formed in his mind, a way to alter the appearance of an ordinary quartz crystal and the means to power the illusion. He looked back at Lyskarion, suddenly aware of its presence in his mind. The crystal was alive! He took a deep breath and focused with the high sight. Then he looked into Lyskarion.

He stood on a vast gray plain, surrounded by a swirling, opalescent mist. He wasn't sure how he knew the plain was vast, as the mist blocked his view beyond a few meters, but he knew. He wasn't alone. The presence with him had no form but he felt its awareness, felt it examining him, cell by cell, molecule by molecule. *"Power,"* thought the entity. *"Develop."*

He forced himself to focus through the mist at an area of the plain. Patterns covered the surface, thousands, perhaps millions, of intricate patterns. He started to examine one, but felt a hand on his arm, shaking him.

He stood in Antram's office with Lyskarion in his hand. There was no gray plain, no mist. Antram was staring at him.

"Are you all right? What happened?" Antram asked. "You looked at the crystal and then you seemed to go into a trance. I couldn't get your attention."

"How long?" Errin asked.

"About five minutes," Antram said.

Errin shook his head. "I think I can fix your fake stone, after all," he said.

"Lyskarion told you how," Antram said, nodding.

"Yes," Errin said with assumed calm, but his mind reeled with shock. What would this do to his relationship with Elise? She feared linking with him, even the way they had linked as children. A link through Lyskarion could never be broken.

BALEN LOOKED AT THE FACES OF THE KINDRED OF MAERA and the ajaren, as the priests of Jehan were called, as they filed into the assembly room of the Sanctuary of Maera in Darenje. The multicolored pastel robes of the ajaren brightened what he remembered as being a sea of white. He recognized most of the kindred and many of the priests. The Sanctuary and the Temple had always worked closely with each other in Darenje. In fact, he noticed a number of ajaren who had come to the party Jerevan attended with him, the night he broke up with Jula. He glanced at Jerevan seated on a bench to one side of the dais, and wondered if he remembered that night and recognized anyone.

Balen looked back at the growing crowd, spotting new faces, both old and young. They would be people who had transferred from other places, and novices who had begun their training since he had left to study with Myrriden.

Throughout most of the human lands, the worship of Maera drew more women, and the worship of Jehan more men, but in Darenje the numbers were traditionally about equal. Still, the present high priest of the kindred was a woman, Gaya Olaven. She was not a native of Darenje; she had come from Lamash before Balen had been born. She was an impressive figure: tall, with long, chestnut hair and red trim on her white robes that marked her as the high priest. Her counterpart in the Temple of Jehan joined them on the dais and nodded to her, his robe a deeper color than the pastels of the lesser ajaren.

She turned to Balen and he noted that the last of the kindred and visiting priests had found seats. "You asked for a full assembly of our joint priesthoods to announce your news, Saram Balen. We are now assembled."

"Thank you, Saram Gaya," Balen said, looking around at the gathering. "I thought it best to speak to you all at once, so you all hear the same thing and rumor doesn't twist my words. My master, the Wizard Myrriden, and members of the Varfarin believe that Aavik of Gandahar plans to invade Darenje. We don't know when, but a legion of isklarin troops are stationed at Nadrum and the port facilities there have been repaired."

Murmurs swept through his audience and Balen held up his hand for silence. "I'm not done. You can all ask questions when I've finished."

"What can you add to top that?" Jula asked angrily from the back of the room.

"My master and I and the other wizards with us have traveled with the carnival through Sardom and Lamash. We found evidence of Gandaharan agents in the region of the Ranaodh. They've been playing tricks on the folks of the city-states, stirring up trouble. We want to know if you've had any similar problems locally, or if any of you have detected unusual numbers of strange isklarin in Darenje." He paused and looked round the room. "That's all I came to say, but I'll be happy to answer questions."

"How could Aavik start trouble in Sardom?" asked a tall, thin blond standing next to Jula. He was one of the people Balen didn't recognize.

"They've been introducing ribald or scandalous parodies of popular music. They insult local political figures and attribute the lampoons to neighboring or opposing political groups," Balen said. "We're sure they're doing other things as well."

The hall erupted with sound as a number of people attempted to speak at once. Finally, Saram Gaya raised her hands and the hall quieted. She pointed to Jula, who had been particularly loud in her protests at the end of Balen's speech.

"You think Gandahar's going to start a war because you heard some satirical music, they have some troops in Nadrum and they've repaired the piers?" Jula demanded incredulously. "Gandahar keeps troops everywhere, and I think it would be more of a shock if they hadn't repaired the port facilities. Nadrum's a seaport, after all. I think your wizard training's gone to your head."

Saram Gaya pointed at another member of the audience who said, "I agree with Jula. I don't see why we had to drop everything we were doing to come and hear this nonsense."

Zenobia said, "It isn't nonsense. I've warned for the past ten years that a dark time comes, but it isn't yet close. We have at least a couple of years before us yet."

Others spoke out, some supporting the Varfarin's record in predicting what the larin would do, and others ridiculing the idea of Gandahar trying to invade Darenje.

Among the whole chorus Balen heard only one piece of helpful information. The musician Petrel Quanat said, "A new musical group did come through here last year." He stood near the front of the assemblage, his black hair falling across his forehead. "Didn't think much of their music or songs, but I did hear some pretty scurrilous parodies relating to members of the Council after they left. Thought it a bit unusual, or I wouldn't have remembered."

Later, when the meeting had broken up, the kindred and the priests all arguing, Balen located Petrel in the crowd and grabbed Jerevan's arm. "Come on, Jere. Petrel's over by the door. Think you can plow a path through the crowd?"

Jerevan heaved himself to his feet. "No problem," he said, and stepped down off the dais into the confused mass of people, forging a path toward the last place Balen had seen Petrel. No matter how fiercely they were debating, both priests and kindred moved aside when Jerevan bore down on them.

They caught up with Petrel just outside the doors in the hall. He was talking intently with a priest from the Temple of Jehan in a powder blue robe. "Saram Petrel," Balen said, as the last few people between Jerevan and his quarry dodged out of Jerevan's way, "I want to talk to you."

"Thought you might," Petrel said. "Why I was waiting here. Think Jula said what she did because you were the one delivering the message. You sure messed up that relationship."

Balen felt a flush spread up this throat and across his face. "Never mind that," he said, avoiding Jerevan's interested look. "We need to know where you heard the musical group, and where you heard the parodies."

"The group played at the Kanakar's Lair on and off for about six months, between doing tours of the countryside," Petrel said. "Lot of foreigners hang out there. Heard the jalith player say they came from Lamash, but the music sounded northern to me. Heard songs like that when we had visitors from Kailane."

"You didn't notice if any of the foreign customers were isklarin?" Jerevan asked.

Petrel shrugged. "Couldn't tell unless one of them changed in front of me. Don't go about giving brain scans to strangers."

"You might have heard them discuss something," Jerevan said.

"Just the bit about coming from Lamash," Petrel said. "Told you, didn't think much of their music, never paid much attention to them."

"You didn't hear the parodies until after they left?" Balen asked.

"Yeah, and I didn't hear them at the Kanakar's Lair. Heard one of the parodies at a village pub way out in the countryside when I was doing my touring healer bit. The other was from a local group who were playing in the Firedrake. Pretty good group. Did tours round the larger country towns; might have picked it up somewhere."

"Where would you suggest we look for Aavik's agents then?" Balen asked.

"Wouldn't hurt to check out the Kanakar's Lair," Petrel said. "You should be pretty good at brain scans by now. Just remember that there's isklarin that've lived in Darenje since the end of the Dragon Wars."

"Don't worry," Balen said, "we won't disturb the locals."

MYRRIDEN FELT VYRKARION FLARE AGAINST HIS CHEST and the knowledge came to him that Errin was linked with Lyskarion. He had expected it for years, of course, but the actuality still came as a jolt. He wondered what had happened to Antram Anifi.

He reached out with his mind to Marion at the inn where they were staying some kilometers across the city. *"It's happened,"* he thought, *"Errin is linked with Lyskarion."*

"Don't tell Elise," she warned. *"Let Errin tell her himself."*

Myrriden looked around the rapidly emptying field where the carnival had set up for its last performances of the tour. *"I thought their problems were over. They've been inseparable the last few weeks."*

"Inseparable, but not linked," Marion thought. *"Elise is still holding back from a complete commitment. I'm afraid the thought of Lyskarion will be too much for her. We must let Errin tell her himself."*

"Very well, but we still need to meet tonight, before my appointment with the Council tomorrow. Do you know if Balen's found out anything about Gandaharan agents here in Darenje?"

"He and Jerevan met with Balen's friends at the Sanctuary last night. Jerevan said they'd given them a lead Balen was following when he set out this morning. That's all I know, but Balen will report at the inn tonight."

BALEN GAPED AT THE HUGE FIVE MASTED BARK flying the colors of the navy of Ilwheirlane tied up in the slip across the street. He had been prepared for many things when he started following the foreign isklarin he discovered in Kanakar's Lair, but five isklarin walking up the gangplank onto a ship belonging to Ilwheirlane with no questions asked by the sailors on duty, that he would not have believed if he had not witnessed it himself.

After a moment he went up to one of the sailors at the foot of the gangplank and asked if he could take a look around the ship.

"Sorry, we don't give tours to the public. This is a naval ship," the sailor said politely.

"But I just saw a bunch of men go aboard," Balen said, wearing his blankest expression. He often found it an advantage that he did not look bright.

"Those were guests of the Admiral. We were notified to expect them, and they had the proper passwords," the sailor said.

"You got an admiral on board?" Balen said, gaping.

"Yes, Admiral Lyle Ortigel. He's reviewing the entire fleet in the southern Thallassean," the second sailor said proudly. "The Maimo is his flagship."

Balen prudently ambled on down the street until he was out of sight of the sailors, then slipped back to where he could watch the gangplank without being seen.

The isklarin remained on Maimo for nearly two hours. When they came back down the gangplank they separated, and Balen followed the one who had most often seemed to be in command, directing the others. He was careful not to let the isklar see him and to use only the most delicate mental touches to keep track of him. He was sure the isklar had some wizard talent, and all isklarin were at least sighted. He followed until the isklar went aboard another ship bearing the colors of Kailane. He took note of the ship's name and the slip it was in and started back to the inn.

When Myrriden joined Jerevan and Marion in the parlor that evening, he said, "I'm happy to report that the last of the carnival people are off to wherever they're supposed to rendezvous next. Massif and his family, wagons and all, are sailing to Lara to start a tour through the Nine Cities of Anat. I've rather enjoyed the last few months, but I'm glad I don't have to be responsible for doing this on a regular basis."

"It would interfere too much with your life of idle luxury," Marion said, smiling.

"Precisely," Myrriden agreed. "Now, what has Balen discovered?"

"We don't know," Jerevan said. "He isn't back yet."

"Yes, he is," Balen said, opening the door. "What's more, he has nasty news." He entered the room and shut the door, then looked around the group before focusing on Jerevan. "You have connections in Ilwheirlane. You'll need to notify Vanda that she has an admiral in her navy who consorts with agents of Gandahar."

"Agnith's fires," Jerevan said. "Who? How do you know?"

"His name's Admiral Lyle Ortigel. He's inspecting the whole fleet stationed in the south Thallassean. His flagship Maimo is tied up in a slip not far from here. And earlier today he met with not just one, but five, foreign isklarin. Now, I can't prove they're agents of Gandahar, but the isklar who seemed to be in charge boarded another ship flying the insignia of Kailane."

"And Gandahar controls large sections of Kailane," Marion said.

———

THE FOLLOWING DAY MYRRIDEN STOOD BEFORE THE COUNCIL of Darenje in the Council Chamber, a large, airy room with high, arched windows down the length of the wall on Myrriden's right. He faced the Chairman of the Council, the Honorable Hathi Beloin, a former sea captain and head of the Merchant's Guild. He and the other eight council members sat around the curved side of a table shaped like a half circle on a raised platform at the end of the room. The Chairman sat at the midpoint of the arc.

Myrriden finished his summation of the evidence regarding Gandahar's plans by saying, "So, while the evidence is circumstantial, the wizards of the Varfarin felt you should be warned that they believe Gandahar plans an invasion of Darenje in the near future."

"But you say you detected evidence of Gandaharan agents in Sardom. Couldn't the invasion be planned for there?" Amale Korsen, the Council representative of the Weaver's Guild, asked. "We've had no report of such agents being active here."

"Aavik isn't a fool," Myrriden said patiently. "He wouldn't attack a position where his enemies could come at him from both flanks as well as the front. Moreover, while we have no proof of hostile behavior, there are quite a large number of foreign isklarin present in Darenje."

After the stir had died down, another Councilman said, "I think we'll all agree that we must increase our militia and start upgrading their training and equipment. However, that by itself won't protect us from an enemy as large and powerful as Gandahar. What does the Varfarin plan to do?"

Myrriden sighed. "Your Honors, the Varfarin has no military branch. We've helped to train troops in Cassinga, and we can give advice, but that's the limit of our capabilities."

"Can you give us any estimate of the timing of this attack?" Hathi Beloin asked. "If we knew precisely when the attack would come, we could hire mercenaries to protect us."

"Supporting a large enough number of mercenaries to protect us from a legion of Gandaharans would bankrupt the state within six months," Bryant Elpine, the Council representative of the Farmer's Union, protested.

"The Varfarin intends to request that Ilwheirlane keep a closer watch than they have in the past on the Strait at Belarrai," Myrriden said. "They may be able to intercept the Senangan fleet that we expect will make up a large part of the invasion force."

"But you can make no guarantees," Hathi said.

"No." Myrriden answered.

XXXII

MONTH OF INGVASH

> *One cannot be overheard when speaking mind to mind, unless,*
> *of course, one deliberately broadcasts one's images to more than*
> *one mind . . .*

— EXCERPT FROM PROBLEMS WITH TELEPATHY, BY THE WIZARD AGNITH

JEREVAN STARED OUT THE WINDOW OF THE CARRIAGE as they approached
Pomorry House, aware of Marion squeezed in beside him. Myrriden,
Balen and Elise sat comfortably on the seat opposite. The carriage was
large and Jerevan knew that, under normal circumstances, Errin would
have come to greet them at the dock. But Jerevan's size was not normal.

Marion had worked him over during the voyage, healing his chronically
strained muscles, and he felt physically better than he had in some months.
Still, he now weighed over six hundred pounds and was still gaining. He
had to think about every move he made.

The carriage drew up in front of the house, and the driver came round
and opened the door. Jerevan waited until everyone else was out before
using the frame to pull himself to his feet. The roof of the carriage was too
low for him to stand erect. He put his head through the door, but the step
to the ground looked a long way down and the opening was narrow so he
could not grip the frame to brace himself. He was grateful when Balen took
his hands and supported him as he stepped down.

Errin, Jao, and a stocky man of medium height Jerevan assumed to be the
Wizard Delanan, waited by the steps leading up to the house. With them
were a middle aged woman with dark hair only lightly touched with gray
and a regal, silverhaired woman, undoubtedly Errin's mother and
grandmother. Jerevan noted surprise at his appearance on the face of the
younger woman, but the older one's face gave nothing away. He paused to
catch his breath before crossing the drive to join them.

"Lord Leyburn, I believe. Welcome to Pomorry House," the older
woman said when he approached, "I'm Aliara Anifi, and this is my
daughter, Nutena Pomorry." She gestured to the middle aged woman. "I
presume you know everyone else. I want to assure you that we're delighted
to have you, and hope you'll make your home with us for a long time."

"Actually," the stocky man said, "Jerevan and I haven't met previously.
I'm Wizard Delanan." He held out his hand, palm forward and fingers
raised, in the salute Jerevan had noticed was common with wizards.

Jerevan touched his fingers to Delanan's, and said, "I'm glad to meet you, too. I've heard a lot about your school."

"Good things, I hope," Delanan said. He looked around the group. "You must all treat the Rakredrem as another home while you're here."

"And when you visit, would you mind teaching a few classes?" Jao said. "Isn't that what you have in mind, Delanan?"

"Jao knows me well," Delanan acknowledged, shrugging. "But it never hurts to ask."

"Marion and I look forward to seeing your school and meeting your pupils," Myrriden said, "but I doubt that I could teach them anything you haven't taught better."

"Different viewpoints are always valuable. We've only got one student capable of attaining the high sight at the moment," Delanan said, "but trained journeymen are needed for many professions."

"Yes," Myrriden agreed. "I once discussed the possibility of opening a school modeled after yours in Belkova with Rand, but he had itchy feet, and it would have been too much for me to manage on my own."

"Balek and I discussed doing something similar in Cassinga before I was captured," Marion said, "but nothing came of our plans after I left Cibata."

Jao snorted. "Every wizard I know talks about starting schools and training apprentices. Jehan knows it's vital we do something to train more wizards, but Delanan's the only one who's actually doing something about the problem." She looked at Delanan ruefully. "All the rest, including myself, get impatient with the weaker students, or caught up in projects of our own."

"If it's so important to train more wizards, couldn't Derwen assign wizards to spend specific periods of time, say one year in five, teaching at a school?" Jerevan asked, shifting uncomfortably on his feet.

Delanan looked at Jerevan, and Jerevan felt himself being evaluated.

"He could," Delanan said, "if it ever occurred to him, but his emphasis has always been on testing for the exceptional rather than training marginal students. Also, Derwen isn't as strong a wizard as most of the other members of the Varfarin, and he knows it. He's never used his authority to command us. But you must be tired after your journey. Jao and I just wanted to meet all of you," his eyes went round the group, "and welcome you to Sussey. We'll see you again another day."

He nodded to Aliara. "You'll excuse us, Your Grace."

Aliara inclined her head. "We'll see you again soon, I'm sure."

When Delanan and Jao had started down the drive, Aliara nudged Nutena. "I'll show you to your rooms," Nutena said, her eyes darting nervously between Jerevan and Elise. "You can refresh yourselves. We'll serve tea or wine, as you wish, in the lounge in about two hours. Any of the servants can direct you."

She led the way into the house and through a large entry area. They proceeded only a short way down a hall to the left before she stopped in front of a door, opened it, and turned to Jerevan.

"Errin said that you'd prefer to be on the ground floor, so I had this suite prepared. Farrell, my brother, used to use it. It has its own entry onto the patio. I hope you'll be comfortable here."

"I'm sure I will be," he said, relieved that he would not have to remain on his feet for a tour of the house. He observed, though, that while she faced him, Nutena's eyes avoided looking at him. He entered the room, glanced around, noted that the furnishings were graceful and the chairs all had spindly legs, and turned back to her. "It's an attractive room," he said, "and I thank you, but I'd be better off with a few benches rather than these chairs."

She flushed. "Of course. I'll see that the seats are changed immediately."

Jerevan nodded an acknowledgment and shut the door. Then he walked through the sitting room of the suite into the bedroom and crossed to the bed. Fortunately, that had been constructed on a more substantial scale than the chairs. He lay down. He felt as though he had been pounded by cudgels, he was so tired. At least he was not yet hungry. He had eaten at the port before coming out to the house. He should be all right for another hour and Otto would arrive with the rest of the luggage by then.

Pomorry House looked comfortable. He would no longer have to cope with sleeping in wagons or on the ground, climbing up or down steep inn stairs, or any of the other inconveniences of traveling. Perhaps now he would be able to concentrate on actually learning to be a wizard, but at the moment all he wanted to do was rest.

ELISE FOUND ERRIN TALKING WITH ALIARA, Myrriden and Marion in the lounge when she came downstairs after changing. She went over and hugged him. "Hi. I missed you."

She was impressed by his home, which was three times the size of her grandmother's, and even more impressed by Aliara, whom she imagined might even be able to face down Mother Adun.

Errin looked around at the others and said, "Excuse us, Elise and I have matters we need to discuss." He took her arm and led her out of the room, down the hall and into another, smaller room.

Elise went willingly, but eyed him in surprise when he turned to her after closing the door. "Wasn't that awfully rude? They'll think we couldn't wait to tear each other's clothes off."

Errin looked rueful. "I wish we could, right now, but I need to talk to you first."

Elise sobered, realizing his purpose was not the romantic one she had supposed. "What's the matter?"

Errin took a deep breath and said, "I'm now the bearer of Lyskarion."

"What?" She stared at him in horror. "But how? Your cousin's still alive, isn't he?"

"Yes, Antram's alive, but he didn't want to bear Lyskarion. Apparently, some strange circumstances have surrounded it in recent years. He believes Lyskarion wanted me as its bearer, so he tricked me into being the first to touch it after his father's death. That makes me his heir."

She looked up to meet his eyes, feeling her whole world drop out from underneath her once again. "It also means that, if I link with you now, it won't be a temporary link but a link to Lyskarion too, isn't it?"

He met her eyes. "Yes, Lise. If you link with me now, we'll be joined for the rest of our lives."

She looked away. She had almost decided she was ready to link with him again. She had been thinking about it ever since he left her in Darenje. But now? If she still wasn't absolutely sure she was ready to link to Errin, she knew positively she wasn't ready to link with one of the karionin. Even the idea of them frightened her. "Can we still make love without linking?" she asked.

"Yes, if I take Lyskarion off," he said. "I doubt it, if I'm wearing it. Lyskarion wants a full linkage, and it has a mind of its own."

She turned back to face him. "What do you mean?" she asked. "I was taught that the karionin only did the will of their bearers."

"Lyskarion has volition," he said. "I wouldn't be its bearer today, if it hadn't been manipulating circumstances rather drastically."

Elise felt as if she had suddenly stepped into one of her childhood nightmares, the kind where she woke up and the world had changed while she slept and she was in a new place, surrounded by strangers. "Manipulating circumstances," she repeated after him. "How?"

"All Inebolu's daughters are sterile, and Ayana went to wizards to guarantee she bore a son for her last two pregnancies. She bore daughters anyway," Errin said.

Elise shut her eyes, taking in the enormity of what Errin must feel being linked to something capable of what he described. She looked back up at him. "How can you bear it?"

"It's part of me now. We're linked," he said.

Elise stared at him, but could not sense his emotions and his face revealed nothing. "One of the karionin caused the Bane," she said, remembering the most terrible thing she knew about the living crystals.

"No," Errin said, and his eyes flashed with a brief burst of emotion. "The Bane was caused by Agnith, not Cinkarion." He hesitated, and suddenly she could see the pain in his eyes. "Still, if you don't want to link with me, it would probably be better if we parted for a time, at least until I can come to terms with Lyskarion. I have to achieve some control, or at least an accord with it, before I can be sure of not forcing you into a linkage."

She shut her eyes, feeling pain of her own. "If Lyskarion can do what you say, why were we taught that the karionin had no volition? That all the things done with them in the past were the acts of their bearers?"

"I don't know," Errin said. "Perhaps what we were taught was true in the beginning, when their only bearers were their creators. Maybe the years without a wizard bearer caused Lyskarion to change. But whatever the reason, Lyskarion has volition now, and I'm not sure how much control I have."

Another thought struck her. "If we formed a link through Lyskarion, how much power would we have?"

"I don't know."

"But even without more training, we'd be the equals of any wizard on Tamar, wouldn't we?" she insisted.

"I believe so," he said. "I'm already much stronger than I was before the linkage. I could qualify as a full wizard today."

"You were only a few years from that before," she said.

"But now I'm on my way to being a great wizard," he said. "With Lyskarion I'll probably make it in another decade or two."

She walked over to the window and looked out blindly. "I was almost ready to link with you when I came here. But the rules have changed again. The power of Lyskarion frightened me even before you told me it had volition. A linkage between us would have been one thing. To link with you and Lyskarion, that's on another scale."

"I love you, Lise."

"But you've changed again. Just when I thought we were getting to know each other, just as we started to be close as we were when we were children, you change all the rules and I'm back where we started."

"I didn't do it deliberately. I was as horrified when I realized what Antram had done as you are now."

"But you can't unlink the link."

"No. Death is the only way to unlink from one of the karionin."

She sighed and shook her head, torn between pain and fear. "Then I think we'd better stay apart for a time. At least until you know you have control. I don't want to be drawn into such a linkage. Not now. Maybe not ever."

ERRIN WATCHED THE CHANGE OF EXPRESSIONS on Elise's face, feeling her pain intensify his own.

"I understand," he said. Elise hated sudden changes, particularly ones she had no control over. It hurt after they had come so far, but he would give her time. After all, they had all the time in the world. Bearers of the karionin could be nearly immortal if they wished. He turned to leave.

"Wait," she said.

Errin stopped and turned, thinking she had changed her mind.

"If you're so much stronger now, could you free Jerevan from Derwen's curse?" she asked.

Errin's disappointment when he realized what she was asking almost choked him and it took him a moment to answer her. Finally, he said, "I don't know. I've never met Derwen, but I understand he's not that strong a wizard, so I probably could. However, according to my knowledge of the placement of such curses, it's designed for Jerevan to overcome. For me to do so, I'd have to break Derwen's will entirely. I'm not sure he could survive that."

"I just thought . . ."

"I understand," he said. "I'll think about it while I'm gone and see what I can find out from Lyskarion. Perhaps, when I have better control, I'll find a way."

"Where will you go?"

"I'm not sure," he said, but even as he said the words, a destination came to mind. "Probably to Cibata. I'm sure the wizards of the Varfarin have some means of keeping track of naval activity in Senanga. A fleet of ships sailing for the Northern Hemisphere wouldn't be something easily missed. Perhaps I can find a way to give warning to Darenje by having the Varfarin track the Senangans. At least it's worth a try."

"That's so far away," she protested.

"Isn't that best?" he asked. "Anyway, this may be my last chance to see the rest of the world. Antram's not a wizard. When he dies I'll have to spend the rest of my life in Sussey. I should see more of Tamar first, shouldn't I?"

Elise bit her lip. "How long will you be gone?"

"I don't know that either. As long as it takes for me to know I have control of Lyskarion, I suppose."

She looked away from him. "I'll miss you."

"Yes. I'll miss you, too."

MYRRIDEN LOOKED AT JAO. "So I need to ask you, Jao, if you'll go to Ninkarrak and speak to Vanda. Tell her about the traitor in her navy and ask for her assistance in the protection of Darenje."

Jao glanced ruefully at Delanan, but said, "I'll go. But I've never met Vanda, it's been years since I've been to Ninkarrak, and I don't imagine Derwen will be glad to see me."

"He's too dedicated a public servant, however, to put spite before his duty," Myrriden said. "He'll get you in to see Vanda. Jerevan might give you a letter and some help as well."

JEREVAN ROSE FROM THE BENCH that had replaced the delicate chair in front of the desk and fumbled in the pocket of his breeches for his signet ring. His finger had grown too fat for him to wear it in the first year after Derwen cursed him. The pocket was tight and he had to struggle to shove his bloated hand in far enough to reach the ring, but he eventually managed. He applied the seal to one of the letters for Ilwheirlane, then cursed as the ring slipped out of his grasp before he could apply it to the second. The pudginess of his fingers interfered with his grip. He looked down, but could not see where the ring had fallen.

Otto was downstairs. Jerevan took a step backward, trying to spot it from another angle. Still no ring. He crossed the room and looked back from there, finally locating it at the edge of the rug, under the corner of the bureau.

He thought wistfully of the days when he could have bent over and picked the ring up with no difficulty. Then, with part of his weight supported by an arm on the bureau, he went down on one knee. He still could not reach the ring. He started to lower himself onto his belly.

Someone knocked on the door. Jerevan pulled himself awkwardly to his feet and went and opened the door. Jao stood outside. "Come in," he said.

She eyed him curiously, and he realized he was panting and disheveled from his struggle to pick up the ring.

"I dropped my ring," Jerevan admitted. "Perhaps you could get it for me. I can't reach it."

Jao looked startled. *"You can't pick up your ring? How much does it weigh?"*

Jerevan flushed, remembering that he was an apprentice wizard. Picking up small objects was something he practiced daily. He turned and focused on the ring with his sight and brought it to his hand.

"Myrriden suggested that I ask you for a letter and advice on how to approach Vanda Cinnac," Jao thought.

Still smarting from his own stupidity, Jerevan answered, *"Of course I'll give you a letter, but as for advice, just tell her the truth. She'll do what she can."*

228

XXXIII

MONTH OF CERDANA

Zaren amin so zaradin ma.

Some problems have no resolutions.

— ESLARIN PROVERB

JAO EYED DERWEN NERVOUSLY AS THEY WERE USHERED into Vanda Cinnac's private sitting room. This was her first meeting with the Estahar of Ilwheirlane, and she wasn't at all sure what to expect. What's more, Derwen had not been inclined to be overly helpful. He knew she was one of the wizards who had been helping to train Jerevan, and he was still furious that Jerevan had not come to him.

Jao's first impression of the room was an air of elegance. The walls were paneled with silvery marin wood and hung with several superb landscape paintings. One was a Creonek seascape so vivid she could almost hear the waves crashing on the shore. The carpet was pale blue and rose, and the chairs and drapes were dark blue velvet. Seasonal flowers arranged in porcelain vases filled the air with a spicy sweet scent.

The only occupant of the room looked almost anemic set against such a backdrop. Vanda sat at a marin wood desk in the only unpadded chair. She was small, with fair skin and pale hair, now more silver than blonde. There was something about the estahar's gray eyes, Jao thought, looking again and meeting Vanda's calm gaze.

Vanda's eyes held wisdom. Jao relaxed. She would be able to deal with this woman.

"Good afternoon, Derwen. You have urgent news for me?" Vanda asked, eyeing Jao curiously.

"Good afternoon, Your Majesty," Derwen said, inclining his head, "but the news is not mine. May I present the Wizard Jao."

Jao said, "Good afternoon, Your Majesty. I'm glad to meet you. I've heard many good things regarding you." She did not bow. No wizard was required to bow to anyone.

"I'm glad you've heard good things," Vanda said. "I'm sure there are uncomplimentary things circulating just as often. But please sit down and tell me your news and how I can assist you."

Derwen sat down, his attitude proclaiming that he had done his duty and was divorcing himself from all that followed.

Jao hesitated. "First of all, Your Majesty," she said soberly, "I need to inform you that circumstantial evidence indicates that an admiral of your navy, one Lyle Ortigel, is either an agent of Gandahar himself or is in their pay or control."

The Estahar stiffened and her eyes widened. "Circumstantial evidence?"

Jao sat down on one of the blue velvet chairs. "While his ship was tied in a slip in the port of Darenje, during the tour of inspection he's currently making of your navy in the southern Thallassean, he met with a group of five isklarin. At the time they were only suspected of being agents of Gandahar, but it's since been confirmed that the leader of the group is indeed an agent of Aavik."

"When did this take place?" Vanda asked.

"At the end of Dirga," Jao said. "The Admiral supplied the day's passwords to the isklarin so they could board the Maimo without comment or escort."

"I see," Vanda said. She reached out and rang a bell on the desk beside her. When a servant opened the door behind her, she said, "Please notify Admiral Parturan that I require his presence immediately."

She turned to Derwen as the servant retired behind the door. "I request a formal test of loyalty be given to Admiral Parturan. You can perform that when he arrives, can't you, without advance preparation?"

Derwen looked uncomfortable, but nodded. "Yes, Your Majesty."

Vanda turned back to Jao. "Now, you may as well tell me what else you've come to tell me. It will take the admiral at least twenty minutes to get here."

"The matter of the probable disloyalty of your admiral came to the attention of members of the Varfarin while they were investigating the possibility that Gandahar intends to invade Darenje," Jao said carefully.

"Darenje?" Vanda repeated, and her eyes narrowed.

"It's a small . . ."

"Yes," Vanda interrupted her, "I know where Darenje is. I thought Aavik's plans were directed northward, into Kailane. Gandahar already controls two of the largest hetrions, after all, but the taking of Darenje would be a brilliant stroke." She paused and rang the bell again. "I have to hear Palus' opinion of this." When the servant appeared she said, "Send for General Braydon, also."

"Yes, Your Majesty."

When the servant had again disappeared, Vanda said wryly, "Palus will beat Parturan here; see if he doesn't."

"But you summoned Parturan first?" Derwen said, startled into speaking out.

Vanda smiled. "But the messenger will have to find Parturan to deliver the message. Palus will be in his office. The messenger won't have to hunt for him. What's more, he'll grumble, but Palus will stop whatever he's doing and come at once. Parturan will posture about finishing some urgent chore before he deigns to heed my summons."

Jao studied the pale, calm face of the most powerful ruler on Tamar and understood why the wizards of the Varfarin held Vanda in such high regard, despite her lack of wizard potential. "Why do you keep Parturan?" she asked.

"Because, aside from the posturing, he's actually quite competent, and I don't make a practice of interfering in the normal course of succession in my military services," Vanda smiled, "unless, of course, I'm given extreme cause."

"What constitutes extreme cause?" Jao asked.

"When I see great talent going to waste because of a superior too incompetent or small minded to appreciate another's brilliance," Vanda said. "For instance, Palus Braydon was my choice for supreme commander of my armies. I forced his appointment over the objections of his predecessor thirty-three years ago. I've never regretted it."

Vanda sighed. "But to get back to the matter at hand, I take it that the results of the Varfarin's investigation were positive? You believe Gandahar will invade Darenje?"

"Yes, Your Majesty," Jao said, "which is why we're also hoping for your assistance in the defense of Darenje."

Vanda frowned. "I don't need Palus to tell me that there's no way Ilwheirlane can send troops there. The neighboring states would take it as an act of annexation."

"No," Jao said, "but you can defend the Strait of Belarrai."

"Against what?" Vanda said. "The navy keeps an eye on the Strait, of course, but it would be very difficult, if not impossible, to stop ships passing through. And it would be counter to our interests to interfere with free trade."

Before Jao could answer the door opened and a short, burly, silver haired man charged in, radiating annoyance. His eyes examined Jao before turning to Vanda. "Summoned me, Your Majesty."

"Palus," Vanda said, "I'm glad to see I can still depend on you to be prompt, that your age has not yet debilitated you."

"Hmmph," Braydon said. "Didn't drag me here to comment on age. Said to retire me. Wouldn't."

"I can't let you retire until I find someone with even a fraction of your energy to replace you," Vanda said, smiling at him, and Jao detected real affection in the estahar's voice and eyes.

"This is Wizard Jao," Vanda continued, nodding toward Jao. "She's brought disturbing news. The Varfarin believe that Gandahar is about to annex Darenje."

"Darenje," Braydon frowned, his heavy eyebrows forming a bristly gray hedge. "Makes sense to take it, opens up whole south. Nasty supply problem overland. Aavik's a shrewd fathik. Took Nadrum. He'll use ships. Where's he getting them?"

Vanda's eyes widened slightly. "I believe from a source outside the Thallassean," she said, glancing back at Jao. "Witness your concern regarding the Strait of Belarrai."

"We believe Aavik's made an arrangement with the Senangans," Jao said. "But we have no idea of the time schedule."

"Senangans?" Braydon frowned. "Large enough fleet. Easy to slip them through Belarrai."

"That's what the Varfarin hoped Ilwheirlane could prevent," Jao protested.

Braydon grimaced. "Navy's business, but doubt they can, unless the Varfarin supplies a wizard for every patrol ship."

There was a knock at the door and Admiral Parturan entered the room and came to attention. "You summoned me, Your Majesty?"

Braydon's opposite in more ways than one, Jao observed. The Admiral was tall and thin, with fine, dark hair brushed back smoothly from a widening forehead. His movements were languid, his attitude implying he found the world around him somewhat tiresome.

"I did, Admiral," Vanda said. "Are you prepared to repeat your oath of loyalty under wizard examination?"

"What, now?" Shock replaced Parturan's disinterest.

"Yes, Admiral. The Wizard Derwen is prepared to hear your oath immediately," Vanda said, her tone level but implacable.

Parturan's eyes flashed around the room, taking in the presence of Derwen, Jao and Braydon for the first time. He looked upset, but not frightened, Jao thought. Lazy and pompous, but not outright disloyal.

"Very well, Your Majesty, but I hope you'll explain what this is all about afterward," Parturan said, regaining his composure.

"Derwen?" Vanda said.

"I'm monitoring him, Your Majesty," Derwen said.

"Your oath, Admiral."

"In the names of Jehan and Maera, I pledge my allegiance to the nation of Ilwheirlane and to Vanda Cinnac, Estahar of Ilwheirlane. I pledge my honor and my life to the purpose of keeping Ilwheirlane a free and independent nation under Vanda Cinnac's rule."

"Derwen?"

"His pledge is sincere," Derwen said. "Admiral Parturan, have you ever had contact with any agent of Gandahar?"

"Gandahar? Great Jehan, no," the Admiral said, his astonishment evident on his face.

Vanda sighed. "Thank you, Admiral Parturan. I'm sorry to have had to put you through such an examination, but the Wizard Jao has just informed me that Admiral Ortigel is, in all probability, an isklarin agent. I needed to be sure the taint had not reached higher."

"Ortigel?" Parturan's forehead creased. "Don't know the man personally. He has an exemplary record. My predecessor was fond of him, I believe."

"Vordal's aide," Braydon said, nodding. "If he's an agent, explain a few things. Handled Vordal's liaison with Shore Guard, for one."

"That would mean he went undetected as an agent for twenty-five years," Derwen said, appalled.

"Probably more," Braydon said. "Check everyone he promoted, too."

Parturan looked dazed. "What do you wish me to do, your majesty? Send out a ship and have him arrested immediately and brought back for trial?"

Vanda frowned. "No, I don't think so. Not quite yet. Palus just brought up a good point. If Ortigel's been an active agent for over twenty-five years, he's bound to have brought other agents into our system. We do have a few apprentice wizards in the service. Put one aboard Maimo with papers that don't show what he is. Let's see if Ortigel flushes out a few other pigeons before we clip his wings. But let our agent have papers authorizing his relieving Ortigel of command when and if he sees fit."

"Very well, Your Majesty," Parturan said, his manner chastened. "I'll see to it immediately." He started for the door.

"Not quite yet, Admiral," Vanda said. "We have another problem for you to deal with, and this one may not have as easy a resolution."

Admiral Parturan halted and turned to face the others again, his expression decidedly anxious. "I'm at your service, Your Majesty."

"The Wizard Jao here," Vanda said, nodding at Jao, "is a member of the Varfarin. She's just informed me that they believe Aavik is planning an invasion of Darenje using Senangan ships for transport. She wants to know if we can intercept those ships before they enter the Thallassean."

"A fleet of Senangan ships," Parturan said blankly.

"Shouldn't think they'd sail as a fleet through Belarrai," Braydon said. "Stupid if they do."

"Quite right," Parturan said, suddenly back on familiar ground. "We could stop a fleet. Our outlying patrol ships are fast, even faster than Senanga's new schooners. We'd have time to put our own fleet across the mouth of Belarrai. Our navy's bigger, and, ship for ship we can match anything they've got."

"But if they come through one or two at a time?" Vanda asked.

"The same problem we've always had with Senangan pirates, Your Majesty," the Admiral said. "Our ships can't identify a linlarin ship without a wizard aboard, and we don't have enough wizards to keep one on every ship patrolling Belarrai."

"But if we put as many wizards as we have on the patrol boats, we'd at least stand a chance of stopping a few, wouldn't we?" Vanda asked.

"What about the wizard you want to send aboard Maimo?" Parturan asked.

"Except for him, of course," Vanda said.

"But that's the point, Your Majesty. Over a period of time, there'd have to be a number of such exceptions. Our wizards are stretched thin now," Parturan said. "Yes, I could assign them all to Belarrai for a short period of time, but then I'd have to shift one of them here, another one there. Unless you can give me a time frame in which to expect this Senangan fleet, what you ask simply can't be done."

Vanda looked at Jao, her expression rueful. "I'm sorry, but I did warn you that would be the probable answer."

"Yes," Jao said, feeling discouraged, "which puts the burden right back on the Varfarin to discover when the attack is planned."

"It might be difficult even then," Parturan warned. "It would depend on how accurately the time is pinpointed. For all our patrol ships to carry wizards, the time would have to be no longer than two to three weeks. If you only pinpoint the time to one or two months, then there would inevitably be some ships patrolling without wizards aboard. Then our ability to stop the Senangans would depend on the power of their wizards. Most of their ships do carry wizards, after all."

"What do you mean?" Vanda asked.

"A Senangan ship carrying a wizard more sensitive than the one in the patrol vessel would be able to detect the wizard aboard the patrol boat before he was detected himself. The Senangan ship could then wait out of range of our wizard until another patrol boat went on duty, one that didn't have a wizard aboard, and sail through then," Parturan said.

Jao nodded. "Very true. That makes the problem much more difficult, however, doesn't it?"

Parturan nodded and turned to Vanda. "That's why my predecessors and I have always assured Your Majesty that such a blockade is impossible."

"Thank you, Admiral. That will be all for now," Vanda said, dismissing him.

XXXIV

MONTH OF ANOR

Then came the plague when millions died and all
Of human life was nearly swept away,
When Agnith and Ilfarnar did conceive
Cinkarion, the Heart of Fire, that they

Might fight for others' lives and never mind
Their own. And Luth and Dirga in despair
Brought forth Lyskarion, the Song of Wind,
To heal the sick and cleanse the world of care.

— EXCERPT FROM "ILKARIONIN, THE LIVING CRYSTALS," FROM LEST WE FORGET: A BOOK
OF TEACHING RHYMES, BY WILTON WIRRAMARETH OF ILWHEIRLANE, 4207

MYRRIDEN FELT VYRKARION FLARE and knew that Cinkarion, the Heart of Fire, had found a bearer. A picture came to his mind: A woman with hair striped like a linlar's, but in black and red instead of black and cream. Faceted rubies filled the empty sockets of her eyes. He gasped. Only one linlar on Tamar looked like that: Saranith Kamrasi. Although young, she was the most notorious of the linlarin pirates, and, if that were not enough, she was also a relative of the royal house of Senanga.

If Myrriden had spent a year thinking of all the worst possible people to take up any of the karionin, he did not think he could have found anyone as disastrous as Saranith Kamrasi. He did not realize he had cried out, until Marion charged into his room crying, "What is it? Are you all right?"

"No," Myrriden said, shaking his head. "Saranith Kamrasi has just taken up Cinkarion."

"What! How did she find it? How do you know?"

"Vyrkarion just showed me the view from Cinkarion as they linked. The feel of that linkage burned me even though I'm not fully linked with Vyrkarion," Myrriden said, shaken by the horror of the memory.

"If she just picked it up a few minutes ago," Marion said, "then she's still in Arduin at the site of the Wizard's Bane. She must have gone ashore from her ship. That means we have a chance to catch her. We can rid the seas of a pirate and free Cinkarion at the same time."

"Then we must try," Myrriden said. "What ships are in port?"

———

ERRIN CRIED OUT IN THE DARKNESS OF HIS CABIN aboard the Gallinule, en route from Candith in Cassinga to Ninkarrak.

Del Maran, soon to be the Wizard Arrun, his cabin mate, woke at the sound from the bunk above and asked, "What's the matter?"

"Cinkarion has a new bearer," Errin said, his voice strangely flat, "one with red striped hair and ruby eyes."

"Jehan's mercy," Del said, shocked, "Saranith Kamrasi. How could Cinkarion have chosen a linlar?"

"Cinkarion was used to cause the Bane," Errin said. Del heard him roll over and sit up in the bunk above. "Cinkarion cares for only one quality in its bearer, that the bearer be incapable of the insanity that destroyed Agnith after Ilfarnar died. Self control, the ability to suppress any and all emotion, that's what Cinkarion wanted. That's what Cinkarion got."

"So much for our hopes that the karionin would choose advocates for peace." Del sat up and put his feet over the side of the bunk, extending his sight to find his slippers in the dark.

"Lyskarion chose me," Errin said. "I'm an advocate for peace. Perhaps the different crystals look for different criteria. A position of strength is better than a position of weakness, whatever your goal."

"Could you read anything more about her, other than her appearance?" Del found his slippers, one of them all the way across the cabin and half under the dresser. He pulled them into position with his will and slid his feet into them.

"I had a sense of a powerful will, but little training," Errin said, climbing down the ladder from the upper bunk. "She hasn't attained the high sight. It will take her a long time to gain full control."

"As you have full control of Lyskarion?" Del asked, being careful to keep his head down as he got to his feet to avoid banging it on the bunk above.

Errin snorted, hauling in his own slippers. "I'm getting there. It no longer acts on its own initiative."

"As far as you can tell," Del said.

"No," Errin said. "I could tell if it tried, but it won't do so now."

They donned their robes and went out onto the deck. Del knew he couldn't simply return to sleep after Errin's revelation, and assumed Errin couldn't either. It was a clear night. He could make out the stars of the constellation Ilgand on the northeast horizon. He was back in the Northern Hemisphere after almost seven years in Cibata.

"How does it feel to be going home after all the time you've spent in Cassinga?" Errin asked, reflecting Del's own thoughts.

"I'm glad I'm going to receive the formal acknowledgment of my elevation to full wizard in Ilwheirlane, where my father can witness the ceremony," Del said. "Otherwise, I don't feel as though Ilwheirlane is my home now. Unless Derwen has something urgent for me to do, I'll go back to Cibata."

"Funny," Errin said, and Del could feel his companion's sight examining him, "I wouldn't have expected you to fall in love with a hot, steaming jungle, teeming with insects."

Del laughed. "It's not the jungle; it's the feeling that I've actually had an effect, that my efforts may have changed the course of the war at least a little bit."

"More than just a feeling, from what Balek said. He didn't like losing you."

"He knows I'll come back. And I don't think Senanga's going to try another invasion in the next year or so, they're still licking their wounds from the last try." Del eyed Errin. "What about you? Will you ever return to Cibata?"

"I doubt it," Errin said. "This was my best chance to see something of the world. I've enjoyed my travels, but I haven't been anywhere I'd prefer to live than Sussey."

"Just as well, as you'll be stuck there after Antram dies," Del said. "I guess you didn't inherit the wanderlust of the wigan folk."

Errin shook his head. "No. I was never really one of the wigan folk, not at heart."

"*And can you control Lyskarion?*" Del asked, feeling that this was as good a time as any to examine Errin as Balek had asked him to do.

"*Yes. I can hold the high sight for nearly an hour now. That's enough to give me full control of the linkage.*"

Del relaxed slightly. That had been the most important question, but not the only one. "*Did Lyskarion kill to get you as its bearer?*"

Errin stiffened, but thought, "*No. It caused sterility in three women it thought unfit to bear children in any case, and it changed the sex of two unborn infants. In no case did it cause physical pain to any living being.*"

"*You're sure of that?*"

Errin nodded. "*Yes. Believe me, I examined Lyskarion most carefully on that point. That thought terrified me when I became its bearer. But it didn't cause Bilsen's death. Bilsen had an aneurysm. He could have died at any time.*"

"*And Izaren Taffen and Farrell and Pendra Pomorry?*"

"*Lyskarion knows nothing about their deaths. They died by accident.*" Errin paused, then added, "*Lyskarion did want me to be its bearer, but its time sense isn't the same as ours. It knew I was studying wizardry. It would have waited decades, even centuries to come to me. It would not have killed.*"

JEREVAN WALKED PONDEROUSLY UP THE GANGPLANK of the Cyring, a ship belonging to Sussey's naval fleet, with Otto beside him. When he reached the deck he found a quiet spot, out of the way of the scurrying crewmen and sat down carefully on the specially built bench that Otto brought. He could see the sky beginning to brighten over the mountains east of Ruffin. There was less than a month to go before the summer solstice, so it was about five thirty in the morning.

Jerevan wasn't sure of the purpose of this expedition. Myrriden had wakened him and told him to tell Otto to pack his things and board the ship as soon as possible as they had to try to intercept a linlarin pirate ship before it left the Thallassean. He had not explained why. That had been less that three hours earlier, but Jerevan and Otto had made it in time.

He had eaten his first morning meal early, however, and that was bound to cost him extra ounces. A pity, he thought, when he was so close to getting his weight under control. The month before last he had only gained four pounds, and it had been half a year since he had gained more than six. He could break the fat down now almost as fast as it was being deposited.

He was much stronger than he had been when he first arrived in Sussey more than four years earlier. Although he now weighed more than Annais, half a ton at the beginning of the month, he was getting around better than during his last month with the carnival. The difference was the massive amount of muscle he had built up under the fat. He had also learned to shift the fat away from places like his inner thighs, so that he could walk more easily.

The constant practice of using his will to shape his body was also having an effect on his development as a wizard. At his current rate of progress, Jerevan would attain the rank of apprentice wizard before the end of the year. He could already lift five pounds with his will and could hold the were-sight for over twelve hours. And he had attained the high sight and held it for almost three seconds on his last attempt. The only test he had not passed was the ability to project mind-speech for a distance of over a kilometer, but he had been working hard on that with Balen during the past month, and his range was increasing.

Balen hurried aboard just before the gangplank was withdrawn, clutching a sack full of things Myrriden had sent him for at the last minute. Crewmen rushed about, casting off mooring lines and running up and down the rigging. The Cyring eased away from the pier, sails unfurled and the ship came about and headed southwest into the Bay of Aelos. After her, the Tolu, bearing Marion and Elise, set sail and followed.

Myrriden came up beside Jerevan as he sat against the cabin wall near the bow of the ship. Jerevan asked, "How did you get approval to commandeer ships belonging to Sussey's navy?"

"I contacted Delanan who contacted a wizard in Krydani who could reach Antram," Myrriden said. "Antram gave the order and the message was relayed back here mind to mind. All the captains of Sussey's navy have enough were-sight to be telepaths. I believe it's a criteria for rising in rank."

"An advantage the larin have over humans," Jerevan said. "Most of them are born with skills it takes us years to achieve."

Myrriden nodded, but added, "They can't attain the higher levels though, unless they give up that natural advantage."

"I suppose that balances things somewhat."

"Jehan, I hope we catch her," Myrriden said, the expression on his face strained. "The Bane must have driven Cinkarion mad or it could never have picked such a bearer."

"Cinkarion is aboard the pirate ship we're chasing?" Jerevan asked.

"Yes," Myrriden thought. *"Didn't I tell you that when I woke you? This is what Vyrkarion showed me."* He projected the vision of the linlar with the ruby eyes and the red striped hair.

"Jehan! What happened to her eyes?"

"We don't know for sure," Myrriden said, "but I've heard rumors from friends who've spent time in Cibata. They say she put them out herself with a poker when she was twelve. She wanted to attain the high sight and knew she never would if she kept her own were-sight."

Jerevan frowned. "Then perhaps we're wrong to chase this Saranith. Perhaps Cinkarion knew what it was doing. Perhaps the Heart of Fire needs someone that strong and that ruthless."

Myrriden shook his head. "The human lands in Cibata have a hard enough time surviving now. Put someone linked to one of the karionin against them, and Cassinga will fall within the decade. We can't allow her to live, not linked with Cinkarion."

"If we to manage to kill her, who will bear Cinkarion?" he asked.

"I don't know," Myrriden said. "We'll have to deal with that problem when we come to it. In the meantime, we need to catch her."

About two hours later, Myrriden, who had been standing near the bow staring at the sea as though he could will the ship to go faster, cried out again.

"It burns! It burns!" he broadcast, and then passed out. When Balen brought him around, his darkly tanned skin had turned gray and his breathing was shallow and erratic. "She killed with it," he said, his voice barely a whisper.

"Saranith killed with Cinkarion?" Jerevan demanded.

"Yes," Myrriden said, too weak to use mind-speech. "She linked with a boy, an innocent. The linkage burned him up. I felt him die through Vyrkarion. His mind burned out completely. It was as though she ate his soul."

After that, Myrriden retired to his cabin. Jerevan remained on deck. Otto had discovered soon after coming on board that the cabin assigned to Jerevan was on a lower deck, and there was no way Jerevan could get down the ladder by himself.

Once in the Bay, the ships clawed their way west and then northwest, almost into the wind, around the Point of Tamul into the southern Thallassean. By then, Vyrkarion indicated that Cinkarion was moving east along the northern coast of Sardom. The Cyring and the Tolu sailed south and then southeast to intercept. Fortunately, the wind stayed favorable, blowing steadily from the northwest.

ERRIN AND DEL HAD GONE BACK TO THEIR CABIN to dress, but neither of them felt like sleeping. They were back on deck near the bow of the ship when Errin cried out the second time.

"It burns," he broadcast.

Del tried to link with him, but felt acid and heat burn him, as though his body and mind were physically dissolving. He threw up a shield and broke away.

Errin seemed to shake himself and Del saw Errin's hand clench around Lyskarion which was ablaze with light and power. *"Break it off. Stop it,"* Errin cried.

Then Errin collapsed on the deck.

Del knelt down and examined Errin with his sight, relieved to find that Errin had only passed out and seemed uninjured otherwise.

"Wake up," Del thought, prodding Errin mentally. *"What happened?"*

Errin stirred, then winced and held his head. *"The bearer of Cinkarion tried a linkage,"* he thought. *"The mind she linked with was destroyed."*

LATE IN THE AFTERNOON OF THE FIRST DAY of the voyage, Otto spoke with Arrai Egan Mareki, the commander of the Cyring, regarding Jerevan's difficulty in gaining access to his cabin. The Arrai ordered some of the crew to lower Jerevan with a cargo hoist to the lower deck so he could rest. After that, however, Jerevan had to stay in his cabin as the ship's passageways were narrow and no one could pass him when he emerged. In any event, there was no place for him to go on the lower deck except his cabin.

The lookout caught sight of the linlar ship on their ninth day at sea, by which time they were sailing almost due east, several hundred kilometers north of Anat.

The Cyring and the Tolu pursued the Senangan ship through the night. Myrriden and Balen took turns with Marion and Elise aboard the Tolu in watching for any change of course. The gap closed a little, but the Senangan vessel, which Balen identified as a three masted schooner, was still well out of range of the ship's cannon or any intense form of wizard attack.

At dawn the Senangan ship's course veered north, almost into the wind. The Cyring and the Tolu, having to tack more frequently, lost ground. "She's heading for the Dalossian Archipelago," Myrriden said, when he came up to relieve Balen.

"She knows we're after her now," Mareki said. He had been talking to Balen. "She can sail closer to the wind than we can, even if we did overtake her running with the wind. Sussey's barkentines are among the fastest ships afloat, and they run closer to the wind than the big square rigged ships, but not as close as a schooner." Mareki shrugged. "Senanga stole that rigging design from Sussey. You could have matched her if you'd been able to commandeer a couple of Sussey's newer ships, but that would have meant your getting to Krydani or Kolwen before you could sail."

He looked back at the fleeing schooner. "Whatever else she may be, she's a canny enough sailor to make the most of her advantage."

Balen, who loved to sail, nodded. "But your hull design is better, isn't it? The Senangans stole the plans for the rigging, but not the rest of ship."

"True," Mareki said. "How good a wizard is this crystal bearer?"

"We don't know," Myrriden said. "We've no idea how much or how little training she may have had. I'm hoping she's never been exposed to the high sight. If she hasn't achieved that yet, she won't be able to fully utilize Cinkarion despite the link."

"Well, we can probably keep her in sight until she reaches the islands. Then it will depend on you wizards," Arrai Mareki said. "The islands belong to Ravaar. My charts aren't good enough for me to maintain full speed through the channels without fear of going aground, but if you can give me bottom depths and warning of shoals, I'll keep up with her."

XXXV

MONTH OF ANOR

A linlar, when his temper's hot,
Is much more dangerous than not.
A tiger's stripy skin he wears,
With fangs and claws with which to tear . . .

And never, ever turn your back
Upon a linlar or you'll lack
Some part of your anatomy,
A fatal risk, you must agree.

— EXCERPTS FROM "THE WERE-FOLK," PUBLISHED IN A CHILD'S GUIDE TO THE LARIN AND OTHER BEASTLY TAILS, BY ENOGEN VARASH OF ELEVTHERAI, 4557

ELISE AND MARION SAT IN THE BOW OF THE TOLU, taking turns reading the depth of the water and the location of the nearest shoals and calling them out. It was a dark night. Ranth would not rise for another hour and the sky was patchy with clouds, limiting even the light of the stars.

Arrai Osan Carthen had taken the helm himself, as his were-sight was the strongest among the crew and it was needed to steer the ship through the narrow channels in the dark. Periodically he called out to the hands on duty to alter the position of the sails as he changed headings.

"*We're gaining,*" Elise thought to Marion just before the break of dawn. Almost a week had passed since Saranith's ship, the Cinhai, had turned northeast toward the Dalossian Archipelago. In the open sea chase heading nearly into the prevailing wind they had lost ground steadily, but since they had entered the narrow channels between the islands, the more streamlined design of Sussey's naval ships and Arrai Mareki and Arrai Carthen's seamanship were closing the gap again.

"*Yes,*" Marion agreed. "*Saranith outsmarted herself. She'd have done better to keep to the open sea.*"

With dawn, however, the Cinhai reached a wide strait amid the islands and widened the gap. Balen, aboard the Cyring, took the watch and Elise and Marion retired to bed.

Another two days passed before the ships from Sussey again drew close to the Senangan schooner. In the late afternoon. Marion and Elise were together on the deck near the bow, communicating with Myrriden aboard the Cyring.

"*We're almost at the end of the Archipelago,*" Marion thought. "*If we don't catch her soon, she'll gain back the advantage.*"

"*We're close enough now, we might be able to do something to her sails,*" Myrriden thought. "*I remember a trick Agnith told me about from the time of the Dragon Wars.*"

Marion brought out her crystal. "*Let's try then.*"

Elise felt a mental touch and joined in the linkage with Marion. She felt Myrriden and Balen join and reach out to include Jerevan. They projected their awareness across the water to the fleeing ship. They had started to examine the sails for weak points when they felt a mental blow, like being hit with a hammer. They tried to shrug it off and rip at the sails, but the mental hammer struck again, harder than the first time.

Their linkage fell apart under the impact and Elise found herself back in her body, lying on the deck of the Tolu. "What happened?" she asked, unable to summon mind-speech.

"I'd say that Saranith expected us," Marion said wryly. "She's very strong, even if she's not using Cinkarion efficiently."

"Just as well," Elise said shortly. "Any more efficiency and we'd be dead."

By nightfall they had closed to almost within the range of the two light, long range cannon, the forechasers, that both the Cyring and the Tolu carried in their bows. Unfortunately, they had also reached open sea.

"Cannon balls can't hurt her," Marion remarked, "not at this range and with only two cannon bearing. She'll just deflect them. She's a strong enough wizard to have done that even before she got Cinkarion. But grape shot might give her some trouble. Deflecting a lot of little pieces is harder than deflecting one big one. At least it may distract her."

Arrai Carthen called his crew to battle stations and they fired off four rounds of shot before Marion reported, "We're not doing any damage. Most of the shot isn't reaching the Cinhai and what does, Saranith's brushing away like the bite of a gnat."

They had begun to drop back again after the Senangan ship reached the open sea, but after midnight the wind shifted. Instead of blowing steadily from almost due north as it had been for nearly two weeks, it became irregular, blowing in gusts first from due east and then from the northeast.

As dawn approached, Elise, whose turn it was to watch, judged that they were keeping at least even with the Cinhai and perhaps closing slightly. She was thinking that they might win after all, when she sighted two other ships approaching from the northwest. The two new ships were sailing northeast, almost into the wind, on a course to meet with Saranith.

"*Arrai Carthen, Arrai Mareki, Marion, Myrriden, Balen, Jerevan,*" she cried out, waking them. "*The Cinhai has company.*" She reached out with her were-sight to examine the crews of the approaching ships and added, "*They're linlarin.*" She yelled to the officer on duty, "Farrail Deshun, two more Senangan ships two kilometers off the port bow."

Even as she called out, the watch in the crow's nest blew his alarm whistle.

Moments later the two new Senangan ships came about to a heading that would bring them past the Cyring and the Tolu.

"All hands prepare for action," Farrail Deshun commanded.

The ship came alive with activity as the crew roused and ran to their duty stations, preparing for battle.

Then the Cinhai also came about, and Elise realized that all three Senangan ships would pass Sussey's naval ships at point blank range. She prepared herself to ward off cannon shot, relieved when Marion emerged on the deck, still in the process of doing up the buttons of her shirt.

The three Senangan ships descended on the Cyring and the Tolu in a line. Arrai Carthen arrived on deck, taking over command from his first officer. The gun crews manning the Tolu's port guns prepared to fire. Elise noted that the new Senangan ships were barkentines of a similar design to Sussey's naval vessels. The first was named the Sukatta Bel, the White Shark, and the second, the Kanakar, for the huge, deep water sea monster.

Then the Sukatta Bel was directly opposite Tolu and the cannons on both vessels fired. Elise concentrated on deflecting the attack, but the Sukatta Bel carried a dozen guns on its port side, and a dozen cannon balls were fired at point blank range. She and Marion did not have time to deflect them all. She concentrated on the four which would have hit the Tolu on the bow end, holing her near the water line, ignoring those she felt would pass above the deck. Marion took the stern end. She reached out with her were-sight and pushed on the approaching iron balls, forcing them down into the water. Then there was an awful crack as one of the cannon balls Elise had ignored struck the foremast and toppled it. The mast fell across the starboard bow and into the sea, but it was still attached to the ship by the rigging. The Tolu lost way as the unwieldy mass blocked the deck and dragged in the water, turning her stern toward the next Senangan ship, the Kanakar.

"Clear the rigging," Arrai Carthen cried. "Cut it free." The hands swarmed over the mass of wreckage, but there was no time to free the Tolu before the next Senangan vessel bore down on them.

The Kanakar fired its broadside into the Tolu and passed on. Again, Elise and Marion could only deflect some of the cannon balls, but, fortunately, this time, the ones they missed passed through the rigging doing only minor damage. Elise shook her head, trying to clear it, her ears ringing from the blast and her sinuses burning with of the acrid smell of gunpowder.

The crew were still cutting away at the foremast. Elise and Marion went to help, but the mast was tangled in the rigging and every line had to be cut. The crewmen were using axes, but that took time and Cinhai bore down relentlessly.

Then the Cinhai passed at point blank range off the Tolu's stern, firing yet another broadside into the crippled ship. Again, Elise and Marion tried to deflect the most dangerous of the cannon balls, but they missed the one that struck the stern, disabling the rudder.

Jerevan lay in his cabin, straining his were-sight to watch the battle. Periodically, Myrriden would link with him and Balen to draw from their energy, but otherwise he felt helpless as the battle waged around him.

Seeing any distance through the wooden side of the Cyring was still difficult for Jerevan, but he made out the crippling of the Tolu. Then the Sukatta Bel was broadside to the Cyring and he lent his strength to Myrriden's efforts to deflect the attack, noting that the Sukatta Bel had not come away from its meeting with the Tolu unscathed. The Tolu's cannon had scored at least two holes in the Senangan barkentine's side near the water line, and the Cyring scored another hit before the Senangan vessel sailed out of range.

Myrriden, with his and Balen's help, succeeded in warding off damage from the Sukatta Bel, but then the Kanakar bore down on them, and the Kanakar was undamaged. Again, Jerevan lent his will to the defense. This time, however, a shot got through, putting a hole in the Cyring on the water line near the port bow.

The Cyring, however, struck back and its broadside did severe damage to the Senangan vessel, causing at least three holes.

Jerevan heard crewmen running past his cabin to man the pumps as Cinhai bore down on them. He helped Myrriden deflect more cannon balls. Another got through, putting a hole in the stern. Jerevan heard a cracking sound and the whole ship lurched. He focused his were-sight above and saw that the mainmast had been hit and had fallen, fouling the mizzen mast.

Elise watched as the Cyring was hit harder than the Tolu had been. She and Marion left the crew to cut away the remains of the wreckage of the foremast and worked at repairing the rudder and the cables that controlled it.

The Cyring floundered in the water as the Senangan ships came about for another pass. The Sukatta Bel put another minor hole in the Cyring's side and advanced toward the Tolu.

Elise felt the ship lurch as the last of the wreckage of the foremast was cut free. Marion cried, "I got it," and finished splicing the rudder cable moments later.

Elise broadcast to Arrai Carthen, *"Rudder is working."*

The Arrai ordered hands to shift the sails of the remaining two masts and the Tolu came about, heading toward the approaching Sukatta Bel.

This time when the two ships were broadside to each other, neither managed to inflict significant damage. Marion and Elise had improved at deflecting the cannon balls, and apparently some wizard on the Senangan crew had also improved.

The Kanakar's second pass by the Cyring also inflicted only minor damage as Myrriden, Balen and Jerevan's defense held, but the Cyring was rolling, crippled in the sea and unable to respond offensively.

Elise felt her head beginning to ache from stretching her will, but the Kanakar approached inexorably. She was sweating, despite the cool breeze that filled the sails. The feel of the ship cutting through the sea and the sound of the water against the hull seemed almost unreal in their normality in the midst of a battle. She looked around and noticed that the top rim of the sun had cleared the horizon and that the eastern sky was pink.

Then the Kanakar came abreast of the Tolu and both ships fired at point blank range. Elise concentrated on focusing her sight yet again and deflecting the attack. Practice had improved her technique, but her mind ached from the strain. Some of the Kanakar's guns had been filled with grape shot. She could do nothing about it except shield herself. She fought the last cannon ball aimed at the Tolu's side down into the water, and heard the sounds of screaming as shot swept across the exposed deck. Then the Kanakar was past, with two new holes in her side and Elise turned with Marion to help the wounded.

"We got her that time," Arrai Carthen called out. "She can't bail fast enough to keep up with those holes. She's listing already. She'll go down."

Two out of three, Elise thought, but the Cyring's crippled. There was a dead man on the deck in front of her. She ignored him, and sought for one of the wounded. She could not help the dead. Another crewman, or woman in this case, she noted, with a bloody gash across her thigh limped up to her. She reached out with her sight and her will and closed the wound. The healing would need to be completed later, but she had stopped the blood flow so the woman would get no worse.

She gave emergency treatment to seven others before Marion summoned her, *"The Cinhai is coming. The Cyring is sinking. We have to inflict damage this time, or we'll go down too."*

Elise pulled herself back to her feet from where she had been kneeling by a wounded crewman. The world smelled of blood and gunpowder. She wondered suddenly where Errin was, what he was doing at that moment. The sky was paling to blue above her, and she heard a gull cry overhead.

She stood by Marion as the Cinhai came abreast and the two ships fired broadsides at each other. Again she estimated trajectories and stopped her half of the cannon balls aimed to cause severe damage, despite the fact that her head was one blinding ache. Then she passed out.

JEREVAN EXTENDED HIS WERE-SIGHT AGAIN to watch the Cinhai bear down on the crippled Cyring. Crewmen labored at the pumps, but he could hear water rising in the bilge underneath him despite their efforts. Other crewmen cut away at the wreckage of the mainsail, trying to clear the mizzen mast and sails. He wished desperately that he were capable of climbing up to the main deck and helping, but he did not dare leave his cabin. He might block the passage of someone needing to get by. And even if he went out into the passageway, he could not climb the ladder to the deck.

The Cinhai came abreast of the Cyring and Jerevan linked again with Myrriden and Balen to deflect the Senangan attack. His head ached with the strain, but they deflected most of the cannon balls. Only one seemed to have been fired with extra power. It drove through their barrier, striking the Cyring amidships at the water line. More water began to flow underneath him. Jerevan felt the ship list to port.

He realized suddenly that he would be trapped in his cabin if the ship went down. *"Can you get me back up on deck,"* he asked Myrriden. *"The ship's taking in water. I think it's going to sink."*

"I'll get some crewmen to hoist you up," Myrriden answered. *"Wait until I call you."*

"I'll wait," Jerevan thought, but he got up off the bed. The mental effort had stimulated his appetite and it was nearly time for his next meal anyway. He opened the chest where Otto kept food and began to eat. If the ship went down, there was no telling when he might get another chance and he did not want his stomach to cramp when his life might depend on his being able to function.

He ate enough to make his stomach feel tight before receiving Balen's thought, *"We've got the hoist ready. Come as quickly as you can."*

MARION WATCHED AS THE CINHAI HOVE to near the sinking Kanakar, sending out boats to rescue the other Senangan ship's crew. The Sukatta Bel came about again. Elise had passed out from exhaustion. Marion was almost as tired, but in a strange way the exertion felt good. She was doing things she hadn't done since before she had been capped, things she hadn't been able to do since that time. She felt stronger for the effort.

The sun cleared the horizon. The sky was a cloudless blue. The wind had died down but still blew from the east. The Cyring had developed a definite list to port. She would sink. The Tolu was closing on her sister ship to take off the crew.

Marion took all this in as she cleaned and healed a splinter wound in the side of another crewman. Blood stained the simple shirt and pants she wore. She had put a coil of rope under Elise's head and covered her with a blanket.

The Tolu hove to one hundred meters off her sister ship's starboard bow. The Cyring was now listing badly, obviously about to sink. Arrai Carthen ordered out the boats to take off survivors. Cyring's boats had already been lowered and were filling with crewmen.

She looked back at the Senangan ships and saw that the Sukatta Bel had not stopped by the Kanakar to help the Cinhai rescue the surviving crew.

The Senangan ship was heading right for the gap between the Tolu and the Cyring.

Arrai Carthen ordered the crew to man the port guns once again, but having come up into the wind the angle of the guns was bad. What worried Marion more were the boats filled with the Cyring's crew dotting the water. She watched the oarsmen rowing frantically for the Tolu, but several of the boats weren't going to make it.

Cyring jerked and settled lower in the water. She saw Myrriden, Balen and a number of the crewmen jump over the side. Where was Jerevan? Then she saw him near the bow of the ship.

"Jump," she thought to him.

Then the Sukatta Bel was close off the Tolu's stern and Marion was again warding off cannon balls. Without Elise there were just too many to block. She figured trajectories frantically to ward off the most dangerous.

The Tolu took two hits, but both were above the water line. When the Senangan ship had passed, Marion looked for the boats that had been at risk. Three of them had sunk and the Cyring had gone down.

Arrai Carthen ordered the boats from the Tolu to rescue survivors. Marion watched the Senangan vessel, but it did not change course to come about again. Instead it sailed southwest toward the distant line of the islands of the Dalossian Archipelago. She checked with her far-sight and saw that the Sukatta Bel was damaged and taking on water, but that act took the last of her energy. She sank down on the deck.

JEREVAN CLIMBED TO HIS FEET ON THE DECK of the Cyring as the net collapsed around him. Boats were being lowered and crewmen were going over the sides into them. As he stood there, the deck beneath his feet heaved, and the ship sank further into the water.

"You all right?" Balen thought.

"Yes," Jerevan responded, *"but I'd nearly fill one of those boats all by myself. I'll have to swim."*

"Good idea. Myrriden's already aboard one of the boats and I'll be on the next one."

Jerevan grunted and headed for the bow, the highest point. His head ached. He did not feel up to using his sight any more, but he wanted to know what was going on.

He saw the Sukatta Bel heading for the gap between the sinking Cyring and the Tolu. *"You'd better be careful,"* he thought, projecting the image of the Senangan ship to Balen, already aboard one of the boats. *"Those boats don't look safe."*

Balen's thought came back to him, *"Maera's mercy! I thought both Senangan ships had stopped to rescue the crewmen from the Kanakar."*

The Cyring lurched again and started to slide down into the water.

Jerevan realized the time had come to leave the ship, or he might be pulled down with it when it sank. He crossed the deck to the side of the ship, but jumping over the railing was not an option for him. He looked around for something he could stand on and finally found a roll of rope that gave him enough lift to enable him to climb over the side. The water closed over him and he swam as hard as he could, away from the ship.

He struggled back to the surface to take a breath and felt the water swirling, dragging at him, pulling him back down. The Cyring was sinking and the waters wanted to drag everything else down after her, but despite the downward pull Jerevan found he could stay afloat if he swam hard. His fat was lighter than water, giving him buoyancy.

He swam on, fighting to escape the whirlpool effect created by the sinking ship, hardly noticing the direction he took. A long time seemed to pass before the drag lessened and he had a chance to look around, sculling to keep himself upright. He could not see any of the Cyring's boats, but the Senangan vessel was bearing down on him rapidly. He tried to swim out of its way.

While his mass made him buoyant, it also slowed his speed through the water. Still, he had almost made it clear of the oncoming Sukatta Bel when he felt a net thrown over him. He tried to dive, but his buoyancy interfered. The net closed. He was hoisted up to the deck of the Senangan pirate ship.

XXXVI

4655, 466TH CYCLE OF THE YEAR OF THE DOLPHIN
MONTHS OF ANOR AND TORIN

Nikta sav po rem, remso e jentay.
Nikta ba asav a tan.

Great pain can eat thought, memory and honor.
Agony is the eater of souls.

— ESLARIN PROVERB

MARION GLARED AT MYRRIDEN. "How could you lose track of him?"

"I'm not comfortable aboard a ship at the best of times," Myrriden said gruffly. "I made sure Balen got him out of his cabin and up on deck before the ship sank."

"Nevertheless, when it sank, you lost him," she said.

"I thought he was with Balen," Myrriden said. "The Sukatta Bel came between us. The Senangans must have fished him out of the sea."

"The Sukatta Bel took a lot of damage," Balen said. "Her arrai will have taken her back into the Archipelago for repairs. If Jerevan's a prisoner, he'll be on one of those islands."

"There's no way we can search the whole Archipelago with only one ship, and the Tolu's damaged as well," Marion said.

"The crew will have rigged a new foremast by the end of the day," Balen said.

"The Cinhai's beyond our reach in any event," Marion said, "which means Saranith will remain the bearer of Cinkarion. We need to warn everyone in Cibata, Maera guard them. I hate to think what this means to Cassinga."

"She has no control at this point," Myrriden said. "It will take her time to gain enough to become a major factor. Maybe we'll get another chance at her before that happens.

"In the meantime," he added, "we need to find Jerevan. And we don't need to check each island physically. We should be able to plot a route that will bring us close enough to every island to far-see for the Sukatta Bel. Why don't one of you ask Arrai Carthen for a map?"

The Arrai, however, when informed of this plan, said that he had no intention of sailing back through the islands. "The Dalossian Archipelago belongs to Ravaar," he said. "If the Tolu is caught in those waters by a ship of Ravaar, it will attack immediately, no questions asked. My ship cannot

250

survive another sea battle before undergoing extensive repairs. We've lost the ship the Tolu was commandeered to pursue. It's my duty now to return to Sussey."

JEREVAN LAY SPREAD-EAGLED ON THE SAND above the high tide line, his hands and feet tied to short posts, his head aching in a silvery cap. He was barefoot, but the Senangans had not removed his pants or shirt. He had lost the suspenders that kept his pants up, however, and his shirt had come unbuttoned, exposing a vast expanse of naked flesh.

He fixed his eyes on a hawk soaring above the trees on an inland hill, and fought to ignore the pain in his belly. It had been nearly six hours since his last meal, the one he had eaten in his cabin while the battle raged around him. Time equaled hunger to his body, so his stomach muscles were cramping. His curse made no allowances for imprisonment or the danger of death. At least, he reflected, he was unlikely to suffer from the heat. Hunger would drive him into a coma long before the sun could hurt him.

Aketi Kamrasi, the arrai of the Senangan ship that had taken him, arrived to view his captive when the sun had reached its zenith. Jerevan knew from the conversation of the sailors that the arrai had commanded the linlarin ship be beached in this cove, on an island somewhere in the Dalossian Archipelago, in order to repair damage received during the battle.

"Agnith's fires! Since when have pirates grown to the size of whales?" Aketi exclaimed. His Eskh was strangely accented, but Jerevan understood him as well as he had understood the sailors.

He shifted his eyes from the hawk to the linlar. He was breathing in short pants, trying to control the pain of the cramping, but he managed to say, "I'm not a pirate." The Senangan arrai had the striped black and cream hair typical of the linlarin, and amber eyes, bright with curiosity. Jerevan expected to die, and found the idea a relief, compared to being at a linlar's mercy.

"You have a tongue? Perhaps you can tell me why there were so many human wizards aboard naval ships from Sussey? And why you were so anxious to capture my cousin's ship?"

Jerevan was silent.

"We'll see if you get more talkative when you've cooked a little longer in the heat. We torture pirates in Senanga."

Jerevan closed his eyes and clenched his jaw as a massive cramp gripped his stomach.

"What's causing the cramps?" Aketi demanded. He turned to the officer at his side. "Gatek, you didn't allow him to take poison, did you?"

"No, rai," Gatek said. "We searched him and tied him up right after you capped him, and you did that the moment we fished him out of the sea. He hasn't taken anything."

Jerevan's stomach cramped again, more violently. He gritted his teeth and panted to ride out the pain. At least he would lose consciousness soon. Then it would be over.

Aketi kicked him. "I asked what caused the cramps, pirate."

"Burn in Agnith's fires."

Aketi laughed. "Oh, no. It's you who'll burn after a few more hours in the sun."

Jerevan shut his eyes again as a new wave of cramps tore through him.

"What would cause stomach cramps, if he hasn't taken poison?" Aketi asked. Even through his pain, Jerevan felt the intensity of the linlar's curiosity. He preferred death to having his condition exposed.

"I suffer . . . from a rare . . . disease," Jerevan said, forcing the words out between spasms.

"No. You wouldn't have been aboard that ship if you were sick." Aketi paused, watching him. "You're so fat. It must have taken a lot of food to get you to that size. Are you hungry, pirate?"

Jerevan tried to repress the rush of saliva the question stimulated, but he had no more control over that than he did over the cramps. He had to swallow or choke. Aketi would notice either alternative. He swallowed.

"How amusing. Your body answers, even when you're too stubborn." Aketi laughed and turned to the guards. "Untie him and take him to my tent." He turned to his second officer. "Gatek, have one of the men fetch some food."

Jerevan felt himself partially lifted then dragged. It took four burly crewmen, but the pain in his stomach monopolized his attention. He was almost unconscious by the time they reached Aketi's luxurious pavilion and the guards heaved him up and dropped him on a carpet.

"Tie him up on the bed," Aketi said.

Jerevan felt himself lifted by his arms and feet and hoisted onto the bed on his back. Then his wrists and ankles were tied to the bed posts. Through a haze of pain he saw a table laden with food pulled up next to him. The sight and scent of it flooded his mouth with saliva, and he choked.

"Feed him some fruit," Aketi said. "We'll see if food is the key."

Jerevan's felt someone pry his mouth open and shove in a section of cotulume. He chewed and swallowed convulsively and another piece was stuffed in. He tried to turn his head away, but a guard held him still and he could not stop himself from swallowing the food put in his mouth.

After a time he could not remember why he had wanted to stop. The food filled the gaping void at the center of his existence. All he could think of was the next bite, and the next. Even when the cramps ceased, hunger dominated him. He ate.

He did not regain full consciousness until the food stopped coming. He opened his eyes. Aketi watched him, stretched out on a low divan. "I see now how you grew so fat." The Senangan grinned. "How much does it take to fill you?"

Jerevan swallowed, realizing how totally his weakness had been exposed. Along with the urgent claw of hunger, he felt nausea. Cats enjoyed playing with their prey.

"You were about to tell me why you and your friends were so anxious to catch my cousin's ship, weren't you?"

Jerevan stared at him.

"How long before the cramps start again?"

Jerevan shut his eyes, praying that his body, for once, might not betray him.

"I think I'll wait and watch for a while," Aketi said.

As Jerevan's stomach had only received enough to stop the cramps, it took fifteen minutes before another rippled across the mass of his exposed stomach.

Aketi's eyes widened. "That was fast. I wonder how long it takes before you lose consciousness?"

Jerevan swallowed convulsively.

Aketi dangled a section of fruit in front of Jerevan's face and watched his belly spasm again.

"You know, I'm bound to find out what Saranith did, or what she took. I mean, we're both Senangan, and I'm her cousin, as well. It's not as though something the linlarin have stolen can be such a big secret."

Jerevan concentrated on remembering The Laws, line by line.

The cramps grew more violent and Aketi stimulated them by dangling pieces of food in front of Jerevan. Every once in a while he fed him a scrap.

Jerevan's world consisted only of the pain in his stomach, until finally he passed out.

He regained consciousness when the flow of oatmeal gruel stopped and nothing replaced it. He felt dazed and disoriented, his hunger dominating his mind, but the cramping had eased.

Aketi asked, "If I allow your hands to be untied, can you feed yourself?"

"Yes," Jerevan said. It was too late for pretense. He would have liked to be able to refuse the food, but if he did, the cramping would only intensify again. As it was, the food on the table would not come close to filling him.

Aketi gestured and one of the crewmen came over and cut the ropes binding Jerevan's hands. Jerevan reached out and ate, hoping that, when Aketi's curiosity was satisfied, he would return to his original plan and put Jerevan to death.

When Jerevan had finished every fragment of the food Aketi provided, he leaned back and massaged his sore stomach, aware of Aketi's intent gaze and that, with the cap on, he could no longer heal his strained muscles or any of the other physical problems his obesity caused.

"Even that didn't fill you," the linlar said. "Guard, bring more food. At least the former amount over again." He turned back to Jerevan. "I'm going to see how much it takes."

Jerevan swallowed the rush of saliva that filled his mouth at the thought of food, aware that the tell-tale working of his throat did not escape Aketi's eye. Never before had his helplessness been more apparent.

When the food came, he ate until his stomach was full. "I've finished."

Aketi nodded. "An impressive performance. How long before you have to repeat it?"

Jerevan hesitated.

Aketi chuckled. "Don't try to lie. It's not something you can keep secret, after all. No matter how hard you try, your body will betray you." The chuckle grew to a roar of laughter and Aketi rocked back and forth on the couch, pounding his thigh. "I've never met a slave like you. You have your own built-in torture system."

Jerevan flinched, hating the linlar, but hating his own body more, and Derwen who had cursed him to become what he was. "Two to three hours," he said.

Aketi sobered, his eyes widening. "You'll need to eat like that again in two hours?"

"No," Jerevan said. "After a fast and gorging as I just did, I'll need to eat again in two hours. Normally, if I eat regularly I don't need to eat that much at any one meal and I can go three hours between meals."

"How long did it take you to get hungry enough to eat as you've just done?"

"Six hours."

Aketi nodded, then turned to the guard. "Tie him up in one of the spare tents with a couple of guards outside. Tell Gatek I want him back in six hours." He turned to Jerevan. "After all, I'm keeping you for your entertainment value. Watching you eat regularly wouldn't entertain me, would it?" He giggled.

As Jerevan's stomach had already been stretched, the cramping started up after only five hours. He was almost unconscious by the time he was dragged before Aketi and tied up on the bed again.

Two of the crewmen helped shovel food into him until the cramping ceased. Aketi studied him as his awareness slowly returned after they stopped feeding him. "About how many pounds do you gain each time you gorge like that?"

Jerevan stared at the ceiling.

"All this food was weighed before you were brought in. I'll weigh what's left when you're full. I should be able to estimate the answer fairly accurately. Of course, your body disposes of a great deal as waste, but we can measure that as well. I'd guess though, that for every four pounds of food, and you went through easily that much your last meal, you must gain at least two pounds of permanent fat. Am I wrong?"

"No," Jerevan said, despising his tormentor, but Aketi obviously had wizard talent and his estimate agreed roughly with Jerevan's experience.

There was no point in denying something Aketi could prove with no trouble.

"How much do you gain when you're allowed to eat regularly?"

"Without the cap and given a proper diet, I'd got it down to about four or five pounds a month."

"Even with the cap on, you probably wouldn't gain more than ten to fifteen then, if I fed you regularly."

Jerevan met the linlar's eyes, "If you fed me regularly with a diet heavy in roughage."

Aketi nodded. "Now, I might be prepared to do that, if you cooperate with me."

Jerevan studied the linlar captain. Aketi was just over medium height and his features were well formed. He did not look to be very old, however, and there were already marks of dissipation on his face, a slackness to his jaw. Jerevan also noted the glinting excitement in his amber eyes. "No."

Aketi smiled. "Untie his hands," he said to one of his crewmen. When Jerevan's hands were free, Aketi said, "Go ahead and eat. I enjoy watching you add to your notable proportions. I'd like to know who worked out such a unique torture. I've examined your metabolism. I think I can duplicate the effect. The beauty of it is that I could do the damage and be gone before the victim even knew anything had been done to him. He might never find out who placed the curse. And if he never knew who placed it, he'd never know who to fight to remove it. Of course, if he were a stronger wizard than I am, he might eventually simply break the effect by the strength of his will, which could hurt me." Aketi frowned, then brightened. "But he'd have to be stronger than I am to do so. Not many are."

Jerevan rolled onto his side so he could reach the table and started to eat. He didn't believe Aketi was as strong a wizard as his boasting implied. Development in wizardry, he had discovered, required self-discipline, a quality he did not think Aketi possessed. Aketi struck him as a spoiled and twisted child. He only prayed that the linlar captain would prove to have a child's short attention span and would tire of playing with him quickly.

In the days that followed, Aketi's enjoyment of Jerevan's condition showed no sign of abating. While he experimented with different fast periods, he rarely fed Jerevan until the cramps were well in evidence. As a result, every meal stretched Jerevan's stomach to new dimensions. Moreover, with the cap on, he could do nothing about healing himself. Within days his clothes were too tight and he could no longer do up the buttons on his pants or shirt.

At the end of a week, after a fast of almost seven hours and a nightmarish period of gorging, his pants split in the seat. Two days later his shirt split down the back.

It took the crew ten days to repair Aketi's ship. During that time Jerevan was kept in a tent on the shore between feedings. However, once back at sea, Aketi had him chained by his ankles on the deck where he could be an object of amusement to the whole crew. A sail was rigged over him for shade, but even with that protection his tender skin, already overstretched, added sunburn to his problems.

Aketi did begin to feed him more regularly, however. "You're going through my stores too rapidly," he commented, eyeing Jerevan's increasingly inadequate rags. "I wish I could take you back to Senanga, but this is a military ship; we don't carry sufficient provisions. But I know where to trade you. I'll restock my supplies, and know you're being appreciated." He laughed.

XXXVII

4655, 466TH CYCLE OF THE YEAR OF THE DOLPHIN
MONTH OF TORIN

Nikta so jecainin win. Quen nalor et ahenilan esamin camio ba esamend nik a remla.

Pain takes many forms. For the wizard or torturer, the most useful is often mental pain.

— EXCERPT FROM THE WRITINGS OF WIZARD RAV

JEREVAN STUDIED THE SHORELINE as the Senangan ship sailed into a large, busy harbor. His position on the deck gave him an unobstructed view, but the harbor was not one he recognized. The Sukatta Bel had sailed northeast since they left the islands and had entered a deep bay. The port should belong to either Khorat or Ravaar, he thought, remembering a childhood study of geography. He tried to make out the flags above the buildings on shore, but without the sight the cap denied him, they were too far away.

Aketi, however, sailed the Sukatta Bel in close to the shore before dropping anchor. The flag flying over the building that dominated the shore line was black, with the symbol of a red eye in the center. Ravaar. Jerevan winced, realizing he should have expected Aketi's destination. Where else, other than Gandahar, would a Senangan pirate ship be welcome?

The next day, after Jerevan's morning feeding, Aketi went ashore with instructions that Jerevan not be fed until he returned. Jerevan was in agony from the cramping when Aketi arrived back on board with three men, who looked like local officials.

"You see his pain," Aketi said to the newcomers. "His own body punishes him with no effort on your part. All you have to do is withhold food for a few hours. But the subtle part of the torture is that it hurts him to eat, also. That pain is mental, not physical, but to men with sophisticated tastes, such as ourselves, that makes it more enjoyable. You see, the more he has to eat to stop the pain, the fatter he gets. The fatter he gets, the more helpless he becomes. Once, he was a proud wizard. Now, his inability to control his own body shames him."

Aketi turned to one of the crewmen. "Bring him his food now, so my guests can watch him eat."

The three men gaped at Jerevan. One, of medium height but plump, said, "He's as big as a whale now. How much does he eat?"

"That depends," Aketi said. "You see how his stomach is cramping. He hasn't been fed since early this morning. The longer you wait after the cramping starts, the worse it gets, and the more he has to eat."

Food was brought and put where Jerevan could reach it. He wished he could refuse it, but if he did he would lapse into unconsciousness and then Aketi would have the crewmen feed him until he regained enough consciousness to feed himself. Coming out of a hunger induced coma, he would have no control at all, and would eat until he could hold no more before regaining full awareness, an aspect of his curse he had not encountered before becoming Aketi's prisoner. He could see from Aketi's expression that Aketi hoped he would try to rebel. Jerevan pulled the nearest plate closer and started to eat.

When Jerevan had finished, another of the Ravaarans, a short, balding man, said, "I won't bid. I couldn't afford to feed him."

The tallest of the three, a huge, burly, black haired man, said, "I'll restock your ship to a value of one hundred rinin. When I get bored with him, I can resell him to a carnival." He laughed.

The man who had spoken first said, "I'll let you have him, Morogo. My wife wouldn't appreciate the entertainment."

Aketi undid Jerevan's chains and had him hoisted over the side and dumped at Morogo's feet in the boat that had brought them from the shore. "I assure you, my friend, he'll provide you with months of entertainment."

"What happens if I don't feed him at all?" Morogo asked.

"First he passes out," Aketi said, "then I presume he dies. I did let him pass out a few times. He has no control at all then, which is amusing on occasion. On the other hand, he's hardly conscious so he doesn't suffer as much and it's too much, trouble stuffing food in him. The fun comes from watching him eat, knowing he hates every bite, but can't help himself."

Morogo grunted. "Your supplies will be delivered in the morning. If nothing else, just looking at him will give my men a laugh."

Jerevan lay in the bottom of the boat until they reached the shore and the boat was tied up at a pier.

Morogo kicked Jerevan. "Get up," he said.

Jerevan lay still.

Morogo called to several men standing on the dock. "Stand him up."

Four men came over and hauled Jerevan out of the boat and onto his feet.

"Load him into the back of my wagon. Two of you can guard him. I'll take him home tonight. He's just eaten. He'll keep til dinnertime."

"I'll need sanitary facilities," Jerevan said.

Morogo looked at him and laughed. "You eat like an animal, you'll shit like one." He turned to one of the men. "Put some straw in the bottom of the wagon. It'll be easier to clean out."

"Yes, rai," the man said.

Jerevan spent the rest of the afternoon in the back of the wagon. At least there had been a couple of sacks of grain to use as a backrest and the vehicle was parked in the shade. Still, his stomach muscles ached and his body was covered with sores from chafing and sunburn. The cap felt like a vise around his head, blinding him. He felt around the edge where it sank under his skin for at least the thousandth time, but there was no way he could remove it. It was embedded into the bones of his skull, and bonded to them.

He looked down at his bloated body and wondered how much he had gained in the weeks since his capture. He also wondered how long he would survive without the ability to heal the damage his obesity caused. Perhaps Myrriden and the others would find him in time to rescue him, but he doubted if they would think to look in Ravaar.

That evening two more of Morogo's men brought out a team of horses and hitched them to the wagon, relieving Jerevan's guards. One of them drove the wagon around to the front of the building. Morogo came out and climbed on the seat in front with his men, and the wagon proceeded north through the town of Ravach into the farm country surrounding it. After an hour, the wagon turned off the main road onto a drive leading to a large house and an extensive series of outbuildings and small houses, almost a little village. Jerevan remembered that in the nations of the Zamargan Peninsula and further south, such estates were called haciendas. The wagon proceeded through a gateway and halted in a paved courtyard between the main house and a large barn.

"Unload him, then see to the horses. When you're finished, bring him into the hall," Morogo said, jumping down from the wagon and heading toward the house.

Morogo disappeared. It was dark, the sunset only a faint lightening to the west. Jerevan decided this was the best opportunity he would have to escape. Only two men guarded him, and he accounted for more than triple their weight. So when they climbed into the wagon bed and tried to heave him to his feet, Jerevan stood and swung his arms around into the man on his right, knocking him backwards out of the wagon. Then he swung around and tried to do the same to the man on the left.

The second man was too quick. He ducked under Jerevan's swing and rammed Jerevan's legs, behind his knees. Jerevan toppled but managed to twist so that he landed on his opponent. The man's head hit the wagon bed and he stilled, unconscious.

Jerevan's breath had been knocked out of him by the fall and his stomach was starting to cramp. It took several moments before he managed to roll over and sit up again. He looked over the side of the wagon, but the man he had knocked over backwards had also landed on his head on the stone paving and appeared to be unconscious.

Jerevan maneuvered to the rear of the wagon and pushed himself off the end onto his feet. He looked around. No one was in sight, but he would not get far on foot. He went round to the front of the wagon. It took him several difficult moments to hoist himself onto the seat, but he managed.

Then he took up the reins and urged the horses forward and in a circle, heading them back down the drive. They tried to balk when they realized they were not on the way to the barn, but he slapped the reins across their backs and they set off again.

At the main road he turned the horses away from the town and urged them into a trot as another cramp contracted his stomach. He panted to ride out the pain. Time passed. Somehow he kept the horses moving, alternating between a trot and a walk, until he came to a place where the fields on either side of the road ended and trees began.

By that time, the cramps were continuous, but he turned the wagon around and climbed down off the seat.

The man in the back was still unconscious. Jerevan slapped the lead horse across its rump and the team headed back to their barn. Then he turned and staggered away from the road into the trees, praying he could get far enough away that Morogo would not find him before his condition killed him. His only regret was that he would now never be able to repay Derwen. Although he fell down several times with the violence of the cramps, he managed to keep going for almost another hour before he lost consciousness.

There existed only a vast hollowness. A trickle came. He swallowed and swallowed. He did not remember who he was or where he was, only that he craved food. When food was placed in his hands he ate. When the food stopped, he opened his eyes and reached for it. He ate, but it took forever before the hollow emptiness began to fill. His awareness of self came back to him slowly as his stomach stretched to satiety. He gulped down the last of a huge bowl of what tasted like some sort of porridge and realized his belly was painfully stretched and he could eat no more.

Conscious again, he looked around and saw that he sat on a stone floor in a large hall, surrounded by the remains of an enormous quantity of food: empty bowls and pie tins, the bones of joints of meat and the carcasses of several fowl, fruit cores and rinds, even an empty milk pail lay scattered around him. Chains attached to his wrists and ankles connected to rings set into the stone wall. Morogo and several others sat at a table nearby. They watched him with various expressions of horror and fascination.

"So you're conscious again," Morogo said. "You injured two of my men. That was foolish. You should have known you couldn't escape."

Jerevan said nothing. He had failed. He doubted that Morogo would give him a second chance.

XXXVIII

4655, 466TH CYCLE OF THE YEAR OF THE DOLPHIN
MONTHS OF AGNITH TO MINNETH

The sea gnaws down, one wave at a time,
Great cliffs of stone, one wave at a time.

And boulders vast, one wave at a time,
Wear down to sand, one wave at a time.

The sea rolls in, one wave at a time,
And slips back out, one wave at a time.

But with each wave, one wave at a time,
It carves the land, one wave at a time.

And so I'll ride, one wave at a time,
The ebb tide out, one wave at a time.

And with the stones, one wave at a time,
It will grind my bones, one wave at a time.

— UNTITLED SONG WRITTEN BY GAREL MARDEK, A POPULAR FOLK SINGER FROM THE
OUTER ISLANDS OF ILWHEIRLANE, HOURS BEFORE HIS DEATH BY DROWNING.

ERRIN STOOD WITH DEL MARAN, soon to be the Wizard Arrun, in the bow
of the Gallinule as it sailed into the harbor of Ninkarrak, late in Agnith.
Some thirty people stood on the pier, waiting for the ship to dock.

"Which one is your father?" Errin asked.

"The tall one in the green coat with the beaky nose and the unruly mop of
silver hair," Del said. "Oh, Tarat's temper, he's got Derwen with him."

"The paunchy one in brown with the salt and pepper hair?"

"That's Derwen."

The gangplank was extended and Del and Errin debarked to the dock. Del
and his father hugged each other. "I've missed you," Orris said.

"Glad I could get back," Del said. "Being elevated to full wizard is an
occasion I wanted to share."

Orris eyed his son carefully, "But you won't stay?"

"No."

Derwen broke into the silence between father and son. "Del, it's good to
see you again."

"Derwen," Del inclined his head. "I don't believe either of you have met Errin Pomorry." He turned to Errin. "Errin, Wizard Derwen and my father, Orris Maran, Lanrai of Luro."

Derwen's eyes went to Errin. Errin felt his evaluation, and his shock when he detected Lyskarion. "I'm," Derwen hesitated, "pleased to make your acquaintance," he said finally. "Jao spoke of you on several occasions. She didn't mention what you carry."

"While my cousin's alive, what I carry is supposed to remain a secret," Errin said. "Although, I admit, it's not a well kept one."

"It would be difficult, if not impossible, to conceal such a thing among wizards," Derwen said. "Will you announce your elevation to the status of full wizard at the same time as Del?"

Errin shook his head. "I can't accept such acknowledgment while Antram is Ahar of Sussey without betraying what he did. I don't need the formal recognition. I won't change my name."

"Except from Pomorry to Anifi," Del said, "and that's out of your control."

Derwen turned back to Del and Errin saw an almost hungry look in his eyes. "I hear you've had a great deal of success in Cibata. You must tell me about your campaigns now that you've returned. I'm glad you've progressed so rapidly, almost as rapidly as Cormor himself."

"I'll be happy to give you a blow by blow description," Del said, "but it's been a long trip. Errin and I would like to get cleaned up and rested first."

"Of course," Orris said. "Let's get you both back to the hotel. I reserved rooms for you, as Derwen said you instructed. A handy thing, the telepathic relay from Nacaonne to Ilwheirlane the Varfarin maintains. If you'll tell me the location of your cabin, I'll have my man load your luggage on the carriage."

"The third cabin on the port side," Del said.

Orris nodded and disappeared into the crowd.

Errin studied Derwen for a moment, then asked, "What news do you have from Sussey since I've been gone?"

Derwen frowned. "You were acquainted with Jerevan Rayne, weren't you?"

"I know him," Errin said, startled by the tense Derwen used. "He's been staying at my home in Ruffin for several years. Why?"

Derwen's eyes narrowed on Errin. "Wearing Lyskarion, you must be aware that Cinkarion chose a bearer."

Errin nodded. "I felt the linkage form back in Anor. I was shocked when Del identified the bearer as Saranith Kamrasi."

"We all were," Derwen said. "Myrriden and Marion tried to stop Saranith from leaving the Thallassean. Antram lent them two ships from Sussey's navy and they chased her more than halfway to the Straits of Belarrai." He sighed, and Errin realized he was very old, and had not been maintaining himself well for a long time. "Unfortunately, they took Jerevan with them."

"Anyway," Derwen continued, "one of the ships sank in the ensuing sea battle. Jerevan was either drowned or taken prisoner by the Senangans."

"I don't believe he could have drowned," Errin said. "He was a good swimmer, and his fat made him buoyant."

He felt a surge of emotion from Derwen at his mention of Jerevan's obesity, a mixture of guilt and something like satisfaction. Derwen, of course, had placed the curse. Errin remembered Elise's question as to whether he could remove it and made his own evaluation of the Esalfar of the Varfarin.

Yes, he decided, he could break Derwen's curse, but Derwen was frail. Such an attempt from anyone other than Jerevan would cause Derwen's death.

Orris returned and led them out to the street where his carriage waited. Once they were all seated, Del said to Derwen, "Errin also has a request to make of Vanda. I told him I thought you could arrange an interview for him, a quick, private one."

Derwen frowned, looking back and forth between Errin and Del. "What is the request?"

Errin said, "Actually it is Varfarin business, although, since our capture in the fall of Nadrum, Rand and I have made it something of a personal crusade. But Jao must have told you about our fears for Darenje when she petitioned Vanda?"

Derwen nodded. "Vanda gave Jao her regrets, but explained that it's physically impossible for Ilwheirlane to detect the Senangan fleet if they sail through one or two vessels at a time."

"I suspected that would be the case," Errin said, "so while I was in Cibata, I talked to members of the Varfarin. They have spies positioned to detect any large fleet movements involving the linlarin nations. However, Cassinga has no ship capable of outsailing the Senangan fleet that could be used to get the warning here. We need Ilwheirlane to supply their fastest courier ship, one capable of reaching the Thallassean ahead of the Senangan fleet."

"I'd be happy to arrange a meeting for you with Vanda," Derwen said, "were she in Ninkarrak. However, she's on one of her progresses and is not expected back until late Redri or early Ilfarnar."

"Then I'll wait until she returns," Errin said. "I'd be staying for a while, anyway, to see Del's elevation."

Del Maran became the Wizard Arrun, the Jester, on a clear, cold day in Redri, the Month of the Harvest. The ceremony was held in the garden of Cliff House, Orris Maran's home in Bria.

The leaves in the woods surrounding the estate had changed from green to yellow and brown, but the lawns and hedges were green, and flowers still colored many of the beds, late blooming chrysanthemums in orange, rust and gold, and akydethin in all the shades from blue to purple. The roar of the waves against the base of the cliff below provided background music.

Since the days of the Council of Wizards, it was customary for those achieving the rank of wizard to choose a single name they wished to be known by for the rest of their lives. While many wizards kept their own names, either first or last, others chose names they felt represented their interests, personalities or goals.

Del had chosen the name he would take years before, when Elise had referred to him as Arrun after she recognized the tricks he had played against his cousins. Much of his success in Senanga was due to subtle psychological attacks and misdirection as much as military force, and he believed his skill with such trickery represented his greatest talent. And Arrun, the Jester, was an aspect of Jehan.

Errin was surprised by the number of wizards attending. Rand he had expected, but not the blonde and beautiful Wizard Vitry, once Rand's apprentice, or the Wizards Beldeth, Basel and Astil, whom he had met while working with Rand. The albino Beldeth, particularly, he had never thought to see outside Lara, where she had lived since finishing her training under Elgan.

The Wizard Basel he remembered for his dark, cadaverous look and for the cataracts covering his eyes, a notable affectation on the part of a wizard. Basel, of course, did not need his physical eyes to see, but the cataracts would be simple for him to remove. He kept them because they reminded him of how he attained his sight, and because he had a strong belief in not altering his natural form.

Errin recognized Astil, the 'Little Worm,' an apprentice of Jao's, because his stocky build and brown hair made him look like an ingvalar, and also like Delanan.

He had not seen Wizards Melanth and Eldana since the day they witnessed his oath. He knew that they had joined the Varfarin, but, when he last heard of them, Melanth had been in Mahran and Eldana had been involved with rescuing children in the regions of Kailane controlled by the isklarin.

Still the guest Errin found most astonishing was the tall, pale figure of Wizard Minlis, the daughter and most powerful student of Wizards Kaaremin and Andamin, the bearers of Belkarion. Her size and coloring was attributed to her mother, Andamin, who was half gamlar. While Minlis, whose name meant 'Snow Cat,' was a member of the Varfarin, she acted more as a liaison between Derwen and the older, more powerful wizards. Errin had met her only once, when Minlis visited Delanan just after Errin had taken his oath.

Hulvar's presence, accompanied by Journeyman Wizard Dinara Harth, one of Derwen's apprentices, was not a surprise, but seeing him sharpened the constant ache Errin felt at being apart from Elise.

There were also many wizards Errin had never met. In fact, he had never thought to see so many wizards in one place in his life.

When Wizard Arrun had retaken the vows he had taken as an apprentice, linked with the entire circle of his peers, over fifteen wizards in all, and assumed his new name, Errin managed to get Rand aside. *"Why are close to half the members of the Varfarin in the Northern Hemisphere here?"* he thought.

"Isn't it obvious?" Rand responded. *"Derwen believes Jerevan is dead. He's decided Arrun will be the next Esalfar. We're here to look Arrun over."*

"I don't see it," Errin thought. *"Jerevan couldn't have drowned and he's too much of a curiosity for the linlarin to have killed him."*

Rand nodded. *"You're probably right, but Derwen's in a flap. He's always resented the fact that Jerevan was being trained by someone else. He knows his curse is the reason Jerevan was captured, but he wants to pass the blame off on Myrriden and Marion for putting Jerevan in danger. While consciously he may hope Jerevan is still alive, some part of him also hopes Jerevan is dead, and all the mistakes Derwen made are dead with him."*

Errin shook his head. *"I once thought I wanted to join the Varfarin. Now I'm glad Delanan kept me from doing so."*

"The Varfarin still serves a great purpose," Rand said, frowning. *"Derwen may be an imperfect tool, but we all have faults and his belief in the Varfarin's goals is as strong as anyone's. Remember that before you judge him too harshly."*

Two weeks later, Errin finally had his private meeting with Vanda Cinnac. Her sitting room reminded him forcibly of the room Aliara used for small, official events. Aliara had described the decor as 'subtle, designed to impress without calling attention to itself or giving away personal information.'

He was more impressed by the small, fair woman seated at the desk. Her aura blazed. While she had only a small amount of wizard power, he sensed another form of inner strength. There was no hesitation in his bow.

"You bear Lyskarion. You'll soon be Ahar of Sussey," Vanda said. "You have no need to bow."

"I don't bow to your position, but to you," Errin said. "Perhaps Lyskarion helps me to recognize wisdom, but I see in you qualities I admire."

Vanda smiled. "I'm just an old woman who's seen too much." She studied him for a moment, then added, "Derwen told me what you want. I've already notified Admiral Parturan to make our fastest courier ship available. If you go to the Naval Headquarters tomorrow, you may speak to the captain yourself, and give him your instructions."

"But you insisted on seeing me first?"

"I was curious," Vanda said. "You're the first wizard other than Kaaremin and Andamin to bear one of the karionin since Cormor died. You and your eventual mate will help mold the future of Tamar. I wanted to meet you, to see if I could sense from you what kind of future you'll try to build."

"The easy answer would be to say I'd like to see a future free of war," Errin said. "I am, after all, a worshiper of Jehan."

Her eyes narrowed. "But you never seek the easy path. What is the more difficult answer?"

"Tamar will never be free of war while her people stress the differences between themselves. To find peace we must all learn to look for what we have in common. But it's easy for an ingvalar of Sussey to say such a thing. My people have never fought in any war," Errin said, "but I've been to Cibata now, and I understand how difficult it will be to find common ground between Cassinga and Senanga."

"Yet from one point of view the Senangans have more in common with the Cassingans than they have with the pure-blooded linlarin of Akasha or Kalat," Vanda said.

"But that's the point of view of a wizard, not of a lar," Errin said.

"But someday almost all the larin will be wizards, will they not?" Vanda asked.

"I stand corrected," Errin said, bowing slightly. "The point of view of a human or ingvalarin wizard."

"Do the ingvalarin of Sussey acknowledge their kinship with humanity?" Vanda asked.

"Those of us who have studied wizardry certainly do," Errin said, "but Kyra has her worshippers on Sussey as well."

"Will Sussey at least maintain its neutrality in the conflict ahead?" Vanda asked.

Errin studied her. "My cousin Antram is Ahar of Sussey. I cannot speak on his behalf," he said carefully.

"You bear Lyskarion," Vanda said. "That makes your cousin a figurehead. The power is yours."

Errin shook his head. "I don't want it."

Vanda laughed. "What sane person would? Your wishes in this matter are quite irrelevant."

Errin felt the truth of Vanda's words pierce him. He took a deep breath, and let it go. "You're right," he said. "I simply didn't want to recognize that fact."

"I can understand that," Vanda said. "But I'm old. I'll be dead long before the minor skirmishes we face today turn into outright war." She paused and he felt her eyes measuring him. "But you're going to be one of the great wizards," she said after a moment. "You'll have only reached your prime when the war is over, which ever way it's decided. Will you be neutral? Or will you stand with one side or the other?"

"For as long as I live," Errin said deliberately, knowing he was making a lifelong commitment, "Sussey will support the goals of the Varfarin."

"You never swore to the Varfarin?"

"My teacher didn't feel it appropriate," Errin said, "but I worship Jehan, so I must believe in the goals of part of his priesthood."

"Will your support be active or passive?"

Errin shook his head. "No one can arm Sussey for a war that hasn't yet begun, but I'll do my best to make my support active."

"Then, on behalf of all the human lands, I thank you," Vanda said.

WHEN JEREVAN HAD BEEN A PRISONER IN RAVAAR for some five months, Morogo devised a new form of torture. He had a shallow, circular pit dug in his courtyard and Jerevan was unchained and put into it.

"You see how generous I am," Morogo said. "You're welcome to leave, if you don't like my hospitality. All you have to do is climb over this little wall." He roared with laughter and pointed to the side of the pit which was lined with bricks and only a meter high.

But Jerevan, who would not have noticed such an obstacle before he was cursed and could have climbed over it easily before his capture, had gained so much weight with the months of being chained and forced to gorge constantly that he was no longer able to raise his body the meter necessary to climb out.

ERRIN ARRIVED BACK IN RUFFIN in the middle of Minneth. Arrun accompanied him, as he wished to see more of the Thallassean region before returning to Cibata.

Aliara greeted them both warmly. "Perhaps your arrival will lift a little of the prevailing gloom," she remarked.

"They've still found no trace of Jerevan?" Errin asked, surprised.

"I gather they've sent word to Cibata, but it's too soon for them to have heard anything back," Aliara said.

"Cibata?" Arrun looked at Errin. "Why would they want word from Cibata?"

"Don't ask me," Errin said. "But I think we ought to ask Myrriden and the others."

"It's nearly lunch time," Aliara said. "I think you'll find them on the terrace."

Errin led Arrun through the house to the terrace overlooking the Bay of Aelos. The sky was a clear, brilliant blue and a light wind frothed the water of the bay into foamy whitecaps.

The beauty of the day, however, was not reflected in the expressions on the faces of the assembled wizards and their apprentices. Errin thought Myrriden, Balen, Marion and Elise all looked as gloomy as they would had Jerevan's death been confirmed.

At least, he noted, Elise's eyes brightened when she saw him. "Errin," she said. "We didn't know you were back." Then she saw Arrun behind him and her smile grew wider. "Arrun. What are you doing back from Cibata? Is Ashe with you?"

Errin suppressed his jealousy. He knew Elise and Arrun were old friends.

In fact, he had pumped Arrun for information about Elise's childhood all through the voyage north.

"Wizard Arrun, now," Arrun said to Elise, smiling. "I came back for Derwen to make the name you gave me official, where my father could witness the ceremony. As for Ashe, he's in Kandorra. He said he wanted to see every part of the world before he decided where he would most like to settle."

"So everyone will call you Jester now," Elise said. "I'm glad for you. And how like Ashe to want to explore. The years he spent with us in Bria must have been frustrating for him." She turned to Myrriden and the others. "This is the Wizard Arrun, a friend of mine. You may remember him as Del. Arrun, may I present Wizards Myrriden and Marion and Apprentice Wizard Balen."

"I'm glad to meet you all again," Arrun said. "Errin and I came back from Cibata together. Derwen told us of your attempt to stop Saranith, but he didn't know much about Jerevan's capture. I've learned a fair amount about the Senangans. Perhaps I can help you find out what happened to him."

"There's not much we can do while he's on his way to Cibata," Myrriden said.

Arrun frowned. "Errin told me about Jerevan's curse, the amount he has to eat. I'm sorry, but there's no way a Senangan ship could have taken him back to Cibata. They don't carry enough supplies and they don't have any place to conveniently restock. If he was captured, he was either killed or traded while the Senangan ship was still in the Thallassean."

Errin looked around at the stunned faces. He said, "Arrun is familiar with a number of the Senangan arrain. Can you tell him the name of the ship you think may have captured Jerevan?"

"The Sukatta Bel," Marion said.

Arrun stiffened. "The arrai of the Sukatta Bel is Aketi Kamrasi, a cousin of both the Estahar of Senanga and Saranith. If he captured Jerevan, given Jerevan's size and the nature of his curse, there's little doubt your friend is still alive. On the other hand, Aketi is known for his sadism. He'd have found Jerevan's condition irresistible, so I doubt Jerevan's enjoying his present existence."

"But if this Aketi didn't take Jerevan with him to Senanga, what could he have done with him?" Myrriden demanded.

"Show me on a map where Jerevan was captured and tell me the condition of Aketi's ship," Arrun said.

Marion fetched a map which Balen spread out over one of the patio tables. "The battle took place just north of that island there," Balen said, indicating one of the dots at the top of the Dalossian Archipelago with his finger. "The Sukatta Bel was badly damaged in the battle. We figure the arrai sailed the ship into the archipelago and beached her for repairs. We found an island where a ship had been careened when we sailed back near the end of Torin."

He pointed to another dot on the map. "But the Senangan ship was long gone."

Arrun studied the map. "Have you checked in Ravach to see if anyone saw a phenomenally fat man brought ashore sometime in Torin?"

"In Ravaar?" Myrriden exclaimed.

"Ravach is an open port even for linlarin pirates," Arrun said. "What's more, the pirate chieftains of Ravaar have no more use for the Varfarin than the Senangans do. I'm willing to bet Aketi traded Jerevan to someone he knew in Ravaar, someone with similar tastes."

ELISE WATCHED ERRIN COVERTLY as the others discussed Jerevan's fate. She had missed him so much. Yet she still feared the power of Lyskarion. But he had come back. He must feel he could control the crystal. She tore her eyes away.

A lull in the conversation brought her eyes back to Errin and this time her eyes met his.

"Excuse us, please, but Elise and I have some catching up to do," Errin said, his eyes holding hers.

Elise inhaled, not knowing what she felt most strongly, joy or panic, but she followed Errin down the stairs from the patio to a path leading along the top of the cliffs. The Bay of Aelos sparkled in the sunlight. Seagulls and keriarin soared in the updrafts above them.

"There's a place inside me that aches all the time I'm away from you," Errin thought.

"Yes," she responded. "I feel the same ache, but I still fear Lyskarion." Her thoughts exaggerated the image of the crystal so it loomed above the other images.

"I can control Lyskarion," Errin answered her, shrinking the crystal's image behind solid iron bars. "We can at least be together as we were in Darenje."

Her eyes met his, their minds on the border of linkage. "Are you sure?"

"Yes."

She went into his arms and laid her head against his chest. "I love you."

"As I love you," he thought, closing his arms around her and hugging her tight. "I can wait for the rest just as long as we never need to be apart anymore." He projected an image of two hearts not quite touching.

She altered the image to two hearts revolving around one another.

ERRIN WONDERED IF ELISE REALIZED that the orbit in her image was unstable and would mean an inevitable collision. He hoped that some part of her did, but he shielded that thought from her as he led her back along the path to the house and his bedroom.

XXXIX

4656, 466TH CYCLE OF THE YEAR OF THE MALIK
MONTH OF DIRGA

Mare rage garth kor lessle garth.

Nothing controls power other than greater power.

— EXCERPT FROM THE WRITINGS OF THE WIZARD RAV

"HEY, KY, COME LOOK OVER HERE. Bet this guy's the fattest man in all the world."

Kymor Dag joined his brother and stared at the enormously fat man lying in the shallow pit with the shiny, metallic cap embedded in his skull. "He's a wizard," he said and shuddered. How could a wizard be reduced to this?

"Nah, he can't be," Heren protested. "He's just a freak."

Kymor shook his head. "A freak wouldn't wear a cap. Only wizards get capped." He wondered if the man had been a member of the Varfarin. Kymor knew how the people of Ravaar felt about the Varfarin. They blamed the followers of Jehan for the destruction of Rav.

Kymor clenched his teeth. Doing something like this to a sentient being was still unconscionable. As far as he could see from the history books he had studied in Esterias before his family moved to Ravaar, Rav was responsible for his own destruction, but he would never say anything like that aloud. He did not intend to be a victim when he grew up. He had been marked by the gods. He would be the greatest wizard ever, as strong as Rav had been. Stronger. He would bear Ninkarion without the weakness the creation cost Rav.

The man in the pit opened his eyes and looked at Kymor. Kymor saw pain; but more, he saw apathy, the loss of hope. He swallowed. No! He would never be like this man, this broken wizard. He turned and grabbed his brother. "C'mon, let's go." They walked away.

JEREVAN WATCHED THE BOYS LEAVE. There had been a quality of awareness and determination about the taller child. The boy might have wizard talent. If so, Jerevan thought, his condition had just supplied the child with an object lesson. He sighed, wishing that he could appreciate the lesson himself. But his fever was high. He must be nearly due for the bimonthly healing session Morogo had ordered.

A lot of people had been coming to see him recently. Jerevan suspected that Morogo was charging money for the privilege, which also explained his increased interest in keeping Jerevan alive. He wondered if word of the spectacle he had become might reach Myrriden and the others. Surely they would still be looking for him. And Derwen as well. After all, if the wizards of the Varfarin hadn't wanted him, he might still be living the life he had planned for himself, unaffected by curses and sadistic linlarin. Of course, at his present weight and rate of consumption, he doubted it would be possible, even if he were rescued, to keep himself alive long enough to complete his training. He shuddered. In all the dreams of revenge he had imagined, he had never considered putting Derwen through anything like the past few months of his life. But, if by some miracle he did survive this, he thought he might make a present of Derwen to Aketi. Aketi was a more imaginative torturer than he would ever be.

ARRUN RODE AHEAD OF THE WAGON and the crew of roustabouts, dreading what he would find when he reached Morogo's hacienda. As far as he knew, they had never met but Derwen had pointed out Jerevan Rayne to him once, years before when he and Elise had visited the court in Ninkarrak. He remembered a handsome, athletic young man. He had trouble reconciling that memory with the images Myrriden had shown him of Jerevan before his capture. Arrun did not want to imagine what Jerevan had since become.

Locating Jerevan had been absurdly easy, once Varfarin agents checked in Ravaar. The retired pirate, now merchant prince, Morogo, was charging money for people to 'Come see the biggest wizard in the world.' Posters advertising the exhibit were displayed all over the city of Ravach.

Arrun remembered what Marion had said on their journey to Ravaar, that Jerevan had once told her that his ability to forgive the Varfarin for what Derwen had done would ultimately depend on what he had to endure before becoming a wizard. Arrun wondered what excuse Derwen would have for his actions if the man he had chosen to succeed him as Esalfar became instead the Varfarin's implacable enemy. Given the circumstances, Arrun knew he would not blame Jerevan if that were the case.

Even after Jerevan had been located, it had taken Myrriden and the others time to decide on a way to rescue him and then to implement the plan. Elise and Errin had taken no part in the discussion, being too intent on each other, but Marion and Balen had come up with several schemes for stealing Jerevan away from Morogo. All of them had been impractical given what they knew of Jerevan's condition. Arrun had reminded them that they had to consider Jerevan dead weight, incapable of assisting in his own escape and unable to fit into one of the trunks the carnivals used to conceal those they rescued.

Arrun had listened to Myrriden, Marion and Balen argue for two days, before saying, "I don't see the problem. Morogo's a merchant. Jerevan's novelty value to him is bound to have worn off by now. He may be making some money from charging people for the privilege of looking at a freak, but given the location of his estate, I doubt he's covering his costs. Send a carnival through Ravach. Have one of the carnival people go out to Morogo's hacienda and offer to buy Jerevan. It'll just be a matter of haggling over price. What's more, if the carnival approaches Ravach overland, no one will find it odd if it leaves by sea on a previously chartered ship."

Everyone had immediately agreed with the suggestion, but Arrun had not anticipated that they would insist he be a part of the rescue. "We all know you think quickly in emergencies," Marion had said. "What's more, Jerevan won't recognize you. Any of the rest of us he'd know. In his current condition, he might give away the fact that he knows us and that could be fatal in Ravaar."

Arrun acknowledged the truth of that and finally agreed, but even with a definite plan there had been delays. Varfarin carnival routes rarely included Ravaar. It had taken over a month to get the only carnival in the region out of Khorat and through Ravaar to Ravach, because, of course, a carnival could not just travel without drawing undue attention. They had to put on shows in every major town on their route.

Still, Arrun reflected, Jerevan had to be alive; the posters advertising his exhibition were still decorating walls all over Ravach. He identified the entrance to the estate he had been seeking by an eye-catching sign. He signaled to his small procession and started up the drive.

Several large, burly men stood in front of the entrance to the courtyard. One of them, tall and black haired, said, "You got to pay us before you get to see the wizard. Price is five rikin. That goes for your men, too," he added, nodding at the wagon and roustabouts behind Arrun.

Arrun said, "I'd be happy to pay to see your show, but first I'd like to speak with your master, Morogo. I have a business proposition to put to him."

"He does his business in town," the man said.

"I checked there," Arrun said, "but they told me I'd find him here today."

The man nodded grudgingly. "He's here, in the courtyard, with the healer and the cleaning crew. If you pay your entrance fee, you can go on through. You'll get twice the show, getting to see the wizard out of his pit."

Arrun managed to conceal his reaction to the mention of a pit and a healer and handed the man two rinin. "That should cover us all."

The man took the coins and nodded.

Arrun rode into the courtyard.

Six large men had rigged a hoist over a shallow pit. They were raising a large mass out of it. Another man in more ornate clothing stood to one side directing the operation, with a healer in the robes of the kindred of Maera next to him.

Arrun dismounted and tied the horse to the hitching rail at the right side of the entryway. Then he walked over to Morogo.

"Quite an operation," he said.

Morogo turned and eyed him up and down. Arrun noted that Morogo's eyes brightened when he took in Arrun's carnival garb. "You're lucky.

You get an extra show for your money. It's the wizard's bath day."

Arrun surveyed the immense bulk now sprawled on the stones of the courtyard and only barely recognizable as a man, and said, "A pity to keep such a display isolated out here, where only a few hardy souls get to see him."

Morogo smiled, "But this way I get the true connoisseurs."

"Only those who live in Ravach," Arrun said. "I assure you there are many who have never heard of your exhibit only a short distance away. I might never have heard of it myself, had not the carnival come to Ravach this year." He walked closer to the mountain of flesh.

Jerevan had been deposited belly down on the stones of the courtyard and the men were pouring buckets of water over his back and the vast expanses of his buttocks and thighs, washing off the smeared mud and feces, and exposing the presence of deep, infected sores, oozing with pus. Arrun almost gagged at the smell. "A bit overripe, isn't he?" he asked.

Morogo, who had followed him, said, "That's why the healer's here."

Arrun turned back to Morogo. "That must get expensive."

Morogo's eyes narrowed. "It's not too bad. The kindred are reasonable in their charges, and he doesn't need it done more than once or twice a month."

Arrun nodded. "The carnival might benefit from such an exhibit, if you'd consider parting with such a novel entertainment."

Morogo frowned. "He's certainly provided amusement, both for myself and my men, but I'll sell him if the price is sufficient. He's unique. I wouldn't consider less than five hundred riktravin."

Arrun's eyes widened. "My dear man, I hadn't considered paying for him by the pound. While the carnival would certainly appreciate such an exhibit, they have other choices. I wouldn't dream of spending more than a hundred riktravin. And for that price you'll have to supply his crystal, to prove he's really a wizard."

"I wouldn't dream of supplying anything for such a paltry sum, but I have no use for a wizard crystal," Morogo said. "You may have him and it for a mere four hundred and fifty riktravin. I'm feeling generous today."

Arrun responded with one hundred and twenty-five riktravin. Morogo blustered that he could not possibly part with the wizard for so little, but reduced his price again by a small amount. Arrun countered and the bidding continued until Jerevan's price was settled at two hundred thirty riktravin.

"And at that you're robbing me blind," Arrun said when the deal had been struck. "Why I bet it costs almost a riktrav a day to feed him. Where's my profit in that?"

Morogo said, "If you feed him regularly every three hours he doesn't eat nearly as he much as does if you withhold food from him for a while before feeding him. At the size he is now, I'd recommend you only make him gorge for special customers."

"How often have you made him gorge?" Arrun asked, feeling nauseous.

"When I first got him, I gorged him twice a day," Morogo said. "Of course, he didn't consume as much then, but it was still quite a show. After he ceased to be able to get up without assistance, I cut it down to once a day. Recently, with him getting so big, I only make him gorge for those willing to pay extra for the privilege. He'll last longer if you do the same."

Arrun took a deep breath and said, "I appreciate your advice."

While he had been bargaining with Morogo, the healer had been working on the sores. The pus had been drained and the flesh repaired. At least, Arrun reflected, Morogo had hired a competent healer. He scanned Jerevan quickly and noted that she had healed some of the worst of the internal damage as well, but she had drained herself and could do no more in one session.

"As he's already in a harness, can you load him on my wagon now?" Arrun asked.

Morogo looked around and appeared to notice the wagon and roustabouts for the first time. "You were pretty sure of purchasing him, weren't you?" he asked, turning back to Arrun with a frown.

"I heard a rumor you were looking for a buyer," Arrun said.

Morogo nodded. "We'll hoist him onto your wagon then. I'll even throw in a bale of straw for bedding."

Arrun inclined his head. "How generous."

Jerevan woke alone in a semi-reclining position on a bed in what looked like the bedroom of an inn. His instinctive attempt to sit up did nothing more than ripple his now mountainous stomach. He rolled over, trying to get onto his hands and knees. Unfortunately, once he was raised up on his belly, his arms had to extend so that his hands reached the bed, which gave him almost no leverage. And, while his legs could raise his lower body somewhat, they couldn't elevate him enough to lift the mass of his flesh off the mattress.

He rolled the other way, trying to get back to the position he had started in, but his struggles had knocked the bolster used to prop him up off the bed and he ended up flat on his back. In that position the massive weight of his belly pressed down on his lungs. His exertions had left him breathless and he nearly suffocated before he managed to heave himself over onto his side. He lay there, gasping, for several minutes.

He decided that the walls of his room had to be thick or the sound of his struggles would have alerted his captors. How much longer he would be left alone? He remembered how hopeful he had been when he had realized he was being purchased by a carnival, but the man who had purchased him was no one he recognized. And Myrriden had told him that the Varfarin rarely sent carnivals through Ravaar. He would rather die trying to escape than live as he was.

But how could he escape if he couldn't even get off the bed? He closed his eyes and tried to control his frustration. Finally, he squirmed sideways to the edge of the bed and rolled onto his back again so he could push his legs over the edge. Then, with his knees bent and his feet on the floor, he tried to raise his upper body to a sitting position by pulling against the headboard. When that didn't work, and his mountainous flesh pressed against his lungs again, threatening to smother him, he tried to roll back.

His legs, however, were over the edge of the bed and he couldn't raise them. He was forced to let go of the headboard and turn over onto his stomach, but, as he was already halfway out of bed, the result was he slid to the floor.

At first he thought being on his belly beside the bed would help him, that he could use the bed to pull himself up, but the enormous mass of his stomach was on the floor and his arms lacked the strength to raise that weight. He could push with his legs, but that only shoved him against the bed, moving it sideways. He could not get his legs under him to push because, lying on his belly, his knees no longer had contact with the floor.

His desire to escape intensified to panic as he struggled to move in any direction at all. He was not sure afterward whether he lay there hysterically fighting his own flesh for an hour, or just minutes. He only knew that he finished up, saturated in sweat and almost suffocated, a mere meter from where he had fallen, with every muscle in his body aching and his stomach painfully empty.

He lay on his side and forced himself to breathe evenly. He couldn't stand up or crawl, but he could still move his arms and legs. There had to be some way he could propel himself.

He suddenly remembered watching sea lions on land when he visited the Outer Islands one summer. They had no legs, but they managed to get around. Perhaps he could imitate them. He rolled himself onto his belly. Pushing down on the floor with both hands, he managed to lift the upper portion of his torso partially off the floor. Then he bent his knees and brought his feet up along the side of his belly as far as he could and tried pushing himself along the floor. He slid a few centimeters. He shifted his body around until he faced the door and tried again. Another few centimeters. He pictured the sea lions and tried to hump himself up and push at the same time. That worked better. A series of humps got him past the end of the bed.

A chair was in his way. Turning was painful, as there was nothing between his flesh and the rough wooden floor, but he managed. Then another series of humps and another turn.

He was dripping sweat and gasping for breath. He tried to hump the last two meters but his abused muscles refused to respond and he nearly passed out. He rolled onto his side and rested until his breath was back under control. Then he got himself back up on his belly. One hump at a time was all he could manage now. His arms quivered from the strain. Still, he made it to the door.

Then he realized that the door opened inward. He could just manage to raise his arm high enough to reach the knob, but he couldn't open the door because his body was in the way.

He wasn't sure how long it took to unlatch the door and move himself enough to get it open, but he managed.

He was lying on his side in the hall, struggling for breath, when he saw his purchaser appear with Otto and Marion. Jerevan stared at them, feeling as though he were hallucinating. Then his stomach started to cramp.

"What are you doing out of bed?" the stranger demanded.

Jerevan stared at Otto and Marion. "Otto? Marion?"

"I'd venture to guess that he was trying to escape," Otto said. "You must not have identified yourself."

"He passed out when I removed his cap," the stranger said. "I didn't have a chance to tell him anything after that. I thought he'd still be unconscious."

Jerevan put his hand up and felt his head. Where the cap had been he felt only smooth flesh. How could he not have noticed that it was gone?

Marion said to Otto, "Find some men to help us get him back to bed and order some food." Jerevan felt her examine his body. "A lot of food," she added, then turned to Jerevan, "We're glad to find you alive. The man who purchased you is Wizard Arrun."

Otto nodded and left.

Jerevan tried to reach out with his were-sight and felt a stab of pain through his head, a pain more severe than the warning cramps in his stomach. He closed his eyes. He had been rescued. Why did he feel no relief?

XL

4656, 466TH CYCLE OF THE YEAR OF THE MALIK
MONTH OF INGVASH

Keren paleles ba proles iresal.

The most important lessons are the most difficult to learn.

— ESLARIN PROVERB

JEREVAN WOKE WHEN OTTO OPENED THE DOOR TO HIS ROOM. He was in a bed, propped up with bolsters in the semi-upright position necessary to keep him from suffocating under the vast bulk of his belly. In the distance, he heard the sound of surf crashing against rocks. He was back in Ruffin. But what good did that do him, when he was still a prisoner in his own body?

"Six o'clock, Your Grace," Otto said, setting a heavily laden tray down on the bedside table.

When the aromas from the food on the tray reached Jerevan, his stomach spasmed and saliva filled his mouth. He hated the reaction, but the constant gorging during his captivity had intensified his body's responses. Even though he had eaten three hours earlier, his body reacted to the sight or smell of food as though he had been starved. Still, he had to eat. Reluctantly, he propped himself up even higher in the bed and started feeding himself.

He weighed nearly a ton. Otto had found a livestock scale and had helped him weigh himself. Almost eight years had passed since he had been cursed, but still his current weight exceeded his worst fears.

What terrified him most, however, was that his stomach was so enlarged from the constant gorging, even eating regularly did not prevent his continuing to gain weight at an incredible rate.

And the cap had caused a setback in his training. He could hardly hold the were-sight for half an hour and had only managed to attain the high sight once for a mere second in the past week. He could no longer lift objects of more than a pound, and his control was pathetic. His captivity had made him so fat and physically helpless that he had to use his will to feed himself, yet he could hardly get through a meal without losing control and breaking something or dropping food all over.

He looked down at his chest, and confirmed his own disgust with himself with the sight of a fresh smear on his bedclothes. Then he looked further. Once he had worried about a double chin. Now his head rested on a series of rolls of fat increasing in size until the bottom one merged into the vast slope of his chest. His breasts were sagging mounds on that slope, which then curved into the mountain of his belly. His circumference at what had once been his waist was now approximately three meters, which made him bigger around than he was tall.

A knock on the door to his suite distracted him from his depressing self-evaluation. His rolls of fat rippled as he tried instinctively to rise, only to be reminded again of his imprisoning flesh. He forced his mind into the were-sight and looked through the walls to the hall.

"Come in, Marion," he thought.

Her face was unusually solemn as she came through the door. *"Very good. You sounded almost like your old self."*

"I've lost a year's progress," he thought.

She shook her head. *"You should be back where you were before your capture in less than five months. No damage was done to your mind's new pathways. Your problem is just that lack of use has weakened them."* She came over to the side of the bed and adjusted the pillows for him.

"No damage?"

"You can see for yourself, Jerevan," Marion thought. *"In fact, you should have done so. You've had five weeks, but you've only worked on your body."* Her thoughts had a cutting bite Jerevan had never sensed from her before.

"I have headaches every time I try . . ."

"That's normal for expanding mental pathways," she thought, interrupting him. *"You know that."*

Jerevan felt her examine him, body and mind. In the past, Marion had always been sensitive to his feelings. He knew he was a disgusting sight, but he had still expected her to remain sympathetic.

"I thought what Derwen did to you was wrong. I felt that so strongly it's made me doubt the trust I had in Cormor's wisdom. After all, Cormor chose Derwen," Marion thought.

Jerevan felt shock and then fury. "But you don't think it's wrong now, when my body's been perverted like this?" he demanded, his bloated hand brushing the slope of his chest to his mountainous belly.

Marion shut her eyes. "No," she said. "As soon as your emotions were engaged, you broke off from mind-speech and resorted to words. After we rescued you, you weren't even aware the cap had been removed until we told you. You've been training to be a wizard for eight years, yet your first reaction to every situation is physical."

Jerevan stared at her, disconcerted. "What does that have to do with anything? I've learned everything I've been taught. Even Myrriden remarked on the speed of my progress before I was captured."

Marion's eyes opened, but she looked sad. "Yes, Jerevan, you learn quickly. Your mind has tremendous power. But your instincts are wrong." She sighed. "In one way, considering your capture, it's a good thing. Your instincts protected you. You never tried to use your will while you were a prisoner, so you never fought the cap and didn't damage your mind."

"Then why are you angry with me?" Jerevan asked, his fat hands unconsciously rubbing the sides of the mass of his belly.

Marion shook her head again. "It's not a matter of being angry, Jerevan. I simply understand now why you must suffer this way."

"Then please tell me. I have a right to know."

"Yes," she said, "but you won't like the answer. You see, when your body can't respond, you'll be forced to use your mind. If your body remains helpless long enough, eventually you'll start using your will before you try using your body. When that happens, you'll become a wizard, not a man trying to learn wizardry to break a curse."

Jerevan lay silent, trying to understand, but his resentment was too great. "You mean, to become a wizard my whole mind, my attitudes and beliefs, must be rearranged?"

Marion frowned. "Not your attitudes or beliefs; just your instinctive choice of a physical response over a mental one."

"You think Derwen thought that out when he cursed me like this?"

"No," she said, "but I believe Cormor understood when he chose Derwen as his tool."

Jerevan stared after her when she left. He had never thought that he would come to hate Marion. She had been his one comfort during the past years, even though their physical relationship had only lasted a few months. But tied to his bed in the prison his own body had become, he found himself hating even her. The Varfarin had wanted a wizard, so he was being tortured to become one. But if he did survive and become a wizard, Derwen would suffer for what he had done, and he didn't think the others would be getting what they wanted either. He was more likely to oversee the destruction of their precious Varfarin than take over as its leader.

4657, 466TH CYCLE OF THE YEAR OF THE BEAR
MONTH OF DIRGA

THE PALE LIGHT OF EARLY DAWN filtered through the curtains as Elise looked down at Errin, asleep in the bed beside her. In one way, the past year spent with him had been the best time in her life, but the closer they grew to each other, the harder it was for her to resist linking with him. And she was still afraid.

Errin lay on his side facing her. Lyskarion lay against his chest, half under him. She had awakened with her back against that chest, her buttocks against his groin, their legs entangled. She had felt warm and safe with his arm about her waist, only half awake, until she had felt the hard shape of the living crystal against her skin.

The feel of it touching her had roused her like a cold bath. She had eased out from under Errin's arm and separated her body from his. Yet now she felt bereft.

She could hear the waves at the foot of the cliff, a constant background murmur. The light filtering through the curtains was beginning to brighten.

What did she really have to fear? Bearing Lyskarion had not changed Errin in any way she could detect, except to enhance his power. She had been afraid when he first came back that he would have changed. She had watched him constantly, waiting to find some difference in his attitudes, his very being. But as far as she could tell without linking with him, he was the same man she had always known. The man she loved.

Could she and Errin have had a life together if she had not been so angry all those years ago on Adun? So angry and afraid? Yes, she had been afraid then, too. Afraid to take the risk of loving, when that love might not be returned as deeply. Her family's record in that regard had not helped.

Elise closed her eyes, but she could not shut off her thoughts as easily. She had been a coward twenty-four years ago, in Adun, and again five years ago in Lamash and Darenje. She had loved Errin, and had known he loved her. He could not lie to her with his mind, but she had lied to him, and to herself. What had she been afraid of then? Afraid of happiness?

No, she thought, I was afraid of admitting to myself what a terrible mistake I made when I was eighteen. I was afraid of looking at that cramped little place inside me where I tried to bury my heart.

She felt tears wash her cheeks and Errin woke, sat up and put his arms around her, as though her pain had wakened him.

"Elise, what's the matter? Why are you crying?"

"I'm crying over lost chances. I should have trusted our love when I was eighteen. I should have trusted it again five years ago. But those chances are gone," she thought, and her mind ached with regret. *"And even knowing how wrong I've been doesn't make a difference, because I'm still a coward. I'm still afraid of Lyskarion."*

Errin hugged her tightly and rocked her against him. *"It makes a difference, Elise. All our thoughts make a difference. And you aren't a coward. You just like to have control of the things that matter to you. Your mother's death, the way your grandmother sent you to Bria, and finding out Brennan wasn't your real father the way you did, all those things chipped away at your basic sense of security. But deep down, you're very brave, and very strong."*

Elise rested in his arms and let his thoughts soothe her. She loved him. Soon she would find the courage to prove it.

MONTH OF CERDANA

JEREVAN WOKE IN THE NIGHT to an empty ache in his stomach. Where was Otto with his tray? He reached out his hand for the bell pull, but it had slipped off the bed where Otto always propped it when he left at midnight. Jerevan stared at it, hanging where any normal man would have no trouble reaching it, about thirty centimeters from the side of the bed, next to the headboard.

But for Jerevan that meant it was nearly half a meter from the tip of his fingers. He would have to move his whole body. He tried to lean forward and push himself sideways with his left arm and leg, but only his head came free of the pillows. His body hardly moved. He tried to roll himself over, but even that only produced wave motions in the mass of his belly.

Although he had converted some fat to muscle over the past year, his weight gain had been so great his efforts had no effect. Simply healing himself and trying to slow the gain by breaking down fat now took most of his energy. He had almost cried at his last weighing. His weight had been precisely the same as before the curse plus a ton.

When Derwen had first cursed him, he had predicted a time would come when he would be a prisoner in his own flesh, yet Jerevan had never really believed his condition would get to that point. Now it had.

He suddenly remembered what Marion had said to him just after the end of his captivity. She had accused him of always trying to use his body, never his mind. He looked at the cord. It weighed almost nothing. He could have brought it to his hand without difficulty by the end of his first year of training. So why had he been struggling to move his body to it? He yanked it with his will and rang the bell.

Otto would come. But Jerevan realized that Marion had been right. He should have used his will immediately. Why hadn't he?

He had a sudden memory of his mother drawing back in horror after he lit a candle with his will. He had been five, he thought. The incident with the candle had cost him his teacher; Kindric had left the next morning. It had cost him his mother, too, he suddenly realized. She had never hugged him again after that night.

Had his mother's attitude to wizardry affected him so much that some part of him shied away from using his powers even now? Jerevan sighed. Apparently it had, but now that he understood the problem, perhaps he could find a way to deal with it.

The next day he called both Marion and Myrriden to his room and presented them with a design for a movable bed. *"I'm tired of this room. I can't walk, and hiring extra men to carry me around isn't practical. Can one of the metal smiths in Ruffin produce the parts for a bed like this?"* he broadcast to both of them.

Myrriden examined the drawing. *"Clever. You'll be able to adjust the angle of the bed yourself unless you tip it too far. I'll take these to Aliara. She knows the local artisans, but I don't believe there'll be a problem. Your design is clear."*

"I'll also be able to push it around by myself eventually, if the wheels are well designed, as long as I'm on a level surface," Jerevan thought. *"It shouldn't require a force much beyond my present ability. Which gives me another reason to practice the use of my will on something other than healing."*

Marion smiled. *"Yes. You'll be dependent on the use of your will to go anywhere."*

"Better than depending on other people and not going anywhere at all," Jerevan thought. *"I'm also working on a design for a curricle, so that I can get around the countryside. I'll have to have a hoist built by the edge of the driveway. Could you ask Aliara if she'll mind?"*

"That will require the help of other people," Marion thought.

"There are always people working in the stable or the garden. Hoisting me into a curricle now and then won't take them far from their work."

Myrriden smiled. *"I'm sure Aliara will have no objection. We've all been concerned by your being shut up in here."*

Jerevan eyed him ironically. *"But I had to act to end my isolation."*

"Exactly," Marion thought.

XLI

4657, 466TH CYCLE OF THE YEAR OF THE BEAR
MONTH OF AGNITH

> Ma nalor pon va bohedal a valodar
> ulen ilvalodarse son end,
> kor quen non du marlin:
>
> Amid marl co nalor pon,
> ful wuno a ilam,
> bohedal va a ayan am.
>
> *No wizard may prolong the life of another being*
> *beyond that being's natural span,*
> *but for these three exceptions:*
>
> *The first exception states that a wizard may,*
> *with the consent of such person,*
> *maintain the life of one servant.*

— EXCERPTS FROM THE LAWS, ISSUED BY THE COUNCIL OF WIZARDS

"YOU KNOW, ELISE," ERRIN SAID ONE AFTERNOON, "we shouldn't be compatible at all. I was born in Theocan a Gand, the year of the Dragon, the sign of change, while you were born in Theocan al Isk, the year of the Lizard, the arch conservative, always resistant to change." They lay side by side on two loungers, basking in the sun like two isklarin in lizard form, on the patio overlooking the Bay.

She laughed. "Or else I'm the perfect balance for you."

"I prefer your interpretation," Errin said, smiling. For once, except for the servants, he and Elise had Pomorry House to themselves. Aliara, Galen and Nutena had gone to some event concerning grape growers and would not be back for over a week. Jerevan was out testing his new curricle with Otto, and Marion and Myrriden were teaching at the Rakredrem. They had agreed to take over there so Delanan could take a short vacation with Jao.

"What made you think about our birth years?" Elise asked.

"I was thinking about changes." He turned his head so he could watch her face in profile. "Everything does change eventually, after all."

Elise shivered despite the heat of the sun. "Do you have to sound so morbid on such a beautiful day?"

Errin shook his head. "But that's just it, Elise. When I say the word, you think I'm being morbid. But many changes are good. Growth requires change."

She sighed, sat up and turned to face him, putting her feet down. Her simple, sleeveless tunic, the color of golden anathallia blossoms, barely covered the tops of her thighs. "I'm not in the mood for a deep philosophical discussion."

"I'm not threatening you, Elise," he said quickly. "I won't say anything about our relationship. Please don't run away."

"Then what are you talking about?" she asked, still poised for escape.

"You've been helping to relay information to Rand through Jao quite a lot lately, haven't you?"

"Yes, of course," she said, frowning in bewilderment at his sudden change of subject.

"How close does she have to be for you to reach her?" he asked, keeping his voice casual.

"I can reach her anywhere Marion or Delanan can," Elise said, "the full distance allowed by the curvature of Tamar."

"Very good," he said. "Now, how much do you weigh?"

"Why do you want to know?"

"Can you raise your own weight?" he asked, sitting up so he faced her.

Her eyes narrowed. "I've never tried levitating."

"Why not, Elise?" he asked gently. "Being able to do so is one of the requirements of becoming a full wizard. Arrun's made it. You trained together. You should be close, but I haven't seen you stretching yourself to reach that point."

She glared at him. "I've had other things to think about."

"How long can you hold the high sight?"

"A little over six minutes," she snapped. "I don't see the point of this. Marion hasn't complained about my progress."

"Marion's also had other things to think about," Errin said. "Why don't you try lifting yourself now?"

"All right, I will," Elise said, and her body rose several centimeters straight up, still in the same sitting position.

"Very good," he said again, grinning. "That means you can do everything necessary to shape-change. Would you like to come swimming with me, Elise?"

She descended suddenly. "You're serious, aren't you?"

"*Come and hear the song of the sea, Elise,*" he thought to her. "*Hear it with me, and we can find ecstasy together.*"

Errin watched her eyes widen and her rate of breathing increase. "*After all, Elise,*" he added, "*I've spent more than a year on land with you. I told you once that, if you were a wizard, I could demand the same of you, that you turn your back on the land and spend a year in the sea.*"

He watched her remember that moment, so many years before. Then he said prosaically, "But we're both older now. I'll let you get off with a day."

His voice and the change in its tone broke the mood he had created. She took a deep breath and let it go. "Why did you do that?" she asked, her voice husky.

"I wanted to reach you," Errin said. "You've been building a shell around yourself. I needed to break through and touch you, if only for a moment. But I meant the invitation, Elise. I want us to swim together in the sea."

"Some people say the song of the sea is as addictive as a drug," she said.

"For some it is," he said, noting how tightly her hands gripped the edge of the lounge. "The sensory input from all an ingvalar's senses can be intoxicating, and there are those who become addicted to the euphoria it causes. But I can't see that happening to you, Elise."

"Why not?"

"The sea claims those who drift through their lives, not those who clutch at reality as firmly as you do."

She looked down at her hands and relaxed them, flexing her fingers to ease the stiffness her tight grip had caused. "I was hanging on, wasn't I?" she said ruefully. She looked up and met his eyes. "The thought of shape-changing scares me."

"I know," he said. *"But you can do it, Elise,"* he thought. *"I'll be there with you."*

"But if I . . ."

"If you turn to me when you need help, you risk linking with me. That's what you're afraid of, isn't it?" Errin demanded.

She sighed and her shoulders slumped. "Yes. That's what I'm always afraid of in these days."

"Will you try it if I promise not to link with you?" he asked, reaching out and taking her hands.

"You'd promise not to complete the link, even if I reached for it?" Her hands twisted in his, gripping him.

"Only for the period of your first attempt at shape-changing," he cautioned her. "I wouldn't want our personal problems to distract you at a critical moment."

She stared at him, and he could see her inner struggle reflected in her eyes. "You have to try a shape-change sometime if you hope to qualify as a wizard," he said. "What better form to choose than one you've been familiar with all your life?"

She turned away from him to look out across the Bay. "If only it were that simple."

"It is that simple, Elise. You just have to make up your mind to do it, and then do it. Just like that."

"Get up and go down to the sea right now?" she asked.

"Why not? I can give you a pattern for a dolphin."

"I already have one," she said.

His chin rose and he smiled. "When did you take the pattern, Elise?"

"Last year," she said. He saw her stiffen as she realized how much she had admitted. She turned back to face him. "Last year right after you came back."

"Then you've thought about changing for over a year," Errin said. "Isn't it time you just did it?" *"Come listen to the song of the sea, Elise."*

She stood up and walked over to the wall at the edge of the patio where it overlooked the bay. The day was calm and clear, with almost no wind. The water of the bay was a brilliant blue and as smooth as glass. "You promise you won't link with me?"

"I swear it."

"Then I'll try," she said.

Errin rose and hugged her. "You won't regret it, Elise," he said. He grabbed her hand. "Come on, I'm not going to give you a chance to change your mind." He pulled her over to the steps leading down to the water.

At the foot of the stairway he shucked off the sail cloth pants that were all he wore and waited while she pulled off her tunic and underthings and laid them on the rocks. They walked across the narrow strip of sand into the water hand in hand, stopping when the water lapped the undersides of her breasts.

"Now, Elise."

For a moment she was absolutely still. Then her body melted and flowed, her face elongating, her skin thickening and changing color, her legs merging. In less than a minute, a small dolphin began to take form in the water in front of him. Errin triggered his own shift.

A dolphin again, he watched as Elise completed her shift. She lay motionless in the water for a moment, and he knew she was hearing the song of the sea for the first time.

She took a breath, then dove, immersing herself in the music. He followed.

Elise dove down through the clear, blue water, enthralled by the delicate melodies all around her. The song of the sea was not what she had expected. She had thought she would be overwhelmed, but instead she felt charmed. True, the slow background pulse of the tidal currents pulled at her until her heart beat in rhythm, but the quick darting notes of the schools of fish reminded her of trills of laughter.

She realized that the calm water of the bay meant this was a quiet movement in the sea's eternal symphony, but there were still a hundred, no a thousand, melodies all around her, a part of her. She listened and let her new form flow with them.

Along with her absorption in the music, she felt Errin swimming with her, his nose even with her tail and about a meter to her right. She knew his heartbeat had slowed to match the rhythm of the sea even as hers had done. She knew he rose for breath and leapt and dived in perfect unison with her. Swimming became a dance she danced with him.

She did not know how long they danced before she realized she could not talk to him in this form except by the use of mind-speech. The thought disturbed her so much that for a moment it blocked her absorption in the song of the sea and her body's rhythmic response to the music. She floundered in the water as though she had forgotten how to swim.

"Elise! Are you all right?"

She recovered her equilibrium and started to swim again. Errin had promised not to link with her. *"I'm fine,"* she thought.

"What happened?"

"I just got distracted," she answered.

A moment passed and Elise began to get caught up again in the rhythm of the sea. Then Errin's mental laughter came to her with his thought, *"Leave it to you, Elise, to hear the song of the sea for the first time, and immediately get distracted from it by an idle thought. Or was it an idle worry?"*

Somehow his laughter eased her fears, and she spent the rest of the day swimming with him in perfect harmony. It was evening when they returned to shore and changed back to human form, emerging from the water as the sunset was painting the clouds on the western horizon in shades of salmon and cerise.

"You see," Errin said as he put his pants back on, "there was nothing to fear. You even enjoyed yourself, didn't you?"

Elise donned her tunic. "Yes," she admitted. "I enjoyed swimming with you."

"Then we'll do it again soon," he said, starting up the stairs. "Teaching at the Rakredrem is all very well, but you need some fun and relaxation in your life."

"You've been out swimming with the sea folk a lot this summer," she commented, following him. "I'm sure you get enough fun without my company."

He paused halfway up the steps to the patio and looked back at her. "So now I'm an idle hedonist again. You'd better watch out, Elise, or I'll corrupt you."

"I know you've worked with Antram and Delanan on starting the new schools," she said carefully, stopping on the step below him. "I realize it must be hard for you, after growing up in a wiga, to stay focused on such a project."

"Even though it's a program I initiated."

She frowned, her eyes meeting his anxiously. "That's why it bothers me that you've spent so much time in the sea this summer."

He turned away and started up the steps again. "But I was raised in a wiga, Elise. What else can you expect?"

She followed him, aware that he was angry, but not sure why. Did he feel guilty about the time he spent in the sea?

JEREVAN USED HIS WILL TO CATCH ONE OF THE REINS as it slipped out of his grasp. When all the reins were again gathered in his swollen, awkward hands, he pulled back on the team of horses, slowing them to a walk. The sensation of the wind blowing through his hair had felt marvelous, but he was exhausted, and the last thing he wanted was to have an accident and damage the vehicle which had brought him so much pleasure.

He had expected to be tired by the end of the day, but not so tired. His hands and arms ached from the strain of holding the reins and controlling the horses, but he could not have controlled them without using his will to supplement his failing physical skills. He had not anticipated so great a drain on his strength, but he had driven the horses nearly twenty kilometers. For minutes at a time, he had almost forgotten that he was a prisoner in his body, unable to so much as stand up by himself.

Jerevan turned the horses into the drive to Pomorry House, drawing them to a halt when the curricle was underneath the winch that had been constructed at the edge of the yard near the stables. His wheeled couch stood near the hoist where he had left it earlier in the day.

He used his will to ring the bell on the post. Otto jumped off the back of the curricle and moved the couch to a position next to the vehicle. Several men emerged from the stable. When Otto had attached the hooks to the harness Jerevan wore, they winched him up out of the curricle and lowered him onto his mobile bed.

Ordinarily Jerevan would then have been able to propel himself into Pomorry House and back to his rooms, but he knew he could not manage on his own this evening. The energy of his will had been depleted by the long drive. He would not even be able to heal himself until he had rested.

"Can you manage, Your Grace?" Otto asked, as though he sensed Jerevan's condition.

"No," Jerevan admitted. "I'm exhausted. I'll need your help." The truth of his words suddenly struck Jerevan and, tired as he was, he made another decision on a subject that had worried him for some time.

Later, when Jerevan had eaten and was back in his bed, he said, "Otto, you've been my servant now for eighteen years."

"Yes, Your Grace."

"I realize the past nine have been difficult for you as well as for me."

Otto's eyes widened in surprise and he looked wary. "Not that difficult, your grace. Nothing I can't handle."

"No," Jerevan agreed. "I can't imagine anything you can't handle, which is why I need to know if you're willing to remain my servant for an indefinite period." Jerevan shook his head, his multiple chins wobbling. "I'm saying this badly. What I mean is, by the laws of the Council of Wizards, a wizard is allowed to prolong the life of one servant. Would you be willing to allow me to prolong your life, as you are now, so you won't grow old until after I die?"

Otto snorted. "You say that as though you expect me to object. Of course, I'm willing. Begging Your Grace's pardon, but what sane man wouldn't want his life prolonged?"

"I don't know," Jerevan said. "When I was twenty-one, I didn't want mine prolonged."

"You'll be thirty later this year. Not so old, but it changes your perspective," Otto said.

"That's not the only thing that's worked to change my perspective," Jerevan said wryly, looking at the enormous mound of his body under the bedclothes.

"You'll come about, Your Grace."

"Thank you, Otto. I expect I will, eventually."

THE FOLLOWING THEOSDAY ERRIN KISSED ELISE AWAKE, but when she started to kiss him back, he withdrew. *"Are you ready for another swim?"* he asked.

Elise sat up and stretched, throwing off the last mists of sleep. "Take the whole day off and swim like we did last week?" she asked, looking up at him wistfully.

"Why not?" he challenged. "Jao's with Delanan. She won't need anyone to relay messages. Marion and Myrriden are teaching at the Rakredrem, and, despite their protests, they're enjoying the experience so they don't need your help. Jerevan said last night he was going to take his curricle out again today, so he won't need anyone but Otto until tonight."

"I have that project Delanan gave me."

"Identifying chromosomes on the new grain he got from Macosia?" he asked, frowning and stepping back from the bed. "Come now, Elise, you can find a better excuse than that. You started a whole new series of sprouts yesterday. The results won't be in for days."

"I didn't know you kept so close a watch on my work," she said.

He laughed ruefully. "I'm the victim of an obsession, Elise. I watch everything about you." He shook his head. "I know you enjoyed swimming with me last week. Why are you hesitant now?"

"I don't know," she said. "I just feel . . ."

"That you should be doing something more meaningful than swimming in the sea?"

She sighed. "Yes." She looked up at him. "I understand why you spend so much time in the sea. You were raised that way, but I was taught that we all need to work at something. Our work is what give us a purpose in our lives."

Errin stared at her, struck by the fact that they had lived together for over a year and yet she had never asked him what he did in the sea. If she had asked at any time, he would have told her. Between the work entailed in starting two new schools to be run by journeymen, due to open in the fall, and his project among the wigan folk, he had been working harder than ever before in his life, but Elise assumed he drifted with the currents.

"You can imagine no work I could do in the sea?" he asked.

She frowned. "Work and the ingvalarin of the wigan aren't concepts that go together."

"No, of course not," he said, swallowing his resentment. "But constant work without relief can turn to drudgery. You really have nothing else to do today, do you?"

She hesitated, then said, "No. I guess it would be all right. I did enjoy the swim we had last week."

"Then come on," he said, grabbing her hand and pulling her off the bed.

ELISE FOUND THE CHANGE EASIER THE SECOND TIME. The music, when it enfolded her, was livelier than it had been the last time. A breeze blew above the water, she remembered, forming white caps across the bay. She took a breath and dove, aware of Errin to the right of her tail, reflecting every movement.

She swam and the music enthralled her as it had before. After a time, however, a new melody impinged on her senses, a melody that sometimes harmonized and sometimes ran in counterpoint to the song of the sea. It was not loud when compared to the other melodies around her, but it seemed to penetrate more deeply.

Her heart still beat with the steady tidal rhythm of the sea, but the new melody made her blood run faster anyway. She rose and leapt and dove with a new urgency, and Errin rose and leapt and dove with her. They danced.

They danced through the clear, blue waters, startling schools of brightly colored fish. They danced in shadowed deeps where shafts of sunlight illuminated strange coral forms. They danced, but the dance was not the same as it had been. Slowly Errin drew closer and the strange, new melody grew stronger. She was not sure the moment she realized consciously that the melody came from Errin, but then she also knew that some part of her had recognized his song from the first note. He sang it for her, and she could not help but answer.

She leapt and dove and he dove with her. They came together where the bright blue of the surface water turned a deeper shade, where the capricious music of the waves faded away, leaving only the more vital melodies. He entered her and his song pierced her, and she could no longer separate her body or her mind from the song.

"*I love you,*" he thought in the midst of the climactic finale.

"*I love you,*" she echoed, reaching out to him. In that moment she wanted nothing more than to be one with him, to end the terrible separation. Her fears were nothing compared to the frustration she felt at being separate from him.

"*I promised not to link with you,*" he thought.

"*Only for the first time,*" she answered.

"*You remembered that when you agreed to swim with me today?*" he demanded, parting from her.

"*I don't know,*" she thought, aching from his withdrawal. She started to swim again. "*I didn't think at all.*" She shivered then at how close she had come, knowing she would have linked with him in that moment, if he had not pulled back.

He swam beside her. *"Do you wish to merge your life with mine?"*

"I did in that moment, but now I'm afraid again," she admitted, sensing an emotion shading his thought images that disturbed her.

"How could you be anything else but afraid?" he demanded. *"How can you trust me enough to link with me, Elise, when you still see me through your grandmother's eyes?"*

"But I don't," she protested, shocked.

"Don't you?"

"Of course not," she thought. *"I love you."*

"Yet you've never asked what I do in the sea."

"Because I know you need time away from all the responsibilities you face on the land," she thought. *"I understand that, Errin, truly I do."*

"Yes," he thought sadly, *"I know you understand that, but what you understand is the heart of what's wrong between us, Elise. When you realize that you don't understand me at all, then maybe it will be possible for the two of us to be one. But, seeing me as you do, I cannot blame you for your fear."*

They swam together for the rest of the day, dancing to the song of the sea, but Errin did not sing to her again. And Elise felt cold inside, despite the warmth of the water.

XLII

MONTHS OF INGVASH AND CERDANA

Yan te aar no Taelessa, ta a at yanse.

We name this water the Sea of Tears,
the symbol of our fate.

— EXCERPT FROM AN ESLARIN LEGEND EXPLAINING HOW THE THALLASSEAN SEA,
  TAELESSA IN ESKH, GOT ITS NAME

E RRIN WAS ON THE PATIO LOOKING OUT OVER THE BAY of Aelos when
Elise joined him. It was late afternoon and there were clouds to the
west. He foresaw a spectacular sunset, but one look at Elise told him that
she had not sought him out just to share the view. Something had
disturbed her, something other than her usual irritation at finding him
looking at the sea.

"What's the matter?" he asked. He rarely tried to use mind-speech with
her these days.

"I've just had a letter from Jorum," Elise said, frowning. "My
grandmother's ill. I haven't been home to Adun since the summer before
you came back from Cibata. That's three years. My grandmother will be
ninety-five this summer. I have to go to see her and Jorum."

Errin nodded. "Of course. I'll arrange with Antram for a ship." He
paused, then added deliberately, "And I'll come with you. I would have
needed to visit the northern Thallassean soon in any event. There are a
number of wigan that never migrate to southern waters."

Elise stiffened at the mention of the wigan. "And I suppose you have to
play with every one of them."

Errin sighed. Once he had hoped that Elise would recognize who he was
on her own, but that was not going to happen. Her grandmother's view of
him was too entrenched in her mind. If their relationship was ever going to
develop, he had to change the way she saw him. Perhaps forcing her to
recognize what he was doing would help. He said, "I wouldn't quite term
what I've been doing play, but yes, I need to meet with all the wigan in the
Thallassean."

Elise's eyes widened. "What about the school project you've been
working on with Delanan? Not that you've spent much time on it anyway
recently."

"I never intended to spend much of my time on it, Elise. I helped to start
it, that's all. I'm a full wizard now, Delanan's equal. You've never heard

Delanan complain about the way I spend my time, have you? Or Marion? Or Jao?"

She shook her head slowly, frowning. "No, but they wouldn't say anything in front of me, would they?"

"Then ask them, Elise. Ask any one of them if they think I'm wasting my time in the sea."

She stared at him, scowling. "You're serious. You actually think you're doing something useful in the sea with the sea folk?"

"Yes, Elise. I'm serious. Come and swim with me again. Come with me to one of the wigan and see what I've been doing among the sea folk. If we leave for Adun soon, my old wiga will still be camped on the shore. You won't even have to swim very far."

She looked both puzzled and disturbed, but she nodded and thought, *"Very well, Errin. I'll swim with you again when we reach Adun."*

THE KERIAR NIN, A SLEEK BARKENTINE, sailed into the cove of the small harbor of the village of Adun on a clear day in the last week of Ingvash. The village lay on the north coast, at the mouth of the island's only watercourse, Sandar's Creek. The road to the Big House, as Mother Adun's home was called, followed the creek for about half its length and then turned west toward the coast.

Errin had insisted on bringing a carriage for transportation, but the small pier used for fishing boats was inadequate for unloading such a large piece of cargo and the crew spent half the afternoon at carpentry, widening and strengthening the structure, before they could get the conveyance ashore.

Elise wondered if the gesture were aimed at impressing her grandmother and grinned. If that had been his reason, it would not work. Mother Adun would not be impressed. But Elise had to admit to herself that the ride up the valley was much more comfortable in the carriage than it would have been in a farm cart, and Errin's horses might impress where the carriage itself would be seen as ostentation.

Jorum came to greet them when they drove up in front of the house where Elise had lived until the age of eight. He had his father's brown hair with only a few red highlights, but he had her hazel eyes, the irises a mixture of green, brown and gold. He was smiling, and somehow Elise was out of the carriage and hugging him before the horses had come to a full stop.

"Jorum," she said, stretching on tiptoe to kiss his cheek and then pulling back from him. "How is she?"

Jorum frowned. "Failing. I doubt she'll live out the summer, but she'll be glad to see you."

"Will she?"

Jorum shook his head, his mouth twisting wryly. "She may not show you how much, but she'll be glad. She's a contrary old woman, but she's proud of you." He hesitated. "We all are."

Elise hugged him again, but asked, "Even though I left you here, and visit so rarely?"

Jorum grinned, deepening the smile lines around his eyes. "It's not as though you abandoned me, Mum. And Granny and Dad were always much easier to manage than you were." His face sobered. "Granny made me her heir. You knew that, didn't you?"

She nodded, glad that her son had inherited none of Timmon's dourness. "I've always known that, Jorum, but you don't have to stay here. If you want to travel, you can find someone to manage the farms for you."

Jorum shook his head. "I love the islands. I always have. I've lived on the mainland, and I've made a few trips, even one to Ninkarrak, but Adun is my home. I'm the healer now. Granny hasn't been able to work at all since just after your last visit. I'm needed here."

Elise nodded. "Yes. It's a good thing to be needed and to have your own place."

"SO YOU'RE LIVING WITH ONE OF THE SEA FOLK after all," Mother Adun said when Elise entered her bedroom some time later. The old woman's voice was a weak thread, but Elise sensed her will. She lay propped in her bed, a wrinkled wisp, but the core was still iron.

"Yes," Elise said, "I'm living with an ingvalarin, but he isn't really one of the sea folk. He lives on Sussey and holds estates greater than Adun."

"But he goes back to the sea, doesn't he, child? He can't stay away from it for long, can he?"

Elise flinched at hearing her own doubts expressed, but found herself saying, "He's stayed away from it for years at a time. He's never shirked his duty."

Moira nodded. "That may be. I knew he was different from the others when he came to my door. I'll never forget the expression on his face when I told him he was too late, and that you were carrying Timmon's child. I should have known then that I'd see him again."

Elise shivered. Her grandmother had never told her that she had seen Errin when he came back. While Elise had known that Errin was telling her the truth about returning to Adun, she had never imagined him actually coming to the house and asking her grandmother where she was.

Moira Adun snorted. "Nevertheless, you won't be bringing him to stay in this house?"

Elise shook her head. "No. He's staying aboard the ship. He has work he'll be doing while I'm here, but he'll be coming to dine. I want him and Jorum to get to know one another."

"I hear you've almost qualified as a wizard," Moira said, changing the subject.

Elise focused on her grandmother's words. "I could qualify now; I've just been putting off taking the final tests."

Mother Adun's eyes, not as bright as they used to be, narrowed. "Why put it off? That's not like you, Elise."

"I'm not sure." Elise shook her head. "No. That's not true. It's just that, if I'm a full wizard, it makes my cowardice that much more blatant."

Moira frowned. "You've never been a coward, child. You were willful, but I don't believe you're a coward. And what can you fear now that you're almost a wizard?"

"Power," Elise said. "I fear power. If I link with Errin, I won't just be a wizard. I'll be a wizard on her way to being a great wizard. Errin and I will be the first since Cormor and Belis. Don't you see? That's too much responsibility."

Mother Adun snorted. "You didn't say 'would be the first,' child. You said 'will.' You're only putting off the inevitable, and in your heart, you know it. But take your time. If you're going to be one of the great wizards, your time will be measured in centuries. You may as well wait until the moment feels right."

IT WAS NEARLY THE END OF THE MONTH OF CERDANA before Errin insisted that Elise keep her promise to swim with him again, and visit with the sea folk she had known in her youth as she had never seen them before.

The shift was difficult for her in the icy water of the northern Thallassean. She had to levitate and suppress her body's need to shiver, but her dolphin form was protected by its natural layer of fat.

The song of the sea was also different in these northern waters. The rhythm was stronger, with great surges from the open waters of the eastern Thallassean crashing against the narrow peaks of the underwater mountains that made up the Outer Isles.

Elise had always known that she lived on top of a sunken mountain, but knowing it and swimming over the ridges and down the valleys forested with groves of dancing kelp, were two different things. Then the land dropped away and she was swimming after Errin through the open sea, the bottom only a faint echo in her dolphin sonar.

She sensed ingvalarin, what seemed a vast number of them, surging through the water toward Errin. "*Esarrage,*" they hailed him, 'High Chief' or 'High Commander.' There were sixty of them, her senses finally registered, three distinct groups of twenty, each wearing the marks of different wigan.

"*Why are they calling you that? I thought we'd be joining a hunt, but they're from different wigan. Since when have the wigan joined for a hunt?*" Elise demanded.

"*I never told you we'd be joining a hunt,*" Errin thought. "*To the contrary, I told you I'd show you what I've been doing spending so much of my time in the sea these past years.*"

"I thought you were resting from your labors on land. Why didn't you tell me you were doing something else?"

"Because, Elise," he thought sadly. *"I wanted you to figure out for yourself that I'm not, and never have been, an idle dilettante."*

She flinched at the bitterness she sensed in his thoughts. *"I never thought of you that way,"* she protested.

"Didn't you?" he demanded. *"What else would you call someone who needs several day's break from just a few day's work? I've spent more time at sea the last three summers than I've spent on land."*

She stared at the approaching ingvalarin, her thoughts filled with confusion. *"But I didn't . . ."*

"I'm a wizard, Elise," he thought, and she sensed a coldness in him that terrified her. *"With the exception of Kaaremin and Andamin with Belkarion, I'm now the most powerful wizard on Tamar. What's more, I'm aware of the responsibility that places on me."*

"What have you been doing with them?" she asked, as the ingvalarin surrounded them, swimming in precise formations.

"I've turned them into a mobile military force," he thought and swam to meet the leaders of the three groups of twenty.

Elise had a sudden memory of Errin's question, "You can imagine no work I could do in the sea?" And there had been other occasions, she realized, when Errin had as much as told her that she was wrong about him. But she had ignored his hints, convinced of her own analysis of the situation, and of him.

What else had he said? "How can you trust me enough to link with me, Elise, when you still see me through your grandmother's eyes?" She had denied his accusation, not even considering the possibility that he might be right. She had been a blind fool.

She watched the units, as Errin referred to them, go through their drill. The Keriar Nin had sailed out to this prearranged location to meet them, and each group of sea folk approached the ship and went through the motions of sinking it. She felt how their minds disappeared as they neared the ship, and appreciated the equipment that allowed them to shift to human form under water. When the drill was over, she even met the commanders of two of the units. The third unit came from farther away and left immediately after the drill.

One of the commanders was Ankor Farswimmer, the younger brother of her old friend Pela. It seemed strange to her that she had never met him, but he had not been born until after she had left to study in Bria. He told her that Tarle was still the arrage, but he had delegated the command of the wiga's unit to Ankor, who was young and strong.

The other commander Errin introduced her to was Lucian Kanakar. Elise recognized the name from her childhood. Errin's age, he was a powerful telepath and one of the few wigan folk who left the sea every year of his youth to attend school. Belonging to a wiga that spent the spring on a neighboring island, he had been one of Errin's few true friends. He was bigger in the water than Ankor, more dominant, but he was still not as huge as most of the mature ingvalarin.

"Errin thought of you often when we were children," Lucian greeted her.

"I heard your name also," she responded.

When they were again alone, swimming back to Adun, Elise thought, *"You told me that I was seeing you through my grandmother's eyes and I didn't believe you, but you were right. I have been looking at you through the eyes of my childhood."*

"Do you really see that now, Elise?"

"I'm sorry, Errin," she thought with a shade of desperation at the coldness she felt from him. *"But I do love you. No matter how wrong I've been in the way I've looked at you, I've always loved you."*

"Then how would you describe my actions in the past four years?" he asked.

"You've accomplished something that's never been done before. You've turned the wigan folk into a military force," she thought with almost a trace of awe.

"Doesn't it occur to you that such a thing may never have been done before because it never should be done at all?" he asked.

Elise's mind recoiled at his anger. *"If you believe so strongly that it shouldn't be done, why are you doing it?"*

"Necessity knows no right or wrong," he answered, and she sensed a vast weariness in him. *"I told Vanda of Ilwheirlane, when I met with her after I came back from Cibata, that Sussey and Lyskarion would stand in support of the human nations in the coming conflict. I keep my word."*

"You met with Vanda?"

"Yes, Elise, I met with Vanda."

"Why didn't you tell me?"

"Why should I have done?" he asked in return. *"You weren't interested in my concerns. You never asked what I did while I was gone."*

"But you must have known I'd be impressed by your meeting with Vanda," she thought.

"Just as it impresses you now," he agreed wryly. *"But what makes you think I want to impress you, Elise?"*

She hesitated, knowing this was another trick question, and that she was still missing his point. *"You said you loved me,"* she thought finally. *"I thought that people who loved each other shared their triumphs and their concerns."*

"Yes," he thought, but she sensed his sadness and knew she had failed to understand him yet again. *"I fell in love with you when I was too young to know better. I haven't been able to break the habit. But, Elise, loving someone doesn't guarantee that you'll like them as well."*

Elise shut her eyes, wishing she could close down all her senses and her mind as well and retreat into the great ball of misery that hovered around her. But if she did that, she knew she would lose him utterly and forever. That she could not face, so she went on struggling with the mind images that seemed to twist into new forms when he received them. *"I told you I loved you,"* she thought. *"I even found the nerve to link with you once."*

"If I'd just pushed you a little in a vulnerable moment," he answered. *"You never came out and said to me, 'Errin, I want to link with you today.' You wanted me to overpower you or trick you into it, so you wouldn't have the responsibility of linking to someone inferior to yourself."*

"I've never thought you were inferior," she protested.

"Haven't you?" he asked. *"Your actions say otherwise. You've always thought me less than your equal, Elise."*

"No . . ."

"Yes," he insisted. *"I've hoped for years that you'd discover your error by yourself. The last thing I wanted to do was to have to prove my worth to you in this way, but the last year convinced me that you'd never really look at me, and judge me by my actions and not my ancestry on your own. So I decided I had no choice."*

Elise thought about that for the rest of her stay on Adun. It explained the growing distance between them, and she knew that the only way to bridge that distance was to demand that Errin link with her. She longed to do just that, but the thought of Lyskarion still terrified her.

Moira Adun died in the month of Torin, and soon after, Elise and Errin returned to Sussey.

XLIII

MONTH OF AGNITH

The range of thought transference is certainly greater than the range of two people shouting at each other. Ultimately, indeed, it is limited only by the curvature of Tamar itself . . .

— EXCERPT FROM <u>PROBLEMS WITH TELEPATHY</u>, BY THE WIZARD AGNITH

RAND WATCHED THE SENANGAN FLEET EMERGE out of the pink and blue haze of the eastern horizon just after dawn on the second Kyrasday in Agnith, the twelfth of the month. He stared in disbelief as they sailed past his lookout point on a bluff southeast of Nadrum's harbor. He should have had at least a week's warning. He had counted on having such a warning. Now he would be lucky if he could give Darenje two days notice of the invasion. He counted the ships. Thirty-nine. Thirty-nine ships could hold twelve thousand soldiers, maybe only eight if the forces included malik cavalry, but malik mounted troops were worth double the number of ordinary foot soldiers, so that was no gain.

Rand closed his eyes, concentrating on an image of Jao, hoping she would not be out of range or so involved in something she would miss his call. He tried for several minutes but could not reach her. It was not yet time for their normal communication. The ship she was on might be too far over the horizon in its patrol of the coast. He would have to try again later.

What had happened to the courier ship that was supposed to give warning? Rand wished desperately that he were a great wizard and could simply shift his body to Darenje in a couple of jumps. Instead, he climbed down the rocks from his vantage point using his hands and feet.

Casting an illusion around himself and his boat, he untied the small yacht and set sail for Darenje. It would take time to load the troops onto the ships. With maliks to load, it might take a full day or longer, then another two days before the fleet could reach Darenje. With luck and a good wind, he might get close enough to give Darenje warning in one day. That might give them two days notice of the invasion.

At least he had been near Nadrum and had seen the fleet arrive. There had been months at a time over the past years when no one had been watching Nadrum. As the courier ship had failed, Darenje might have had no notice at all.

"*THE SENANGAN FLEET is already at Nadrum?*" Myrriden felt stunned. All their plans for dealing with the invasion of Darenje had depended on their having at least a week's warning. With that warning, they could have arranged for Darenje to hire mercenaries. There were always troops available among the Nine Cities of Anat.

But now? "*What happened to the courier ship?*" he demanded of Jao, who had relayed the message from Rand.

"*Rand doesn't know,*" she thought, and he sensed her despair. "*All he knows is that the fleet sailed into Nadrum this morning. He's on his way to Darenje, but he won't be close enough to warn them until tomorrow. Depending on how long it takes to load the troops, the Council will have two days or less to summon the militia from the outlying regions. I don't think they can do it.*"

"*If only we'd managed to set up a telepathic relay along the coast like the one the Varfarin maintains between Nacaonne and Ilwheirlane,*" Myrriden thought.

"*There aren't enough of us,*" Jao thought.

"*I'll get permission from Antram to take the naval ship in Ruffin to Darenje as soon as we can get aboard. At least we may be able to evacuate a few survivors,*" Myrriden thought. "I don't see how we can get there any earlier than the morning of the sixteenth, Taratsday."

"*Will you have room for Delanan and two of his best students?*" Jao asked.

"*Of course,*" Myrriden said.

"*At least I was able to reach Errin,*" Jao thought. "*He said to tell you that he thought he could reach Darenje by the evening of Tamarsday. He's put out a call and hopes to have at least twenty-three units of the wigan folk with him.*"

"*Yes,*" Myrriden agreed. "*If the legion takes more than a day to load, the ingvalarin might get there before the army can land. They might be able to sabotage the landing enough to give the militia a chance.*"

THE CALL FROM MYRRIDEN REMINDED JEREVAN too much of the summons he had received before the disastrous chase after Cinkarion. He did not want to leave Sussey again. Still, he reached out with his will and rang the bell for Otto.

Jerevan required the help of Otto, four footmen and the hoist now kept in one corner of the bedroom to dress himself and transfer to his wheeled bed. Once transferred, however, he could move the sliding weights and adjust the bed to raise his upper body with his will. He then removed the blocks that stopped the couch from rolling and propelled it across the room and out of his suite. He was proud of his dexterity at opening and closing the doors as he came to them, again through the use of his will.

He found Myrriden in the entrance, directing the footmen on the disposition of his luggage. "Why do you want me to accompany you?" he demanded.

"Because you have the most power, if we have to defend ourselves against wizards," Myrriden responded. "Neither Marion nor I could survive a wizard battle without your backup."

"Even with this couch," Jerevan protested, "I'm not very portable. There's no way I can go ashore in Darenje."

"We don't intend to go ashore," Myrriden said. "Without the warning we expected, we have no troops to support Darenje's militia. The only hope we have are the ingvalarin troops Errin's bringing, and they'll only be effective in the water against the Senangan fleet."

Jerevan nodded, and told Otto to pack what they would need.

As soon as Myrriden persuaded Antram to put the Keriar Nin under their command, they put to sea. When they were headed with all possible speed for Darenje on the barkentine Errin had been using all summer, Myrriden called for the wizards and their apprentices to meet in the arrai's cabin.

As the arrai's cabin opened on the deck, Jerevan managed to fit his wheeled bed through the door. He maneuvered it into a corner, to take up as little space as possible, but Elise still thought it made the small room feel crowded.

Myrriden had the chair by the arrai's desk. Marion and Delanan's two students sat on the bed with Elise, while Delanan occupied the only other chair. When Balen came in, he had to stand.

"I couldn't reach Errin," Elise said, when they were all assembled. "He must be with a distant wiga."

"That's all right, Elise," Myrriden said. "Jao reached him. He'll be in Darenje ahead of us. I only hope he gets there in time to disrupt the landing."

"What can he do by himself?" Balen asked.

"He won't be by himself," Marion said. "Hopefully he'll have a small army of wigan folk with him." She turned to Myrriden. "Did Jao say how many units he thought he could bring?"

"Twenty-three," Myrriden said. "That means quite a force, given the lack of notice. They should be able to sink a few Senangan ships."

"Errin's been training the wigan folk?" Balen asked, his expression one of amazement. "Why didn't he tell me?"

"He's been trying to keep the project secret." Delanan said. "He felt that surprise would make it even more effective."

"I wondered about all the time he spent at sea the last few years," Balen said.

"He's been working his fluked tail half off turning the wigan folk into mobile military units," Marion said.

Balen looked at Elise. "Did you know about this?"

She met his eyes. "He showed me something of what he was doing last summer, but I don't think I grasped the scale of it. He's going to bring nearly five hundred of the wigan folk to fight to defend a human city?"

"How large a force has he trained?" Balen asked. "And how did he get ingvalarin, who've been pacifists throughout history, to agree?"

"At the time of Errin's last report to Antram," Delanan said, "he had trained one hundred forty-seven units, each consisting of twenty ingvalarin."

Balen whistled. "Nearly three thousand."

"Furthermore, he trained the best telepaths in each unit in the use of crystals, and supplied the crystals," Marion added. "Errin even persuaded some of the wigan to alter their routes to cover the greatest area of the Thallassean possible, given their seasonal preferences. He also supplied every unit with all the tools necessary for sinking ships and trained them in mental shielding, so any unit should be able to take a ship, even if the ship has a wizard aboard."

Balen looked stunned, but said, "That still doesn't answer the question of how Errin persuaded the wigan folk to agree to fight?"

"According to Errin," Delanan said, turning to Balen, "the wigan folk understand and appreciate the concept of freedom more than most land dwellers. They don't like the idea of war, but most of them were willing to take a stand against both Gandahar and Senanga when the conflict was explained to them as a matter of freedom of choice. There were, of course, a number of wigan who refused to participate, but they made up less than twenty percent of the wigan Errin contacted over the last four summers."

JULA MOREC TURNED, STARTLED, when one of the younger brothers came running into the hospital. He cried, "They're coming. The army of Gandahar. They started boarding troop ships yesterday morning. They'll be here the day after tomorrow, or the next day at the latest."

It was three o'clock in the afternoon of Miunesday, and Jula had just started her shift. She was supposed to work until midnight. "The Varfarin said they'd give us warning," she protested, forgetting for a moment how publicly she had sneered at the idea of an invasion.

The brother stared at her, and she remembered his name was Aldan, Aldan Yosevi. One of the young trainees, he had only recently qualified as a Healer. With his unruly blond hair and the dusting of freckles across his nose, she thought he looked an unlikely messenger of doom.

He said, "No, Jula, they said they'd try to give us warning. They did try. Vanda of Ilwheirlane sent a courier ship all the way to Cibata, but something must have happened to it. Wizard Rand mind-sent to Latrem on the Council that thirty-nine Senangan ships sailed into Nadrum yesterday. The alert's gone out to assemble the militia, but there's no way troops from outlying areas without journeymen can make it here in time."

"Just the fact that troops are boarding at Nadrum doesn't guarantee Darenje's their target," Jula said, remembering her position, but her words sounded weak even to her. The truth was that she was afraid of even the thought of war.

One of the patients, a woman who had almost died of burns from a fire started by a spilled pot of oil, said, "The isklarin destroyed the Sanctuaries in Nadrum and Ardagh, didn't they? Will the hospital here close?"

Mekan Roka, the senior attendant on duty with Jula answered, "We don't know yet. The Kindred will call a meeting, I'm sure, to discuss the emergency and make contingency plans." He looked around at the dozen patients occupying the beds, people whose conditions were such that their healing took more than a day. "If we have to close this facility, however, we'll find some other location for all of you."

Jula envied Mekan his calm assurance when all she wanted to do was run screaming from the hospital and find somewhere to hide. He looked at her and she knew he felt her fear. His mind touched hers with a sense of encouragement. *"Will you be all right?"* he asked intimately, so the knowledge of her near panic would not upset the patients.

Jula nodded stiffly. She had never before thought of Mekan, with his brown hair, brown eyes and only medium height, as a tower of strength, but she was grateful for his presence. Without it, she knew she would have lost control.

Mekan turned to Aldan. "Tell Sister Gaya we can't leave our posts, but we'll be alert for the signal to link when the time comes for a vote on any decision."

Alden nodded, and continued through the hospital to the rear door leading into the less public portions of the Sanctuary.

ON THE MORNING OF TAMARSDAY, the fifteenth day of Agnith, Errin was swimming in rhythm with Zetan Kelpdancer's unit, with fourteen other units spread out in the waters around them. Most of the military units he had trained were led by young hunt masters. Zetan had been one of the few arragen to insist on commanding his wiga's unit. *"Always lead my own hunts,"* he had thought when Errin suggested he delegate the fighting to a younger ingvalar. *"See no reason to change now."*

Errin had not argued. Zetan was a reliable sub-commander. Despite his size, which was only average for the arrage of a wiga, he had a commanding personality and his presence reassured the younger commanders. He was one of their own, while Errin, despite his background, was considered one of the landborn.

Zetan was also one of the stronger telepaths, and Errin linked with him lightly to check the progress of the other units. For a moment he was linked to twenty-three minds in a network that spread out across hundreds of kilometers of the Thallassean.

"Report estimated arrival times," Zetan thought to the nine commanders whose wigan had been in southern waters when the summons had been issued.

When the commanders had reported, Zetan thought to Errin, *"Four units should be there by noon or a little later. The rest won't make it until after the sun sets."*

Errin entered the linkage and thought to the commanders of the units that would arrive early, *"Do not approach the fleet if it's already there. Our greatest asset is surprise. To take full advantage of that, we need to attack all at once. I don't want the Senangans to suspect that they need to watch out for enemies in the water."*

Later that day, the first unit to reach the port area of Darenje reported in. *"Only two ships of the Senangan fleet are anchored in the harbor, but there are sounds of fighting in the city,"* Zetan relayed to Errin.

"Send a scout to find the location of the rest of the fleet," Errin sent back, *"but don't get too close to any of the ships. There are bound to be wizards aboard. Don't let any of them notice you."*

Throughout the afternoon, as Errin and the main body of his troops swam steadily closer, the reports from the units arriving ahead of them kept coming. Errin was particularly shocked by the news of the location of the main body of the Senangan fleet, anchored off shore, ten kilometers north of the city.

"They must have loaded the entire legion within hours of the fleet's arrival in Nadrum," he thought, *"and unloaded it as quickly."*

"Probably been practicing loading and unloading procedures for years," Zetan commented. *"I would have, if I'd been in command of that army in Nadrum. Not much else to do."*

XLIV

MONTH OF AGNITH

The malik is a fearsome beast
With taloned claws and horny beak,
All ready to make you his feast,
If him you're fool enough to seek.

Part bird, he'll leave a three clawed track,
Or with his lizard tail he'll whack
You on your head, or 'cross your back,
And either way, your life you'll lack.

— EXCERPT FROM "THE MALIK," FROM <u>A CHILD'S GUIDE TO THE LARIN AND OTHER</u>
<u>BEASTLY TAILS</u>, BY ENOGEN VARASH OF ELEVTHERAI, 4557

THE FIFTH LEGION OF THE ESTAHARIAL ARMY of Gandahar landed on the shore of Darenje, ten kilometers north of the city, on the morning of Tamarsday, the fifteenth day of Agnith, a full half day before Rand's estimate of their earliest time of arrival. Isklarin scouts went ashore before dawn to kill the militiamen manning lookout points along the coast who might have witnessed the landing and given warning. The legion had time to order its ranks before it marched on the city.

The earliest warning Darenje had of the actual landing of the troops from Gandahar came from a few farmers on horseback fleeing the advance. There was barely time for a third of the troops of militiamen to form ranks in the lorsk fields on the plain north of the city before Gandahar's regiments of malik cavalry advanced upon them.

A double rank of well trained and experienced halberdiers could stop the charge of malik cavalry. Such feats were accomplished many times during the latter years of the Dragon Wars, when mankind fought free of the yoke of Gandahar, but that was the stuff of legends. More recently, in Cassinga, halberdiers had defeated Senangan malik cavalry on a number of occasions.

The troops of Darenje were trained. One or two of their instructors had even fought in Cassinga, but the militiamen had no experience at all. Only a few of them remembered to keep the halberds low on the ground until the maliks were almost upon them. They forgot that, if a malik sees the halberd in time, unlike a horse, it can shift sideways and reach out its head and bite the shaft, tearing the halberd out of its wielder's hands.

The militiamen had never known what it felt like to kneel on the ground with only thin, pointed stakes in their hands while a host of the most feared predators on Tamar charged at them, predators with armed soldiers mounted on their backs. The militia was made up of young men and women fresh off the farms. A few of them might have sighted a wild malik in the hills, but most of them had never seen one before that morning.

As a result, the malik cavalry cut through the militia almost as though they were not there. After a few moments of bloody carnage, the survivors broke and fled.

The city of Darenje had no walls to defend it. The troops of militia trying to reach the plain from their barracks or from outside the city, seeing what had happened to their fellows, tried to set up barricades in the streets, but there was no time to do more than shift a few carts or wagons sideways. A malik, even carrying a rider, can leap over a cart, or onto a wagon bed.

By midafternoon on the day of their landing, the army of Gandahar had put down all armed resistance. Darenje had fallen. The Councilors stood together on the steps of the Council Hall to proffer their surrender.

Jula, dressed in a plain, yellow cotton dress and feeling strange without her white robe, watched the ceremony from a nearby rooftop with the family who had given her temporary refuge. The Sanctuary of Maera had been one of the invading army's primary targets, and everyone the Gandaharan soldiers found there had been slaughtered. Fortunately, with plans for such an event already prepared, all of the kindred and patients in the hospital had escaped, as she had. Those killed in the Sanctuary had been those who took refuge there from the fighting in the streets, unaware of the isklarin hatred of Maera.

Despite the success of the escape plan, Jula wondered how long any of them would be able to stay out of Gandaharan reach, now that the city had fallen. The hospital had been moved to the Temple of Jehan and many of the kindred had taken refuge there as well, but the Temple could not double its priesthood without a number of people noticing. How long would it be before someone reported the discrepancy to the Gandaharan troops?

A black haired man with intense amber eyes, mounted on a large gray stallion, rode into the square in front of the Council Hall. Jula identified him as Aavik Ziakar by the insignia on his uniform. He was flanked by several dozen officers. Ranks of foot soldiers lined the sides of nearby streets.

There were no maliks in sight. She had never seen a malik before that morning, but she had heard about them, so she knew why the cavalry had disappeared as quickly as they had come. They were too dangerous. A malik would attack its rider as willingly as it attacked the enemy. They were used for war and rapid patrols, but then they were put back in their pens or staked out away from the troops. Malik cavalrymen usually died in service. Those who survived long enough to retire rarely retained all their fingers or hands. The officers of the Gandaharan army rode horses.

Aavik's horse halted at the foot of the steps leading up to the Council Hall. "Your city has fallen," he said. "Do you surrender?"

"It appears we have no choice," Amale Korsen, the current Chairman of the Council, said. "Will you now march us all in chains up your Road of Masters?"

Jula focused her sight on Aavik's face, catching his smile, before he said. "On the contrary, none of you need to leave your homes, or even your offices as Council members. The kulhar I shall appoint to rule Darenje will undoubtedly wish to consult with your Council on local matters. Your knowledge should prove invaluable to him."

"You would have us become puppets?" Amale demanded.

"Not puppets," Aavik said, "public servants. Without your assistance, anyone I appoint as kulhar will have no way of knowing your local traditions. He may make mistakes. Surely you wish to avoid such unpleasantness?"

Amale's hand fingered the medallion symbolizing her office hanging from a gold chain around her neck. She lifted the chain over her head and descended the steps to drop both chain and medallion in the dirt in front of Aavik's horse. "I hereby resign my office," she said. "Your kulhar will do what you tell him to do, but I'll not lend my countenance to your act of tyranny."

"Then you shall walk in chains up the Road of Masters," Aavik said, "for you've proved yourself a traitor to the new state." He looked at the remaining eight Councilors. "Those are your choices, too. Remain in your offices and assist whomever I shall appoint as kulhar, or be condemned to slavery in Gandahar." He looked at Amale again. "You may change your mind, but you must do so now. Even an hour from now will be too late."

"I'd rather be a slave than a traitor," Amale said. "However you word it, anyone who stays on this Council will be a traitor to Darenje."

Fellis Latrem, the representative of the independent merchants on the Council, said, "Darenje has many customs and traditions. I see the importance of the new function you would have this Council serve. As I have dedicated my life to public service, I will remain."

Three of the other Councilors removed their symbols of office and descended the steps to drop them in the dust beside Amale's.

Jula felt her lip curling as she watched Latrem kowtow. He was a handsome man. She had thought him a romantic figure years before, when he had still been a Healer protesting the rules of the Sanctuary. Of course, she had been a child of thirteen. She remembered her disappointment when he resigned from the kindred upon completing his training, the same year she had been admitted as a trainee. She shook her head at her own naivete, realizing it had been simple greed and selfishness he had romanticized.

Yet he had leadership ability, she reflected. Four of the other Councilors were shifting their positions on the steps to stand by Latrem.

"Very well," Aavik said, "you've made your decisions." He gestured to one of the officers behind him. "Have these four," he indicated Amale and her companions, "taken to my ship and put in the brig. I'll take them back to Gandahar with me."

AS SOON AS ERRIN AND THE UNITS HE HAD ASSEMBLED joined the nine already patrolling the coast of Darenje, he ordered the commanders to meet with him. Full dark had fallen. His sight showed him the heat shadows of the warm bodies of his twenty-three officers arranged in a semicircle before him, floating in the cooler, black, silt laden water of Darenje's harbor.

"Have they moved more of the fleet up the coast into the harbor?" Errin asked, after all the status reports were completed, closing out his awareness of the profusion of melodies created by the movement of the sea against the shore.

"Five," Lucian Kanakar reported, his fins and tail stroking the water to keep him in place. One of the younger commanders, he was a powerful telepath and one of the few wigan folk Errin had met who had left the sea every year of his youth to attend school. Errin had found him quick thinking and inventive, and had given him temporary command of the units that had arrived at Darenje before he could. "The other thirty-two are still anchored offshore of where the legion landed. I took the liberty of sending one of my unit ashore when we spotted a group of people fleeing the city."

"What did he find out?"

"Darenje has fallen," Lucian thought. "The Council has given its formal surrender."

"So quickly?" Errin thought, his tail stroking the water violently in reaction. It took him a moment to regain his position, but most of the other ingvalarin had reacted the same way. He performed a calming mental exercise, while his mind insisted on recalling the fall of Nadrum. But Nadrum had been a mere shadow; Darenje was a thriving city with a population of over a hundred thousand.

"Gandahar brought a full regiment of malik cavalry," Lucian thought. "The coastal lookouts failed and the militia didn't have time to fully assemble. Those that reached the plain north of the city broke on the first charge."

"Aavik is efficient," Errin thought, "but this changes our priorities. The Keriar Nin should be here early tomorrow morning. Our main purpose now must be to rescue key personnel of the city government and those of the kindred of Maera who wish to escape. The destruction of as much of the Senangan fleet as we can manage must take second place."

"Aavik gave the Councilors a choice," Lucian thought. "They could keep their positions as Councilors and serve under his kulhar, or they could be sent in chains to Gandahar."

"*Interesting,*" Errin thought. "*If he doesn't intend to reduce the citizens of Darenje to slavery, he must want very much to keep its economy intact.*"

"There's been no looting," Lucian confirmed. "*They broke the militia with malik cavalry, but the maliks disappeared after the first hour of the takeover. The foot soldiers have acted more like police since then, ordering people to their homes and only fighting after being attacked.*"

"*Why did the refugees flee then?*"

"They were known worshipers of Maera," Lucian answered. "*The Sanctuary was the exception to Gandahar's attempt to limit the violence. Everyone found there was slaughtered.*"

"*How many Councilors chose chains?*" Errin asked.

"*Four.*"

"*Less than half the Council?*" Errin exclaimed. "*Aavik or the maliks must have been persuasive.*" He released air and heat limned bubbles spiraled up through the dark water.

He signaled and they all rose to breathe, then reassembled. "*If four chose to resist, then those are the four we must rescue,*" Errin thought. "*Did the refugees know where they were being held?*"

"*They didn't,*" Lucian thought, "*but one of the observers I kept in the harbor saw prisoners taken aboard the largest of the ships anchored there.*"

"*The flag ship,*" Errin thought. "*Aavik would want his prisoners close.*"

"*Shouldn't we send someone else ashore?*" Zetan asked. "*We need to notify the kindred of our presence, so that those who wish to escape in the morning may do so.*"

"*The survivors will be in hiding after the massacre in the Sanctuary,*" another of the commanders thought. "*How can we contact them?*"

"*The priests of Jehan will know how to do that,*" Zetan thought. "*I've swum in Darenje's waters. The kindred and the ajaren are closely allied here.*"

"*True,*" Errin thought. "*Send your scout then, but he must be back before dawn. Our attack must take place the moment the Keriar Nin enters the harbor, which should, at the present rate, be just after dawn.*"

"*The wizards can conceal their ship, can't they?*" another of the commanders thought.

"*Not for long, if Aavik isn't distracted. He's a powerful wizard with full command of the high sight,*" Errin thought. "*Any of the kindred, or others with reason to fear for their lives under Aavik's rule, should plan on being on the docks at dawn. They must arrange for their own boats to take them out to the Keriar Nin when it arrives. We'll sink the Senangan ships in the harbor, but we won't be able to sink a third of the ships up the coast. The Keriar Nin will have to turn about and leave the harbor immediately. Those unable to board immediately will have to be left behind. Have your scout make that clear.*"

Zetan indicated acknowledgment of the order with a gesture of his fins.

XLV

MONTH OF AGNITH

Yet in the end the wizards fought each other,
For power unchecked will often madness cause;
So Rav conspired and sought to reign supreme,
Despite the Council's strict and binding laws . . .

They met upon a field in Arduin,
Where Agnith, mad with rage and bitter hate,
Called down the very power of the sun.
So did the Age of Wizards meet its fate.

— EXCERPTS FROM "ILKARIONIN, THE LIVING CRYSTALS," FROM <u>LEST WE FORGET: A</u> <u>BOOK OF TEACHING RHYMES</u>, BY WILTON WIRRAMARETH OF ILWHEIRLANE, 4207

"I DON'T LIKE SPLITTING OUR FORCES," Errin thought to the circle of his unit commanders in the early hours of the morning of Taratsday, *"but I don't see that we have a choice in this situation. We have to take out all the ships in the harbor, and, if we don't attack the main fleet at the same time, they'll have warning and our attack won't be effective."*

"There are seven ships in the harbor," Zetan thought. *"I recommend we keep eight units here, so one can act as a backup, if needed."*

"Nine," Errin thought, *"One of the ships in the harbor is the flag ship. Aavik himself may be aboard as well as the prisoners. We have to board that ship as well as sink it."*

"That leaves twelve units to attack the main body of the fleet. They'll have to be in and out quickly," Zetan thought. *"I'd recommend they try for ten ships and keep two units for backup."*

"Sounds reasonable," Errin thought, *"but feel free to improvise when you're on the scene. You'll be in command of the units attacking the main fleet."*

Zetan signaled acceptance with his fins.

OVER A HUNDRED PEOPLE WERE GATHERED in the secret room beneath the main building of the Temple of Jehan, all but a few of them wearing gossamer veils that concealed their features while allowing them to see what was going on. They had been entering the Temple one or two at a time since late in the afternoon of the previous day. Now, in the early hours of the morning, the room was so full there was no longer room for chairs, and everyone was forced to stand. Ajaren of Jehan, in their pastel robes and the kindred, many still in white robes, made up a large percentage, but Jula saw several in the uniforms of the defeated militia, and her sight enabled her to recognize a number of well known merchants, craftsmen and farmers despite their veils. Most of the militiamen and merchants were gathered around the stout, silver haired figure of Hathi Beloin, who had been Chairman of the Council until he retired three years earlier. The farmers and craftsmen were gathered around the tall, angular figure of Bryant Elpine, once head of the Farmer's Union and another ex-Councilman. Beloin and Elpine were among the few who wore no veils.

Escan Jabiren, the High Priest of Jehan in Darenje, also lacking a veil, called the meeting to order from the raised platform at the end of the room farthest from the door. He was a small, nondescript man with light ginger hair and brown eyes, much younger than the high priest he had replaced the year before. Jula often wondered how such an unimposing figure could produce such passionate music, but Jabiren's musical compositions had made him famous all over Tamar. Everyone in Darenje had felt honored when he came to live and serve in their city.

"Your attention, please," Jabiren said when no one else had arrived for some time. His voice was not loud, but some quality in it drew the attention of the crowd. They quieted and turned to face him.

"As you are all aware," he said, when he had everyone's attention, "Darenje has fallen to Gandahar. We're here to decide what to do now. Will the people of Darenje accept isklarin rule, or will you resist and begin this night to set up the machinery of that resistance?"

"Resist," the crowd cried out with one voice.

Of course, Jula thought, they would not have been invited to this meeting if there had been any doubt about their reaction to the invasion.

"Darenje threw off the rule of the isklarin once. We can do it again," a voice shouted. Jula thought it sounded like Petrel Quanat's.

"Then I give the floor to Hathi Beloin," Jabiren said.

Beloin stepped up onto the platform and looked around the room. "You have reason to despise most of your City Council this day, but those of you who know me know that I'd have joined Amale and accepted chains." His frown caused his gray, bushy eyebrows to meet above the curved beak of his nose.

"Saram Gaya," he nodded toward the tall woman standing behind him and to his left on the platform, "has warned the members of the Varfarin on their way here not to communicate again with Councilman Latrem or the others who joined him. She tells me that, despite the lack of warning and the failure of the militia, there'll still be a blow struck against the invaders."

A ragged cheer went up from the crowd, and Jula felt her own spirits rise. She hated violence. The thought of a long term struggle against Gandahar appalled her, but still, the isklarin takeover had been bloody and ruthless and altogether too easy for them. They were the aggressors; they deserved to suffer some retaliation.

When the crowd quieted, Beloin said, "Although Ajare Escan," he nodded toward Jabiren who had remained on the platform, "has been generous in sheltering the kindred and offering to take over the hospital and a staff of healers, the Temple can't safeguard all the kindred. Moreover, we need to send witnesses to what has happened here to Ilwheirlane and the other human nations, both to warn them of the danger they face, and to urge them to aid us in once again throwing off Gandahar's yoke. Therefore, those of you who don't feel able to face the coming conflict, or have friends or family you wish sent to safety, get them or yourselves to the harbor at dawn. If possible, have boats prepared. A signal will be given for the moment you should take to the sea. Are there any questions?"

"How many will the Varfarin be able to take?" a voice asked from somewhere in back of the room.

"No more than two hundred, and conditions will be cramped if that many seek to flee now," Beloin said. "But there'll be other ships taking refugees in the future. This one should only take members of the kindred who cannot be absorbed by the Temple and are unfit for the road, or well known worshipers of Maera and high ranking officers in the militia whom the isklarin may recognize."

"Why were we given these masks and told to wear them?" one of the merchants asked.

"So at least none of the non-sighted here can tell the isklarin who attended this meeting should any of you be taken captive," Beloin said. "Bryant and I," he nodded at the tall, gaunt ex-Councilman with his shock of silver hair standing in the front row of the audience, "will be interviewing all of you and assigning you contacts and passwords, so that you can each work with your own groups. After tonight, there'll be no other mass meetings."

"Why'd you let us see your faces then?" asked a voice from the crowd.

"Bryant and I will be going into hiding, but we felt you had a right to know who'd be in charge for the time being, until we can free Amale and the other Councilmen."

"The system they taught us in school, the way they organized the rebellion during the Dragon Wars," someone called out.

Beloin nodded. "That's right. If a system worked once, it will again." He looked around the room. "Never forget: Our ancestors bore Gandahar's yoke having never known freedom. They freed themselves. Having known freedom, can we do less?"

"Will the priest be going into hiding, too?" another voice cried from the audience.

Beloin stepped back and allowed Jabiren to step forward. Jabiren said, "No. I'll be playing my jalith in the Temple tomorrow as usual. I have no desire to hide from Aavik or his underlings, but many isklarin still worship

Jehan. The buildings errected to honor the gods are supposed to be safe havens for all who enter them, despite what was done in the Sanctuary of Maera yesterday. I doubt I'll be harmed or arrested. On the other hand, I'll undoubtedly be watched, so I'm not a safe person to contact except in an emergency." His eyes scanned the crowd and he added, "I wish all of you good luck. Would all the ajaren and the kindred assigned to work with us in the Temple please meet with me in the meeting room upstairs."

When Jabiren stepped back, Gaya Olaven stepped forward. "Would all of the kindred who haven't received assignment to work in the Temple please join me in the back of the room." She looked around at the rest of the crowd. "Anyone who wishes to leave should leave now. The rest of you should form a line. You'll each be called up to be interviewed and receive your assignments. I, myself, will also be going into hiding, but there will always be healers available for those who need them. Your group leaders will tell you how to contact a healer in your district when you've been assigned."

She stepped back and the crowd began to churn as various people sought to exit the room or position themselves as they had been instructed. Jula let herself flow with a group in the pastel robes of the ajaren. She broke away from them as they approached the exit and moved to join the clump of people gathering in the right corner of the back of the room.

Saram Gaya joined the group only moments after Jula. She looked around and Jula saw her eyebrows rise when she noticed the cocky, angular figure of Petrel Quanat.

"Petrel, what are you doing here?" Gaya asked. "I know you were offered a place in the Temple."

"I refused," Petrel said. "I've decided to take up the position of wandering minstrel."

"But you're the best musician to ever join the Sanctuary," Gaya exclaimed. "I thought for sure you'd be thrilled to study with Ajare Jabiren."

Petrel shrugged. "I would be, but I chose healing ahead of my music long ago. If I stay in a Temple, particularly with Jabiren, the music will eventually take me away from being a healer. That's not what I want. You and the ex-Councilmen," he nodded toward the front of the room where Beloin and Elpine were meeting one by one with the new conspirators, "you'll need couriers. Who better than a strolling player? I'll be able to act as a healer as well."

Gaya smiled ruefully. "You're wise to know yourself so well, and you're right that we'll need couriers. I accept your decision." She looked around at the others, and Jula felt herself flinch under Gaya's eyes.

"Zenobia," Gaya said, and listed off over a dozen other names, "you'll all be coming with me, unless, like Petrel, you've made other plans or wish to leave with the Varfarin on the morning tide."

Those named all indicated assent.

Gaya turned to Jula and the remaining group around her, most of them elderly or infirm. "The rest of you must be at the harbor before dawn. It will be your job to spread the news of what happened here in Darenje to all the human nations around the Thallassean."

Jula bowed her head. She felt ashamed of her cowardice, and that Gaya had sensed her fear and was sending her away because of it. Being exiled now might shame her, but it was just as well. She would not have been strong enough to endure the coming conflict. Keeping her in Darenje would only have endangered those in the resistance around her.

LUCIAN KANAKAR, ALONG WITH THE OTHER UNIT COMMANDERS, was linked with the ingvalar perched on an upthrust of rock outside the harbor of Darenje. Through the sentry's mind he saw the lightening of the eastern horizon that meant dawn.

"*The Keriar Nin is here,*" the lookout thought, and Lucian sensed the form of a ship emerge out of the darkness.

He signaled his unit, knowing the other units were doing the same, and they rose through the dark, silty water to the surface for air, being careful not to splash. Then they dove and swam for the ship they had been assigned to sink, the Illod Ing, or Flying Fish, the flagship of the Senangan fleet.

Lucian felt honored that his unit had been assigned the largest ship, the one ship certain to have wizards aboard. Granted Esarrage Pomorry would be boarding the Illod Ing with another unit, and thus might be there to supply backup if Lucian's unit needed help, but Lucian's unit's assignment was still the most difficult because of the timing involved.

The other units only had to sink the ship they were assigned to sink. Lucian's unit had to sink their ship at a precise moment, in time to cover the escape of the prisoners. And, if the unit boarding the Illod Ing had difficulties, his unit would be the first to supply backup.

He linked mentally with his fellows. They erected the shield around their minds that they hoped would keep even wizards from noticing them. When he felt the presence of the Senangan ship above him, Lucian shifted to human form, suppressing the instinct to inhale, and signaled to the others of his unit who had also been assigned to drilling holes. He twisted until he could reach his backpack and took out an auger, aware of others doing the same. They each went to predetermined points of the hull and bored into the wood.

Lucian worked carefully, trying to make as little noise as possible. His pack contained a bladder full of air from which to breathe. His mind maintained a tenuous link with the other unit commanders and with Errin who was boarding the ship above him.

ERRIN SHIFTED TO HUMAN FORM and levitated out of the water and up the side of the Illod Ing while maintaining an illusion of non-being. Once aboard, he sent his awareness out and identified the location and awareness levels of the sentries. When he was sure he had not been discovered, he took a rope ladder from his pack and attached it to the ship's railing before lowering it into the water for the unit to climb when he signaled that the way was clear.

He crossed the deck to the location of the closest sentry. This, he knew, would be the greatest test he would meet this night. Could he use his power to kill? The great wizards, even the most noble of them, had often done so. They had dominated all of Tamar with their ability to kill with a thought. Through Lyskarion he knew how, but was he, an ingvalar who believed above all in peace, capable of reaching out and killing with his mind?

The sentry was looking toward the shore and Errin followed his gaze, afraid he would see a boat full of refugees pulling out too soon into the harbor. There was nothing, and the sentry shifted, looking across the water at the other ships in the harbor. His gaze passed through Errin. Errin clenched his teeth and reached out with his will to stop the sentry's heart.

The effort of breaking through the linlar's defenses was more than he had expected. The guard gasped, and his weapons' harness clattered as he fell to the deck. Errin checked instantly to see if the other sentries had been alerted, but they had not been. He had killed, but it had cost him a drain in energy and will. Would he have enough strength to finish? As Jehan wills, he thought, and moved on to the next guard.

When all the sentries had been eliminated and the twenty ingvalarin were safely aboard, Errin had the two smallest ingvalarin don the sentries' harness and insignia. Then, he went to the hatch closest to where the prisoners were being held and had the ingvalarin wearing the linlarin insignia open it. He slipped through, again assuming the guise of invisibility, and levitated himself to a position behind the guards at the foot of the ladder, where they had moved to question the opening of the hatch. Again, he stopped their hearts, although killing two so quickly strained his ability. Even the second one, who turned when he heard his companion fall, had no chance to cry out.

Leaving the two ingvalarin in linlarin harnesses on deck to stand guard, Errin led the rest of the unit below. He met the first real obstacle to his plan at the hatch to the lowest deck, where someone with a strong wizard talent was on guard. When the hatch had been opened, he attacked the Senangan wizard directly with his mind, pushing the globe of force he had already formed to overwhelm the linlar. The Senangan's mind collapsed under his attack, but even as he died the linlar sent out a mental cry Errin could not block.

"Hold the hatches," Errin warned the ingvalarin with him. *"That one got off a warning."*

He dropped through the hatch, levitating again for speed, and moved down the passage to the grill above the space where the prisoners were being kept, stopping the hearts of two more guards as he went.

Errin had to pause for a moment over the grill before he could calm his mind and recover enough energy to unlock the padlock. Then he tore the grill open and yelled down to the prisoners. "I'm dropping a ladder down. You all have to move quickly if you hope to escape." He took the second ladder he had brought with him and dropped one end down while attaching the other to the grill.

He waited while the four Councilmen and five others, three of them in military uniforms, climbed up, thinking to Lucian, *"How soon before you can hole the ship?"*

"Five more minutes, then we'll be ready on your command," Lucian thought.

"Should be perfect," Errin thought, *"but hold off until I signal or you feel me die. I've got the prisoners, but we still have to get out of here, and one of the guards gave a warning."*

When the last of the prisoners had climbed up into the passageway, Errin led them toward the hatch. As they reached the ladder, there was a shout from the deck above. Errin levitated up to the higher deck and saw at least a dozen Senangans advancing toward the hatch from the forward half of the ship, two of them wizards.

He reformed the ball of energy he had used to destroy the other Senangan wizard and sent it down the passageway. The oncoming Senangans slowed their charge at the sight of the ball of force, all but the two wizards stopping. Errin moved forward making room for the prisoners to climb up the ladder behind him. The ingvalarin who had been guarding the hatch took up the weapons of the dead guards.

The two wizards linked and sent their combined will to meet Errin's, but Errin had Lyskarion, and the two who faced him had not attained the high sight. The war of wills took little more than a minute or two. Then the linlarin wizards fell. The other linlarin fired their muskets and charged.

Errin deflected the round of musket balls and managed to stop the heart of another Senangan before they could close, but there were too many for him to be able to stop them all and his energy was dwindling rapidly. A shot fired after the first volley struck one of ingvalarin nearby high on the arm. He felt the pain as his own. Then the eight ingvalarin with him charged to meet the Senangans.

He pushed the prisoners back from the fighting and led them toward the hatch at the other end of the passageway that more of his men still guarded. "We have to get you out of here quickly," he said, and did not wait for them to climb the ladder, but lifted each of them up to his men in the upper passageway, then levitated himself after them.

He felt one of the guards he had left on the main deck die and screamed a mental warning to the other, then another ingvalarin in the passageway below died. He threw up a partial shield, but he could not block out the pain without blocking out the contact he needed to maintain control. "Have to get up on deck," he said to the ingvalarin guarding the hatch. "Senangans above us."

He felt two more deaths from the passageway below before the signal came to him that the linlarin who had attacked in the passageway were dead and the surviving ingvalarin were coming after him. He sensed the whole ship stirring now, Senangans starting to pour out of the forward hold where their bunks were located. *"Hurry,"* he thought.

Then he was at the foot of the hatch leading up to the deck. He levitated himself up, again assuming the appearance of non-being and stopped the heart of one of the Senangans waiting on the deck. He stabbed another with his knife. The surviving ingvalar guard, in a Senangan harness, stepped out from behind a barrel and killed the third linlar, the last guarding the hatch. Lucian's unit and the backup unit were coming over the side where Errin had hung the ladder, racing to reach him before the horde of Senangans coming from the bow.

Errin levitated two more ingvalarin up onto the deck to face the Senangans closing on them, then started levitating the prisoners up. He could hear the rest of his men below fighting another group of Senangans in the passageway.

"Now," he thought to Lucian. *"Sink her now."*

The Illod Ing shuddered as the charges in the holes in her hull exploded.

"Run for the stern and jump into the water," he yelled at the prisoners. "You'll be safe once you're in the sea. There's a boat coming to pick you up."

He saw Amale, who seemed to be their leader, nod, then turned to face the oncoming Senangan marines, an unending stream of them, charging toward him from the hatches near the bow of the ship. He had no more energy to stop hearts, or even maintain the illusion of invisibility. He would have to fight hand to hand now, just as the ingvalarin emerging onto the deck from the hatch near his feet, and the backup units coming over the side, would have to do. They needed to give the boat from the Keriar Nin time to pick up the prisoners from the water without interference before they could escape themselves.

Jula huddled with the seven others in her group in the black shadows next to a warehouse across the street from a pier where a number of small boats were tied. The night was perfect for their purpose, with clouds concealing Ranth and most of the stars. A pervasive aroma of rotting fish filled the air. She shivered despite the warmth of the night, remembering why so much of the previous day's catch had been left to decay. But that, too, worked to their advantage. Even if the isklarin patrolled the harbor with their were-senses, the heat from the bodies of the refugees would be difficult to distinguish from the heat of the heaps of putrefying fish.

"Does anyone know what the signal will be?" she thought to the leader of the group, Saram Debran, a diminutive, gray haired man with stooped shoulders.

He thought, *"No, my dear, but I'm sure we'll recognize it when we see or hear it."* He sent reassurance to calm her.

Again Jula felt humiliation that she should be included in this group of refugees. All of the others were simply too old to fight; most of them had been retired. She was the only member of the group under fifty. There was no reason for her to be included with these refugees, except that everyone in the Sanctuary knew of her cowardice and feared that her fear would betray them.

And here she was, the strongest of them all physically, yet she was the one who was trembling, while they waited patiently for whatever was to come.

Then she felt a familiar mind touch, and Balen thought to her, *"Pass the word. It's time for the refugees to get into their boats. Head due east."*

"But the Senangan ships in the harbor," she protested. *"They're bound to see us."*

"In another moment or two they'll be too busy to worry about a few small boats. But you have to hurry. We only have one ship and we can't do much about the fleet up the coast. We're coming about and leaving here almost immediately. So move," he thought urgently.

Jula turned, still dazed about the fact that it had been Balen who contacted her, and thought to Saram Debran and all of the other leaders, *"It's time. I've heard the signal. We have to hurry."*

They slipped across the street and onto the pier. Then, one by one they boarded the rowboats tied up and waiting for them. Jula and an elderly man still strong for his age took up the oars of their boat while someone else cast off the ropes. Then they began to move across the black water. Despite Balen's claim, she used all her skill to row without splashing, uneasily aware that not all the other boats around her were being as careful.

Then she heard sounds of fighting from the largest ship in the harbor followed by a muffled explosion. There were cries aboard several of the other ships. She rowed harder. Another muffled explosion came from another ship. There were cries and more sounds of fighting from the largest ship. Then she heard splashing as though several people had jumped overboard.

ELISE STOOD IN THE BOW OF THE KERIAR NIN as it sailed into Darenje's harbor. She was dressed for combat, as they all were, in dark leggings, a long sleeved shirt, calf high leather boots, and a weapons belt with two muskets and a sword. If she had not been linked with Marion, Myrriden, Balen, and Jerevan in the effort to keep the ship invisible to the Senangan sentries, she would have been using her sight to watch Errin and his ingvalarin troops board the Illod Ing. Even now, when she was seeing the plans he had discussed with her put into action, she found it hard to understand how he had managed to turn the carefree spirits of the sea into an effective military force. Her doubts heightened her fears for his safety.

The harbor was dark, with scattered clouds concealing Ranth and most of the stars, but her were-sight enabled her to see the anchored Senangan ships. The water blocked sight deeper than a few meters, but she sensed no unusual concentration of life forms. Still, without using the high sight and probing for mental shields, she would not be able to detect anything. After all, if she could see the ingvalarin, so would the Senangan sentries.

The Keriar Nin had furled almost all her sails and was coming about. All hands remained on duty, ready to unfurl the sails again and leave Darenje the moment the refugees were aboard. Elise heard the boats being dropped and added extra energy to the shield that protected them from the Senangan sentries, muffling sounds as well as sight and heat patterns.

"I want to be aboard one of the boats," she thought to Myrriden. "I have to be able to reach Errin if something goes wrong."

"Very well," he responded. "We'll let you out of the link, but you must supply cover for the boat you're on. You'll be taking on Aavik's prisoners after Errin gets them out of the brig and off the Illod Ing. Balen will be on the other, picking up the refugees on the shore who couldn't find a boat."

"I can manage that," she thought. "Won't some of the prisoners want to go ashore, though? I thought the Councilmen at least would be joining the resistance."

"We'll swing south before heading back to Sussey," Marion thought. "We can put off anyone who wants to go ashore along the coast where the Gandaharans haven't had time to take control."

"Won't the Senangan fleet be after us?"

"We should still have time to put a boat ashore," Myrriden thought. "The fleet will have problems of their own, and they'll have to come into Darenje's harbor before chasing us. Aavik will want some of his own officers involved. From what I'm hearing from the ingvalarin, there are only Senangans aboard the ships in the harbor. I'm sure that's true of the fleet as well. All of the isklarin are still ashore."

Elise eased herself out of the shield link, feeling Balen do the same. She hoped Marion, Myrriden and Jerevan would be enough; Jerevan's will felt strong as a rock.

She loaded both muskets before she climbed down a rope ladder into the waiting boat, then she reached out to find Errin. The Illod Ing had a shield around it. She went to the high sight and felt her way through the intangible barrier. There were bodies on the deck and a confusion of forms within the hull. Errin had been discovered, and the Senangans on the ship were rousing like one of Arrun's hornet nests.

"Hurry," she said to the oarsmen who had cast off from the Keriar Nin and were rowing toward the Senangan flag ship. She dropped back into ordinary were-sight to conserve her energy. She had not found Errin in her brief scan, but somehow she knew he was tiring.

She sensed motion from the shore. A number of small boats had put out from the docks and were heading out to sea. Balen was directing them.

There were a series of splashes as nine bodies flung themselves over the side of the Illod Ing. "Pick them up," she said to the oarsmen.

The boat was close to the side of the Senangan ship now and she could see the released prisoners floundering in the water, but her attention was up on the deck where less than fifty ingvalarin, determined to cover the prisoners' escape, were fighting over a hundred roused Senangans.

Elise had never levitated more than to hold herself up when she changed shape, but now she lifted herself out of the boat and all the way up to the deck of the Senangan ship. Errin was fighting along with the other ingvalarin but their position was being enclosed by the Senangans. They would soon be surrounded and cut down.

Elise reached out to Errin. *"Link with me and use my energy. The prisoners are boarding the boat now. You need to get yourself and your troops out of here."*

"Elise? What are you doing here?" he thought, and she felt his surprise.

"Trying to help you escape," she thought, *"unless you're determined to make a martyr of yourself and the rest of your ingvalarin."* She pulled out the musket she had brought and blasted a Senangan who had spotted her arrival and who was charging her. He fell, and she jumped over his body, heading for Errin's position in the melee.

"I can't link with you," he thought.

"You'd rather die?" she demanded. She fired her second musket at point blank range into the back of another Senangan who had an ingvalarin down on the deck and was about to kill him.

"If we link now, the link will be permanent," he warned.

The ingvalarin she had saved shoved the dead linlar aside and rose, taking the Senangan's saber and nodding to her. "Thanks."

She nodded back at the ingvalar and thought to Errin, *"I'm aware of that."*

A gap appeared in the swirling mass of bodies and Elise followed the ingvalar into the center of the fighting, shoving the empty muskets back into her belt and drawing her own sword. The Varfarin had given her years of training in self defense, but she had never expected to use those skills in a combat situation. Still, she clenched her teeth and parried the thrusts as they came at her, trying to get closer to Errin.

"Why now?" he demanded.

"Because I'd rather live than die," she thought, suddenly impatient with him. *"And we're both likely to die without the link."*

There was a lurch and the whole deck of the Senangan ship tilted beneath her feet. She caught her balance and thrust at the Senangan nearest her, who had not been as quick to recover.

"We may die anyway," he thought. *"I don't have much energy left and I don't know how long it takes to form such a link, or if I'll be able to use your energy quickly enough to make a difference."*

Elise withdrew her sword from the dead linlar in time to parry another attack, but her arm was tiring and she had never learned any methods of fighting with her will. Yet she was close to Errin now. She thought, *"Then it's time we found out,"* and dodged another ingvalarin to reach Errin's side. She was still behind him, but he had just dealt with the opponent he had been fighting. She reached out her hand and touched his neck, the only point she could reach, opening her mind to Errin completely, almost forcing him into rapport with her.

As she touched him with her mind open, she felt Errin and another force reach out to her. Then she felt herself falling though a whirlpool of spinning, opalescent mist. And in that mist flowed music. Arpeggios and crescendos played around and through her, and Errin was with her, his mind also caught in the spinning, nacreous vortex that sang with all the music of the song of the sea. They were two minds intertwining, and for a moment she was not sure which thoughts were hers and which were Errin's. Then they stood alone on an opalescent plain, surrounded by swirling mists. *"So,"* he thought, *"it's done. We're linked."*

Elise was appalled at the sadness she felt in him, but he felt her reaction even as she felt it and thought, *"No, Elise, it's not the link itself I regret, but the way we came to it."*

"The battle," she thought. *"Where are we?"*

"Our minds are inside Lyskarion, but you needn't worry. Time is relative here, Lyskarion tells me. Less than a second has passed outside, and neither of our bodies are in immediate danger."

"But how can we escape when we're back in our bodies? The Senangans were all around us."

Elise sensed Errin reaching out into the music and mist that surrounded them and information entered her mind like a memory she had just recalled. *"Lyskarion will sing for us,"* she thought, stunned by the simplicity of crystal reasoning.

Then Elise was back in her own body on the deck of the Senangan ship hearing a strange, haunting melody. The music that to her ears seemed harmless was reducing the Senangans to writhing bodies on the deck. Errin turned and took her hand, and they followed the remaining ingvalarin over the side into the sea where the boat waited for them.

XLVI

> Bagor ilamlarin u bipar tem al at.
> Ileanse vailin ba ma daca e bohe nik
> a rhamin arto a ean.
>
> *Avoid those who wear the brand of destiny.*
> *Their lives are seldom happy and bring pain*
> *to those close to them.*
>
> — ESLARIN PROVERB

JEREVAN LAY ON HIS MOBILE BED ON THE DECK of the Keriar Nin, watching the events in the harbor and extending his will to support the illusion Myrriden and Marion had designed to conceal the ship from the Senangans. The effort was draining him, but not as severely as it was draining either Myrriden or Marion. The realization startled him. While he lacked much of their training and skill, in some respects he was already stronger than either of his chief instructors.

The knowledge disturbed him. It forced him to recognize the validity of Derwen's motives. Jerevan did have more pure power than any of the other wizards he had met, except, perhaps, for Wizard Arrun and Errin Pomorry, but Errin's power was enhanced by Lyskarion.

His thoughts were interrupted by the battle breaking out on the deck of the Illod Ing, and the sounds of muffled explosions as charges exploded in the hulls of the Senangan ships around the harbor. He felt the impact of the moment when Elise linked with Errin through his own linkage with Myrriden. The effect was so strong it acted like a psychic shock, and Jerevan had to compensate quickly when Myrriden broke out of the linkage in reaction.

Soon after, Errin and Elise came aboard. He heard Errin broadcast the release call to the ingvalarin, telling them that they had done their part and should swim as rapidly as possible back to their wigan. Boatload after boatload of refugees were hoisted up, and Jerevan was conscious of their curious stares. Balen came back aboard with Jula, and the sails were unfurled as they sailed out of Darenje. Jerevan did not relax and lower the shield until the Keriar Nin was back in the open sea. By then his head ached from the strain.

BACK IN HER CABIN WITH ERRIN, Elise hardly knew what to say. They were linked. She could feel the link. But she felt no major change in herself.

The cabin was small with only one narrow bunk. Morning light came through a porthole in an almost solid looking beam spotlighting a dusty seascape on the opposite wall. Errin's presence made the room feel small, almost claustrophobic.

Elise crossed into the light to look out the porthole. For years she had dreaded being fully linked with Errin because of the overwhelming effect she had thought Lyskarion would have on her, but now she felt little different than the way she had felt before. There had been a moment of respite in the midst of the battle, then the linlarin had been incapacitated by the sonics the crystal produced. She had sensed the crystal then. But she felt no awareness of the crystal now. She did not even feel as though her relationship with Errin was resolved.

"Is this all there is to it?" she asked.

"Is this is all you wish from it?"

Elise remembered Errin telling her that, while he might love her, he would not have chosen to do so. Looking back on her behavior over the years, she couldn't blame him. Elise had never realized before how much her grandmother's bitterness had affected her own attitudes and opinions. Seeing her behavior objectively, she didn't like herself.

"No, Lise," Errin thought, but she felt his thought in her mind as though he were another part of herself, *"don't be so hard on yourself. You do well enough when you're not echoing your grandmother."*

He was now a part of her, she realized. He had responded to thoughts she had not projected, thoughts she had considered solely in her own mind.

"But we'll always be able to hear each other's thoughts now."

"Then why don't I hear yours?" Elise demanded.

"You aren't listening. You're trying to withdraw, pull back into yourself, just as you've done for years," Errin thought. *"Part of us has been linked since we were children, Lise, but you've always rejected that linkage, so a part of your mind is trying to reject the stronger linkage now."*

Was she rejecting their linkage? Even a few days ago she would have denied such an accusation at once, but Errin's insight into her motives and rationale had proved so accurate in the past she could no longer deny any opinion he expressed out of hand.

She stared out the porthole blindly. She loved Errin. She had adored him as a child, chased after him and sought his attention. She had loved linking with him when they had both been children. She had been devastated when he refused to link with her that final summer.

She had fallen in love with him when she had been eighteen, but then her own fear and her grandmother's bitterness had forced her to reject him. Had she feared the link, or that he would deepen the link and then leave, as he had when she had been a child?

She had grown to know and love him again during the halcyon months of their journey with the carnival, yet she had withheld a major part of herself from him, and then she had sent him away when she learned of Lyskarion. She had known he loved her then, she had read it in his mind, but she had still been afraid.

She had been living with him now for several years, and, despite her love, she had consistently turned away from recognizing his real nature or sharing the major part of herself with him. Why? She had always told herself that she was afraid of the linkage, but was that really what she feared?

"Why did you stop linking with me when we were children?"

"We were too young. It was dangerous."

She could feel his presence just a step behind her. She turned to face him and put her hands up to rest on his shoulders. *"But the damage had already been done."*

He lifted her right hand off his shoulder and kissed her on the palm, a wet kiss that sent a shock through her whole body. *"I know that now, but I was too young to understand that then."*

"It's not the linkage I've been afraid of, is it?"

"Childhood fears are often the strongest," he agreed, *"but I can't leave you now. Wherever I go, I'll still have you with me, and wherever you go, I'll be there too."*

Lyskarion hung from a chain around his neck and she could feel its heat against his chest, see its swirling colors with her eyes. She suddenly saw herself through his eyes and bent down to complete the kiss they both desired.

Then they were back in the opalescent whirlpool she remembered from the battle, except this time the music sounded erotic. Somehow she pulled back from the vortex and clutched at Errin. He took her hand and pulled her toward her bunk, but she felt the sensations in his body, the feel of her hand in his, the tightness in his groin, as clearly as she felt her own reactions.

They undressed each other, although she was never sure which hands, his or hers, performed which act. Still, what gave pleasure to one, gave pleasure to both. They sank down together on the narrow bunk.

He felt her sensations as well as his own as his hands explored her body. She felt his feelings when she ran her fingers down his chest. In this dual exploration, they each found new ways to arouse and heighten each other's pleasure. They became one totally self-involved creature intent on fulfilling its most erotic dreams. Time and self ceased to have meaning. There was only sensation, and a tension that spiraled higher and higher until they exploded together into ecstasy.

They regained consciousness together, as they had lost it.

"You never explained that the linkage would include something like that," she thought.

"*I never knew,*" Errin laughed. "*The experience gives me a whole new concept of the creators of the karionin. I used to think of most of them as dry and dusty, prone to stay at home and do nothing.*"

"*They just didn't need to go far to get satisfaction,*" Elise said, grinning.

She was back in her own body, but she could still sense a faint shadow of Errin's thoughts and feelings. She knew suddenly that she could tune into those feelings if she wished. Read his every thought, as he had read hers. It was just a matter of focus.

Errin frowned and she sensed him receiving a message from one of the ingvalarin through Lyskarion.

"*We got the first ten ships just fine and another three for good measure as the backup teams wanted a try when the first teams were done and Kekar lost his head and tried for two, but by then the Senangans figured out what was going on and we had to get out fast. Kekar's team lost two, his team was the last to go, and there are some other cuts and scrapes, but everybody else is fine,*" Zetan thought.

"*Good job,*" Errin thought, but Elise could feel his pain at the thought of the two deaths. "*Spread out and head back to your wigan. Sussey and the Varfarin thank you.*"

Elise felt the connection break and Errin took a deep breath. "The Senangans still have nineteen ships. They'll be on our tails soon."

"Those are troop carriers," Elise said. "They'll never catch us." It felt strange to feel his reaction to her words, but she didn't feel her identity threatened. She realized that she could put as much or as little into the linkage as she wished.

"So are we now the most powerful wizards on Tamar?" she asked, only half joking.

Errin grimaced. "We may have the potential to become such, but at the moment I don't think I could light a candle."

"What will we do with that power?"

Errin sighed. "I suppose we'll just go on doing what we've been doing. It will take years for us to actually reach the level the Great Wizards did."

"You're not afraid?"

Errin looked her in the eyes. "Elise, I was afraid when I realized what Antram had put in my hand. I was terrified then that we'd never be together. Right now I'm sad, and elated, and exhausted. Let's just go to bed and get some sleep and worry about the future when it comes."

BALEN SLIPPED OUT ONTO THE STERN DECK where Darenje's refugees were staring back at the retreating shore. Jula was standing by herself, a little apart from the others. He went up to her. "I hope you didn't mind my asking for you as a contact on the shore."

Jula turned to him, her face expressing surprise. "Was that why I was assigned to go with the refugees?"

"Didn't they tell you?"

Jula bit her lip. "No. I thought it was because they knew I was a coward and didn't want to face the violence that's sure to come."

Balen shook his head. "Jula, you're not a coward. Hating violence doesn't make you a coward. It just means you've got good sense."

"You don't understand. I was relieved to be assigned with the refugees. I was a little hurt, ashamed that my fear was so apparent, but I was glad, too, because it meant I wouldn't have to face what's going to happen to Darenje."

"What is going to happen, Jula?"

"Gandahar won. The militia was mowed down and the maliks ran through the city killing everyone who tried to resist." Jula sighed. "But most of the people of Darenje won't accept that. They'll go on fighting, and more people will die. I don't want to watch that, Balen. I don't think I can bear to watch that or live in the middle of it."

"Most of the militia wasn't destroyed, Jula, because most of the militia never got to fight. I heard Amale talking to the wizards and only about a third of even the town militia made it into the field. None of the militia in the countryside was mustered in time. Gandahar may have conquered the city of Darenje, but they don't control the country. We'll be letting Amale and the other Councilors off on the shore south of town. They'll be helping to organize the resistance. Yes, there will be deaths, but Gandahar will never benefit as much as they expected to from this conquest. Instead of a breadbasket, they'll have a thorn in their side."

Jula sighed. "And the thought of that kind of struggle makes you happy?"

Balen shook his head. "I was horrified when I learned that Gandahar was planning to invade. I helped all I could to try and stop or defeat the invasion. None of this makes me happy, Jula. But I grew up in Darenje. I love Darenje. Our ancestors fought to free themselves from the isklarin before; we can do it again. Would you have wanted all of humankind to just stay slaves?"

"No," Jula said. "I know you and the others have to fight, but I can't bear to be a part of it. I just want to practice healing."

"Then you better tell Amale that. I think she's expecting you to go ashore with her and the other Councilors," Balen said.

"Yes," Jula said. "I will." She turned away from him and Balen turned and left her.

MARION LOOKED AROUND AT THE SALOON of the Keriar Nin as Myrriden ushered her in. Errin and Elise were already seated, entwined, on a padded sofa.

Marion smiled. She was glad to see that Elise and Errin's problems had been resolved. She sat on the sofa opposite the one the newlyweds occupied and asked, "Why are we here? I don't have much time before I'm due to help Jerevan with his healing. He overstrained himself holding that shield for so long."

"Jerevan's condition is the reason I asked you all to meet with me," Myrriden said. "The effect of the strain he suffered while covering our escape from Darenje points out how dependent he is in his current state. After an exertion like that, he can't even survive without assistance."

"I'm aware of that," Marion said.

"Then you'll understand why I want to ask Errin to enable Jerevan to shape-change into a dolphin. Errin told both of us that such a solution was possible when he returned to Sussey after his trip to Cibata, but you, Marion, objected. I need to know if you still feel as you did then?"

"No," Marion said. "My reason for that objection is no longer valid. Jerevan does everything now with his mind. In just three years he's forced that to become his instinctive reaction. I've always recognized the power of his will, but what he's done took more than strength of will."

"Discipline," Myrriden said. "Jerevan has the most disciplined mind I've ever met. Cormor had genius, but I don't think even he had the discipline Jerevan has achieved."

EPILOGUE

4659, 466TH CYCLE OF THE YEAR OF THE GRIFFIN
MONTH OF REDRI

Wheir so jecainin e jen win.

Freedom has many forms and variations.

— ESLARIN PROVERB

ERRIN KNOCKED ON JEREVAN'S DOOR.

Jerevan's mind touched him. *"Come in,"* Jerevan thought.

Errin opened the door and crossed the sitting room to the bedroom. Jerevan took up most of his wheeled bed. A huge, tent-like garment covered his upper body and the sheet covered the rest, but neither could conceal the sheer mass of him. Errin estimated that Jerevan now matched the largest of the wigan folk, but he lacked the musculature to go with such weight. Nor, from what Marion and Myrriden had told him, had Jerevan been strong enough to reshape his body and create the muscles he needed while keeping up with the healing his body required even before the conflict at Darenje. And at his current rate of gain, even an expanded musculature would only work for a short time before he became completely bound in by his swelling flesh.

"Any further suggestions as to how I handle my obesity problem?" Jerevan asked.

"As a matter of fact, yes," Errin said. "That's precisely why I've come to see you."

Jerevan glared, his blue-gray eyes looking smaller than Errin remembered them, sunk in the bulging roundness of his cheeks. He had no neck, only expanding rolls of fat. "I hope you'll excuse me, but it's a little hard for me to appreciate your home these days despite this." His bloated hand patted the edge of his wheeled bed.

"Yes. So I understand," Errin said. "Your bed's a clever notion, though. I plan on suggesting similar devices to certain members of the wigan, for when they have to come ashore. But what I'm offering this time isn't a change of scenery, but a change of form."

Jerevan's body rippled as he stiffened. "A change of form?"

"Yes," Errin said. "I've studied what Derwen did to your system. I can't alter the curse, but it shouldn't interfere with your becoming a shape-shifter. Linked to Lyskarion, I can do things I couldn't have dreamt of doing when we first met."

"Can you break the curse?" Jerevan asked, his fat hands clenching into fists.

Errin hesitated, then said, "I could, but I won't. If I break the curse Derwen put on you, he'll die. Believe me, I examined him and that would be the result. You will some day be able to break the curse without killing him. I can't, and I'm not willing to kill him to save you discomfort."

"Discomfort?" Jerevan's chins jiggled as looked down at himself.

Errin shrugged. "I know you see it as more than discomfort now, but you have a long life ahead of you. Some day you'll be able to look back on this and see it as only a temporary inconvenience. In the meantime, I can make it much less uncomfortable for you, if you wish, by enabling you to become an ingvalarin shape-shifter."

"How can you do that?" Jerevan demanded, shifting weights to raise himself to a more upright position. "Myrriden said it would be years before I could learn to change my shape. And if it involves being able to lift myself, I'll never be able to change my form."

"I'm not talking about shape-changing as a wizard does it," Errin said. "I'm saying that, if you request me to, I can insert into your brain the same control that a natural ingvalar possesses. Then you'll be able, simply by stimulating the switch, to change your shape whenever you want."

"But that entails your altering my brain?" Jerevan's mass seemed to deflate as he slumped in the bed.

"Yes. That's why you have to fully understand and ask me to make the change," Errin said, eyeing Jerevan closely. "Under ordinary circumstances, I'd never think of modifying another wizard. To do so is counter to the laws of the Council of Wizards. But your natural form has already been grossly distorted. Therefore, although it's a gray area, I believe it wouldn't violate my oath if I gave you a better way to cope with the changes already imposed on you. I've discussed the ethical question with both Myrriden and Marion and they agree."

Jerevan's soft, bloated hands began to rub ineffectively at the upper slope of his stomach in what appeared to Errin to be an unconscious habit. "How would I continue my wizard training as an ingvalar?"

"You can practice all the things you're practicing now in the ingvalar form: mind-speech, moving objects, healing, even the high sight," Errin said. "You'd have to disable the natural were-sight that goes with the dolphin form to practice were-sight with your inner vision, but that's a simple adjustment made frequently by ingvalarin who study wizardry."

"But who would supervise my training? I can't imagine Myrriden changing his shape."

Errin chuckled. "No, nor can I, at least not to a dolphin. I might be able to imagine him as a lizard lying out in the sun, but nothing else. I've wondered ever since I met him if he has isklar blood somewhere in his background." He sobered. "But Myrriden isn't the only one supervising your training now. Marion has said she'd be willing to live as a dolphin for a time, and Elise and I would join you, if you wish, for at least the first year. She's promised, now that we're linked, to come with me among the wigan folk, to listen to their songs, and see the part of their lives that she's never seen before. You'd be welcome to swim with us. I'm qualified as a full wizard, even if I haven't taken the title."

Jerevan studied him for several moments, then asked, "If I made the request, how long would it take? How soon before I could change into a dolphin?"

"It would take only a few moments to insert the control. As for how soon you could change, that would depend on how quickly I could gather enough men to carry you down the stairs and into the sea. Probably about twenty minutes," Errin said.

Jerevan stared at him for a long moment. "Then do it," he said finally.

Errin nodded and pulled out Lyskarion from where it hung against his chest. He expanded his vision into the high sight and examined Jerevan's brain, finding a group of cells in one of the areas of Jerevan's brain that still seemed semi-dormant. *"Examine these cells,"* he thought to Jerevan, *"and record them so you can undo what I'm doing now when you're able to shift on your own."*

Jerevan nodded. Errin monitored him as he exerted himself to attain the high sight. He managed it finally and held on long enough to record the pattern on his crystal.

Errin looked into Lyskarion at the place he had previously prepared. Then he copied the pattern into the group of cells he had pointed out to Jerevan and made the necessary connections.

"Can you sense the switch now?" he asked.

Jerevan frowned and shut his eyes. Moments later he opened them and nodded. "Yes. I can sense it. That's all it took?"

"That's all," Errin said, turning to the door. "Now I'll fetch some strong men to help you down to the beach."

TWENTY MINUTES LATER JEREVAN FELT THE PLATFORM on which the men had carried him down the stairs lowered into the water. The buoyancy of his fat reduced his weight and Otto removed his bed robe. Then the men carried him, naked, out into the bay. He waited until the water was above their waists before he stimulated the new switch in his brain.

The shape-shift flowed through his body, an incredible twisting sensation that was almost painful, and yet almost pleasurable at the same time. Then, suddenly, he was no longer a helpless mass of flesh, but a large, sleek creature of the sea surrounded by the most fantastic music he had ever heard. Instinctively, he took a deep breath and dove down toward deeper water.

The music enfolded him. His whole body seemed to be permeated with astonishing rhythms and rippling crescendos. He rose to breath and dove again, and still the music was all around and through him, ever changing.

Jerevan was never sure afterward how long his intoxication from his first exposure to the song of the sea lasted, but it ended when he felt the familiar sensation of hunger, only slightly mutated by his new form.

He rose to the surface and looked around, realizing that he had swum a long way from shore, and that he was not certain which way he had come. There was land to the north, and Ruffin was on the north shore of the Bay of Aelos. Jerevan dove back down and started north.

He had not gone far, however, before he sensed a large school of fish. He dove among them and began to eat. He was startled by how quickly his stomach filled.

Jerevan really examined his new body for the first time. He realized immediately his new stomach was not enlarged in comparison to his body. He felt a sudden surge of exhilaration, boosted higher by the climactic music all around him. In this body he would be able to control his weight. He let the glory of the music absorb him again.

He did not make it back to the shore, or contact Errin, Myrriden, or Marion, for nearly a week – a week devoted entirely to the pleasure of being free.

APPENDIX

TAMARAN CALENDAR AND GLOSSARY

TAMARAN CALENDAR

There are ten years to a Cycle, named as follows:

1. YEAR OF THE DRAGON   Theocan a Gand
2. YEAR OF THE EAGLE   Theocan a Hai
3. YEAR OF THE LIZARD   Theocan al Isk
4. YEAR OF THE TIGER   Theocan a Lin
5. YEAR OF THE DOLPHIN   Theocan al Ingva
6. YEAR OF THE MALIK   Theocan a Malik
7. YEAR OF THE BEAR   Theocan a Gam
8. YEAR OF THE MOLE   Theocan a Fal
9. YEAR OF THE GRIFFIN   Theocan a Caral
10. YEAR OF THE OX   Theocan a Bekasar

The planet Tamar has one moon, Ranth, which goes through eleven cycles of waxing and waning. Tamar's year is divided into ten months. Below are the Tamaran months and their approximate Earth equivalents:

1. ISKKAAR   January – February   35 days
2. DIRGA   February – March   35 days
3. INGVASH   March – April   35 days
4. CERDANA   April – May   35 days
5. ANOR   May – June   35 days

6. TORIN	July – August	35 days
7. AGNITH	August – September	35 days
8. REDRI	September – October	35 days
9. ILFARNAR	October – November	35 days
10. MINNETH	November – December	39 days

Each month consists of five weeks of seven days, with four days that are not counted in the week at the end of Minneth. These days are mathedin, 'not days,' and are holidays. Every eight years there are five mathedin at the end of Minneth. Although there are only 354 days in the Tamaran year, the time involved is very similar to Earth's year as Tamar's rate of spin is slightly slower and, therefore, each day on Tamar is roughly fifty of our minutes longer than an Earth day.

The days of the week can be thought of as follows:

1. TAMARSDAY	Monday
2. TARATSDAY	Tuesday
3. MAERASDAY	Wednesday
4. JEHANSDAY	Thursday
5. KYRASDAY	Friday
6. MIUNESDAY	Saturday
7. THEOSDAY	Sunday

In Eskh Tamarsday would be Tamarthed. Theothed is the Eskh way of saying Sunday. Weekends aren't a concept familiar to Tamarans. It is usual, however, for Tamaran employees to be given the day off on their god's day. Thus a worshiper of Miune would usually have Miunesday off of work and probably one other day off as well. Someone like Balen, who worships both Maera and Jehan, would have Maerasday and Jehansday off.

There are only twenty hours in a Tamaran day, by their reckoning. However, as using Tamaran time might have been confusing, Earth equivalents have been used throughout.

GLOSSARY

A *(or al)*: from, out of, of, by

A- *(or al)*: 1) Prefix of nouns denoting persons concerned or connected with something, as in alfar, ahar, etc. 2) Prefix of verbs denoting persons who habitually perform such action. (Also *y-* if verb begins with vowel.)

ABWIN: among

AC: to, toward,

ACADAM: every

AGNITH: 1) 7th and hottest month of the Tamaran year, named for the wizard who was the Council of Wizards' Monitor for this season. 2) The wizard who took the name 'Fire Newt.' With Ilfarnar, she created Cinkarion.

AHAR *(pl. aharin)*: ruler, king

AJARE *(pl. ajaren)*: 1) one who plays a musical instrument 2) priest of Jehan

AL *(or a)*: from, out of, of

ALFAR *(pl. alfarin)*: 1) wanderer 2) title of an officer of the Varfarin.

AM *(pl. amin)*: one *(pl. some)*

AMID: first

AMVALOD *(pl. amvalodin)*: universe

ANATHALLIA *(pl. anathallian)*: A flowering plant with gold and white showers of blossoms

ANDRIONANTH *(pl. andrionanthin)*: gardener, a term of honor in Eskh): Among the eslarin, an andrionanth is the head of a house, or clan grouping.

ANOR: 1) 5th month of the Tamaran year, named for the wizard who was the Council of Wizards' Monitor for this season. 2) The wizard who took the name 'Warm Rain.' With Torin, she created Vyrkarion.

AODH: The longest river on Tamar - empties into Thallassean Sea in Sardom. Lara, the city at its mouth, is the largest city on Tamar.

ARDAGH: Human pirate city taken by the isklarin of Gandahar in the 458th Cycle of the Year of the Malik, 4576, and renamed Kavarna.

ARGERIUM: Refers to the plant and its spicy leaves which are dried and used in cooking.

ARRAGE *(pl. arragen)*: water master, chief of a wiga

ARRAI *(pl. arrain)*: captain, commander of a ship among the larin

ARRUN *(pl. arrunin)*: jester

AT *(pl. atin)*: future, fate

BA *(p.t. bat, f.t. bara)*: is, are *(p.t. was, f.t. will be)*

BAJAL *(p.t. bajalt, f.t. bajala)*: dance *(p.t. danced, f.t. will dance)*

BAL *(p.t. balt, f.t. bala)*: go *(p.t. gone, f.t. will go)*

BEL: white

BELKARION: White Crystal, the 2nd living crystal made by Iskkaar and Minneth, also known as the Heart of Snow.

BOHEDAL *(p.t. bohedalt, f.t. bohedala)*: keep *(p.t. kept, f.t. will preserve)*

BORES *(p.t. borest, f.t. boresa)*: carry *(p.t. carried, f.t. will carry)*

BORIL *(p.t. borilt, f.t. borila)*: cost *(p.t. cost, f.t. will cost)*

BORUN *(p.t. borunt, f.t. boruna)*: own, possess, hold *(p.t. held, f.t. will hold)*

BORVAJENDO *(pl. borvajendoin)*: betrayal, treachery

CASSINGA: Only surviving human country in Cibata.

CAURAK *(pl. caurakin)*: skin house, teepee, tent

CER *(pl. cerin)*: seed

CERDANA: 1) 4th month of the Tamaran year, named for the wizard who was the Council of Wizards' Monitor for this season. 2) The great wizard who took her name from the time of sowing. With Redri she created Kaikarion.

CHRYS *(pl. chrysin)*: multi-colored, rainbow *(pl. rainbows)*

CHRYSKARION: Rainbow Crystal, the 7th living crystal created by Lindeth and Ingvash, also called the Rainbow Crown.

CIBATA: Southern continent of Tamar ruled by the linlarin except for the human country of Cassinga and the Nyali Coast, a melting pot for misfits of all races.

CIN: red

CINKARION: Red Crystal, the 5th living crystal created by Agnith and Ilfarnar, also called the Heart of Fire.

COTULUME: Hybrid fruit from the eslarin isle of Isin. It has segments like an orange but is not a citrus fruit. It tastes like a combination of a kiwi fruit and a pear.

CUNA: Designates the plant and its spicy seed, used frequently in hot regions.

CYR: blue

CYRKARION: Blue Crystal, the 8th living crystal created by Cormor and Belis, also called the Sword of Cormor.

-D (or -od if the verb ends in a consonant) Suffix of nouns formed, from verbs expressing the action of the verb or its result.

DALES: best

DALNE: well

DEBARRA (pl. debarran): Large food fish found in schools in the Thallassean Sea and the northern reaches of the Jevac Lessar.

DIRGA (pl. dirgan): hurricane

DIRGA: 1) 2nd month of the Tamaran year, named for the wizard who was the Council of Wizards' Monitor for this season 2) One of the great wizards who named herself 'Hurricane.' With Luth, she created Lyskarion.

DUBAREM (p.t. dubaret, f.t. dubarema): forget (p.t. forgot, f.t. will forget)

E (or ev): and

EA (pl. ean): he, she, him, her - referring to a being with full awareness (pl. they, them)

EASE (pl. eanse): his, her - referring to a being with full awareness (pl. their)

EGASTI (pl. egastin): sand worms

ELANDA (pl. elandan): Tall, graceful tree common to tropical and semi-tropical zones of Tamar.

END (pl. endin): time

ES: high

ESALFAR: Title of the chief officer of the Varfarin.

ESAMEND: often

ESAMIN: most

ESKH: Common language of the larin of Tamar, literally, 'high tongue.'

ESLA (pl. eslain): High sight, the sight of the eslarin and the sight a wizard must achieve to be considered a true wizard. Beings with esla can sense all the spectra of energy and see into the structure of matter down to the atomic level.

ESLAR (pl. eslarin): High being, one of the firstborn of the gods. Eslarin were the first race created by Tarat and Maera. Tarat intended them to be the ruling race. Of all the eleven sentient races created by the Lorincen, only eslarin are born with high sight, the full vision of the gods.

ESTAHAR (pl. estaharin): emperor, high king

EV (or e): and

FAL (pl. falin): mole

FALLAR (pl. fallarin): mole person

FATHIK (pl. fathikin): A small carnivore known for its bad smell and viciousness.

FINGOE: Human country in Macosia, second of two founded by Ilwheirlane. Originally a penal colony.

GA: strong

GABO: madness

GAM (pl. gamin): bear

GAMLAR (pl. gamlarin): bear person

GAND (pl. gandin): dragon

GANDAHAR: Ancient empire of the isklarin, once ruled all the lands around the Thallassean Sea and still rules vast lands to the southwest of the human lands.

GANESH (pl. ganeshin): war

GANOD (pl. ganodin): fighting, violence

GAO (pl. gaon): strength

GARTH (pl. garthin): power, force

GRES (p.t. grest, f.t. gresa): know (p.t. knew, f.t. will know)

GWATAR: River of Yellow Clay - Gandahar's main access route to Thallassean Sea. The marshes at its mouth cover the site of ancient Sikkar.

HAI (pl. hain): eagle

HAILAR (pl. hailarin): eagle person

HE (p.t. het, f.t. hesa): give (p.t. gave, f.t. will give)

HEDAL (p.t. hedalt, f.t. hedala): rescue (p.t. saved, f.t. will rescue)

HENILAN (p.t. henilant, f.t. henilana): torture (p.t. tortured, f.t. will torture)

HETRI (pl. hetrin): Literally 'grain giver,' the highest level of the human nobility under an estahar or ahar, roughly equivalent to a margrave or duke. During the Dragon Wars, when most of the hereditary grants of nobility were made, a hetri commanded all the lanrais in his region (generally between 5 and 10) and was responsible for supplying his forces with food and certain other staples. Thus, the original hetrin were given ownership of vast tracts of the most fertile lands.

HETRION: territory ruled by a hetri, dukedom

HUNICA (pl. hunican): Plant grown in warmer regions of Tamar similar to corn. A type of meal is made from it.

I- (or in-): Prefix of verbs creating the infinitive form.

IDOM *(pl. idomin)*: love

IFLA *(p.t. iflat, f.t. iflea)*: dream *(p.t. dreamt, f.t. will dream)*

IKVAL: ancient

IL- *(or ill-)*: Only article in Eskh, it means 'the noble one,' or 'such a one.'

-IL *(or -ill)*: 1) Suffix denoting 'the little one,' diminutive. 2) When used in connection with a title, as in naharil or hetril, it indicates that the person so named is the consort of the holder of the title, not the actual holder thereof.

ILFARNAR: 1) 9th month of the Tamaran year, named for the wizard who was the Council of Wizards' Monitor for this season. 2) The wizard who called himself 'Migrating Goose.' With Agnith, he created Cinkarion.

ILL *(or il)*: Article, it means 'the noble one,' or 'such a one.'

ILWHEIRLANE: The first country of free humans on Tamar. The name means 'the noble free land.'

IN- *(or i-)*: Prefix of verbs creating the infinitive form.

INGVA *(pl. ingvan)*: dolphin

INGVALAR *(pl. ingvalarin)*: dolphin person

INGVASH: 1) 3rd month of the Tamaran year, named for the wizard who was the Council of Wizards' Monitor during this season. 2) The wizard who called himself 'Dying Fish' for the fish that ran in the season when he presided over the Council. With Lindeth, he created Chryskarion.

ISK *(pl. iskin)*: lizard

ISKKAAR: 1) 1st month of the Tamaran year, named for the wizard who was the Council of Wizards' Monitor during this season. 2) The wizard who called himself 'Ice Lizard.' With Minneth, he created Belkarion.

ISKLAR *(pl. isklarin)*: lizard person

ITNE: also, in addition to

JALITH *(pl. jalithin)*: Hollow, pear-shaped instrument similar to a lute but having twelve strings.

JAO *(pl. jaon)*: song

JAO *(p.t. jaot, f.t. jaora)*: sing *(p.t. sung, f.t. will sing)*

JATHEV *(pl. jathevin)*: thunder

JE *(pl. jen)*: bend, variation

JECAIN *(pl. jecainin)*: shape, form

JEHAN: One of the Lorincen, the Five Gods, with Kyra he created the were-peoples. Patron god of the Varfarin.

JENTAY *(pl. jentayn)*: honor

JERAM *(pl. jeramin)*: cripple, bent one

JIDTHE *(pl. jidthen)*: flash

KAI: gold

KAIKARION: Gold Crystal, the 3rd living crystal, also called the Harvest Stone, it was created by Cerdana and Redri.

KAILANE: Human country on the west coast of the Thallassean Sea.

KANAKAR *(pl. kanakarin)*: A creature related to a giant squid but less mobile due to armor of bony plates. Found in deep water in the warm regions of Tamar; deadly enemy of dolphins, whales and the ingvalarin; kraken.

KANDORRA: Small southern continent of Tamar colonized by Ilwheirlane in 2893, the 290th Cycle of the Year of the Lizard. Particularly hard hit by the plague, by the time of Vanda III most of the population is of mixed blood.

KARAD *(pl. karadin)*: sword

KARION *(pl. karionin)*: crystal

KATH *(pl. kathin)*: lightning

KERE *(pl. keren)*: lesson

KERIAR *(pl. keriarin)*: A shore bird known for building its nest in the cracks in cliff faces, but where cliffs are unavailable they will use hollow trees.

KOR: but

KULHAR *(pl. kulharin)*: governor, under ruler

KWALUCCA *(pl. kwaluccan)*: Cherry-like orange fruit grown in the tropics of Tamar.

KYRA: One of the Lorincen, the Five Gods, with Jehan she created the were-peoples. She is also the keeper of the Rhystallin, the Book of Changes. Worshipers of Miune call her 'the Destroyer,' but her worshipers are divided into two sects: those who worship her as 'Destroyer,' and those who worship her as 'Chronicler.'

LA *(p.t. lat, f.t. lasa)*: see, sense *(p.t. saw, f.t. will see)*

LANRAI *(pl. lanrain)*: The rank of human nobility between a hetri and a tamrai, roughly equivalent to an earl or a count. A lanrai, during the Dragon Wars, commanded the forces of ten tamrais and was responsible for supplying them with arms and, in some cases, mounting them as well.

LANRION *(pl. lanrionin)*: territory ruled by a lanrai, earldom

LAR *(pl. larin)*: Sentient being, one who has full awareness (humans, other than wizards, are not considered larin).

-LE: a suffix forming the comparative degree of adjectives or adverbs, *-er*

-LES: a suffix forming the superlative degree of adjectives and adverbs, *-est*

LESS: great, huge

LESSA *(pl. lessan)*: sea, ocean

LESSKA *(pl. lesskan)*: penis, prick, vulgar slang for a man

LIN *(pl. linin)*: tiger

LINDETH: One of the great wizards, she called herself 'Tiger Flower.' With Ingvash, she created Chryskarion.

LINLAR *(pl. linlarin)*: tiger person

LOKAMDEM *(pl. lokamdemin)*: whetstone, sharpener

LOKAN *(p.t. lokant, f.t. lokana)*: sharpen *(p.t. sharpened, f.t. will sharpen)*

LOMCAN *(pl. lomcanin)*: Fruit native to Tamar, it tastes like a sweet lemon.

LOMCAUL *(pl. lomcaulin)*: pleasure

LOMKAS *(pl. lomkasin)*: musical instrument, literally 'sweet horn,' it has a sound similar to a clarinet.

LOMMAS *(pl. lommasin)*: Fruit native to Tamar that tastes like a cross between a sweet quince and a nectarine.

LOR *(pl. lorin)*: god, creator

LORDOM *(p.t. lordot, f.t. lordoma)*: worship *(p.t. worshiped, f.t. will worship)*

LORINCEN: Five Gods – the five deities of Tamar.

LORSK *(pl. lorskin)*: A tuber remotely similar to a potato but nuttier in flavor.

LUTH: One of the great wizards, he called himself for the final fruits of the harvest. With Dirga, he created Lyskarion.

LYS *(pl. lysin)*: wind

LYSKARION: Wind Crystal, the 6th living crystal. It was created by Dirga and Luth. Also known as the Singing Stone or the Song of the Wind, it was the only one of the living crystals that produced sounds.

MA: no, not

MAERA: One of the Lorincen, the Five Gods, she created the eslarin, aarlarin, tamlarin and valarin with Tarat, and humans with Miune. Because she later left Miune as well as Tarat, the worshipers of both call her 'the Great Whore.' Her worshipers are dedicated to healing, regardless of race.

MALACAB *(pl. malacabin)*: despair

MALAIR *(pl. malairin)*: Eskh name for human women - the addition of the 'i' indicates the feminine. None of the larin distinguish between masculine and feminine. An eslar is an eslar no matter what sex. Gender is only relative to the lower orders of life. An exception are the karothin who were deliberately bred by the eslarin. The distinction between the sexes has survived their sentience.

MALAR *(pl. malarin)*: Eskh name for human men.

MALIK *(pl. malikin)*: A large, carnivorous bird used by the military of many larin nations to mount their soldiers.

MARE: nothing

MARIN *(pl. marinin)*: Tree that the eslarin brought to Tamar; it has edible nuts that are often ground into flour for rich breads and cakes.

MARION: chaos

MARL *(pl. marlin)*: exception

MAJENALAD *(pl. majenaladin)*: illusion

MATHEND *(pl. mathendin)*: One of the days at the end of Minneth not counted as part of the fifty weeks of the Tamaran year, sometimes slang for a day off.

MAWHE *(pl. mawhen)*: slave

ME *(p.t. met, f.t. mea)*: Verb form used to form present, past and future perfect tenses.

MEK *(p.t. mekt, f.t. meka)*: do, act *(p.t. did, f.t. will do)*

MELDARCAN *(pl. meldarcanin)*: honey round, a Tamaran pastry

MELDETH *(pl. meldethin)*: honey flowers (scarlet)

MEND: old

METELLA *(pl. metellan)*: One of a breed of long-haired, sheep-like ruminants native to Sussey.

MINNETH: 1) 10th month of the Tamaran year, named for the wizard who was the Council of Wizards' Monitor during this season. 2) The wizard who called herself 'Snow Moth.' With Iskkaar, she created Belkarion.

MIT *(p.t. mitet, f.t. mita)*: stop *(p.t. stopped, f.t. will stop)*

MIUNE: One of the Lorincen, the Five Gods, with Maera he created humanity.

NA *(pl. nan)*: child

NAHAR: Child or heir of an ahar or estahar, equivalent of prince or princess as Eskh does not distinguish the sex of sentient beings.

NALOR *(pl. nalorin)*: Child of a god, wizard as wizards are larin, no gender applies and they take the ea form of pronoun.

-NEAD: verbal suffix, can be added to almost any descriptive adjective, *-ly*

NENAKA *(pl. nenakan)*: Hardwood tree found most commonly in Nacaonne known for beauty of its wood.

NIK *(pl. nikin)*: pain, hurt

NIKTA *(pl. niktan)*: agony

NIN: black

NINKARION: Black Crystal, the 4th living crystal, also called the Eye of Rav. It was created by Rav and Sugra.

NITH *(pl. nithin)*: fire

NO *(pl. non)*: this *(pl. these)*

-O: Suffix used to form, from adjectives and participles, nouns denoting quality or state, or exemplifying quality or state, *-ness*.

OA *(pl. oan)*: he, she, him, her, it - referring to lower orders of living things. The were-peoples use this form to refer to humans, plants and animals *(pl. they, them)*

-OD *(or -d if the verb ends in a vowel)*: Suffix of nouns formed from verbs, expressing the action of the verb or its result.

PALE: important

PAPAIL *(pl. papailin)*: burden, responsibility

PO *(p.t. pot, f.t. posa)*: can *(p.t. could, f.t. will be able)*

PON *(p.t. pont, f.t. pona)*: may, is allowed *(p.t. was allowed, f.t. will be allowed)*

PRO: difficult

PUAT *(p.t. puatet, f.t. puata, must)*: have to *(p.t. had to, f.t. will have to)*

QUA: like, as if, as though

QUEN: for

RAGE *(p.t. raget, f.t. ragea)*: master, control, rule *(p.t. mastered, will master)*

RAI *(pl. rain)*: lord, master

RANTH *(pl. ranthin)*: moon

RAVAAR: Human pirate stronghold on the southeast coast of Thallassean Sea by the mouth of the Bay of Khor, called Yesil before it was taken over by Rav during the Age of Wizards. Ravach is the capitol and major port city.

REDRI: 1) 8th month of the Tamaran year, named for the wizard who was the Council of Wizards' Monitor during this season. 2) The wizard who called himself 'Rich Harvest.' With Cerdana, he created Kaikarion.

REM *(pl. remin)*: thought, idea

REMLA *(pl. remlan)*: mind

REMSO *(pl. remson)*: memory

RESRION *(p.t. resriont, f.t. resriona, intend)*: plan *(p.t. planned, f.t. will plan)*

RHE *(p.t. rhet, f.t. rhea)*: change, alter *(p.t. changed, f.t. will change)*

RHYSTALLIN: Book of Changes - the history of the universes of the Lorincen.

RIK *(pl. rikin)*: Main monetary unit of all of the lands of Tamar (10 synin=1 rik, 10 rikin=1 rin, 10 rinin=1 riktrav).

RIN *(pl. rinin)*: 10 rikin

SAV *(p.t. savet, f.t. sava)*: eat *(p.t. eaten, f.t. will eat)*

-SE: Suffix indicating the possessive form of nouns, state of belonging to.

SEN: if

SENANGA: Aggressive linlarin empire in Cibata known for piracy and continual warfare with Cassinga, the sole remaining human nation in Cibata. As with Mankoya and Gatukai, the other linlarin pirate nations, the population is not pure-blooded.

SENIT: although, even though

SERAL *(pl. seralin)*: A herd animal native to Tamar, about one meter high at the shoulder and stockily built. Easily domesticated, seralin form a staple part of the diet of all the peoples of Tamar.

SIC *(pl. sickin)*: Smallest unit of money on Tamar (10 sickin=1 syn, 10 synin=1 rik).

SIKKAR: Ancient capitol of Gandahar, before it was sunk by human wizards.

SO *(p.t. sot, f.t. soa)*: have, own *(p.t. had, f.t. will have)*

SON: own (adjective)

SUKATTA *(pl. sukattan)*: shark

SULCATH *(pl. sulcathin)*: Domestic Tamaran bird - similar to a duck or goose, but the size of a turkey. Used for down and meat.

SYLVITH *(pl. sylvithin)*: Tree native to Tamar but hybridized by the eslarin. It bears pods containing nuts that taste like nutty mushrooms and contain a complete protein. A staple in the diet in all mountainous regions near where eslarin dwell.

SYN *(pl. synin)*: 10 sickin; 10 synin = 1 rik

TA *(pl. tan)*: word, essence, symbol, soul

TAMAR *(pl. tamarin)*: world

TAMAR: Tamaran name for their world.

TAMRAI *(pl. tamrain)*: Lowest rank of human nobility on Tamar; literally 'landlord;' roughly equivalent to a baron. During the Dragon Wars, a tamrai was responsible for recruiting and commanding one hundred soldiers.

TAMRION *(pl. tamrionin)*: territory ruled by a tamrai, barony

TAN *(pl. tanin)*: reality, truth

TARAT: One of the Lorincen, the Five Gods. With Maera he created the eslarin, the aarlarin, the tamlarin and the valarin.

THEOCAN *(pl. theocanin)*: year

TOLU: peace

TONOD *(pl. tonodin)*: enjoyment

TORIN: 1) 6th month of the Tamaran year, named for the wizard who was the Council of Wizards' Monitor during this season. 2) The wizard who called himself 'Growth.' With Anor, he created Vyrkarion.

U *(or ue)*: who, which

UA *(pl. uan)*: you - referring to larin folk

UASE *(pl. uanse)*: your - referring to larin folk

UE *(or u)*: who, which

UOA *(pl. uoan)*: you - referring to lesser beings

UOASE *(pl. uoanse)*: your - referring to lessar beings

VA *(pl. van)*: breath, life

VYR: green

VYRKARION: Green Crystal, the 1st living crystal, also called the Talisman of Anor. It was created by Anor and Torin.

WANE *(p.t. wanet. f.t. wanesa)* temper, as a sword *(p.t. tempered. f.t. will temper)*

-WE: passive suffix

WHEIR: freedom

WIGA *(pl. wigan)*: tribe, family-kinship grouping, clan (used particularly by the more primitive of the were-folk)

WIN: many

WUN *(p.t. wunt, f.t. wuna)*: consent, agree *(p.t. consented, f.t. will consent)*

Y: of noble spirit, generous

Y-: Prefix to verbs beginning in a vowel, meaning one who habitually performs an action. (Also *a*-).

YA: *(pl. yan)* I, me *(pl. we, us)*

YAN *(p.t. yant, f.t. yana)*: serve *(p.t. served, f.t. will serve)*

YAR *(pl. yarin)*: A large sea creature resembling a plesiosaur or sea monster found only in the tropical regions of Tamar.

YASE *(pl. yanse)*: my *(pl. our)*

YESIL: The original name of Ravaar before the Wizard Rav went to dwell there.

ZAMARGA: Peninsula dominated by humans located between the Thallassean Sea and the Jevac Lessar south of the Zamargan Sea and the Strait of Belarrai.

ZAND: when

ZARAD *(pl. zaradin)*: solution, resolution

ZARE *(pl. zaren)*: problem